AF278810

SMOKE & MIRRORS
(book 3)

KR Bankston

All rights reserved. No part of this book may be used or reproduced by any means, graphic, electronic or mechanical, including, photocopying, recording, taping or by an information storage retrieval system without the written permission of the author or publisher except in the event of quotes embodied in articles and reviews.

The work is a work of fiction. All of the characters, names, incidents, organizations, and dialogue in this novel are either the products of the author's imagination or are used fictitiously. Any similarity to any person living or dead is purely coincidental.

The views expressed in this work are solely those of the author and do not necessarily reflect the views of the publisher, and the publisher hereby disclaims any responsibility for them.

Printed in the United States of America

Copyright © 2009 KR Bankston. All rights reserved.

Kirabaco Publishing 12/2009

**Liberation is not a gift bestowed upon us
from our oppressor.
It is taken and owned by the decision that
NO ONE can keep them from it.**

For too long we've watched silently as we've been violated by our government at every turn. The rights and needs of the poor, minorities, and women have been ignored and trampled upon. It's time to stand up and say no. You have the power to make a difference and it is as simple as casting a ballot in your local, state, and federal elections.

If you haven't registered to vote, you may do so in the following ways:

- Contact your Secretary of State and request a voter registration form by mail
- Register at your Public Library
- Register at the DMV when you renew your license
- Register when you renew your TANF/Food Stamp benefits

Registering to vote doesn't automatically sentence you to jury duty. If you get a jury summons, don't avoid it! We need rational voices to keep our men and women from behind bars!

Convicted felons are not barred from registering! States such as Rhode Island, South Carolina and Utah automatically restore your voting rights upon completion of your sentence. Check your state laws for complete information on restoring your voting rights if you've been convicted of a felony.

To Report Voter Issues: call the Civil Rights Division toll-free at (800) 253-3931, or contact them by mail at:
Chief, Voting Section
Civil Rights Division
Room 7254 – NWB
Department of Justice
950 Pennsylvania Ave., N.W.
Washington, DC 20530

Your right to vote was secured through blood, sweat, and tears. Exercise it to the fullest without relenting. Social change and justice for people of color is not optional: it is mandatory. Make them know this by registering your voting voice today!

For Nikki, Dee, and Shunte'
Because you all said so!
For my Readers In Motion Family!
Thanks for all the love!

The Gianni Legacy

D ezi Gianni arrived in Virginia Beach again for the first time in more than twenty years. Big D was there to meet him. He ended up actually walking up and introducing himself.

"Wow," Big D exclaimed. "I didn't even recognize you man," he grinned, as they embraced.

Dezi smiled.

"That's a good thing. It means no one else will either," he replied.

At least not until I want them too, Dezi thought. They arrived at Big D's apartment, went in, and made themselves comfortable.

"Man," Big D told Dezi, looking at him. "It's good to see you again," he went on. "I was so glad to hear from you and know you weren't really dead all those years ago."

"I knew I could trust you to keep my secret," Dezi told him. "Thanks again for the knowledge about Aidan, and the pictures of him, and Kayla."

"Tell me about the boy's mother," he said quietly.

Dezi remembered Liv from the hotel, and their daily sex sessions. He also remembered how cold and heartless he was to her about her possible pregnancy. Big D sighed deeply thinking about Liv.

"She was a good woman," he said simply and Dezi knew he cared for her intensely.

"She did a helluva job raising that boy," Big D went on. "She was good people," he told Dezi. "I actually loved her a lot," Big D finished sadly.

"Did you pay the debt," Dezi asked, looking at him evenly.

"In spades," Big D said coldly. "They buried his ass a week after they buried her," he finished, the hatred still raw in his words.

"So man," Big D began, looking at Dezi. "What name are you going by now?"

"Dante Enzo," he replied smoothly.

"Why did you pick that," Big D asked, thinking it was an odd name.

"Because," he began. "In Italian, Dante means lasting, and Enzo means winner," Dezi finished chuckling lightly.

Big D got it, and began to laugh too.

"Well, you are surely right about that one man," he continued laughing.

Dezi would spend his first few months in the states here with Big D, while they got his house ready in Chapel Hill. It was in a new subdivision, less than a half mile from Kayla. Dezi smiled thinking about her again. *Now I just have to figure out how to get rid of the husband,* he formulated. Dezi managed not to kill anyone for a while, not in the states anyway, but he wasn't beyond it. He wasn't beyond anything when it came to getting Kayla back. *I'm not leaving without you this time baby,* Dezi vowed as he got up, stretched, and headed for the room Big D was showing him.

•••

Collins looked at the manila envelope the younger agent placed on his desk. He opened it, hoping it wasn't another summons to appear in court for a case. He looked at the report and sighed. It was sent by a friend, the last contact left in the bureau from the old days. *I knew he would come back,* Collins thought tiredly. He sat back in the chair, and let his mind wander back twenty years ago to a life changing conversation with his superior.

"What are you saying, sir," Collins asked the superior agent he was addressing.

"I'm saying that for all intents and purposes, this investigation is over, and Dezi Gianni is off limits," he finished evenly, looking Collins in the eye.

Collins knew he was defeated. Whatever Gianni held on the powers that be, it must have been good for them to turn a blind eye, and let him walk away. They pronounced Gianni dead at the scene, but later detected a faint heart rhythm at the hospital. Collins never told Black. It would have destroyed him. He figured they would be all right because Gianni was out of the country and no longer a threat. Now his friend was dead, and this clown was back.

"Dear God," Collins mused half aloud "What is he back for now," he questioned, knowing the answer all too well.

Gianni was still after her. Collins kept in touch with Kayla after Black's death. He even attended her daughter's wedding. *Maybe I should warn her,* he thought, but decided against it. Collins didn't want to alarm her for no reason. Gianni didn't use his real name when he came back, and that was a problem. He bought the ticket with cash. Collins was effectively searching for a ghost. They didn't even have any recent photos of Gianni since his surgery. Collins knew the only way they would find him was to wait on him to make his move. Collins thought about how he would keep tabs on Kayla and her family. He needed to be close to Chapel Hill. His wife separated from him, so there was no real reason for him to remain here in California. Collins headed to personnel to request a transfer to the North Carolina office. *Please let me get there before he does,* he prayed silently, stepping onto the elevator.

Dezi awoke from his nap refreshed. He called the builder to check the progress of his house.

"Good morning, Tinsley Builders," the receptionist answered.

Dezi smiled at the deep southern accent. He himself adopted an island accent that he used when necessary to disguise his own voice. He would need to use it all the time once he introduced himself to Kayla again.

"Good Morning," he began, accent in place. "This is Dante Enzo, and I'm calling to check on the progress of my house."

"Oh hello Mr. Enzo," she greeted him by name. "Please hold for just one moment."

The next voice he heard was that of the salesman, Wayne Crimmons, who sold him the plans.

"Mr. Enzo," he boomed into the phone. "The house is almost complete," he went on. "We ran into a little backorder problem with the Italian marble tile you asked for, but we have it now, and the house is still on schedule to be completed in the next month or so."

Dezi smiled again. "Good, that's wonderful news."

They talked a moment about other minor matters concerning the house, and disconnected. He designed the house to be almost an exact duplicate of the homes they lived in before. *I wonder if she even thinks about the times we shared,* he thought about Kayla.

"Well, no matter," Dezi said aloud. "I'll make you remember baby and this time no one is going to interfere," he finished irritably as he headed for the kitchen.

After retrieving himself a beer from the fridge, Dezi made another call to the bank to see if the money was transferred. The teller he reached confirmed the transfer and told him the funds were available. Dezi thanked her and hung up. The phone rang as soon as he placed it in the cradle. Dezi looked at the ID, Preston A., it read. *It's my son,* he thought excitedly. It would be his first time talking to the young man. He thought of changing his voice, but decided it wasn't necessary.

"Hello?" Dezi answered smoothly.

Aidan was a bit surprised. He hadn't expected anyone other than Big D to answer the phone. *Guess he's got company.*

"Hey, can I speak to D please?"

Dezi smiled. "He's actually out right now. Is there a message?"

"Yeah," he began. "Would you tell him Aidan called, and that Mariah had the baby this morning."

Dezi was smiling again, pleased to hear his son's voice, and equally pleased that his grandchild arrived.

"Yes, I'll be sure to tell him," he replied, wanting to ask what the baby was.

"Oh, and tell him I'll call him later with details," the young man said warmly, as he hung up.

Well, guess I'll have to wait until he calls back, Dezi thought excitedly, as he grabbed the key Big D left him. He needed to get out and look around for a while.

●●●

Mariah was exhausted but happy. She endured a long labor and delivery, but Olivia was here now. The baby was beautiful, a perfect combination of both Aidan and Mariah. Even her eyes were light brown with flecks of gray. She inherited Mariah's dimples, and so far Kayla's disposition. Everyone left her to rest now, except Kayla. Mariah and her mother were talking quietly.

"I wish daddy, and grandmother, could have seen her," Mariah said softly, looking at her mother holding the baby.

Kayla's eyes misted as she thought of Black, and her mother in-law, who passed suddenly during Mariah's pregnancy. She still thought of him, even more now, since she and Thomas were apart so much.

"Yes baby, I wish they could have seen her too," she went on. "But I know they're looking down and smiling right now," Kayla finished, looking up from Olivia to Mariah.

"When is Dad getting back," Mariah inquired.

Kayla sighed. Thomas was gone more and more these days, doing various things involved with his ministry. It wasn't that she resented what he did. Kayla simply wished he were home more. He missed Olivia's birth. Not to mention, all the other nights he missed lately.

"He should be back in about three days."

Mariah knew her mother was becoming increasingly unhappy with Thomas's travel schedule. She hoped that now with Olivia being born, she could help Kayla fill some of the empty time.

"I'm thinking of going back to work," Kayla said quietly.

Mariah frowned at that statement. She knew Thomas was opposed to it, and she herself wanted her mother around to help her care for Olivia.

"Mommy, do you think that's a good idea," Mariah asked gently.

Kayla sighed again. She knew Mariah was thinking of Thomas, as well as herself.

"Well," she began. "I wouldn't go back fulltime, just part time," Kayla went on. "And of course, I can still work independently, so my schedule would still be my own."

Mariah didn't argue with her. She knew her mother was just lonely, and wanted something to do. She made a mental note to speak with Dad when he came home. *Maybe he can take her on some of these trips, or find something she can help with to keep her busy.* Kayla placed the sleeping baby back into her crib, and kissed Mariah goodnight.

"I'll be back in the morning," she spoke sweetly. "Get some rest."

"All right mommy," Mariah replied. "Be safe driving home, and sweet dreams."

"I will," Kayla smiled, as she closed the door behind her.

●●●

Kayla was thoughtful on the drive home. *Jackie's leaving and I don't really have any other friends,* she thought. Chris accepted a Pastor's appointment in Georgia, and they were moving at the end of the month. *I've got to do something to occupy my time. I haven't felt this alone in a long time,* Kayla sighed sadly, getting out of the car and entering the house.

She checked the machine. Thomas left three messages. Kayla smiled as she listened to each of them, declaring his love for her. It wasn't that she felt any less love for Thomas. She just felt very much alone these days. Kayla began to cry softly from her sadness, as she headed upstairs to bed, alone again.

●●●

Thomas was lying in bed at the hotel, thinking of his wife. *I've got to stop neglecting her,* he thought guiltily. He knew his schedule was taxing, and he was spending too much time away from her. Kayla always understood when he left, but he knew she was upset. *It's almost finished though,* Thomas thought again. *Just a couple more months, and I won't have to travel as much.* The question was, would his marriage survive another couple months of him being constantly absent from home? He recalled their last conversation, before this trip.

"Thomas," Kayla began quietly. "Why do you have to go to every meeting or conference personally?" He was impatient, and snapped at her that it was what he did, and that she knew that before they were married. Thomas could tell he hurt her, but Kayla didn't say anything else. She even packed his things for him, made

his favorite dinner, and made love to him the night before he left. Thomas felt like a royal ass for treating her that way. *I love you so much Kayla,* he thought once again. *Please God, help me and my marriage make it through this trying time,* Thomas prayed silently, as he closed his eyes and let sleep take him.

•••

Collins couldn't believe how easy getting his transfer was. *Guess they want some new blood in my spot here, huh,* he chuckled. He still wouldn't be able to leave for another four or five weeks. In the meantime, he would arrange his housing, and maybe make a couple of visits. *I've got to make sure Kayla, and her family, are safe,* Collins thought as his mind went to the young man, Aidan, Gianni's son. *I wonder if he knows about him,* he pondered again, knowing he did. If Gianni knew where Kayla was, he knew all about her family too. *How,* Collins wondered again, as he picked up the phone to call a realtor.

He talked at length with the agent about what he was looking for, and the agent agreed to send him brochures, photos, and information, on various properties he may be interested in. Collins also needed to find Kayla's new address. He knew she gave the house she shared with Black, to her daughter and new husband. Collins used the FBI locator to find her current address, and phone number, putting them in his files for use later. He would call Kayla once he got there and settled in. They were old friends, so she wouldn't be suspicious of his transfer, or his contact. *Why can't this guy just let go,* he wondered disgustedly as he headed to the target range.

Collins needed to make sure his skills were as sharp as possible. Gianni was determined, and deranged. Collins would need to be prepared, or he wouldn't survive this encounter. He thought of Black, and the secret he kept from him all these years. Collins owed his partner big, and he was determined that nothing would hurt the one person he knew Black loved more than life itself.

Smoke & **1** Mirrors

Dezi was finally settled. The house was completed, and he finally got it furnished and decorated, the way he wanted it. He thought about Kayla often, and was anxious to finally see her in the flesh. It was Sunday, and Dezi was headed to church.

"I hope the building doesn't catch fire when I walk in," he chuckled, as he looked at his reflection in the mirror.

Dezi decided he passed inspection in the charcoal Armani suit he was wearing, and Kayla wouldn't suspect he was anyone other than who he would tell her he was. He thought about the last time he touched and held her. She would have gone with him then, if it wasn't for that Agent Black. *She probably thought I would hurt her because of the baby,* Dezi surmised. He wouldn't have. He could forgive Kayla anything. *This time she'll go with me,* Dezi smiled, as he headed out the door.

The church wasn't far, and he found it with ease. Dezi never went to a Christian church. He was raised Catholic, but found his use for God very limited, if at all. He didn't see the purpose of praying to a being you couldn't see or touch. *No, his god was a gun and money. They could both do amazing miracles quickly when necessary,* Dezi thought, chuckling once more, as he got out going inside. He entered the sanctuary, and found a seat near the front, with a good view of the entire congregation and pulpit.

The sanctuary was nice, Dezi thought taking it in. It was very colorful; with the purple and gold he saw everywhere. There were big, beautiful, flower arrangements on either side of the pulpit, and a magnificent painting of Christ above, what Dezi assumed, was the baptismal pool. He saw himself getting admiring stares from some of the female members, and smiled within. *Guess good Christian women need sex too huh,* he deviously thought, barely suppressing the laughter that came.

The laughter left quickly as Dezi saw Kayla enter, and take her seat. He couldn't stop staring. She looked absolutely amazing in the navy blue suit. Kayla aged very little, and her figure was still perfect. Dezi took her in and forced himself to turn his attention to the other woman who entered with her. *She must be Liv's sister,* he thought looking Jackie over. She was also an attractive woman. Honey Almond complexion with nice shapely legs, big brown eyes, and an eye-catching, shoulder length, bob haircut. Dezi knew she was married to the assistant pastor.

Then he saw the young woman who could have been Kayla's twin twenty years ago. *There's my daughter in law,* Dezi thought wistfully, as he looked her over. *No wonder my son fell in love with her,* he sighed gently. Then he saw Aidan and Olivia. Aidan was carrying the small baby, and now handed her carefully to her mother, who smiled at him. Dezi took in his son, and felt that familiar longing in his heart to get to know the boy. Aidan was a very handsome young man who favored Dezi tremendously. *If he had dimples,* he was thinking, until the choir singing broke his thought. Dezi made himself turn away and pay attention to the singers.

His mind was spinning in a thousand different directions. Dezi saw the two men come into the pulpit. He never saw her husband. Big D was careful to send him only photos of Kayla, or her with the kids, never with him. Dezi watched the taller of the two men as he stood at the podium. He followed the man's gaze, and saw it resting on Kayla. Thomas smiled at her, and Kayla gave him a weak return smile. *Hmmm,* Dezi supposed. *All is definitely not well at home.* He knew Kayla, and as he looked at her eyes, he saw the sadness. He smiled again, thinking how easy her husband was going to make this. Dezi sat back, and actually began to relax, and enjoy the service.

●●●

Rachelle saw the handsome man she met a few days earlier, sitting in service. *Well,* she thought, looking him over. *Maybe I'll get a chance to get his number today,* she smiled, recalling their earlier meeting.

"Hi," she said to the man, as he paid for his purchases.

He smiled graciously, and returned her greeting. She noticed the accent. "Where are you from?" "Pembroke Parish," he told her, and they chatted pleasantly for a few moments before he excused himself, and left.

Rachelle got nothing other than his name, and she definitely wanted a lot more from this man than that. Pastor Bradford was calling her name to give the announcements, which brought her back to the present.

Dezi remembered the woman from the store where they met. She was fairly attractive; nice haircut and cute face, full pouty lips, and almost slanted eyes. Her figure was agreeable enough, nothing spectacular to make her stand out. He also saw she was the church secretary. *Might come in handy later,* Dezi thought, making a mental note to talk to her after service.

Rachelle was sitting again, as she felt the man's gaze on her. She looked up to find him staring directly at her. *He is so delicious,* she thought lustfully, as she returned his gaze. *He has the most amazing hazel eyes,* she thought as Dezi smiled at her. Rachelle smiled back, as he returned his attention once more to the service. *Oh yes,* she thought again *I've got to get into those pants and see what's really going on,* Rachelle finished wickedly, also returning her attention to the service.

●●●

Thomas knew Kayla was still hurt. They quarreled last night. He was wrong, and he knew it. He apologized again and again. She accepted it, but he could tell the hurt was still there. Thomas tried to explain to her, there was only one more month of heavy traveling, and then he would be home all the time. *I shouldn't have yelled at her,* he thought sadly. She told him she wanted to go back to working, at least part-time. He blew up, and screamed at her. He basically forbid her to do any such thing, and she grew angry.

"I'm not a child Thomas," Kayla screamed at him.

"No, but you are my wife," Thomas yelled back. "And you will obey what I tell you!" he finished, and slapped her hard across the face. She fell to the floor, and he immediately wished he could take it back.

Kayla was crying, and trying to get away from him.

"Please honey," he pleaded. "I'm sorry," he went on. "So sorry baby, please forgive me," he finished, near tears himself at that point.

How could I have done that to her, Thomas was thinking as he watched Kayla playing with Olivia. *You're going to lose her if you don't get it together man,* he scolded himself. Thomas vowed never to put his hands on Kayla ever again. He rearranged his schedule to have this week free. They were going on a pleasure cruise to the Caribbean. He made the arrangements quickly this morning, actually waking his travel agent from sleep. He would tell her during dinner, after service today. *Please,* Thomas began to pray. *Let her pain be healed, and let her realize once again, how very much I love her. Above all, please let her forgive me completely, for what I did to her,* he concluded, turning his attention to Chris, who was beginning his message.

●●●

Kayla was fighting back tears, as she held the baby. She could barely look at Thomas. She still couldn't believe he hit her. Never in her wildest imagination would she have thought him capable. *What is going on with him,* she wondered, still hurting from last night's confrontation. He hit her so hard it knocked her down. She was scared to death of him at that point. He immediately apologized, picked her up in his arms, and held her. *What did I do to deserve that?* She wondered if he were seeing someone else or if he was just sorry he married her. All Kayla knew was she was in pain, and unhappy.

Kayla thought of Black all night last night. She missed his gentle touch, his loving voice. Even when they argued he never hit her. Kayla even found herself thinking of Dezi. She thought of the times he was angry with her, not once, ever, did he touch her like that. *God,* Kayla began praying to herself. *I need your help with this marriage. I don't know what I'm doing wrong, but please help me to be a better wife. Most of all please protect me, and don't ever let Thomas hit me again,* she finished, a small shudder going through her body.

Kayla felt someone staring at her and turned around. Her eyes met the man's hazel stare. He was a visitor she could tell. She couldn't recall seeing him before. He looked vaguely familiar, but she couldn't place him. Kayla smiled at the man and he smiled back before dropping his gaze, embarrassed that he was caught. She chuckled lightly, and turned her attention back to the pulpit, finding Thomas still watching her intently.

● ● ●

Thomas saw the man looking at her, his jealousy instantly kindled. *It's your fault so stop it,* he chided himself again. He knew his wife was absolutely gorgeous, and if he didn't get it together fast, she would be gone. Kayla saw the jealousy in her husband's face. *Well, at least I know he still cares a little,* she thought as she returned a genuine smile to him this time.

● ● ●

Dezi was still trying to recover from their contact. She looked right at him. He saw that she was trying to place him. He also saw the jealousy on her husband's face, serving further confirmation that things were not good between them right now. Dezi calmed himself. He needed to stick to his plan for this thing to work out. When everything fell into place, he would have not only his love back, but also his son, and his new family, together all in one place. Dezi saw the secretary still watching him intently, that all too familiar look on her face. *I'm going to have to sleep with her,* he thought, sizing the woman up. *Hmm,* Dezi thought looking her over again. *She might do nicely for a moment. Kill two birds with one stone,* he finished thinking as he slyly winked at the woman, recalling his lack of sex since returning to the states.

Rachelle smiled fully, and Dezi knew she was his for the taking. *Damn! That was almost too easy,* he thought and chuckled internally. Dezi looked again at the assistant pastor. There was something very familiar about this guy. He looked at his program, and found the man's name.

"Chris Lynch," he said softly, almost inaudibly.

His memory snapped, and he remembered exactly who he was. Dezi found himself immediately angry. *This is the son of a bitch that raped her,* he fumed. He knew from what Big D told him, that Kayla and the man's wife were friends. He guessed she forgave him. Dezi knew it without a doubt. Kayla was one of the most loving, and forgiving people he knew. Dezi wasn't, and he was pissed that Chris was still alive. *I may have to remedy that shit real soon,* he thought hatefully, flexing his fist open and closed.

The pastor, whom he now knew was Thomas Bradford, Kayla's current husband, was giving the benediction. He was a big man, about the same height as he at 6'2", in good shape, which led Dezi to believe he worked out. Thomas was distinguished looking, with a hint of gray at his temples, and a well-manicured mustache. Dezi decided he would make his way to the secretary. He needed information first before he approached Kayla. Seeing her today was wonderful. He would come back again of course, if need be. *After I fuck this secretary, I should hopefully have Kayla's schedule, and I can see her whenever I want,* Dezi thought as he walked up to Rachelle.

"Hi," he greeted her, accent in place.

"Hi there," Rachelle smiled. "It's so nice to see you in service today."

"So perhaps you would like to go grab a bite to eat," Dezi asked her, feigning shyness.

Rachelle smiled again at how sweet he was. *As good looking as he is, he shouldn't be shy at all,* she thought as she told him yes. Dezi smiled as he followed her in his car to the restaurant, actually laughing out loud at how gullible she was.

"This arrangement should work out nicely," he said to softly, getting out of the car.

Smoke & 2 Mirrors

Everyone came over for dinner, having a wonderful meal. Thomas saw that Kayla was trying hard to be as normal as possible. He knew she didn't want to answer any questions about their relationship, just as he didn't right now. They were gone now, leaving the two of them alone. Thomas found Kayla in the kitchen, finishing up the dishes. He walked up behind her, putting his arms around her waist. He felt her tense.

"It's just me, sweetheart," Thomas said softly, as he kissed her neck.

Kayla was still anxious, and Thomas knew she was afraid. His heart sunk. Thomas turned her around to face him. Kayla wouldn't look at him, so he lifted her face toward him.

"I should never have hurt you like that last night, baby," he told her evenly, the pain evident in his words. "I was a petty man last night. I hurt the one person I love more than anything else in the world last night," Thomas went on. "Please, give me another chance to love you Kayla. I promise you won't regret it," he finished, kissing her on the lips.

He saw her eyes welling as he talked. Thomas hoped against all hope, she would forgive him. He hugged her close to him, and Kayla sighed softly.

"I have a surprise for you honey," Thomas began again.

"What is it?"

He smiled as he held her. "We're going away for a week."

She pulled away, and looked at him.

"When," Kayla asked cautiously.

He smiled again and caressed her face.

"We leave Tuesday," Thomas said simply.

"Really? Where," she asked, delighted.

Thomas felt a weight lift from his shoulders, seeing her happy like this again.

"Yes, really," he began. "We're going to the Caribbean, on a cruise."

Kayla squealed her delight, and hugged Thomas again. He hugged her fiercely, and told her he loved her so much. They began to kiss passionately, and their desire overtook them. Thomas picked her up, and took her into the den, where they made love in front of the fireplace. Thomas held Kayla afterwards, telling her again and again, how much he loved her.

"I forgive you Thomas, really," she said softly, looking him in the eye.

Kayla kissed him again, assuring him of her total forgiveness. They fell asleep together, still lying in front of the fireplace.

●●●

"Did mommy seem different to you today?" Mariah was asking Aidan.

She noticed her mother a little out of rhythm today. Mariah knew they were having problems. She also knew it all surrounded Thomas, and his constant travel. She spoke with him about it when he returned, after Olivia was born. He assured her he would be finished in a month and able to spend more time with her mother. Mariah hoped they would last another month. She knew her mother was unhappy, and lonely. Kayla wanted to go back to work. She wondered if that's what they quarreled about. Mariah didn't want to see her mother unhappy, or go through any more pain.

"Maybe she was just distracted honey," Aidan said simply.

He noticed Kayla was a little different today too. Mariah smiled at her husband, and nodded. He was probably right. Her mother did after all, have a right to have bad days too, she supposed. Mariah chuckled to herself at the thought, and went to check on the baby.

●●●

Aidan was thinking about the visitor today. The man seemed so familiar to him, yet he knew he never met him. They spoke only briefly after service, as he held Olivia. He thought about the conversation.

"Hello," the man greeted him, with a heavy island accent.

"Hi there," Aidan returned.

The man asked if he might see the baby, and Aidan obliged. He saw the man's face change, and become pained. He assumed there was something personal, dealing with his own family perhaps.

"It's a nice town, this place," he'd told Aidan.

"It is," Aidan agreed. "I'm glad you chose to visit today, hopefully you'll come back."

"Yes, I think I might," the man smiled. They parted ways, and he saw him talking to Rachelle. There was nothing unusual about the conversation, Aidan

supposed. There was just something so very familiar about the man himself. He dismissed the thought, and went to find his wife and daughter.

•••

Dezi was pleased with the day's events. He just arrived home from Rachelle's. He managed to learn her name before he slept with her. He laughed silently at how eager she was to be with him.

"An absolute slut," Dezi declared aloud, thinking of her.

Rachelle was however, very useful information wise. She told him all about the Pastor, and his extensive travel of late. She informed him that the Assistant Pastor was leaving in a few weeks for a new church. *Lucky for his ass,* Dezi thought angrily, still wanting to punish Chris for ever touching Kayla. She told him about Kayla's schedule, and that she volunteered at the children's hospital weekly. Rachelle talked a lot, which got on his nerves at times. Dezi thought about the sex once they arrived at her place. He told her he lived with three other people. Dezi chuckled again, at how quickly she believed him. Rachelle was an average lay. *Too much noise and not enough skill,* he thought, as he made his drink.

Dezi sipped the cognac, and thought once again of Kayla. She looked so beautiful today. He was a bit undone by the conservatism of her dress, but she still looked great. Dezi wanted so much to hold Kayla again, to kiss and caress her, to run his fingers through that long, thick, beautiful hair she had. Her husband was obviously stupid. Why else would he ever make her unhappy? *No matter,* Dezi thought, *Big Daddy is back, and I'm all she needs.* He drained his glass, and headed for the gym he installed in the house. He kept himself in excellent shape. Dezi chuckled, thinking about Kayla's love of his body. He was still formidable at 6'2", his hair was still thick and curly, cut close to his head, making it appear wavy, just the way she loved it. Thick and muscular arms, legs and thighs, with a well-defined waist and butt Dezi knew Kayla would still find attractive, just as he found her.

I can't wait to be inside her again, he thought, as he pounded the weights onto the floor. Dezi was still contemplating how he was going to run into her. He needed to gain her trust, her friendship. He didn't want to come across as hitting on her. Dezi knew that would immediately turn Kayla off. He would continue to sleep with Rachelle. That way he wouldn't be over anxious, and ruin his well-laid plans. *I bet that bastard Black is spinning in his grave knowing I'm alive and this close to her again,* Dezi thought, chuckling heartily. He finished his workout, and headed upstairs to rest. He was going out tonight. He needed to know the layout of the land. *Time to get moving man! We've already wasted enough time,* Dezi chastised himself.

His phone rang. He looked at the ID. It was Rachelle.

"Hello," he answered, accent once again turned on.

"Hi Dante,'" she purred into the phone.

"Hello Rachelle," Dezi replied smoothly, wondering what she wanted.

"I was wondering if perhaps, I could interest you in returning. Maybe even spending the night, hmm?"

Dezi chuckled silently. He really had other plans for tonight, but he needed to keep her talking, and at some point even helping him, so he agreed.

"Wonderful," Rachelle replied delighted. "I'll expect you in about an hour?"

"Yes, I'll be there," he replied and they hung up.

"Well, I still have time for a quick run by Kayla's house," Dezi mused aloud, heading to his bedroom to grab his overnight bag.

He drove by the magnificent stone front home, with the beautiful manicured front lawn. It heralded a generous array of blooms, complimented by a lake on the backside of the house, where the deck connected. Dezi saw only one light as he passed. He sighed, and headed for Rachelle's. *I'll definitely have to think of Kayla while I'm screwing her this time*, Dezi thought.

"The things you do for love," he sighed softly, turning into Rachelle's driveway.

●●●

Thomas was just putting Kayla gently into bed, when he heard his cell. She stirred slightly, but didn't wake. He snatched the phone up, placing it on vibrate, and crept out of the room before answering.

"Hello," Thomas answered quietly, as he walked further away from their bedroom.

"I asked you never to call me this late," he told the caller angrily. "What is it?"

The caller stated the purpose of the call, and Thomas listened in dismay.

"I can't this week. I'm taking my wife on vacation," he replied.

The caller continued to speak, reminding him the urgency of the situation. Thomas sighed heavily, knowing he was defeated.

"All right," he said quietly. "I'll fly out in the morning," he went on. "How long am I staying this time?"

The caller answered his question, and told him goodnight. He sat down in his chair. He made it to his study to complete the call. *How the hell am I going to tell her I have to leave again?* If that wasn't enough, he also would be forced to tell her how long this time. Thomas found himself praying again. She was going to be hurt. He knew that already. Thomas just hoped Kayla would still be there when he came back. *Maybe I should let her work part time,* he thought again. It would give her something to do, and maybe she wouldn't be so upset about his traveling anymore.

Thomas didn't really want her to work. It wasn't that he was old fashioned; honestly he was scared. Kayla was the most beautiful woman he ever met. Thomas supposed he liked keeping Kayla close to him, so no one else would take her away. He felt very vulnerable since learning he couldn't give her a child. They talked about it, and she agreed that it would be nice for them to have one together. *You couldn't even do that for her,* Thomas chastised again.

True, Kayla was no different, and she loved him just as much, Thomas still felt that he let her down. He was doing all the things he was doing now, for her. He wanted to give Kayla everything. She deserved that and so much more. *Please,* he began to pray again. *Let her understand one more time, when I tell her this tomorrow,* he fervently prayed, heading for their bedroom. He kissed Kayla gently on the cheek, and she stirred a tad. Thomas lay down beside Kayla taking her in his arms, and closed his eyes to sleep.

Smoke & **3** Mirrors

Hi Dad," Mariah greeted him, "May I speak to mommy, please?"

Thomas sighed deeply. He didn't want to have to tell anyone, but he knew he would have to tell Mariah.

"She's not here," he said quietly.

Mariah thought that was odd. Where could her mother be this early?

"Oh," she replied. "When do you expect her back?"

Thomas really didn't want to get into this.

"I'm not sure Mariah," he replied. "Do you want me to tell her to call you," he finished, hoping he could avoid any more questions.

Mariah was completely perplexed. It wasn't like her mother to go anywhere, and not at least tell Thomas what time she would be back.

"Is everything alright Dad?"

Thomas took a deep breath. He didn't want to lie, but he wasn't ready to answer any questions right now either.

"She just went out for a while, that's all," he replied evasively, trying to keep his tone even.

Mariah was getting a bad feeling. This wasn't like her mother at all, not to mention how evasive Thomas was being.

"Did you two argue again," she asked him softly.

Thomas sighed deeply, and Mariah knew they did.

"What happened, Dad?"

He didn't want to tell her, but he knew she wouldn't stop until he did.

"I've been called out of town again," Thomas told Mariah. "And I'll be gone for three weeks."

Mariah sighed but didn't speak as he continued.

"I promised to take her on a cruise this week, but of course I had to cancel because of the trip."

"I've never seen her that angry, Mariah," Thomas said resignedly.

Mariah exhaled again. She only recalled seeing her mother really angry a couple of times, herself.

"Did she say where she was going?"

"No," he replied sadly.

Mariah knew this was hard for him.

"Can you take her with you this time, Dad," Mariah asked hopefully.

Thomas sighed heavily again.

"No, unfortunately I can't, Mariah."

Thomas heard a car in the drive, and looked out the window. He breathed a sigh of relief.

"She's home now. Let me go," he told Mariah, who was also relieved.

"OK Dad," she replied. "Call me later, if you need me."

Thomas went to the door, and opened it for her. Kayla walked in, and passed him without acknowledgement. *She's still angry,* he thought sadly, as he followed her into the kitchen. It was usually a warm and comfortable place, with all the bright sunflowers she collected, and displayed on the walls, mixing in watermelon and strawberries for color. Kayla loved all her collectibles, and spent a lot of time here, cooking and creating wonderful meals for them to enjoy. Today it felt cold and sterile, given the mood she was in.

"Honey," Thomas began. "Please don't be angry," he went on. "I swear to you this will be over soon, and I'll make it up to you."

Kayla took a deep breath, and loosed a sound filled breath as she turned to face him.

"I'm going back to work," she said simply, watching him intently to see his reaction.

Thomas swallowed hard. He was defeated, and he knew it. As much as he hated the idea of Kayla being out working and meeting other people, other men, he had no choice if he wanted to save his marriage.

"All right baby," Thomas replied gently, hoping that would make her happy, and he wouldn't lose her.

Kayla continued to watch him. He was getting uncomfortable, not knowing what she was thinking behind that gaze.

"Are we alright baby," Thomas asked her, concerned.

"I honestly don't know," she returned, matter-of-fact.

Thomas didn't like that answer at all. He needed to know she would be here when he returned. He walked to her, and reached out for her. Kayla didn't push him away, nor did she step any closer. Thomas took her in his arms, and tried to kiss her. This time Kayla did push him away.

"I can't," she said simply, and walked away.

Thomas was devastated. He couldn't lose her. He was doing all this for their future.

"Honey," he began, following her into the sunroom.

Here the light sparkled, and made the room come alive, it was where they spent time together almost daily, during the first year of their marriage.

"Please try and understand," Thomas went on. "I know you're hurt, I know you're angry, but baby I love you so much," he finished, putting his arms around Kayla's waist standing behind her.

She was looking out of the window at the ducks that were gathering in the yard, eating the bread she threw out earlier. Thomas heard her sigh softly. He turned her to him, and kissed her.

"Baby, please," he said gently. "I can't lose you," he finished, lifting her head to kiss her again. She didn't push him away this time. Thomas kissed her gently, and hugged her close to him. Kayla began to cry. He led her to the couch and sitting down, continued to hold her.

"Is there someone else, Thomas," Kayla asked quietly.

He was dumbstruck. He never dreamed she would think he would cheat on her.

"No baby, absolutely not," Thomas replied emphatically.

Kayla looked him in the eye.

"Are you sure," she asked again, continuing to look at him.

"There is no one else in the world for me but you, Kayla," Thomas told her again, kissing her for emphasis.

She seemed satisfied, and lay in his arms again. He felt her breathing become even, and realized she was sleeping. He didn't move. He held her, and watched her sleep. *This has got to be the last trip,* Thomas thought, realizing just how close he actually came to losing her this time.

●●●

Dezi was delighted. He saw her this morning as he made his usual bagel run. She was going into the business license office. Kayla was dressed impeccably, in an all business black skirt and white blouse, with sterling silver accessories. Even in that plain ensemble, she was absolutely gorgeous. Dezi suspected she was going back to work. *Prefect,* he plotted. He would hire Kayla as his broker and financial specialist. Dezi chuckled, remembering how hard it was this morning not to run up and say hello. He was having lunch with Rachelle later today. He wasn't really looking forward to it. She was already becoming a headache. She wanted to see him constantly, and now she wanted to define their friendship. Rachelle was shopping for a relationship. Dezi knew that already, although he held other plans. Still, he would humor her for the time being. His phone rang. He looked at the display. *Speak of the devil,* Dezi mused, as he answered.

"Good morning," Rachelle quipped.

He frowned slightly, but returned the greeting.

"Would you like to join me for breakfast?"

"I've already had my breakfast," he replied smoothly.

"Oh," Rachelle sighed, sounding disenchanted.

"Why are you up so early anyway," Dezi asked. "I thought you were off for the week."

"Yes well plans have changed," Rachelle told him. "Seems Pastor is going out of town again so I have to be in place on time, and keep things flowing."

Dezi was intrigued that he was leaving town, yet again.

"Is his wife going with him this time?"

"No," Rachelle told him. "He normally makes these trips alone."

Dezi was getting happier by the moment.

"Well I guess that's okay," he began. "Since I'm sure he's not gone long," he fished.

Rachelle took the bait.

"Please!" she began. "He's gone for weeks at a time," she went on. "This trip is three weeks all by itself," she continued. "Kayla's a good woman, because I wouldn't put up with that nonsense, personally."

Yes she is a good woman. Better than you'll ever be, Dezi thought.

"Well, I'm sure she must love him then," he replied.

"Yes, I suppose she must," Rachelle said, and turned the conversation back to them.

"When can I see you again? Besides our lunch date today I mean," she asked.

Dezi wasn't going to let Rachelle monopolize all his time. He was just given three good weeks to work on his friendship with Kayla.

"I have to go out of town for a few days," he replied "I'll call you when I come back, OK?"

"OK," Rachelle sighed softly.

Dezi could hear the disappointment in her voice, but he didn't care. His mind was on his love, and getting closer to her.

"Well alright," she replied again. "I'll see you later."

"Okay, see you," Dezi told and disconnected.

His mind was going in multiple directions. He needed to go back to the license office, and see if Kayla did indeed register again. He was going to be her first client. *I'm going to make you happy again Kayla. We're going to be together,* Dezi thought as he headed to his home office. There was other business he was working on too, and he needed to make sure everything continued to move according to plan. It was all going to come together soon, and he didn't need to leave anything to chance.

●●●

"Hey youngblood," Big D greeted Aidan cheerfully.

The young man called him this morning needing to talk.

"It's good to hear from you," he continued. "How's the baby and the wife?"

"They're both fine," Aidan laughed. "Livvy is growing every day."

"It's just so amazing when I look at her sometimes D," he told him. "To think, I actually helped create something that perfect," Aidan mused.

Big D laughed.

"Yeah, just wait until she starts dating."

"That won't be happening until she turns thirty," Aidan replied.

They both laughed heartily at that. Aidan began to tell him the reason he called. He needed his advice. Aidan received the opportunity to go to school out of the country, fully paid.

"Do you think I should take my wife and daughter away from their family?"

Big D thought about it, and decided it might be for the best, since he already knew Dezi was back, and what he planned.

"Where are you talking about going?".

"It's a school in Bermuda, place called Pembroke Pines, is the town," Aidan told Big D.

He almost laughed aloud. Big D knew then that Dezi set this up.

"It sounds like a great opportunity, Aidan," Big D told him.

"I mean it is," Aidan went on. "Mariah could go to school free too. I guess I just don't know how she will feel leaving her mother, since they're so close, you know?"

"Well youngblood," Big D told him. "She's a wife and mother now. So you, and that baby, have to be her first priority," he went on. "I'm pretty sure she'll be alright though. Her mother can always come and visit, and they can always come visit her," Big D finished, knowing full well Kayla would be right there with them, if Dezi had his way.

"Thanks D," Aidan returned. "For the great advice and helping me make a good decision."

"I'll talk to Mariah about it this evening and help her see how positive this would be for all of us," Aidan added.

"Anytime youngblood, anytime," Big D returned, as he and the young man disconnected.

He immediately dialed Dezi's cell.

●●●

"Hello," he answered.

"You still got it man!" Big D laughed, when his friend answered.

He told Dezi about his conversation with Aidan, and they both laughed.

"So, is he leaning toward going?"

"Yeah he's sold," Big D told him Aidan. "He's going to talk to his wife about it later this evening."

"That's excellent," Dezi replied. "I'm going to have them gone first," he continued. "Then Kayla won't feel guilty about leaving them here, when she comes with me."

"I got a good feeling about it this time man," Big D told Dezi. "I think everything is going to work out for you."

"Yeah I think it's going to be all good too," Dezi replied.

"Call me in a couple days," Dezi told Big D.

"No problem," he replied as they said goodbye and disconnected.

Dezi sat back, and reflected on the events. *Things are going very well and right on schedule,* he mused, getting up to ready himself for his lunch date.

Smoke & 4 Mirrors

idan went into the nursery to find Mariah looking worried, as she held the baby.

"What's wrong," he asked gently.

She sighed and told him about her conversation with Thomas. Aidan was worried too. They were fighting a lot lately. He hoped Pastor Bradford would stop, or at least slow down on the travel. He hoped they weren't headed for divorce. Aidan knew Mariah would be devastated. He also knew she would never leave then.

"I'm sure they'll work it out, baby," Aidan tried to reassure Mariah, even though he wasn't all that sure himself.

He got the uneasy feeling Kayla was about at her end with the whole thing. He hoped with everything in him, that he was wrong. Aidan took Livvy, and left Mariah to her thoughts. He would feed her and give her a bath. He absolutely adored his daughter. Aidan often thought about his own father, and wondered how he would have reacted if he ever met him. He wanted to know everything about the empire he built. Aidan wanted to follow in his father's footsteps but he didn't have a clue how to even start. He sighed deeply. No use wondering about what ifs. He was dead now, so it didn't matter. Aidan kissed the happily squealing baby and took her from the tub back to her room to dress her.

Mariah watched him with the baby. She wondered if he would accept the offer from the school in Pembroke Parish. She knew he thought she didn't know, but she found the papers when she was cleaning. *I don't know if I can leave mommy with all she's going through,* Mariah thought, knowing full well Kayla would be the first to tell her to go. *I won't worry about it until he brings it up, I guess,* she thought again, leaving the room to go make them lunch.

•••

Dezi was in an extremely good mood. His son was coming home, bringing his daughter-in law and granddaughter, with him. The love of his life was indeed working again, he found out after a quick trip to the license office. Things were going perfectly. He could even endure sitting here listening to Rachelle drone on, and on, about nothing. He told her he was leaving after lunch, so he wouldn't have to worry about sleeping with her again.

He really grew to detest it. She wasn't very good at all, and Dezi arousal was arduous and hard to maintain, when he slept with her. He was going to call Kayla after lunch, and set up an appointment. Dezi was excited just thinking about seeing her, and being alone with her again, after all these years.

"Do you want desert," Rachelle asked, bringing him out of his thoughts.

"No, nothing for me thanks," Dezi replied.

Rachelle looked him over, and spoke.

"Trying to stay fine, no doubt," she replied lustfully.

"Something like that," he laughed.

She ordered strawberry shortcake, and continued to chatter as she ate it. Finally lunch was over, and Dezi was walking Rachelle to her car.

"Have a safe trip, Dante," she told him, as she gave him a quick kiss.

"I will," Dezi told her, as he closed her door and leaned in, to give her another quick peck.

He waved as Rachelle drove down the street.

●●●

"Damn!" he swore aloud. "I thought she would never leave," he chuckled.

He got into his car, and pulled out his cell, dialing the number she listed on the business application.

"Hello," Kayla answered amiably.

Dezi was speechless. He was experiencing her voice again after twenty years. She still sounded heavenly.

"Hello," he returned, accent carefully in place. "I'm looking for Kayla Bradford."

"This is she," Kayla replied.

"I got your number when I visited the license office to inquire about a financial broker," Dezi told her.

"That's wonderful. When would you like to get together?"

Dezi was trying to not blurt out how much he still loved her, as he thought.

"How about tomorrow, for lunch perhaps," he replied.

"That will be fine," Kayla told him. "Any particular place you favor?"

"Champions Green," Dezi asked.

"Sounds wonderful, " Kayla told Dante. "Thank you for calling and I will see you tomorrow."

"Yes, I'm looking very forward to it," Dezi replied, as he let her go.

He needed to go home and hit the gym. He was fully aroused just from the sound of her voice. *I'm going to have to smoke, or take something, before I meet her tomorrow*, Dezi thought, seeing the effect she had on him. He laughed at himself, started his car and headed home. There were still details and plans that needed to be made.

●●●

Trying to relax before his next meeting, Thomas was lying in his hotel room thinking about his wife. He was none too thrilled that Kayla was going back to work. He accepted it though. He couldn't lose her, and she was livid this morning. He called her earlier, and knew she already received a call from a perspective client. *It just had to be a man too huh*, Thomas thought angrily. He was jealous as hell when it came to her. He made up his mind that whether this trip was successful or not, it was the final one. His marriage wouldn't stand the stress of another trip, and he couldn't stand the stress of knowing Kayla was around other men, client or not. The phone rang. *I hope this is my wife*, Thomas mused thoughtfully.

"Hello?"

"Hey Pastor," Rachelle returned.

He sighed softly, and returned her greeting. She call to update him on the church, and some things that needed his attention at the moment.

"Are you alright," she asked concerned.

"Yes, Rachelle I'm fine," Thomas returned. "It's just been a long day, that's all."

"OK, well if you need anything, give me a call," Rachelle offered.

"Thank you, Rachelle. I will keep that in mind," Thomas replied and ended their conversation.

He looked at the clock, and saw it was almost time for him to leave. Thomas rose, and headed for the shower, dressing shortly afterward and leaving for his meeting.

●●●

Kayla missed her husband and they parted awkwardly as he left. She got up to shower and get ready for her day tomorrow. She was looking forward to getting back to work. She was also pleased that Debbie looked out for her. She was the girl at the license department, and she told Kayla she would send her as many clients as she could. Mr. Enzo was very charming. *You have to do a good job for him, so he'll recommend you to friends.* Kayla thought as she stepped into the shower. Today was a good day, and tomorrow promised to be even better.

Smoke & 5 Mirrors

Aidan was trying to figure out how to broach the subject with Mariah. He needed her support on this. He knew it was going to be a hard sell as it was, but now with trouble between Thomas and her mother, it was going to be almost impossible. Mariah came into the sunroom where he was sitting, waiting for her. She already knew what he wanted to talk about. She was just waiting on him to say it.

"Livvy asleep," Aidan asked.

"Yes, soundly," she smiled.

"I think she's actually snoring a little," Mariah chuckled, as Aidan joined her.

"Baby I've received the most exciting offer," he began, watching her intently, as he spoke.

"I've, I mean, we've, been offered the opportunity to go to school free of charge," he went on. "The package includes room and board too, which in our case, would be couples housing," Aidan finished, and waited for a response.

Mariah already knew what he was talking about, so she wouldn't make him suffer through all this explanation.

"I know about the offer, Aidan," she said softly.

"How did you find out?"

"I found the letter when I was cleaning," Mariah smiled.

"I should have known," he smiled back.

They both chuckled.

"So, have you decided you want to go?"

He looked at her for a moment before answering.

"Yes," Aidan replied mildly.

Mariah sighed deeply.

"I know you don't want to leave your family baby," he began. "But you know as well as I do, your mother would be the first to tell us what an excellent opportunity this is for us."

Mariah smiled somewhat, knowing Aidan was right.

"I know," she replied. "I'm just scared."

Aidan understood as he came to her, taking Mariah in his arms.

"Baby I'll be here for you, and protect both you and Livvy," he spoke soothingly. "We can have a great life and get our degrees at the same time."

"Baby, we can always come back once we're done with school," Aidan began again. "Plus, we'll visit, and you know your mother will always come see us, as much as she loves water."

Mariah smiled again, knowing he was right.

"So when do we leave?"

Aidan smiled brightly, and hugged her again.

"In about a month," he replied. "We need to get some stuff in order first."

"Thank you baby," he added, as he kissed her.

●●●

Dezi gave himself quite a workout. He was exhausted now and ready to sleep. He didn't need to worry about Rachelle. She thought he was out of town. *Thank goodness,* he sighed relieved. He really didn't know how he was going to continue sleeping with her. He would think of something he supposed. Dezi thought ahead to the meeting he would have with Kayla tomorrow, as he went to his closet and picked out just the right suit. *Blue is her favorite color,* Dezi thought, taking the tailor made suit out of the closet. He chose the accessories, and headed to the shower. He would have a drink and unwind, after his shower. His phone rang before he could get in.

Dezi looked at the display. "Yeah," he answered.

"Everything is set and in place," Big D told him.

"That's good," he replied, "When?"

"Tomorrow night," Big D answered.

"Thanks man, I knew you could take care of it," Dezi laughed.

"It's straight and you should have exactly what you want," Big D told him another time.

"Yeah, it's the icing for my cake," Dezi said chuckling again.

Big D laughed.

"I'll call you once everything is complete."

"That's fine," Dezi told him, and they hung up.

Nothing like a little insurance policy, he thought about the call, heading to the shower once again. Dezi found himself thinking of Kayla again while he showered. He thought of the times they made love in her shower, his too for that matter. *We'll be back together baby,* Dezi thought again, *and I'll make you remember all those delicious times together.* He turned the cold water up, as he felt himself once again, becoming seriously aroused.

●●●

Finished with his shower, and now sitting in front of the TV enjoying his cognac. Dezi picked up his cell, and dialed.

"Hey," the man answered.

"You have everything you need for tomorrow?"

"Yeah its straight, I just need her kept busy for the allotted time."

Dezi smiled. That wouldn't be a problem. He knew how much Kayla loved what she did, and Dezi was walking in with a substantial amount of money for her to work with.

"I'll take care of that," he replied. "You just don't mess up, or it's your ass. You got me," he finished icily.

"I got it," the man told him.

These fuckers are going to make me kill somebody before I leave this piece, Dezi thought crossly, as he made himself another drink. He wanted to be gone within the next couple of months. He knew if Aidan took the offer, which Big D assured him he would, they would leave in the next month. Then he would really shift into overdrive getting her ready to leave too. *You're going to love your new home Kayla,* Dezi thought, bringing a smile to his face.

"Ahh baby," he said softly aloud. "It's been too long."

Dezi drained his glass, and headed for his bed. He was anxiously waiting the new day.

●●●

Thomas was exhausted. It was a very long night. He looked at the clock, finding it was after midnight. He wouldn't call and disturb Kayla this late. Thomas realized the broker was a side of Kayla he didn't know well. He made a mental note to talk to her when he returned, and get to know all about what she did. *She worked when she was married to Donovan,* he thought. He was just paranoid, he supposed. Kayla never gave him any reason to think she would ever be unfaithful. Thomas knew a lot of his fear was from his own past experience, and he needed to get a handle on it. Thomas thought of hitting Kayla, again bringing a new round of guilt and shame.

He was having a flashback from his first wife, and Debbie, the woman from his last enduring relationship with, before marrying Kayla. She was nothing like them, yet he treated her like she was. Thomas was glad she gave him another chance, vowing he wouldn't mess up again. He needed to go pick her up something nice tomorrow, while he had a little free time.

Thomas would be in meetings off and on all day and it was really beginning to take its toll on him. He was told this was the last set, and the outcome would happen after this particular one was ended, in two weeks. He certainly hoped so. Otherwise it was all in vain as far as he was concerned. He wasn't going to leave his wife alone anymore, and that was final. *Please protect my wife from any unscrupulous characters,* Thomas prayed silently, having a bad feeling. He couldn't explain it, but his mind held a premonition something very dark was on the horizon, and it was headed straight for them.

●●●

Kayla woke refreshed, but nervous. She didn't work in the five years since Black's death. She was still on top of her game though. She made sure she kept up on what was going on in the market faithfully. *You can do this,* Kayla thought, laughing at how silly she was being. The phone rang.

"Hello?"

"Hi, Mommy," Mariah returned cheerfully.

Kayla smiled, and returned her daughters greeting.

"What are you doing today," she asked, unaware that Kayla was working again.

"I have a meeting with a client today," she replied smoothly.

There was silence for a few moments, until Mariah spoke again.

"Does Dad know you're working again?"

Kayla chuckled lightly.

"Yes, he does, and he knows I have a client already too."

Mariah assumed Thomas agreed to her working because he cancelled their trip, and she was angry.

"Are you sure you want to do this again mommy?"

"Yes, I'm sure," Kayla sighed.

"I need to do something I enjoy Mariah," she explained. "I'm good at this, and I love it!"

Even though Mariah didn't really want Kayla to work, she was happy for her mother.

"I'm proud of you for going back, Mommy."

"Thank you, honey," Kayla replied happily.

"Well, will you call me after you come back?"

She needed to tell her about them moving away to complete school.

"Yes, of course honey," Kayla replied.

"Is something wrong," she asked, picking up the tone of Mariah's voice.

Mariah smiled. Her mother knew her so well.

"No, not really mommy," she began. "I just need to tell you something."

Kayla wasn't sure she liked where this was going.

"So tell me now," she told Mariah, becoming anxious.

"What time is your meeting," Mariah asked.

"It's not until noon," Kayla told her. "I have time."

Mariah took a deep breath, and told her about the school, as well as the fact that it was out of the country.

"So you and Aidan think this is a good opportunity?"

"Yes," Mariah told her. "We would get to enjoy a wonderful year round, warm climate."

Kayla smiled, thinking how much she would like that herself.

"I think it's wonderful honey," she replied good-naturedly.

Mariah wondered if her mother were telling her the truth.

"Really?"

Kayla laughed.

"Yes girl," She replied. "It gives me a lot of reasons to visit you all the time, and enjoy that sun and surf!"

After she settled down, Kayla spoke seriously.

"Mariah, baby," she started. "You have to live your life. I know you love me, and no matter where you are, I know that will never change," she continued. "You must also know within yourself that I feel the same for you, Aidan, and Livvy," Kayla finished gently, hearing Mariah crying softly.

"Thank you mommy," Mariah said simply.

"You're welcome. When are you all leaving," Kayla asked.

"Not for another month," she replied.

"Well that's good, gives you plenty of time to get everything together so you can be ready for my first visit," Kayla told her.

Mariah laughed aloud. Kayla knew she was feeling better now, and she was glad. She didn't want Mariah staying here because of her.

"Well, I better go. I have to get my portfolios and computer equipment together," Kayla told Mariah. "I'll call you later honey, OK?"

"That's fine mommy," Mariah told her as they said goodbye.

Kayla reflected on what she just learned. *Well you knew she would leave one day*, she thought, fighting back tears.

"Good thing I decided to go back to work, huh," Kayla said aloud, as she went to get her things together.

•••

The phone was ringing again.

"Hello?" she answered.

"Good morning, baby," Thomas greeted lovingly.

Kayla smiled, and returned his greeting.

"How was your evening?"

"The usual," he chuckled.

"I wanted to call and tell you good luck with your meeting," Thomas said amiably.

She thought that was a very nice gesture.

"What time is your meeting?"

"In about an hour and a half, so I better get moving," Kayla began. "We're meeting at Champions Green."

Thomas knew it was a far distance from their home, and she would need to go ahead and leave.

"OK," he replied. "Go and do what you do honey," he continued. "I love you."

She chuckled softly.

"I love you too," Kayla told him. "Call me later tonight, after your meetings."

"I will," Thomas promised, and they disconnected.

She grabbed her equipment and headed for her car. Kayla popped in a jazz CD, and was soon speeding toward the restaurant, completely absorbed in her thoughts.

Smoke & **6** Mirrors

Dezi watched Kayla pass him on the interstate. *She's still a speed demon!* He chuckled silently. He only caught a glance, but no matter, he would get to enjoy the total package once he arrived at the restaurant. Dezi chose this particular one because of the distance, and the privacy it offered. He reserved one of the smaller meeting rooms. Dezi wanted very much to be alone with Kayla, and this would also accommodate them the space they needed to cover all his paperwork.

He needed to give the men he hired time to do what they needed to do at her house. His cell rang as Dezi glanced at the display. It was Rachelle. *Not now, no bad karma,* he thought, letting her go to voicemail. He already told her he would be out of town. Dezi supposed she was calling to double check. His cell rang again. *If this is Rachelle again,* he was thinking ominously. It was his worker.

"Yeah?"

"Do you know if she's gone yet?" he asked.

"Yes, she's gone, go ahead and handle everything," Dezi told him.

"OK," he replied. "Remember, we need a solid two and half hours to get this done right."

"You will easily get that," Dezi assured him.

"Make sure all the devices are working correctly," he instructed the man.

"We'll go to your house after we're done here, and check the equipment," the man replied.

"Fine," Dezi replied again. "After I get home and check everything out, I'll call you for your payment," he finished and disconnected.

Time to get everything up and running. Dezi thought.

He was having Kayla's house wired for sight and sound. He would have monitors in his viewing room, so he could see every room in her house, as well as hear everything that was said. Dezi needed to get inside her world, to find the cracks he would exploit to get her back. *I can't wait to see you up close and personal again baby,* he thought excitedly, as he exited the freeway headed for the restaurant.

●●●

Collins couldn't believe his luck. He landed in North Carolina for three days, before managing to somehow break his leg. For the last month plus, he was confined to a desk, and was forced to limit his search for Dezi to the computer and telephone. Collins hated using crutches and not being able to get around. *I need to get to her house and stake it out for a while,* he thought, of Kayla.

They considered the case closed years ago, so of course he couldn't officially investigate, but Collins knew Gianni was back, and he knew why. He managed to get Kayla's new address and phone number. He planned to call her later today. He would tell her he transferred, but of course he wouldn't tell her about Gianni. Not yet. Collins knew Kayla would invite him over, and he needed to get there. He needed to know all he could about her, and her comings and goings now. He wondered if she was back at work. So far, Gianni was keeping one seriously low profile. No one matching his description was seen in the area. *Of course, he probably looks completely different now.* Collins thought disgustedly, knowing he underwent some surgery, and they possessed no current photos.

"This is gonna require a whole lot of luck," he said aloud.

Collins still didn't know why Gianni chose Virginia to return. He contacted a couple of friends at the bureau there, who owed him a favor, to chase a couple of hunches. He was waiting to hear from them. Collins couldn't let Gianni harm Kayla. He still felt so guilty for lying to Black all those years. He was not only his partner, but also his friend and Collins let Black believe that lie to his grave. *I'm gonna make it right though,* he vowed another time.

Collins was determined to find Gianni, and put an end to him, once and for all. His computer beeped, and he saw the email icon. Collins opened the electronic message, and found some interesting information.

"So," he began aloud. "Big D is still around is he?"

He smiled. Now he knew why Gianni chose Virginia. Collins picked up the phone and made a call. He arranged for his friends to pick up Demetrius Wilson, aka Big D. Then he made a plane reservation for himself. Collins was going to Virginia, and find out just what Gianni was up to, broken leg and all.

●●●

Kayla was waiting in the lobby when Dezi walked in. He caught his breath. She was here within arm's reach, after all these years. Dezi quickly gathered himself, and approached her.

"Mrs. Bradford," he queried, accent in place.

She smiled, and he almost lost it.

"Yes, I'm Kayla Bradford," she replied, extending her hand.

He took her hand, and shook it. Dezi was still reeling standing this close to her, and now he actually touched her again. The hostess came over and interrupted his thought.

"Your room is ready now," she informed them cheerfully.

"After you," Dezi said politely, allowing Kayla to walk ahead.

He was taking her in all over again as she walked. She looked stunning today, professionally dressed in a soft pink blouse, and black tailor fitted skirt. Her legs were still shapely, with the three-inch stiletto heels, making them look even sexier.

"Here we are," the hostess was saying, as she opened the door.

They entered and made themselves comfortable. Their waitress came, and took their drink orders.

●●●

"So Mr. Enzo," Kayla began. "Tell me about yourself, and what you hope to accomplish with your investments."

Dezi sat back in his chair thoughtfully for a moment.

"Well, I'm from Pembroke Parish, it's in Bermuda," he began.

Kayla recognized the town from her conversation earlier with Mariah. *Maybe he could tell them what to really expect once they get there*, she was thinking.

"I'm single now," Dezi went on.

Kayla wondered if were ever married or just dating someone.

"I simply want my money to work for me, and afford me the lifestyle I've become accustomed too," Dezi went on to tell her.

"Well, I'm sure we can definitely make that happen for you," she replied, smiling again.

"Mr. Enzo," Kayla began, before he cut her off.

"Please call me Dante," Dezi replied smoothly.

Kayla smiled, and corrected herself.

"May I ask you a personal question?"

"Certainly," Dezi smiled.

"Why did you leave Bermuda, for here?"

He chuckled lightly before answering.

"It's not a permanent move for me," Dezi began. "There is some unfinished business I need to attend to, then I'm going back home," he replied, looking Kayla directly in the eye as he spoke.

What beautiful hazel eyes he has, Kayla remarked inwardly. She noticed Dante Enzo was a very attractive man in general. He reminded Kayla of Dezi actually, once she thought about it. He shared the same structure and build. The only thing she didn't care much for was the beard. She was never a big fan of facial hair. She would tolerate a mustache, but she didn't like beards at all. *No matter,* Kayla thought again. *I'm sure whomever he dates, or marries, will like it.*

"Oh, well now I understand a little better," she replied.

"Why do you say it that way," Dezi asked.

"Oh, it's just that I love water, tropical climates, and things like that," Kayla told him. "I miss it a lot actually, living here."

"Perhaps you will come and visit sometimes?"

She smiled.

"Well actually, my daughter and son in-law are moving to Pembroke Parish, to complete their schooling," Kayla told him.

Dezi smiled again.

"Hmm, perhaps I could meet them, tell them a little about the place before they arrive."

"That sounds like a wonderful idea," Kayla returned. "I'll arrange a nice dinner party for us, and we'll all get together then."

"I'm looking forward to it," Dezi replied smiling another time.

The server brought their lunch and they began to eat, talking more about Bermuda, and the wonderful climate. Dezi was in a state of total bliss sitting here having lunch with Kayla. He forgot how engaging she could be in the art of conversation. Here was a woman he could actually sit and talk with for hours.

Dezi thought about the wistful look on Kayla's face when she talked about her love of the water. *Don't worry baby, the house overlooks the ocean*, he thought, watching her get up. She excused herself to the restroom. They were going to have dessert, then begin working on his portfolio. Dezi checked his watch. They were already well into two hours. He knew going over his paperwork, would take at least another two. Dezi never wanted the afternoon to end. He loved being here with her.

Patience man, Dezi chided himself. Everything was lined up, he couldn't let his emotions take over, and make him take a wrong turn. His cell rang. He checked the display. It was Rachelle again. *Damn!* Dezi thought. *This bitch is like a bad case of hemorrhoids*. He changed the setting from ring to vibrate, and placed the phone back in his pocket.

"Let her leave another message," Dezi said half aloud, as he heard Kayla opening the door.

●●●

Collins hobbled into the interrogation room. His friends unofficially detained Demetrius Wilson for him, but they could only hold him a couple of hours. Collins decided he needed to make those hours count.

"How are you today Mr. Wilson," he addressed the man sitting across the large, worn, wooden table from him.

Big D regarded him with a look of utter disdain, and didn't answer. Collins sat down and took his time opening and reading the file in front of him. There was really nothing in it. He was just bluffing trying to rattle the man.

Big D relaxed in his chair. He knew they didn't have anything on him. He hadn't done anything on their level in years. *This one is looking for something*, Big D thought, watching Collins intently. Big D remained deep in the game a long time, and it took a lot to shake his cage. Collins finally looked up and cleared his throat.

"So tell me," he began. "Where is Gianni now," he asked, never taking his eyes of the man in front of him.

Big D didn't flinch. *So, that's what he wants*, he thought inwardly. He wondered why? He knew there couldn't be any official investigation. So what was this guy up too?

"Man, you're kidding me right," Big D replied coolly. "You pick me up, hassle me to bring me here, and ask me about a guy who's been dead for twenty years?"

Collins knew he was lying. He must be. *The guy didn't even react though*, he observed. Maybe Gianni came here and didn't let anyone know. Maybe it was just a coincidence after all. He decided to try again.

"Look Wilson," Collins began again, a little more forcefully. "We know Gianni came back to the states. We also know you and he are friends. So stop trying to con me, and tell me where he is," he finished, looking at the man hard.

Big D smiled again.

"Like I said, the man you're talking about is dead, unless you know something I don't," he continued, giving Collins a quizzical look.

Collins didn't reply. Big D nodded knowingly.

"So now, if you're done hassling me, I would like to leave," he finished.

Big D knew they couldn't keep him if he didn't want to be here. They held absolutely nothing on him. Collins was frustrated. This guy knew something, he could feel it. He sighed deeply, and told him he was free to leave. Big D hurriedly gathered himself, and left. Collins already asked one of his friends to follow him for a while. *Maybe he'll meet Gianni somewhere, and we'll at least see what he looks like now*, he thought dejectedly He made his way back to an empty office, and waited for his cab. He still needed to call Kayla once he made it back to North Carolina. *I could sure use some help on this one*, he thought reflectively, looking up at the ceiling of the office.

Smoke & 7 Mirrors

The afternoon was wonderful. Dezi never wanted to say goodbye, but he let her leave. Kayla promised they would all have dinner later this week. Dezi relaxed in the oversized desk chair, as he flipped on all the monitors in front of him. He saw every room of her house. He saw Kayla coming out of the bathroom. She just showered, and was wrapped in a towel.

"This view alone is worth the money I paid," Dezi said aloud, as he watched her.

He turned on the sound monitors, and heard Kayla humming softly. Her phone rang and Dezi flipped the phone monitor switch, so he could hear her conversation.

"Hey girl!" Jackie greeted her.

Kayla smiled.

"Hey yourself," she replied cheerfully.

"So how was it," Jackie asked, chuckling.

Kayla laughed lightly, and began to tell her all about her afternoon with Dante.

"Oh, so its Dante now, is it," Jackie teased.

Kayla laughed.

"It's not like that Jackie. I have a husband remember?"

"You're not dead either, honey," Jackie quipped back, asking Kayla to describe the man.

Dezi was very interested in her answer. He turned the volume up on the monitor.

"He's very attractive," she began. "He has beautiful hazel eyes, very nice body, especially his chest and butt," Kayla continued, both she and Jackie giggling.

"He reminds me of someone I knew a long time ago," she said tenderly.

Jackie noticed the tone, and called her on it.

"Someone you once loved?"

Kayla smiled gently.

"Yes, I did love him very much at one point," she replied thoughtfully.

Dezi smiled. He needed to thank Jackie for this trip down memory lane she was taking Kayla on. *One less thing I need to do,* he thought, continuing to listen to them talk.

"The only thing I don't like about him," Kayla began, as Dezi sat up to take note. "He has a beard."

Jackie laughed.

"Girl is that all," she laughed harder. "Can you say, shave," Jackie finished, still laughing.

Kayla caught herself. She was a married woman, and she and Jackie were acting as if she were single.

"Jackie, I'm not trying to date the man, for goodness sake," she told her, laughing lightly herself.

Jackie calmed herself, and became serious.

"Maybe you should think about it."

Dezi was completely enthralled. *Why would her friend say something like that?*

Kayla sighed.

"We're doing okay now, Jackie," she said evenly.

"I don't like what he did Kayla," she replied, annoyed.

What did he do, Dezi wanted to know.

Kayla sighed again.

"I know Jackie, but he promised," she replied softly.

Jackie was quiet for a moment, before she spoke.

"Did you ask him?"

"Yes, and he said no," Kayla told Jackie.

"Hmph," Jackie replied. "Well, just because I won't be here, doesn't mean I can't get to you if you need me," she went on. "If he ever and I mean ever, does that again Kayla, I want you to leave," she continued. "Do you hear me?!" Jackie finished, waiting for an answer.

"Yes, I hear you," Kayla replied.

"Promise me," Jackie said evenly.

Kayla sighed deeply.

Dezi knew she didn't like making promises like that, but he also knew she would do it.

"Yes, I promise," she replied.

Dezi smiled, as Kayla caved.

"OK, now that that's settled," Jackie began again. "Let's talk more about Dante," she giggled.

Kayla laughed, and told her there was nothing else to tell.

"So is he well endowed?"

Kayla blushed.

"How would I know that?"

Dezi laughed heartily. He liked Jackie, even if she were married to Chris.

"Oh, you looked. Don't act like you didn't," Jackie replied. "You're still a woman," she finished, still laughing.

Kayla laughed, and admitted she did.

"So? What's the verdict?"

"I don't think a woman would be disappointed when he undressed. Let's just leave it at that," Kayla replied laughing.

They continued talking a little while longer, as Kayla told her about Aidan and Mariah leaving too.

"Oh," Kayla began, as they were about to hang up. "I'm having a dinner party Friday night. Dante is going to tell the kids about Pembroke Parish. Why don't you and Chris come too," she asked. "I want to spend some time with you, before you guys leave."

"I'll be there but Chris will be out of town making last minute adjustment and preparations," Jackie told her.

Dezi was glad he wouldn't be there. He wasn't sure he could sit that close to Chris, and not kill him.

"OK that'll be fine," Kayla replied, gave her the time for the dinner and said goodnight.

Dezi was pleased with what he heard. *Maybe I can find a way to get Jackie to tell me what Thomas did to Kayla,* he thought, watching intently as she applied her lotion. He wanted to touch, and hold her again. *Soon man,* Dezi thought, as he got up to get himself another drink. He needed to go cool off for a few minutes, after watching Kayla's beautiful body on his monitor.

$$\bullet\bullet\bullet$$

The phone rang again. Kayla answered, not recognizing the number on the ID.

"Hello?"

"Hi, Kayla," Collins responded.

She smiled, as she recognized his voice.

"Hi, Maurice," Kayla greeted him warmly. "Wow, long time no hear from," she told him laughing.

"I'm sorry about that," Collins apologized. "Been super busy."

"I have a surprise for you," he told her, still chuckling lightly.

Kayla was intrigued.

"What is it?"

"I've transferred here," Collins told her. "Of course as soon as I got here I managed to fall and break my leg," he ended, chuckling.

Kayla was still laughing at him falling, when she spoke.

"I'm so sorry Maurice," she replied, trying to gather herself. "Why don't you come by Friday?" she went on. "I'm having a dinner party, and most of the people you'll know," she went on. "I know Mariah would love to see you, as would I," she finished, waiting for his answer.

Collins thought that would be an excellent time to come by. He could check out her home, and gather information without alarming her, or Mariah.

"I'd love that," he told her.

"Great, we're gathering around 7:30," Kayla explained. "Do you know how to get here?"

"Yes, I have directions," Collins told her. "I'll see you Friday," he added as they disconnected.

He was sitting thinking about their conversation. *She sounded fine*, Collins mused. He didn't think Gianni would just come right out and tell her he was back for her. *He's got to be somewhere close though*, Collins thought again, as he hobbled into the kitchen to eat his dinner.

●●●

Dezi was curious. He returned with his drink, to find her on the phone. *Who the hell is Maurice*, he jealously wondered. Dezi didn't want anyone else to take her attention away. He was plotting for Friday night. He knew there was a crack in their marriage, and he was fully ready to exploit it for his own purpose. *Well he better be gay, or otherwise not interested*, Dezi thought coldly about the newly invited guest. He still loved to kill, and he would definitely kill anyone who tried to get in his way when it came to Kayla.

Dezi saw her sitting in bed watching a movie. He chuckled as he watched Kayla fighting to stay awake, only to lose the battle a few moments later.

"Sweet dreams baby," he said aloud, as he headed downstairs to his gym.

His cell ringing interrupted his workout. Dezi looked at the display. It was Rachelle. She left him a total of six messages already.

"Hello," Dezi answered sighing heavily.

"Hi baby," Rachelle replied excitedly, completely missing the sigh. "I'm glad you're back," she went on. "I've really missed you."

Dezi frowned, and rolled his eyes. *She is really beginning to irritate the shit out of me*, he thought disgustedly.

"Yes, I just got back, I'm exhausted," he replied, hoping Rachelle would take the hint.

"Well, why don't you come on over here, and I can help you relax," she replied, obviously missing the point yet again.

Dezi sighed.

"Sure, I can do that," he replied half-heartedly.

He supposed he could make it through the night with her. He spent such a wonderful day with Kayla. He didn't want to think about sexing Rachelle tonight.

"Well, I'll see you in a little while then," she told Dezi, jarring him back to the present.

"Sure," Dezi told Rachelle, as they disconnected.

"How the hell am I going to get hard with this bitch," Dezi groused aloud, as he grabbed his bag and tossed clothes into it.

•••

Rachelle was putting the finishing touches on the fruit tray she prepared. She included wine and cheese too. She wanted Dante to relax, and enjoy being with her. She was completely smitten with this man. Rachelle wasn't stupid either. She did her homework, and found out Dante had quite a bit of money. That made him even more attractive. Rachelle didn't plan to spend the rest of her life working, or scraping by. *Kayla beat me to Thomas, but I'm going to snag this one,* she thought inwardly chuckling.

She put on her sexiest nightie, her favorite scent, wearing her hair down tonight. *I want him to be blown away when he sees me,* Rachelle thought again, as she saw the headlights in the driveway. She smiled, thinking of the wonderful lovemaking she was in for tonight. The bell rang, and Rachelle went to answer the door.

Smoke & **8** Mirrors

It was finally Friday. He didn't know how he did it, but he managed to get through all the meetings and interviews. Thomas was exhausted. There was one final meeting tonight, and he would be done for the weekend. He would fly out to the next city on Monday morning, but for now Thomas was going to enjoy resting. He was going shopping this morning to get Kayla something nice. She told him about the dinner party tonight, and about Aidan and Mariah.

Thomas was surprised, but pleased for the kids. They were taking a big step, venturing out on their own like that. He asked Kayla about her meeting, and she filled him in. He was glad Mariah and Aidan were meeting her client. Thomas was curious about him, and of course he still didn't trust any man around his wife. He missed Kayla desperately, wanting to make love to her in the worst way. *Well no use lying here dwelling on it,* Thomas thought, as he got up and dressed to head out.

●●●

Elise saw him get off the elevator. She was waiting for the last two hours to get a look at her mark. *Very nice,* she thought, looking Thomas over.

"I might actually enjoy this particular job very much," Elise said aloud.

Thomas left the hotel, and she followed. Elise always liked to get to know as much about her marks as she could, before she finally approached them. She wondered what he did to make them hire her. *No matter,* Elise shrugged. *Money is money.*

Thomas went to several shops, and Elise surmised he was looking for something for his wife. He was selective however, and that pleased her. Thomas was very meticulous, finally finding what he was seeking at a small boutique. He paid for it in cash, and had the girl gift wrap it. Elise followed him for another hour before deciding she gathered all she needed. Thomas seemed like a very decent man to her. Of course she was wrong before, but Elise hoped this time she wasn't. *Maybe this one will restore my faith in mankind hmm,* she thought as she chuckled quietly. Elise left to do some shopping of her own. There was a job to do.

●●●

Thomas returned to his hotel and called home.

"Hello?"

He smiled at the sound of her voice.

"Hi baby," Thomas replied.

Kayla giggled slightly, and returned his greeting.

"Are you alright," she asked. "You sound exhausted."

Thomas smiled, thinking how well Kayla knew him.

"I'm okay honey, just a little tired," he replied. "Everything underway for tonight?"

She laughed lightly. "Yes, everything is underway."

They chatted a few moments more.

"Thomas?"

"Yes, honey," Thomas responded.

"Is this the last trip for sure," Kayla asked softly.

He sighed. Thomas knew Kayla was tired of him being gone. He wanted to be there with her, just as much as she wanted him to be.

"Yes baby, I promise," Thomas replied.

Kayla smiled, and he heard it in her voice.

"Good," she said simply.

Thomas looked at the wrapped gift he bought. He loved his wife so much. He couldn't lose her.

"I bought you something today," he teased, knowing Kayla couldn't stand the mystery.

"What is it," she asked excitedly.

"I'm not telling," Thomas replied, chuckling lightly.

"That's not fair," Kayla whined.

He laughed heartily.

"Still not telling."

"Oh, you are such a stinker," Kayla pouted.

Thomas continued to laugh. Finally he collected himself, and spoke.

"I miss you so much baby," he said candidly.

"I miss you too Thomas."

"Well I have a luncheon to go to, honey," he began. "So I'll call you back later, before the party OK?"

"That will be fine," Kayla told him.

"Oh, did I tell you Maurice will be here," she asked, as he was about to hang up.

Thomas smiled. Maurice was good people, and he would make sure no one tried to put a move on his wife.

"That's wonderful honey," Thomas replied. "What brought him out?"

"He transferred, he said he wanted a change of pace," Kayla explained.

"I can understand that," Thomas replied. "Well tell him I said hello," he finished as they hung up.

●●●

Dezi was still frowning. He didn't like the conversations between Kayla and Thomas. He endured them the last few days. He needed to find out what he did, and use it to his advantage. Dezi was just glad Thomas was out of town. He didn't think he could take watching, hearing, or knowing they were making love to each other.

Dezi got up and switched off the monitors. He was having lunch with Rachelle. He needed some information, and of course Rachelle held what he needed. He made a mental note to call Big D. He left a message saying it was important a few days ago. He was caught up with Rachelle, and forgotten. He wouldn't forget today though.

●●●

Rachelle was chattering as usual and getting on his nerves. *If I didn't need this bitch right now*, Dezi was thinking.

"So," he interrupted, temporarily ebbing the flow. "Why didn't you ever date one of the Pastors?"

Rachelle was surprised. *Where did that come from,* she wondered. *Careful girl, He may be trying to see how many men you've been with,* she was thinking, wanting to make sure Dante Enzo didn't get away.

"Well, I was never interested in Pastor Lynch," Rachelle replied.

Dezi sipped his tea.

"What about Pastor Bradford," he returned, noticing she didn't mention him in her response.

Rachelle sighed, and Dezi knew she was at least interested. If he were lucky, maybe they slept together.

"I was interested in him once," she replied. "But it wasn't a mutual attraction."

Dezi had more questions. There were things Rachelle wasn't saying, and he wanted to know why.

"Because of his wife now?"

What is he after, she wondered. Rachelle didn't want to admit what a shameless flirt she was, in trying to get Thomas to sleep with her.

"Yes, I suppose," she replied vaguely.

She's still not telling me something, Dezi thought, and decided to play it another way.

"Why are you lying to me Rachelle," he asked her, sounding irritated.

"How are we supposed to be together, when you won't tell me the truth," Dezi continued, sounding angrier "Did you sleep with him? Are you still sleeping with him and me too," he finished, breathing hard and looking at her evenly.

Rachelle was terrified, and pleased all at once. She never ever saw Dante angry like this, but he was also jealous, and that let her know he cared about her.

"No, Dante," Rachelle replied sincerely. "It wasn't like that at all," she went on. "I wanted to be with Thomas, but he was in love with Kayla. He turned me down flat," she continued. "I've never slept with him. Please believe me," Rachelle finished, looking at him for his response.

Dezi was thoughtful for a moment before he spoke.

"Do you still want to be with him?" he asked, before adding. "And don't lie to me Rachelle, I can tell when you lie."

Rachelle didn't want to answer the question. She did still have feelings for Thomas. She couldn't shake them for some reason, but she didn't want to tell Dante and lose him. *Please make him believe what I'm about to say,* Rachelle prayed silently.

"No, Dante," she began. "I want to be with you, and only you," she replied, looking into his eyes.

This bitch is lying to my face, Dezi thought, wanting to laugh aloud. He procured what he was looking for though, so he would play along for now. He sighed deeply, before speaking again.

"All right Rachelle," Dezi replied. "I believe you."

Rachelle let out the breath she held, and relaxed. *That was too close,* she thought, as she watched Dante finish his desert.

Dezi knew she was plotting. He rattled her, and he knew Rachelle didn't want to let him get away. She already made up her mind she was going to marry him, probably have babies with him. He almost laughed aloud again at that. Rachelle was going to play into his plan rather nicely, now that Dezi knew she still wanted Thomas.

"You ready to go," Dezi asked her pleasantly.

"Yes," Rachelle smiled.

Dezi knew he would have to sleep with Rachelle now, to reassure her he was still hers. He would do his usual and think of someone, anyone else, while he was with her. Dezi pulled her chair out, and allowed her to get up. *Well here's the medicine before the treat,* he thought glumly, thinking ahead to tonight and Kayla.

Dezi hoped everything went according to plan. It would prove to be a very good night indeed.

●●●

They arrived at her house, and Rachelle excused herself to the bathroom. Dezi used the time to call Big D.

"Wassup man," he asked when Big D answered.

"You got a bloodhound," he said simply.

Dezi didn't like the sound of that at all.

"Who," he questioned, fully alert now.

"FBI man," Big D returned.

Dezi was getting angry. He knew they weren't investigating him anymore. He was dead for all intents and purposes. This must be someone from the original case.

"You get a name," Dezi asked icily.

Big D cringed. He hoped Dezi would get in, get Kayla, and get out without spilling blood, but now it looked like that plan was out the window.

"Collins," Big D replied, "Ring any bells?"

Dezi knew exactly who he was.

"Yeah, I know the fucker," he replied coldly.

So he's fishing huh, Dezi thought.

"What did he want?"

"They know you came back and that you landed here in Virginia Beach, but that's all they know," Big D told him.

"This one is trying to figure out where you are now," he spoke another time.

"I overheard them talking," Big D was saying. "They don't even know what you look like now," he began to chuckle. "Shit, you could walk right up to this Collins, and he wouldn't know who the fuck you were," he finished, laughing harder.

Dezi smiled. Big D was right.

"Thanks for the info man," he replied, feeling better about the situation. "I know what he looks like though," he told Big D. "And this time, I'm going to kill him," Dezi finished, in a no nonsense tone.

Big D knew he wasn't kidding.

"Well, man, do what you need to do," he replied. "How are things moving along by the way?"

Dezi smiled, and told him about their meeting, and about the things Kayla told her friend.

"Sounds like everything is going your way man," Big D told him, chuckling again.

"Yeah, except for the fact I'm at this tricks house and I have to figure out how to get a hard on to fuck her," Dezi told him.

"Man, smoke some," Big D told him.

"Doesn't help," Dezi told him. "She just doesn't turn me on."

"Make her suck your dick first," Big D told him plainly.

Dezi never thought of that. He wasn't even sure she would.

"Trust me, that will get you up and then you just concentrate on getting your nut, not the bitch you're fucking," Big D told him again.

"Thanks, you just saved the day man," Dezi laughed.

"Don't forget to check your phone later," Big D reminded him.

"Yeah, I will," Dezi replied, and they hung up.

Rachelle returned moments later, and began trying to arouse him.

"Baby, how about some head," Dezi asked, as he caressed her face.

"Of course baby," Rachelle smiled at Dante. "Whatever you want."

They went into her bedroom, and undressed. Dezi lay back on the bed, and closed his eyes, as Rachelle began to pleasure him. *Thanks again D, I owe you one*, he thought, as he felt himself come to life.

Smoke & **9** Mirrors

Jackie was thinking about Kayla and Thomas. She was still angry that he touched her. *I don't care what he told her, he's messing around on her,* she thought angrily. Kayla was a wonderful woman, and she deserved only the best. *She had that with Donovan,* Jackie fumed again. It wasn't that she disliked Thomas, she just felt there was something hidden beneath the surface that was ugly. Jackie thought about Kayla calling her in tears, telling her he hit her. *Why would anyone want to hit Kayla? She's got to be the nicest person in the world.* That was the sort of thing she was talking about. Thomas was also extremely possessive.

Jackie was glad Kayla was working again, but she bet Thomas wasn't. She knew the only reason he gave in, was because of this last trip he took. Kayla came over that morning, and they talked. She was ready to leave him. Jackie talked her into working, and giving Thomas an ultimatum instead. *Stupid me!* she chided herself then thought again.

Well, she wouldn't have met Dante then would she? Jackie secretly hoped the man was everything Kayla told her. She also hoped he was attracted to her friend. As wrong as it seemed for her to wish their marriage ill, Jackie was afraid for Kayla. *He has the capacity for violence. I can just feel it,* she thought another time of Thomas, shuddering lightly. Jackie also knew Kayla was a little curious. She wouldn't have bothered to assess the man's physical appearance at all, if she weren't. *Maybe I can help her curiosity along tonight,* Jackie thought wickedly, as she headed out to the mall to get something new to wear tonight.

•••

Once she arrived at the mall, Jackie found herself looking at several dresses that would actually be better suited for Kayla. Subconsciously she was trying to set her friend up. Jackie picked out the soft blue low back dress, in Kayla's size, and purchased it, along with her own. She stopped at Catessa's, the shoe store, and bought them both shoes to match their outfits. Jackie knew Kayla would balk at first, but she would wear the outfit.

Now I just need to make sure neither Aidan, nor Mariah, run interference. She chuckled again; thinking how she already decided Dante was going to be Kayla's new man.

"Or at the very least, her new lover," Jackie chuckled out loud, and headed for the door.

She went straight to Kayla's to drop off the outfit.

"Jackie," Kayla breathed, when she saw the dress. "This is beautiful."

"Glad you like it, because that's what you're wearing tonight," Jackie replied, looking at her evenly.

Kayla knew what Jackie was up too.

"I can't," she said quietly.

"Why the hell not," Jackie asked, cornering her.

Kayla laughed. Jackie put her so much in mind of Taea sometimes.

"Because I'm married Jackie," she replied lightly.

"And?" Jackie demanded. "Look, you are not a troll Kayla," she began. "You need to stop acting like you're a hundred years old," she went on. "There is nothing wrong with you being attractive, contrary to what Thomas has convinced you of," Jackie finished, angry that her friend was so caught up in this lie Thomas was trying to make her believe.

Kayla sighed softly. The outfit was amazing, and she knew she would look great in it.

"OK," she said quietly. "I'll wear it tonight."

Jackie smiled.

"Glad that's settled," she said chuckling. "I'll be back in a little while," she told Kayla, heading out the door. "Oh, and wear your hair down," Jackie yelled back to her, as she got in her car.

Kayla laughed. *That is Taea reincarnate,* she mused, heading back inside to get dressed.

●●●

Mariah was excited in spite of her earlier trepidation about moving. At least now, she would get the opportunity to meet someone who actually lived there, and could tell her what it would really be like. Mariah also wanted to meet her mother's client. She didn't want someone coming in, and taking advantage of her mother's vulnerability. She would keep an eye on this man tonight and make sure he knew without a shadow of a doubt, that her mother was married, and planned to stay that way. Mariah heard Aidan and Livvy coming and turned her attention to her husband and daughter.

"Well, don't you two look nice," she remarked laughing.

Aidan took a bow, with Livvy dipping as well. Livvy was inspecting her fingers, as she drooled on her outfit.

"Somebody needs a bib," Mariah laughed.

Aidan handed her the baby, while he went to find one.

"I'm excited about meeting Mr. Enzo tonight," Aidan remarked, when he came back.

Mariah smiled.

"I am too actually."

"This is going to be a wonderful adventure for us honey," he said thoughtfully.

"Did you send for our packets, so we could see where we would be living," Mariah asked.

"Yes, and they actually came back already," Aidan told her.

He went to retrieve the packet.

"I'm glad you mentioned it," he told Mariah. "I want to see if Mr. Enzo knows where they are, and what kind of area they're in."

Mariah handed Aidan the baby, as she went to get the casserole she prepared for the dinner. They headed out to the car.

"I'm going to miss mommy," Mariah said quietly.

Aidan took her hand.

"I know baby," he said softly. "We'll get her to come often and visit," he returned. "And you and Livvy can visit too. Plus there's email, chat, and the ever popular telephone," he finished, chuckling.

Mariah laughed heartily at Aidan for that last statement.

"I don't know why I didn't think of that," she said sarcastically, and laughed again.

"I love you, you nut," Mariah told him, and Aidan smiled.

"Love you too baby."

●●●

"Looks like we're the first to get here," Mariah remarked when they arrived.

She let herself in. Kayla gave her a key when they first moved in, for emergencies.

"Mommy!"

"I'll be there in a minute honey," Kayla replied.

Mariah went into the kitchen, and began getting the entrées together. Jackie drove up shortly after Mariah and Aidan.

"OK," Jackie began, talking to herself. "Let's make sure this evening goes as planned," she finished, chuckling devilishly as she rang the bell.

Aidan answered, with Livvy still in his arms.

"Hey pumpkin!" Jackie said, addressing the baby.

"So what am I? Invisible," Aidan asked, feigning hurt.

Jackie laughed.

"Hello nephew," she greeted as she hugged him.

"Where's everybody?"

"Mariah is in the kitchen, and Kayla is still upstairs," Aidan told her.

Jackie went to the kitchen to deal with Mariah first.

"Hey there," she said, smiling at the young woman.

"Hi Aunt Jackie," Mariah said happily. "Wow, you look really nice," she told Jackie, looking her over.

"Why, thank you," Jackie replied. "You looking forward to getting some information from Mr. Enzo tonight?

Mariah smiled.

"Yes, but I also want to see what he's up to where mommy is concerned," she spoke.

Exactly why I'm running interference tonight, Jackie thought.

"Mariah, he is just a client, and he happens to live where you're moving," she replied. "I'm sure your mother is just trying to be social."

Mariah sighed.

"It's not mommy I'm worried about," she replied with a look.

"Mariah, there are a lot of things you don't really have a full understanding of," Jackie said simply.

Mariah gave Jackie a new look. *What is mommy keeping from me*, she wondered.

"Do you know something I should know Aunt Jackie?"

"Probably," Jackie answered honestly. "But, until your mother either tells you, or gives me permission, I can't say anything."

Mariah thought for a moment before speaking.

"Are they getting a divorce?"

Jackie sighed.

"Not that I know of, Mariah," she answered honestly.

"Listen," Jackie began again. "All I want is for your mother to enjoy this evening. I don't know if Mr. Enzo has any interest in your mother outside of business, but if he does, is it so wrong for her to enjoy some much needed, and deserved attention," she finished, looking at Mariah trying to gauge her response.

Mariah thought long and hard about that. She knew Thomas neglected her mother for a while now. She saw the sadness in Kayla's face, heard it in her voice. If anyone deserved to be happy, it was her mother, besides there was no harm in talking to someone.

"No, I guess you're right Aunt Jackie," Mariah replied.

They heard Kayla laughing with Aidan, and decided to end the conversation. Jackie was glad Mariah wouldn't interfere, and of course, she would control Aidan.

"Hi, you two," Kayla greeted them smiling.

Mariah was impressed with how beautiful her mother looked. She hadn't seen Kayla this radiant in a long time. The dress was absolutely to die for.

"Wow, Mommy," was all Mariah could say.

"Do I look alright," Kayla asked them both fearfully.

"Hell yes, you do," Jackie blurted, and laughed.

Mariah joined her, and Kayla relaxed.

"Well as soon as Maurice and Dante get here, we can get ready to eat," she replied.

Mariah took note that her mother called Mr. Enzo by his first name. She hoped this didn't turn out badly. Mariah promised herself she would support her mother though. Kayla wasn't this happy in her own skin for a long time now.

●●●

Dezi was just about ready. He arrived home a little late fooling around with Rachelle, missing what Kayla was wearing. He wanted to match her. He decided to stay with blue. *You can't go wrong with her favorite color,* Dezi thought chuckling. He put on the soft powder blue tailored cut shirt with navy blue pants, also hand tailored. This particular ensemble showcased his toned, muscular, body. *This should take her mind back,* he thought, as he added the accessories and cologne.

Dezi was looking forward to spending the evening with his family. This would be the first time he would be with his son. He wanted the chance to talk to Aidan one on one. He decided he wouldn't reveal who he was to him until they moved to the Island. Dezi also wanted to talk to Jackie. He liked her already. *She reminds me a lot of Taea,* he thought wistfully. That thought of course bringing back memories of his friend and partner, Dirty. Even after all these years, Dezi still missed him and was yet to meet anyone else quite like him. He shook the sadness, and took a deep breath. *Tonight is a whole new beginning,* Dezi thought, at the prospect of being with all the people he loved. He was also going to find out who Maurice was. *He better not be trying to get close to Kayla,* Dezi thought angrily, as he headed out the door.

Smoke & **10** Mirrors

Dezi arrived a few minutes later and rang the bell. Jackie made sure she was positioned to see his reaction when he saw Kayla. Aidan answered the door, and invited him in, remembering him from church.

"Good to see you again Mr. Enzo," Aidan told him, as he shook his hand.

"Thank you, and please, call me Dante," Dezi smiled.

Aidan showed him into the living room where everyone was conversing. Aidan introduced him to Mariah, and Livvy.

"May I," Dezi asked to hold the baby.

"Sure," Mariah gave her to him.

Livvy smiled at him. *Guess she recognizes her blood,* Dezi thought as he smiled back, and began to talk to her. *I'll teach her Italian when she gets a little older,* he thought, handing her back to Mariah moments later.

"She's beautiful," Dezi said softly, still looking at the child.

"Thank you," Mariah smiled.

Dante seemed like a very nice man so far. *He is extremely attractive too,* Mariah thought, as she looked at him. *Obviously works out and takes good care of himself.* Jackie heard Kayla ending her call and knew she was on her way. She sat back, and watched.

"Why, hello Dante," Kayla greeted the man, as she entered the living room.

Dezi turned at the sound of her voice, and froze. His mind went back twenty years to the club, and their first date. Kayla was wearing a soft blue dress amazingly close to the one she wore that night. *My God she is stunning,* Dezi thought as he gathered himself, and returned her greeting.

Jackie smiled. *Oh hell yes, he is very interested,* she thought cheerfully, noticing Dante never took his eyes off Kayla the entire time she was in the room.

"I'm going to get the table set," she told them.

"Mommy, what about Uncle Maurice?"

"He called, he won't be joining us, "Kayla told her. "He's getting his cast off," she chuckled lightly.

Dezi knew Kayla didn't have any blood brothers. Perhaps he was her husband's brother. He needed to know.

"Your brother hurt himself?"

Kayla smiled at him.

"No, he's not my brother," she went on. "He's my late husband's old partner," she continued. "My first husband, Mariah's father, was with the FBI," she told Dante.

Collins, Dezi thought. *And the fucker was gonna be here tonight. Good thing for him he cancelled.* Dezi decided he would kill Collins before he left, owing him that much.

"Oh, I see," he told her and smiled back.

●●●

Kayla left to handle dinner. Mariah also left to help her, and Aidan was putting Livvy down to nap. *Finally!* Jackie thought gleefully. She wanted to talk to Dante, and now was the perfect opportunity.

"So Dante," Jackie began, looking directly at him.

Dezi wondered what was on her mind.

"Are you interested in Kayla," she asked straightforwardly.

He was expecting something like that. She watched him all evening.

"Yes," Dezi replied just as honestly.

He already knew he liked Jackie, and she was going to be his one help in his pursuit of Kayla. Jackie smiled. She liked his honesty.

"She seems very happily married, however," Dezi said, looking directly at Jackie now.

She smiled again, before replying.

"Things are not always what they seem, Dante," Jackie said plainly.

Dezi could tell she really didn't like Thomas, and he wanted to know why.

"Why do you dislike her husband," he asked, still watching Jackie intently.

"If I tell you, you hafta swear never to let Kayla know I told you."

"This is our conversation, Jackie," Dezi assured her.

"He hit her," Jackie said, with an irritated edge to her voice.

Dezi was careful not to overreact. *I'll kill his ass,* he thought, feeling the familiar coldness begin to overtake him.

"Thomas tries to keep her in this isolation," Jackie went on, bringing Dezi back.

"He's very possessive. The only reason she's working is because he feels guilty about leaving her alone so much," Jackie finished bitterly.

Dezi saw that he was right about Jackie. He made a mental note to invite her to the parish, whenever she wanted to get away from Chris for a while.

"He should be careful," Dezi said quietly. "Something that beautiful should be treasured, not neglected," he finished softly.

Jackie smiled, as she looked at him.

"Exactly," she replied. "And that Dante, is where you come in." Jackie finished, with a knowing look.

Before Dezi could reply, Aidan returned and told them dinner was ready to be served. They all enjoyed dinner and desert.

●●●

"No, mommy," Mariah told her mother, taking the dish from her. "Aidan and I will clean up," she continued. "You go relax."

Kayla smiled. "Thanks."

Jackie excused herself, and left them alone in the living room.

"Dinner was wonderful," Dezi told her.

Of course I already knew it would be, he thought, recalling the wonderful meals she made for him before.

"Have you lived here always?"

Kayla chuckled softly.

"No," she replied. "I actually lived in a few other places on the coast, before settling here."

"Did you like the coast," Dezi probed, hoping to stir more memories.

"Yes, I really enjoyed it." Kayla replied.

He didn't want to push. Dezi knew there were also some very bad memories she would rather forget.

"Mariah is your only child?"

Kayla smiled, but her eyes didn't Dezi noticed.

"Yes," she said softly.

"Your husband didn't want any?"

Dezi saw the tears then.

"I'm sorry," he said softly. "I didn't mean to pry."

She smiled. "It's alright."

"Yes, we decided to try and have one, but there were medical reasons we couldn't," Kayla said simply.

Dezi didn't push. Mariah and Aidan returned, as did Jackie, and they all began to discuss the Parish. Dezi answered all their questions, and looked over the information he ordered sent to them. He paid for their home of course, and made sure it was in the best of areas, with the best of amenities.

"Mommy, we're going to leave now," Mariah said.

"It's getting late and Livvy gets cranky if she gets off her schedule," Aidan added.

"Alright, don't want that," Kayla laughed. "Goodnight you three."

"Thank you again for all your help, Dante," Aidan spoke.

"You have all my information," Dezi questioned.

"Yes, I have them all stored in my phone," Mariah spoke this time. "We'll definitely be calling once we arrived," she added as Dezi smiled.

Jackie left soon after, asking Dante to walk her out. Kayla was upstairs, and didn't hear the request.

"This is your opportunity," she told him bluntly. "If you really want her, go for it," Jackie finished, looking Dante in the eye.

Dezi smiled.

"Thank you, Jackie," he said, as he looked at her. "I hope you're right about what you think."

Jackie chuckled, and got into the car. Dezi watched her back out, and returned to the house.

●●●

Kayla was coming back downstairs, as he sat on the couch.

"So, are you bailing out on me too," she teased.

"Not right now," Dezi laughed.

"Would you like to sit in the sunroom?"

She liked the breeze from the evening, and it was always so peaceful.

"That would be nice," Dezi told her.

"Is your husband gone often?".

Kayla sighed. "Unfortunately, lately he has been."

"I suppose work keeps you busy though," he replied.

She smiled. "I actually just started working again."

"How fortunate for me," Dezi replied softly.

He was sitting right next to her, and she was beginning to feel things. Dezi saw Kayla's discomfort, and knew she was getting turned on from his closeness.

"Kayla," Dezi said softly.

She turned to his voice, and he kissed her. It was a soft, gentle kiss, and Kayla was surprised at how much she enjoyed it.

"Dante," she began, pushing him mildly away.

Dezi couldn't let her stop now. He knew the kiss awakened something in her. Dezi pulled Kayla to him, and kissed her again, more insistently this time. He felt her body relax, and her nipples harden against his chest.

"Dante please," Kayla began again, after Dezi released her. "I'm married, and this is wrong."

He looked at her. She wouldn't look at him. Dezi turned Kayla to him.

"Do you really want me to stop," he asked, looking right at her.

Kayla bit her bottom lip. She couldn't do this. Yet, Dante was so attractive and she was so lonely.

"Yes," she lied.

Dezi almost laughed. *She is still the world's worst liar,* he thought, looking at Kayla.

"We don't have to do anything," he said softly. "Let me pleasure you," he went on. "Don't you want that? Need that?"

Kayla swallowed hard. She was extremely needy, but she couldn't could she? Dezi watched her wrestling with the idea. He leaned down, and kissed her again passionately, picking her up, took her into the living room. He laid Kayla gently on the couch, and began to undress her.

"We shouldn't," she said quietly.

Dezi kissed her again, effectively silencing her as he completed his task. He looked at Kayla once she was naked. She was still absolutely beautiful. Dezi began to kiss her neck, and work his way down her body. He settled himself at her sensitive spot, and began to bring her to multiple orgasms. He wanted to make love to her, but he would wait. Dezi simply thought about Rachelle, whenever his erection became unbearable. He did all the things to her he knew she loved. Everything he ever did to bring Kayla pleasure, he did tonight.

Dezi knew once she was alone, she would think of him and it would make her remember once again. He needed Kayla to remember him, and all the good times they shared. Once Dezi was sure Kayla was completely spent, he gently kissed and dressed her. She was embarrassed he could tell. Kayla wouldn't look at him. Dezi took her face in his hands, as he made her look at him.

"I understand about your being married," he began. "But tonight, you needed this. You needed me," Dezi went on. "I want you to know, whenever you need me, I'm always at your service," he continued. "Anytime, day or night. Pick up the phone, and call me. Understand?"

"Yes," Kayla smiled. "And I will."

"Promise," he asked, looking into her eyes.

Kayla knew what she did tonight was wrong, but this man pleasured her in ways she hadn't been in years, and as wrong as it sounded, she wanted it again.

"Yes, I promise," she replied.

Dezi believed her. He kissed her softly, and told her goodnight. Kayla heard him drive away, and made her way upstairs to shower.

"You did a terrible thing tonight," Kayla chided herself, secretly glowing from the things he did to her.

Smoke & **11** Mirrors

Elise was waiting for Thomas. She knew about his meeting, and what time she should expect him. Spotting him coming into the lobby of the hotel, Elise took the service elevator, so she would be ready when Thomas got off the main elevator.

•••

Thomas was exhausted. He would get two days of rest though, and he was very much looking forward to that. He looked at his watch. It was after one a.m. He wouldn't call Kayla tonight. He didn't want to disturb her rest. Thinking about her was causing an arousal, and Thomas definitely didn't need that. The doors opened on his floor, and he saw the distraught young woman huddled in the corner.

"What's wrong," Thomas asked concerned.

Elise continued to rock back and forth, eyes closed, not answering.

"Please, miss," he said again. "I can't help you, if you don't talk to me."

Elise stopped rocking, and looked at Thomas.

"Who are you," she asked frightened.

"I'm a Pastor, I'm here for some meetings," Thomas explained.

"Are you a guest?" he asked her.

"No," Elise told him. "I was visiting a friend, and he just flipped out on me," she spun the web. "He really lost it, I thought he was going to hurt me."

Thomas was sorry the young woman had gone through so much. She was obviously still very upset.

"Do you need to call someone," he asked kindly.

"I'm alone," Elise said plainly. "Can I maybe use your bathroom and clean myself up, so I can go home?"

Thomas saw no harm in that.

"Certainly," he replied.

He took her arm, and gently helped her off the floor. Elise followed Thomas to his room. He opened the door, and told her to go ahead. Elise closed the door and began to wash her face. *OK, let's see if he passes or fails.* Elise knew the cameras were already in place. She saw to that personally, earlier this evening while Thomas was out. Her partner, Charles, was in the adjacent room monitoring the action. If anything went down, he would be over here in a flash. They obtained an extra key for access, just in case.

"Thanks," Elise said softly, as she emerged from the restroom.

Thomas was standing by the window looking out. He turned at hearing her voice.

"You're more than welcome," he replied, still looking at her. "Are you sure you're going to be OK?"

She sighed, and sat in one of the chairs.

"Yeah, I guess," Elise said evenly.

Thomas came over, and sat in the other chair across from her.

"Do you want to talk about it?"

Time to earn your money girlie, Elise thought, as she began to haltingly speak, fighting tears. Thomas felt bad for the girl, listening to her talk. He guessed she was somewhere around twenty-seven or so. She was very attractive, and he assumed the guy she was talking about was much older.

"Is it wrong that I'm attracted to older men," Elise asked, bringing him out of his thought.

"Well no, I don't guess it really matters," Thomas replied. "I'm sorry I never got your name."

Elise smiled.

"Oh, sorry," she said, chuckling lightly. "It's Elise."

She never used a fake name. It wasn't necessary. Elise seldom saw any of her marks again.

"Well Elise," Thomas said, using her name this time "I don't think love or attraction knows age," he went on. "You just have to be careful, that's all."

Elise smiled again.

"I guess you're right," she told him rising to leave. Thomas rose too.

"Thank you so much Thomas," Elise said, hugging him tightly.

Thomas was surprised by the hug, but he hugged her back. He figured she needed comfort right now. *OK, it's now or never girl,* Elise told herself. She pressed her breasts against his chest, and sighed quietly. Thomas felt himself starting to become aroused. He was missing Kayla, and thinking about sex all day. He needed to get Elise out of here. Thomas went to pull away from her, when she looked up at him.

"Did I do something wrong?"

"No, Elise," he replied. "I just think it's better if you left."

"Why, Thomas," she asked. "Because you want me," Elise finished, looking at him evenly.

Thomas took a deep breath.

"Yes," he said plainly.

She smiled.

"What's wrong with that," Elise inquired. "You're a man, and I'm a woman."

"I'm a married man," Thomas reminded her.

"I still don't see a problem," Elise went on, as she began to stroke his chest. "I'll never meet your wife, and if you don't tell her, she'll never know," she finished, still touching Thomas.

Elise unbuttoned his shirt, and licked his nipple. *She's got to get outta here now,* Thomas thought, feeling himself becoming fully aroused. *Well he hasn't failed yet, but we shall see,* Elise thought, as she continued to kiss his chest. She undid his pants, and Thomas grabbed her hands.

"No," he said hoarsely.

Elise smiled and shook his hands from her. She continued with his pants, and soon held his fully aroused manhood in her hands.

"Mmm, this looks delicious," she murmured, pushing Thomas onto the bed in a sitting position.

Elise was immediately on her knees, with him in her mouth. Thomas groaned in pleasure. He closed his eyes, and enjoyed what she was doing to him. *OK, you still have the opportunity to stop,* Elise thought, as she began to work more aggressively on him. Thomas was moaning his pleasure, holding her head as she worked. Elise teased Thomas almost to orgasm, before suddenly stopping. She deftly pulled out the condom she concealed in her bra, and slipped it on him.

"I can't," Thomas told her, trying to take the condom off.

"Stop it," Elise told him sternly. "I'm about to give you what you really want," she told him, as she turned her back to him and sat on his erection, allowing Thomas to enter her anally.

Oh my God! Thomas screamed in his head. Anal sex was his favorite dark pleasure, but Kayla wasn't into it and he never tried to force it on her after his initial inquiry early in their marriage.

She was almost beside herself with pleasure. Elise was actually close to orgasm, as was Thomas. She felt him getting faster, and knew he was about to cum. *Shit, so am I,* she thought as Thomas reached around finding her on switch and massaging it sensuously. Elise felt the orgasm hit her hard, as she screamed his name in pleasure. She heard Thomas cry out and shudder. They collapsed together, and she had to catch her breath.

After they both calmed down, Elise spoke.

"See, that wasn't so bad was it?"

"No, not at all," Thomas responded.

"So, do you want to see me again tomorrow," Elise asked, after she was dressed.

"Yes, very much," Thomas told her softly, as he kissed her goodnight.

Elise smiled, and told him what time she would be by.

●●●

Sorry Thomas. You failed, she thought, although this time she wasn't really sorry. She really enjoyed being with Thomas, and was looking forward to tomorrow night. Elise went into the room with Charles, and made the call.

"It's done," she said, when he answered. "The DVD is printed, and on its way out to you."

"Excellent," he replied, giving further instructions, as she went to the lobby.

●●●

Dezi was watching Kayla now. She showered he saw, and put on a very sexy nightgown.

"I should have stayed around," he chuckled lightly.

He heard the phone ring. She answered.

"So what happened," Jackie asked Kayla point blank.

Dezi laughed out loud, almost spitting out his liquor. Kayla laughed lightly.

"You are terrible," she told Jackie.

"Yeah OK, I'm terrible," she replied. "Now what happened," Jackie asked again.

Kayla laughed again, and told her about them being together.

"Wow," Jackie said softly.

"He reminds me so much of another time, and place, Jackie," Kayla confided in her friend.

"Tell me about it," she pressed gently.

Dezi sat attentively. He wanted to know what Kayla remembered.

"His name was Dezi," she began, and went on to tell Jackie all about their relationship, and how wonderful it was at the beginning.

"Well, did they ever prove he did any of those things," Jackie asked.

"No, not to my knowledge," Kayla told her.

"So, did he ever actually hurt you Kayla?"

"No, Never," Kayla replied honestly.

Jackie was quiet for a moment.

"Maybe this is your second chance," she replied matter-of-fact.

"I mean, it sounds like maybe you were misinformed, and based your fear on that instead of what you really knew about Dezi," she continued. "I mean, you do have to remember by this time, Donovan had developed very deep feelings for you."

Kayla never thought of it that way. She admitted, even when Dezi found her in Virginia, all he talked about was being with her.

"He was always telling me how much he loved me," Kayla said softly.

"I believe he really did Kayla," Jackie replied. "And if Dante reminds you of him, it's not crazy that you find yourself so attracted to him."

"It's just scary Jackie," Kayla went on. "Dante did things to me tonight that only Dezi would have known to do."

"Pure coincidence girl, and total skill on his part," Jackie told her, and chuckled.

"Are you going to see him again," she asked, hoping Kayla was going to say yes.

"I think I might," Kayla replied.

Jackie was satisfied with that for now. She wanted Dante to be the real thing. She still felt in her gut Thomas was bad news for Kayla, and he would end up hurting her badly.

"Well missy, I'm going to go now," Jackie told her. "You get some sleep, and I'll see you tomorrow."

"Good night," Kayla responded to Jackie and they hung up.

Dezi watched Kayla as she thought.

"Who are you Dante," she said aloud.

Dezi smiled at the monitor.

"You already know the answer to that baby," he said softly. "You'll let me know when you're ready to admit it," he finished, and drained his glass.

Kayla closed her eyes to let sleep take her. Dezi blew her a kiss through the monitor, and turned it off.

"It won't be long now," he said again.

Dezi still had a couple of loose ends to tie up, Maurice Collins being one of the bigger ones.

"I owe you death fucker," Dezi growled, his gray eyes going flat and cold.

He would deal with that starting tomorrow. Right now, he just wanted to close his eyes, and remember tonight with her. Dezi turned out the light, as he climbed into bed and pulled the covers up, a small smile playing on his face.

Smoke & 12 Mirrors

Mariah and Aidan were set to leave in another week. They packed everything they were shipping, and it was being sent out early next week. Aidan was spending considerable time with Dante, finding himself inexplicably drawn to the man. They shared a lot in common he found, during the course of conversation.

Aidan also found out Dante was very interested in Kayla. It wasn't his place to interfere, so he said nothing. He noticed how they were with each other, and assumed they already were together. Aidan secretly suspected Pastor Bradford was cheating on Kayla for months now anyway, so why shouldn't she be with someone she cared for too, he'd surmised.

He and Dante were hanging out this weekend. Aidan was going to take him to the track in Charlotte for one of the races. It was an overnight trip. He was glad Mariah didn't balk when he told her he was going. Aidan suspected she was secretly glad for the opportunity to spend the entire weekend with her mother. He chuckled thinking about it.

●●●

"Hi honey," Mariah said cheerfully, coming into the bedroom where he was.

"Hey," Aidan replied. "Where's Livvy," he asked, not seeing the baby.

"She's with mommy," Mariah replied.

Aidan smiled, knowing Kayla was surely enjoying spoiling the child more.

"Are you staying over there for the weekend?"

"Yes, Dad is due home Monday," Mariah told him.

Aidan thought he heard a tone and called her on it.

"Is something wrong baby," he asked looking at Mariah intently.

She sighed heavily before answering.

"I'm not sure," Mariah replied. "I think Mommy may ask Dad for a divorce."

Aidan was stunned. He suspected Kayla and Dante had something going, but nothing to this magnitude.

"Why do you say that?"

"Just some of the stuff Mommy has been saying lately," Mariah told Aidan.

"Maybe she's just really tired of being alone all the time honey," he replied.

Mariah knew Aidan was right. Thomas was gone for three weeks this time. During the whole year he remained home less than four full months.

"I want mommy to be happy," Mariah told her husband. "I just want her to be sure she's doing the right thing."

"Baby," Aidan began. "I've never known your mother to be hasty about anything," he replied. "I'm sure whatever Kayla decides, she will think about long and hard."

"Yes, as usual, you're right," Mariah smiled.

She helped him finish packing. He just sat his bag in the living room, when Dante arrived.

"Hi," Dante spoke to Mariah.

"Hello," she smiled back.

"Are you ready," he asked Aidan.

"Yep," Aidan replied smiling and giving Mariah a hug and kiss goodbye.

"Oh yeah," he said, kissing her again. "That one is for Livvy," Aidan finished as he headed out.

"You two be careful," Mariah admonished them both.

"We will," Dezi smiled.

●●●

They were enjoying the ride when Aidan questioned him.

"Are you and Kayla having an affair," Aidan asked calmly.

Dezi was surprised. He didn't think they were that obvious.

"Why would you ask me that," he returned to the young man.

Aidan smiled.

"I see how you look at her. How you talk to her. I know a man in love when I see one," Aidan teased.

Dezi chuckled aloud.

"Is it that obvious?"

Aidan laughed again.

"Probably only to me."

"No, Aidan, we're not having an affair," Dezi replied, which was true.

Kayla called him once after they were together that night, and he pleased her again, but she wasn't ready yet. Dezi knew she was still trying to do the right thing and save her marriage, so he didn't press her. Besides, he already made plans for that.

"Well, Mariah thinks she's going to ask Thomas for a divorce," Aidan said simply, looking at Dante for his reaction.

Dezi was thrilled at the thought, but he didn't show it.

"Hmm," he began. "I'm sure Kayla will do what she feels is best for her and her life."

Aidan chuckled again and changed the subject.

This is definitely my son, Dezi thought content, marveling at the young man's adept ability to disturb thoughts like he was able to do. He was pleased they were taking this weekend together. Aidan was very relaxed and comfortable with him. Dezi hoped it would make the news easier when he finally told him the truth.

•••

Thomas was looking forward to getting home. Kayla secured three more clients now she told him when they talked last. Two of them were women, and the other a man. Thomas was glad she was doing so well. Now that Kayla was busy, she wouldn't be lonely and she wouldn't be as upset that he was traveling. He promised her no more trips, but Thomas was slated to take at least two more. They would be short though. Only two weeks each. He wasn't going to tell Kayla until he returned.

He thought of Elise then. He saw her every night after his meetings. The sex was fantastic. She made the nights bearable for him. Thomas would never leave Kayla for Elise, and he already told her that. She was fine with their arrangement just the way it was she told him. Thomas hoped Kayla would understand, and allow him these two trips. Now that he was pretty much assured he would get what he was seeking, he needed to secure it.

Thomas knew Mariah and Livvy would be spending the weekend with her. That would surely put Kayla in a good mood for Monday, when he arrived. He would at least spend the rest of the week with her. He didn't need to fly out until Friday morning. Thomas wanted to see Mariah and Aidan too, since he would be out of town when they actually left. He heard a knock at the door. Thomas smiled knowing it was Elise. He was taking her to do a little shopping today. Thomas figured it was the least he could do for her, since he knew Elise was single, and trying to make ends meet on her own.

●●●

You're getting in too deep. Elise thought, as she tried on the different dresses and modeled them for him. Thomas was very good to her, and she felt badly taking advantage of him. She knew that someone was going to use their first session against him. Part of her wanted to warn Thomas and tell him to confess to his wife. Elise still thought of her livelihood, and that would be professional suicide for her. She sighed deeply and vowed to just enjoy the time she spent with Thomas, and pray that when the DVD did surface he would be all right.

●●●

They were finished now, and he helped her choose four new dresses.

"It's off to the shoe store now," Elise laughed.

"OK, but I need lunch first," Thomas chuckled.

They stopped at a bistro and were having a nice lunch, when he noticed Elise studying him intently.

"What's wrong?"

She smiled weakly.

"Nothing," Elise replied.

Thomas knew. He saw it in her eyes. She was developing feelings for him. It was bound to happen.

"It's OK, Elise," he said softly, not pushing the subject any further.

She was grateful for that. *He is such a nice guy,* Elise thought, sorry all over again, for what she knew was going to happen to him.

●●●

Collins was frustrated. He still had absolutely nothing. He was standing at Black's grave marker talking to his friend.

"He's here man," he said aloud. "I know he is. I just can't find him," he went on. "I won't let him hurt them though, I promise you that," he told him, praying his spirit heard.

69

Collins went on to apologize for lying to Black all those years.

"I've got to warn Kayla about any strangers she may meet," Collins said again.

He called her earlier, and found out Mariah was staying the weekend. They all agreed to get together and spend some time. *If I only knew what Gianni looked like now,* Collins thought, as he drove. They were watching Wilson since his visit, and he led them to nothing. *Maybe he was telling the truth,* he thought again. Collins knew Gianni was extremely paranoid, and maybe he didn't trust anyone any more. Collins just carried a feeling in his gut that Gianni was here, and he was close.

"Why won't you just die," Collins asked aloud, to no one in particular.

●●●

He arrived at the house and took a deep breath. He wanted to act normally. *No need in alarming them if I don't need too,* Collins thought, as he rang the bell. Mariah opened the door, and hugged him excitedly.

"Hi, Uncle Maurice!"

Mariah motioned Collins in, and showed him to the den. Kayla was there with the baby.

"Hello, Maurice," she greeted him warmly, as she hugged him.

Collins took them both in, and told them how wonderful they looked.

"Sit down," Kayla told him.

Mariah was gone to the kitchen to get their drinks.

"Tell me everything that's been going on with you," she told him, still smiling.

There wasn't much to tell as far as he was concerned, but Collins did the best he could.

"Where are you living," Kayla asked.

"Longbow," he told her of the condo community.

"Oh I know where those are," Kayla told him.

"Are you dating," she pried.

"No, and I'm not looking to either," Collins laughed.

Kayla laughed heartily at that. They chatted on for a while longer, and he asked her about business.

"Well I just recently started again," she replied. "I have four clients, and two more prospective ones."

"I'm proud of you," Collins smiled. "You were always fabulous in business."

Collins found out from Mariah, about her and Aidan's impending move. He never connected the Pembroke Parish she told him about, with the city of Hamilton. No one ever told Collins they were the same city in Bermuda, where Gianni maintained residence for the last twenty years.

"Are you really okay with them leaving," Collins asked Kayla.

She sighed gently.

"Well, they have to live their lives," she replied. "It gives me an excuse to visit often," Kayla finished, chuckling lightly.

Collins knew she was trying to be brave. Mariah was all Kayla had left from Black, and it couldn't have been easy watching her go. He definitely needed to make sure Kayla stayed all right, and that Gianni didn't harm her.

"Well, I better be going," Collins told her, as he rose to leave.

Kayla hugged him again, as did Mariah.

"Now that you're living here, I better see more of you," Kayla chided him playfully.

"I promise, you will," Collins laughingly returned.

"When is Thomas coming back," he asked.

He met her new husband, and he seemed to be an okay guy.

"He'll be back Monday," Kayla replied lightly.

"Tell him hello for me," Collins told her as he left.

They waved, as they watched him back out and drive away.

●●●

Kayla and Mariah returned to the house. Livvy was still sleeping, so it gave them a chance to talk.

"Mommy?" Mariah began "Are you going to divorce Thomas?"

Kayla was surprised.

"Why would you think that?"

"Well, I know you're tired of his constant travel," she went on. "And I think there are some things you're not telling me too," she finished, watching her mother's reaction.

Kayla tried to not allow her emotions to show on her face. True, she was having some issues with Thomas, but she wanted to try and work on them when he returned this week. He promised no more trips, so they would have plenty of time to try and rescue their marriage.

"I think Thomas and I can work out our problems, honey," Kayla told her gently.

Mariah smiled, and breathed a small sigh of relief. It wasn't that she didn't like Dante; she just didn't want her mother to be with him on the rebound.

"I'm going to lay down for a bit," Kayla told Mariah.

"OK, mommy," Mariah told her, as Kayla ascended the stairs.

●●●

She was thinking of what Mariah asked her. She was going to have to do something. Kayla found herself increasingly attracted to Dante. She went to see him a few nights ago, and he did the same wonderful things to her he did the first time. *I must be going crazy,* she thought. She bit her lip hard to keep from calling out Dezi's name during her orgasm.

Kayla loved Thomas, but she was falling in love with Dante too. He reminded her so much of Dezi, and after talking to Jackie, thinking about the things she said, Kayla couldn't help wondering if she was indeed getting another chance to make it right. She was exhausted from thinking about it, and from thinking about her marriage. She closed her eyes and drifted off to sleep.

Smoke & **13** Mirrors

The weekend was wonderful. Dezi thoroughly enjoyed spending quality time with his son. He knew Aidan enjoyed it too. *I think it will be all right when I tell him,* Dezi thought. He needed to get home and check his mail. He was expecting a package from Big D. He also knew Thomas was due home today. Dezi dreaded it, and found himself getting angry, the more he thought about it. *Relax Dezi. She's thinking about you every day,* he told himself and smiled. He heard Kayla telling Jackie, how she almost called him Dezi, the last time they were together. He knew once they made love the farce would end. There was denying who he was once Dezi made love to her. Kayla would know. He wondered if she would leave with him then.

Dezi would need to take care of this marriage nonsense between her and Thomas very soon. He also had that unfinished business with Collins to consider. *Don't forget Rachelle,* Dezi reminded himself tiredly. He needed to go see her today. He put her off for the last week. He still had to keep Rachelle dangling, until he accomplished his mission.

Dezi dropped his bag at the door, once he entered the house. He headed to the bar and fixed himself a drink, then made his way to his mail. He found what he was looking for and headed to his monitor room. Dezi made himself comfortable, and opened the package. He put the DVD in and pushed play. The images spilled onto the screen and Dezi smiled. There in living, breathing color was Thomas, having sex with Elise. Dezi chuckled.

"Gotcha, preacher man!" he said aloud, as he turned on the house monitors.

●●●

Thomas just arrived home. He didn't tell Kayla what time his flight got in. He wanted to surprise her. He heard the shower running, as he went upstairs. Dezi was enjoying watching the lather run down Kayla's beautiful body. He saw Thomas on the other camera coming down the hallway. He saw him enter the bathroom. Dezi didn't want to see what was going to happen next, but he wanted to know what the competition was bringing to the table. He saw Thomas undress, and slip into the shower while Kayla washed her hair. After she rinsed it, Kayla opened her eyes and found him standing there.

"Hi," Thomas said softly, looking her over.

Kayla smiled; happy he was home at last. Thomas kissed her and pulled Kayla to him. He began to arouse her. Dezi noticed she wasn't really responding. He smiled, knowing he was responsible for that.

●●●

She had to put Dante out of her mind and allow Thomas to make love to her, Kayla told herself. She pulled him to her, and Thomas began kissing her.

"I've missed you so much, baby," he said softly, as he picked Kayla up and placed her against the shower wall.

"I've missed you too, Thomas," she replied in between kisses.

Thomas slowly entered her, and Kayla cried out.

●●●

Dezi knew it was from pain, not desire. She wasn't ready. *She doesn't want him. She wants me,* he thought, as he watched her suffering through the act she was forcing herself to endure.

"Baby, no," Dezi said softly, watching her fighting back tears.

●●●

Thomas's pace quickened and Kayla knew he was almost spent. She wanted it over. She just couldn't get into it when he tried to arouse her. Finally he came, and began kissing her again. Kayla kissed him back, as Thomas got out to dry off.

"I'll be there in a minute," she told him.

"Okay baby, take your time," Thomas told her, and kissed her again.

Kayla put her face under the spray to wash away the tears that were still coming.

●●●

Dezi hated watching Kayla suffer like this. *Baby, just say the word,* he thought. He couldn't push her. This time she had to come to him on her own. Dezi knew it wouldn't be long, not with what he just witnessed. Kayla was in the bedroom with Thomas now, and he was talking to her.

"So baby, tell me what I've missed since I've been gone," he told her, as she toweled her hair.

Dezi saw the look on her face.

"No baby, you can't tell him that," Dezi said aloud chuckling.

Kayla told Thomas about Maurice's visit, about the dinner, minus the Dante part of course.

"Come here," Thomas said softly.

She came and sat on the bed beside him. He began stroking her hair. Kayla sighed and looked at him.

"How long this time?" she asked, looking at Thomas evenly.

Dezi was incredulous. *I know this asshole is not leaving again!* he thought, as he watched the scene unfold.

"Two weeks, each," Thomas replied quietly.

She sighed deeply.

"So, another month?"

Thomas looked at her. He couldn't tell what she was thinking.

"Yes, something like that," he replied.

Kayla swallowed hard, and chose her words carefully. There was a lot going on in her mind right now.

"OK," she said simply, and got up to leave the room.

●●●

Thomas was stunned. He was also frightened. At least if she'd yelled at him, he knew what she was thinking, but this reaction left him completely in the dark. Thomas got up and put on his pants. He needed to talk to her. He needed to know what was going on. He was not going to leave Kayla here, and come back to find her gone.

●●●

Dezi saw him follow her. He fixed himself another drink, and was sipping it as he watched intently. *He better not fucking hit her again,* Dezi thought coldly continuing to watch.

"Baby, is that all you're going to say?" Thomas asked Kayla after he found her in the kitchen.

She was sipping the tea she just made.

"What do you want me to say, Thomas," Kayla asked without emotion.

Dezi laughed at how in the dark this man was.

"She's angry fool," he said aloud.

He saw her like this only once in their history, but he never forgot it.

"I know you're tired of me traveling," Thomas began, and she turned to look at him.

"Yet, you continue to do it," Kayla said again without emotion.

Thomas was frustrated. He didn't know what to say to her right now.

"Are you going to be here when I come back?"

She sipped her tea, and took her time answering.

"I don't know," Kayla told him honestly, as she went into the den.

Dezi continued to watch.

Thomas didn't want to hear that. He got angry.

"I'm not divorcing you, Kayla," he said, through clenched teeth.

Dezi began paying closer attention, seeing that Thomas was angry.

Kayla exploded.

"No, of course you wouldn't!" she screamed at him. "You've already left me!" she continued. "Who is she Thomas?!" she yelled. "Who are you screwing when you're not here?!" she finished, as she slapped him hard across the face.

Thomas grabbed her, and threw her on the sofa.

It took everything in Dezi not to get up and go over there, but he saw Kayla wasn't hurt. Thomas came over, and tried to talk to her again.

"No!" Kayla screamed, and hit him again.

"How dare you come here and tell me you're leaving again for a month, and expect me to sit in this damned house and rot," she continued, crying hysterically.

Dezi was angry. He couldn't stand seeing her cry. *This fucker has about one more time to put his hands on her,* he thought irately.

"I won't do that!" Kayla screamed.

Thomas took a deep breath, and tried again.

"Kayla, please," he began.

"I don't want to hear any more Thomas!" she screamed, and bolted upstairs.

Thomas sunk into the chair, and put his hands in his head.

Dezi smiled, and turned his attention to the monitor from their bedroom. Kayla was still crying, sobbing deeply now. His heart was breaking watching her, but Dezi knew she needed to let it all out. *Well there is no saving it now is there,* he thought. Dezi knew for certain Kayla would be calling again soon. This time he would make love to her, Dezi decided, heading to the kitchen to drop his glass off. He was headed to Rachelle's. Dezi needed one more piece of information from her, and then he would dump her and move on.

●●●

I need to know who he's seeing. Rachelle was thinking. Dante put her off almost the whole week, before calling tonight. There was someone else, she was almost positive. *This bitch has picked the wrong man!* Rachelle furiously formed. She wasn't letting anyone take Dante from her. *If I could just get him inside me without that damned condom,* she plotted. Rachelle made plans tonight though. She knew Dante loved getting head before they made love. Tonight she would slip him inside her, right as he was getting ready to cum. He won't be able to pull out, because he'll be so close to his peak. *What if you piss him off,* Rachelle thought again. She didn't want to lose him. She caught only a small glimpse of his anger, but it was more than enough for her. *He'll be all right once he calms down. It will be in the heat of passion. No one's fault, it just happened,* Rachelle reasoned, as she opened the door to let him in.

"Hey, baby," she smiled and kissed him.

Dezi smiled and returned her greeting.

"Would like something to eat," Rachelle asked Dante.

"Mhmm, but it's not in the kitchen," he replied, looking her over.

Rachelle laughed and took his hand as they went to the bedroom. *This man is absolutely wonderful,* she thought as she hit orgasm number three. It was her turn now. Rachelle got Dante comfortable, and took him in her mouth. She began to work him aggressively. He sighed softly, and she knew he was almost there. Dante didn't make noise. Rachelle learned to read his body, to know when he was about to cum. She knew it was almost time as she continued her rhythm, and Dante sighed again. *Now!* Rachelle thought as she mounted him.

Dezi figured she would try something like this. He was almost ready to cum, but stopped himself. Dezi maintained control if nothing else. He thrust into Rachelle a couple times then pushed her off.

"What are you doing," Dezi asked calmly.

He was pissed.

"You're trying to trap me huh," he asked coldly.

Rachelle realized, too late, that she made a mistake. She just didn't realize the magnitude of it.

"So, you're one of those bitches, hmm," Dezi asked acidly.

She was crying now. He didn't care.

"Please, Dante," Rachelle began.

"Shut the fuck up," he snapped. "Here I am caring for you. Making love to you and you pull this bullshit on me," Dezi finished, looking at Rachelle hard, fully dressed, with his keys in hand.

"Please, I only wanted to be with you," Rachelle said pitifully.

"Really," he asked harshly "Then why are you trying to fuck me without a condom, and I'm telling you I don't want any babies?"

Rachelle tried to explain that she was on the pill, and wouldn't get pregnant.

"Yeah, right," Dezi told her, and laughed coldly. "You haven't taken them for the last three weeks," he replied.

Her mouth fell open. He saw she was surprised.

"Yes, I keep track. I'm not stupid," he finished, turning to leave.

Rachelle was crushed. She followed Dante into the living room.

"Well, who the hell is she then," she yelled at him.

Dezi spun on her, and Rachelle was scared. He looked at her hard.

"What are you going on about," he asked icily.

"I know you're seeing someone else. That's why you haven't called me all week," Rachelle told him, calmer this time.

She never witnessed anyone be this cold, and she was frightened. Rachelle loved Dante though, so she risked it to confront him. Dezi continued to stare at her. He didn't need the information that badly. He was sick of her. She got on his nerves, and he didn't even enjoy screwing her.

"Yes, there is someone else," Dezi replied coldly. "I only came over here out of pity for you," he told Rachelle, as she cried harder.

"Do you know why I started asking you to suck my dick," he went on cruelly. "Because I couldn't get it up any other way to fuck you. You are a complete turn off sexually," Dezi finished, as he walked over to her.

Rachelle was hurting. She couldn't believe Dante said all those things, and he was being so cold to her. Dezi slapped her hard across the face, drawing blood from her. Rachelle screamed and tried to get away from him. He hit her again and again. He finally stopped hitting her, as she lay on the floor whimpering.

"Don't ever call me again bitch," Dezi said quietly in her ear. "If you tell anyone I did this to you, I'll kill you," he said evenly, and Rachelle believed him.

She drew herself tighter into a ball, and shrunk away from him. Dezi chuckled, as he washed his hands in her sink.

"Stupid bitch," he mumbled, as he closed the door behind him.

Rachelle dragged herself into the bathroom, closed and locked the door. She was terrified. She stayed there until she was sure he wasn't coming back, and gingerly ventured out.

"He's crazy," she spoke aloud to the empty room.

She would stay inside for the next couple days, and she would definitely keep her mouth shut. Rachelle had absolutely no problem believing Dante would kill her. She began to cry again, as she a lay down and let sleep take her.

●●●

Dezi arrived home, and made himself a drink. He went to the monitor room. He needed to check on Kayla, and make sure everything was all right. Dezi saw Thomas in the guest bedroom and chuckled.

"Guess you're in the doghouse, huh?"

Kayla was on the phone downstairs in the den. Dezi turned up the phone monitor.

"He's leaving again tomorrow," she said flatly.

Jackie was pissed.

"Who is he screwing, Kayla," she said evenly, trying hard to contain her anger.

"He swears no one, but I don't believe that anymore," Kayla replied.

"So what are you going to do?" Jackie asked, glad Kayla was finally awake and not believing Thomas's lies any longer.

"I think I'm going to leave," Kayla said simply.

"Why do you have to think," Jackie replied.

She missed what Kayla was really saying, but Dezi didn't. He knew her, and what she just said was that she was leaving North Carolina.

"Because, I'm not sure where I want to go," Kayla replied, and this time Jackie got it.

"Well," she began slyly. "I hear Bermuda is lovely," she replied, chuckling.

Kayla giggled.

"It's on the list," she replied.

Dezi smiled.

"That's what I want to hear," he said aloud sipping his drink.

"Did you sleep with him," Jackie asked.

"Who?"

Jackie laughed, "Your husband, nut case!"

Kayla laughed too.

"Yes, he found me in the shower," she replied.

"From that answer, I would say you didn't enjoy it much," Jackie replied probing.

"No, not really," Kayla replied honestly.

"Why do think that is," Jackie continued to push.

"Because we've been having so many problems," Kayla replied.

Jackie sighed.

"Stop lying to yourself, Kayla," she went on. "You didn't respond, because he wasn't Dante," she added. "Be honest, and admit it."

Dezi was waiting for that answer too. Kayla sighed deeply before she answered.

"I guess that's part of it too," she replied.

"Where is he now, Thomas I mean?"

"Guest room," Kayla answered flatly.

Jackie roared.

"I'm so impressed," she told Kayla. "You're going to have to make some decisions while he's gone you know."

"He said he wouldn't give me a divorce," Kayla told Jackie.

"Whatever!" she replied. "You can get a divorce, even without his signature," she went on. "Granted, it may take a little longer, but you can get it."

"Okay, I'm going to check into it," Kayla told her. "I'm going to sleep now."

"Listen to me Kayla," Jackie began again. "Do what's best for you, not anyone else, you!" Jackie told her. "Whatever you decide, make sure it's what, and who, you really want, OK?"

"I will, I promise," Kayla told Jackie. "I'll call you tomorrow."

They hung up and Kayla headed up to bed.

Thomas obviously heard her go into their room. He waited fifteen minutes, and carefully came inside. Thomas gently slid into bed beside Kayla, and put his arms around her. Kayla heard him come in, and felt him get into bed. She was too tired to fight anymore. Kayla closed her eyes and went back to sleep.

Dezi saw him too. *It's too late for you preacher man, She's already gone, and you don't even know it yet*, Dezi thought blowing Kayla a kiss, and turned off the monitor, heading upstairs to finally sleep himself.

Smoke & **14** Mirrors

Dezi was sick of Collins snooping around, and decided he would go ahead and tie up that loose end now. He needed to make a couple of trips. He called Big D and told him he was on his way. Big D warned Dezi that wasn't a good idea. He saw a couple of suits watching him. Big D gave him an alternate meeting place. Big D knew how to lose a tail so that wouldn't be a problem. *Yeah, the sooner I kill this fool the better,* Dezi thought. Kayla called earlier. He knew Thomas was gone. He also heard him threaten Kayla before he left. Dezi thought about it and got angry again.

"Kayla, I meant what I said about divorcing you," he told her evenly.

She just looked at him. Thomas came very close to Kayla then and spoke.

"I won't let you go. If you run, I'll find you. If you find someone else, I'll kill them," he told her harshly.

Dezi could tell Kayla was frightened. He was proud of her for holding her own, in spite of the fear.

"So are you going to kill me too, Thomas," she asked, looking back at him.

He sighed then.

"Don't be stupid," Thomas replied. "You know I would never hurt you."

He kissed Kayla, and hugged her tightly.

"Be here when I come home Kayla, please don't do anything you'll regret," Thomas told her softly in her ear, before releasing her.

Dezi wasn't sweating that crap. He was going to show Kayla the DVD soon, and Thomas could blow all the smoke he wanted. Thomas was clueless who he was messing with, and he didn't want to find out. Dezi grabbed his bag and jumped into the car. He heard nothing further from Rachelle. *Guess her stupid ass finally got the message,* Dezi chuckled, as his cell went off. It was Kayla.

"Hello?"

"Hi, Dante," she replied. "Do you think we could get together this evening, to talk?"

Dezi had an idea what Kayla wanted to talk about. *Well if she's ready, so am I.*

"Yes of course," the replied.

"Is eight good for you?" she asked.

"Yes, that's good," Dezi told her. "I'll see you then."

He spoke again as an afterthought.

"Can we meet at my house," Dezi threw out. "We can have complete privacy there."

"Um yes, that will be fine," Kayla agreed.

I'm going to make love to her tonight, Dezi made up his mind, as he hit the expressway. The trip was uneventful.

●●●

Dezi and Big D were sitting and talking as they enjoyed their meal.

"So what's the progress," Big D asked Dezi, who brought him up to speed on everything.

"Shit man, you don't even need the DVD," he told Dezi. "Sounds like old boy is messing up all on his own," Big D finished, laughing out loud.

Dezi smiled, and told him he agreed.

"The DVD is so that fucker doesn't hold up her divorce," he told him.

Big D nodded his understanding.

"You don't think he would try to hurt her, do you," Big D asked.

He saw Dezi change, and already knew the man better not, if he wanted to live.

"She's coming over tonight," Dezi told him.

Big D smiled. "So, y'all finally gonna get to business?"

"If I have anything to say about we certainly will," Dezi laughed.

He collected what he came to get from Big D, and they parted.

"Call me later," Dezi told Big D.

"Well, if I get the machine, I'll just leave a message," he told Dezi, chuckling heartily as he drove away.

Dezi turned the car back toward Chapel Hill, thinking about his evening with Kayla all the way there.

●●●

Kayla looked at herself in the mirror. She thought she looked very nice, and of course Jackie told her she did. Kayla was wearing a sexy turquoise wrap skirt, with a matching sleeveless chemise top. She wore all the matching turquoise accessories, and the stiletto sandals set the outfit off. *He's sure to love this outfit,* Kayla chuckled, thinking of Dante. Jackie stayed with her most of the afternoon. The kids were leaving in the morning, and she wanted to be there to say goodbye.

Dante agreed to drive them all to the airport. Thomas called them and said his goodbyes already. He called her too. He threatened her again, but she didn't care. Kayla made up her mind, and she was going to get out while she there was still life worth living. She grabbed her keys, heading over to Dante's, and opened the door to find Thomas standing there.

"Where are you going," he asked her harshly.

Kayla was stunned. He left this morning. She saw him get on his flight.

"Surprised to see me," Thomas asked still looking at her. "Where are you going," he asked again.

"I'm going over to Jackie's, and we're going out for a while," Kayla said calmly.

"Call her and cancel," Thomas told her, handing Kayla the cordless.

She started to balk, but the look on his face made her change her mind. Kayla dialed Dante, and he answered on the second ring.

"Hi Jackie," she said, and Dezi immediately knew something was wrong. "I'm going to have to cancel tonight," she said simply. "I'll call you tomorrow," Kayla told him, and hung up.

Dezi kicked up the speed on the car. He was still fifteen minutes from his house.

Thomas continued to look at Kayla. She was trying to leave him. He couldn't allow that. A divorce right now would devastate his career, not to mention the little thing of Thomas being totally in love with her.

"Take your clothes off," he told her firmly.

Kayla was scared. She didn't know what Thomas was planning, or even thinking. She never saw him like this.

"Please, Thomas," Kayla began.

"Take them off," he told her sharply.

Kayla began to cry as she undressed. Thomas looked at her standing in front of him naked. He was completely aroused. He stepped to Kayla, and wiped her tears, kissing her in the process.

●●●

Dezi made it home and went straight to the monitors. He saw Thomas carrying Kayla upstairs. *Not this bullshit again!* Dezi thought, loading the clip in the .10mm he just got from Big D.

Thomas laid Kayla gently on the bed. He stood up, and undressed himself. Kayla was terrified. She hoped he didn't hurt her. Thomas kissed her, and felt her trembling.

"I'm not going to hurt you," he said softly.

Kayla let out a breath, and Thomas felt her relax a little.

"Kayla, I absolutely adore you," he told her gently. "Don't you know that?" he continued, kissing her neck and her breasts. Kayla found herself getting turned on.

"You're all I've ever wanted," Thomas murmured again, close to her ear. "Let me show you, Kayla," he continued. "I came back for you, baby," he said gently. "Because I love you so much," he kissed Kayla passionately, and felt her body respond.

Dezi didn't like what he was seeing. *You knew some part of her still loved him,* he told himself, but that didn't help the jealousy and anger he felt watching Kayla respond to Thomas's lovemaking. Kayla began to moan softly, as Thomas sucked her nipples and stroked her. She was getting hotter by the moment. He moved his mouth down, and began to lick her there. She was sighing softly. Thomas began to kiss her again, as he slowly entered her.

Kayla had the same reaction as before, and Dezi saw it. *She was fantasizing about me during the foreplay,* he thought, as he saw her desperately trying to make herself respond. She closed her eyes and let her mind drift.

Kayla imagined Dante inside her, and began to enjoy herself. She was getting closer to her orgasm, and bit her lip again, as Dante almost slipped from her mouth. Dezi saw her on the monitor, and knew without a shadow of a doubt what happened.

She wants me, he thought and smiled. Thomas of course was oblivious, and thought she cried out from his lovemaking. He kissed Kayla gently, and told her he loved her. Thomas held her as she drifted off to sleep. He kissed her forehead, and laid Kayla gently on her side of the bed. He got up and headed downstairs. Dezi watched him intently. Thomas called Jackie and apologized again for Kayla canceling. Jackie was smooth as butter; never once letting on that she didn't have plans with Kayla. Dezi chuckled again. He really did like Jackie. Thomas was satisfied that Kayla told him the truth, and headed back upstairs to her. He slid in beside her, and fell asleep.

You interrupted tonight fucker, Dezi fumed. *But you'll be gone soon enough, and there will be no interruptions this time.* He finished, heading up to bed. Dezi needed to be up early so he could drive them to the airport tomorrow. If he were lucky, Thomas would be on a flight too.

●●●

Kayla was still scared. Thomas was his usual cheerful self this morning as he dressed.

"Good morning baby," he said softly, as he kissed her.

She returned his greeting, and finished getting dressed.

"So are you staying home now," Kayla asked softly.

Thomas looked at her. He desperately wanted too, but he knew he couldn't. He made up the excuse of an emergency to return last night.

"I can't baby," he said gently.

Kayla sighed heavily, and Thomas knew she was hurt again.

"Listen honey," he told her, as he went to hug her. "I promise it's almost over, just another week, and few days. You're working now, so that should help fill some of the time while I'm gone, shouldn't it," he finished, kissing her again.

Kayla didn't respond.

"Please, say something honey," Thomas pleaded.

"Why are you doing this to me, Thomas," she asked, looking intently at him.

He sighed this time.

"Baby, I know you're tired of me traveling, and you think I'm neglecting you," he went on. "You're probably a little scared of me now, after what I said yesterday," Thomas continued. "But I love you more than anything, and I'm not trying to hurt you."

Kayla looking into his eyes, believed his declaration of love, but she also saw something else. There was something dark inside Thomas, and it frightened her.

"All right," she replied, and sighed again. "I'll try to understand. Like you said, I have my work now."

Thomas smiled brightly, and kissed Kayla again passionately. His cab blew for him, and he told her goodbye.

●●●

Kayla called Jackie as soon as Thomas left.

"Hey girl" she said as Jackie answered.

"OK, so what the hell was he doing back," Jackie asked instead of a greeting.

Kayla was stunned.

"How did you know he was back?".

"He called, wanted to apologize for you standing me up," Jackie told her.

"Oh my god," Kayla gasped.

"I figured you actually were supposed to be with Dante, so I knew you used me as the alibi," Jackie returned.

"Thanks so much, Jackie," Kayla spoke.

"Girl, you know that is never a problem," she said before asking. "So what are you going to do?"

"I've got to get out," Kayla told her. "He frightens me Jackie," she added quietly.

"Did he do something to you last night," Jackie asked, alarmed.

"No, just made me have sex with him," Kayla told her.

"He's been threatening me though," she began anew.

"You need to leave while he's out of town," Jackie told Kayla.

"I know, and that's what I need to talk to Dante about," Kayla replied.

"You're going to Bermuda with the kids?"

"No, I don't want them to know right now," she replied.

"What then," Jackie asked again.

"I'm going to ask Dante if I can stay at house until he returns to the island himself," Kayla explained.

"Where will you go then," Jackie asked, after telling Kayla it sounded like a good idea.

"I'm not sure, but it will give me a chance to think, and get my head together," she told Jackie.

Kayla heard Dante drive up.

"Dante just got here."

"OK girl, I'll see you at the airport." she replied and hung up.

Jackie was going by and pick up Aidan, Mariah and Livvy, since she was closer. Dante and Kayla would come together. Dezi rang the bell, and she answered looking beautiful as usual.

"Hi," he said, smiling.

Kayla smiled and returned his greeting.

"So, do you want to tell me what happened last night," Dezi asked as they rode.

"My husband surprised me," she sighed lightly.

"Oh, so he's home early," Dezi asked.

"No, he just came back last night," Kayla replied. "To try and repair our marriage, I suppose."

Dezi heard the finality in her tone.

"Did it work?"

She sighed sadly.

"No, not really," Kayla said softly.

Dezi was elated, but careful not to show it.

"That's part of what I wanted to talk to you about."

He was intrigued, and asked Kayla to continue. Before she could reply they were already at the terminal parking area.

"I'll tell you later, I promise," Kayla replied, as they got out of the car headed for the airport terminal.

Mariah was waiting for her when she rounded the corner.

Smoke & **15** Mirrors

ommy, I can't do this!"

Kayla knew Mariah would be emotional, but she needed to make her see this was something she could do.

"Honey, what's wrong," she asked gently, as she hugged Mariah.

"I can't leave you here alone, and I can't stand being that far from you," Mariah cried.

Kayla smoothed her hair. "Baby, you can do this," she told Mariah. "I'll always be near, you know that."

"Mommy, please," Mariah continued to cry.

Dezi came over to see if he could help.

"Mariah," he said gently.

She turned to him, still sniffling.

"As you know, I own a home in the parish, and I've already told your mother it's available for her, any time she wants to visit," Dezi told her gently. "I myself will be returning in a little while, and you will have someone you know around again," he went on. "Perhaps, I can even persuade your mother to come with me for a visit when I return."

Mariah looked at Kayla hopefully, and her mother smiled.

"Yes, baby, I'll come I promise," she told her.

Mariah brightened, and allowed them both to lead her back to her gate, where Aidan was waiting with Livvy. Kayla hugged them both, and kissed her granddaughter.

"I'll see you all really soon, I promise," Kayla told them, looking into their eyes.

●●●

Aidan didn't like the way she looked. He knew something was wrong. He asked Dante if he could speak to him alone for a moment. Dezi readily agreed.

"Dante," Aidan began. "I think there are some things going on with Pastor and Mrs. Bradford that she's not telling us," he went on. "I'm scared for her. Do you think you could keep an eye on her for us, please?"

Dezi smiled. "Yes of course."

"I promise you Aidan, I will not allow anything bad to happen to Kayla," he said matter-of-fact.

It was the look in his eye and the tone of his voice that made Aidan believe this was more than just an idle promise. Aidan knew how much his father once loved Kayla, and would never allow anything to happen to her. Since Dezi was dead now, it was up to him to make sure she was all right.

"Good," he replied. "That makes me feel a whole lot better about leaving her here with him."

They boarded the plane, as Kayla, Dezi, and Jackie watched them fly off. *I'll be with them again soon*, Kayla thought, trying to keep the tears at bay. Dezi soon found himself comforting them both, as they broke and couldn't stop the flow.

●●●

Elise watched Thomas intently during their meal. There was something heavily weighing on his mind.

"What is it," she asked gently.

Thomas looked up, as his thoughts were interrupted.

"Excuse me?"

Elise chuckled lightly.

"What is going on with you today," she asked again. "You are totally not in this place," she chided him gently.

Thomas sighed. He didn't want to get into this with her.

"Just got some personal stuff going on," he replied.

Elise understood. There was something going on with his wife. She was secretly pleased. Maybe they would divorce. She found herself falling hard and fast for Thomas.

"Are you sure you don't want to talk about it," Elise asked again gently.

Thomas looked at her for a moment. *You know she's fallen for you don't you*, he told himself. He didn't want to hurt Elise. She was a very nice young woman, but Kayla was the woman Thomas wanted by his side. She was the woman all of his ministry contacts approved as the perfect companion. Thomas absolutely adored Kayla, yet all he could seem to do lately was hurt her.

"No, I'll be OK," Thomas told her calmly. "I think I want to be alone for a little while," he said gently, as he rose to leave.

Elise didn't push. She knew he would open up when he was ready.

"Will you call me later if you want some company?"

"Yes," Thomas smiled and caressed her face.

●●●

"How am I going to fix this," he spoke into the atmosphere, once he was alone in his hotel room.

Thomas couldn't run out on the meetings he was having, he was too close to success.

She's the key to that success. You can't let her leave you, he thought, growing angry again. He needed to call Kayla and check on her. *What if she decides to leave while you're gone*, Thomas thought. He decided to call Jackie, and ask her to keep an eye on Kayla for him. Then he realized Jackie would be gone in a couple days herself.

"Maurice!" Thomas said excitedly.

Kayla told him Maurice was back, and he would be perfect to keep an eye on her for him. Thomas would tell Maurice a little of what was going on, and ask him to watch her. He and Maurice got along well, and he would do this for him he was sure.

"I can't let you leave me baby, I just can't," Thomas said aloud, as he dialed Collins number.

"Hello," Collins answered.

Thomas greeted him and they began to talk.

"I know it's asking a lot, Maurice," he went on. "But she's been very erratic, and I'm worried about her."

"Sure man no problem," Collins told Thomas.

Collins loved Kayla, and he knew Thomas did too.

"I won't let her do anything crazy," he told Thomas. "The two of you deserve a chance to work this thing out."

Thomas smiled, and thanked him as they disconnected. *Now I can take care of this business, and my wife and marriage, will still be there when I get back*, he thought, relieved that she wouldn't be gone.

Thomas called Elise and asked her to come over. He needed to be with her. *You need to wean yourself from her*, he reminded himself. After these two weeks were over, he wouldn't see her anymore. He would be too out in the public eye for anything to come up, he continued to brood as he headed to the shower to wait for her.

•••

Collins called Kayla. *What is going on with her*, he wondered, waiting on her to answer. He got the machine, so he left a message asking her to call him. Collins didn't suspect anything was wrong between Kayla and Thomas when he visited. *Well, she obviously didn't want you to know either huh*, he thought. Collins was actually glad Thomas called. Now he would have an excuse to hang around more. He needed to be close in case Gianni tried to contact her.

"Where is that snake," Collins asked aloud.

They found neither hide nor hair of him. His friends at the Bureau in Virginia told him they were forced to call off the tail on Wilson. The manpower was needed elsewhere. Collins told them he understood, and thanked them for all their help. He was truly on his own now.

"I've got find him," Collins said again.

Collins knew if Gianni ever found out he was looking for him, he would try and kill him too. Collins knew Gianni hated him. He was the one who kept pursuing him, and finally succeeded, in breaking his cartel.

"I bet he would love to put a slug or two in my head," Collins said again, taking a long drink from his beer.

The thought frightened him a little. Gianni could be a very vicious man. Collins knew he wasn't a young man anymore. *Maybe you need to give this up and live your life.* He knew he wouldn't. Collins felt too guilty still. He bowed down to pressure, and allowed his best friend to think he, and his family, were finally safe. Now, the one nemesis they both hated the most was back, and he was threatening yet again, the one thing Black held dear.

Collins was glad that Mariah and her family were gone. *At least Gianni can't bother them*, he thought, grabbing another beer from the fridge. Collins headed into the den to watch the game, and wait on Kayla to call him back. *Thomas better bring back one helluva present this time*, he chuckled, thinking of the doghouse the man put himself into. He soon drifted off to sleep.

●●●

"Shh, man be quiet," the man told his partner, peeking into the window and seeing Collins asleep in his recliner.

They were here to do a job, and he didn't want to get caught. Jail was definitely not on the agenda. Neither was getting shot. Dante warned them this guy was a federal agent.

"Hand me that wire over there," he told his accomplice.

They wired the house outside, and were now preparing to enter.

"Remember to be death quiet," he told his partner once again, as they entered the house through the garage.

Collins was snoring fitfully, and they knew they would be able to complete their task. They placed the tiny cameras and mics throughout the house. Once they were finished and outside again, they made a call. Dezi answered on the second ring.

"Check the monitors," he told him.

Dezi turned on the monitors, and the sound, finding them all in working order. He saw Collins sitting in his recliner sleeping, and chuckled.

"Everything is fine," Dezi replied. "Come get your money," he finished, as he disconnected.

They gathered their equipment and headed out, talking during their ride.

●●●

"Man what is up with this dude, and surveillance," Cedric asked K.C.

They were partners in crime, and this was one of many jobs they handled together.

"I dunno, but he gives me the impression he can be lethal, if you know what I mean," K.C. replied, and his friend concurred.

They both found Dante to be personable enough, and he definitely paid well. He just gave off that air that he was not one to be messed with, if you wanted to keep on living and breathing.

●●●

"Gentlemen!" Dante greeted them smiling, as he invited them in.

He went and retrieved their monies, and brought it to them. They both smiled, as he gave them each an envelope.

"If you need anything else, Mr. Enzo," Cedric began. "Please call us, anything at all," the meaning of the statement very evident.

Dezi thought about that for a moment, and decided it might come in handy later.

"I'll certainly keep that in mind, gentlemen," he replied making it known he understood completely.

They both smiled, and exited the home.

●●●

Dezi returned to the monitors, and watched Collins continue to snore blissfully. *You're going to soon be out of my hair,* he thought confidently, as he turned on his other monitors, finding Kayla napping herself. Dezi smiled, thinking how beautiful she looked resting on her side. *I can't wait to get you home baby,* he thought, bringing yet another smile to his face. Dezi was still wondering what she wanted to talk to him about. She was too upset after the airport to talk, and he didn't press. He picked up the phone. There was one person he could think of who would know, Dezi smiled, as he dialed Jackie's number.

Smoke & **16** Mirrors

Mariah was absolutely delighted. The Parish was extremely beautiful. She was taking in all the sights and sounds as they were driving to their home. They arrived a few moments later and she was once again incredulous at the beauty of the place. The house was stone front, with brick sides. The yard was immaculate, with beautiful green grass and colorful sweet smelling blooms.

There was a two-car garage attached to the house, and a beautiful rounded smoked glass window at the attic top. Palm trees lined the driveway, from the road to the front yard. There was a small white gazebo on one side of the yard, and a wonderful tree swing on the other.

"This is student housing," Mariah asked amazed.

The structure was absolutely marvelous. Aidan himself was in awe.

"Wow!" he said aloud, taking in the house and the view.

They were right on the ocean, and the breeze was magnificent.

"Your mother is going to absolutely flip, when she gets here," Aidan laughed, as he and Mariah were standing on their deck.

"Yes," she agreed. "I can't wait for her to see it."

Livvy was still napping. The flight was a little long, and she was off her schedule.

"Do you think Mommy will be alright," Mariah asked Aidan, looking concerned.

They talked on the flight, both relaying their concerns and fears about Kayla and Thomas's marriage.

"I think she'll be fine," Aidan replied. "I also asked Dante to keep an eye on her," he went on. "He promised he would, and I'm sure he will."

Mariah smiled.

"Yes, I'm sure he will," she said chuckling lightly.

Aidan looked at her quizzically.

"Come on, Aidan," she began. "Surely you know he's in love with Mommy," Mariah finished, still chuckling.

Aidan laughed. "Yeah, I called him on it earlier, when we went to Charlotte."

They both laughed heartily.

"Wouldn't it be nice if she came here with him," Mariah asked.

She accepted the fact that her mother and Thomas would more than likely divorce. Mariah was scared for Kayla. She witnessed Thomas's temper once at church. It was a very ugly scene, and she never let on she knew, nor had she told her mother. *Please God protect my mother,* she prayed silently. *Help her to get away from him,* she finished, as she and Aidan returned inside the house to look around some more. They were both exhausted from their trip, so they knew there would be no unpacking today.

"I want to call Mommy and Jackie," Mariah said, as she was up righting a chair to sit in.

"That's fine, but wait a couple of hours, you know the time difference," Aidan told her.

"Aidan, I cannot believe how amazing this place is," Mariah breathed, thinking of how fortunate they were again.

"It is wonderful, isn't it," Aidan replied. "We need to go out and look around tomorrow."

Dante promised to send a guide to them tomorrow, who would show them around, and help them get everything they needed. Aidan thought of what a nice man Dante turned out to be. *I sure hope we can still be close when he returns,* Aidan thought. He knew the man had no family. He found that much out, that and how much money Dante possessed. *He did mention a son, but he never told me much else,* Aidan thought again thinking there was an unspoken darkness about the man that reminded him very much of his father.

●●●

Jackie answered and Dezi greeted her.

"What's going on with you Dante," Jackie asked amiably.

"I'm fine, all is well," he chuckled lightly.

"How are you?" Dezi asked.

"I'm good," Jackie replied.

"I understand you're leaving in a couple of days," he told her.

She sighed lightly.

"Well Dante," Jackie began. "Between you and me, that's the story."

Dezi was intrigued.

"What do you mean, Jackie?" he asked. "You can trust me. I won't tell anyone. I promise."

She took a deep breath. Jackie thought Dante was good people. He never breathed a word of any of their other conversations about him and Kayla, so she figured it would be all right.

"Chris and I are divorcing," Jackie said. "He's moving to Georgia," she went on. "I'm going somewhere else."

"Why didn't you tell Kayla?"

"Because, she would never leave Thomas if I did," Jackie replied.

"I don't understand."

She chuckled lightly.

"If she knew I wasn't sure where I would be, or how stable I was going to be, she wouldn't go," Jackie went on. "Kayla is leaving, because everything and everyone she has leaned on is gone, or soon will be," she continued. "It's forcing her to finally think of, and take care of, herself."

Dezi understood. She was right. Kayla would stay simply to help Jackie, and make sure she was all right.

"Do you need money Jackie," he asked her evenly.

She sighed. "Yes,."

"Not a problem," Dezi replied.

He thought for a moment, and decided Jackie and Big D might just hit it off. He was once in love with her sister, and they were sort of alike.

"What are you talking about, Dante," Jackie replied, shaking him out of his thoughts.

"I will give you some money," Dezi replied. "I have plenty of it, and you've been nothing but helpful to me since I've been here."

Dezi heard Jackie sniffle, and knew she was crying.

"Why don't you go to Virginia?"

"I actually thought about it," Jackie told him. "My sister had a friend there I might look up," she added softly.

Dezi knew she was talking about Big D.

"Well, I'm sure they would be glad to see you, and help you get settled." Dezi told her.

"So, do you think two hundred fifty thousand will do you for a while?"

Dezi heard Jackie gasp, and caught himself before he could chuckle.

"Uh, yes Dante," she replied, laughing lightly. "It will probably last me the rest of my life."

"Good, set up and account that you can either transfer or in Virginia and I'll put the money in tomorrow," Dezi told Jackie.

"Thank you so much, Dante," she told him, genuinely moved.

"You're more than welcome," he replied genially.

"What did you call me for, originally," Jackie laughed, thinking how they moved completely off track.

Dezi laughed himself, and told her.

"Well, I won't tell you, because Kayla needs to do that herself," Jackie replied. "But, believe me when I tell you, it will be very pleasing to you," she finished, chuckling.

Dezi was definitely curious, but he decided not to push.

"All right, Jackie," he replied. "I'm going to hold you to it," he finished, laughing lightly himself.

"Don't forget to call me with the account information," Dezi reminded Jackie, as he let her go. *What in the world are you up to baby*, he thought, heading to the bar to make himself a drink.

●●●

Kayla woke with a start. She was having a nightmare. She dreamed Thomas was strangling her, trying to kill her. She was breathing hard, and needed to collect herself. The phone rang, and she jumped. Kayla slowed her breathing, and answered.

"Hello?"

"Hi Mommy!" Mariah said happily.

Kayla smiled brightly, hearing her daughter's voice.

"Hi, baby!" she returned, genuinely happy to hear from her. "How is everything?"

Mariah told her excitedly, how wonderful everything was, and how much they loved the house and the Parrish itself.

"Mommy, you are going to absolutely love the view we have!"

"I can't wait to see it," Kayla laughed.

"Are you alright," Mariah asked, becoming serious.

"I'm fine, Mariah," Kayla assured her daughter.

"I'm scared for you," Mariah said quietly.

Kayla sighed again.

"I'll be just fine, I promise."

"OK Mommy," Mariah told Kayla. "I'll call you again tomorrow and check on you."

"That will be fine honey, give Livvy a big kiss for me," Kayla told Mariah, as they said goodbye.

●●●

You've got to talk to Dante soon, she thought, as she rose from the bed. Kayla saw the machine blinking, and checked the message.

"How nice," she said aloud, after hearing the message from Maurice.

Dezi also heard the message.

"This fucker is becoming a real nuisance," Dezi said simply, breathing deeply.

He watched Kayla call him back, and monitored the conversation.

"Hi, Maurice," Kayla greeted Collins warmly.

He returned her greeting.

"Can we get together for lunch, tomorrow?"

She thought that was a great idea.

"Oh, yes of course!" Kayla returned, and they made plans.

Dezi made note of the time and place. He thought he might want to crash.

"Thomas is worried about you, Kayla," Collins told her.

She sighed.

"He's just worried about you being alone," Collins told her.

Kayla sighed heavily.

"I really don't want to talk about it anymore," she went on. "Tell me about you, and what's going on with you," Kayla finished. "Are you dating yet?"

"No, and would you please stop trying to set me up," Collins told her exasperated.

Kayla laughed.

"I would never do that," she assured Maurice.

He scoffed, and they both burst into laughter.

"I'll see you tomorrow, Maurice," she told him.

●●●

"I'm going to kill him by the weekend," Dezi said flatly.

So, Thomas is calling in reinforcements, is he, he thought. *Maybe it's time I dealt with that fucker too,* Dezi continued thinking, as he sipped his drink and watched Kayla shower.

"When are you going to call me," he said aloud, as he watched her dry off.

Kayla dressed for bed, and headed downstairs.

●●●

"I need to call Jackie," Kayla said aloud, as she cut her sandwich.

She picked up the phone, and dialed. Dezi was still watching and listening.

"Hey girl," Jackie greeted her.

Kayla returned her greeting.

"You got everything ready for your trip?"

"Yes, I do actually," Jackie told her.

"Do you need me to help you with anything?"

"Nope, I'm done, just chilling and relaxing until I leave," Jackie informed.

"Are we getting together tomorrow night?" Jackie asked.

"Yes," Kayla laughed.

"So have you talked to Dante yet?"

"I'm scared to," Kayla told her. "What if he says no?"

Jackie sighed, "Yeah right! He is going to be absolutely thrilled!"

"It's a lot to ask though," Kayla said again.

Dezi was definitely intrigued. *What could she possibly want from me?*

"Girl, do I need to come over and kick your ass myself," Jackie asked, laughing.

Kayla laughed. "No, that won't be necessary."

"OK, I'll talk to him," she replied.

"When," Jackie threw back.

"This weekend," Kayla replied, still chuckling.

"OK," Jackie told her. "Don't make me come back to Chapel Hill, and beat you down girl, you hear?"

"I'm going to, I promise," Kayla laughed heartily.

"So, is Chris ready for you to be there yet?"

"Yes girl, more than ready," Jackie replied smoothly.

Dezi smiled at her deception. He knew Jackie would tell Kayla the truth later. *Of course, that will be after she tells Jackie she's with me*, he chuckled at the thought. They said their goodbyes, and Kayla headed into the den. Dezi had some business to attend to himself. He finished his drink, and turned off the monitors.

Smoke & 17 Mirrors

Jackie awoke with an agenda. She called the number she kept for Big D. She got it from Aidan, who asked her to check on him from time to time. She heard him pick up after the third ring.

"Hello," Big D said, recognizing the number but knowing Aidan was gone.

"Hi D," she replied. "This is Jackie. Aidan's aunt."

"Yes, I remember you Jackie," he said. "How's it going?"

She laughed lightly. "It's going."

Big D chuckled himself.

"Listen D," she began. "I'm thinking of moving there, and wondered if maybe you could help me get settled."

Jackie wasn't sure if he would. They hadn't spoken really since Liv died, almost three years ago.

Big D already knew Jackie would call. Dezi clued him in last night. He always thought she was good people. He liked her immediately when he met her. Dezi also told Big D about her and the husband divorcing. Jackie was a good-looking woman. *Maybe we could hit it off,* he thought plotting.

"Sure Jackie," Big D replied amiably. "That wouldn't be a problem at all," he went on. "Do you have somewhere to stay yet," he asked, knowing she didn't.

"I haven't really gotten that far yet," Jackie told him honestly.

"Well, that's cool," Big D began again. "I have a spare room, and you're more than welcome."

"Wow, thanks D," Jackie said gratefully.

She already opened her account this morning with a bank that kept branches there. She called Dezi earlier, and gave him the info.

"You flying or driving," Big D asked, bringing Jackie back to now.

"Oh, I'm driving," she told him.

"Cool. When should I expect you?"

Big D wanted to get the house straightened up, and buy a few groceries.

"Would tomorrow be okay," Jackie asked.

"Sure, it would be perfect," Big D laughed.

He gave Jackie exact directions, and told her to call him if she got lost.

"I will, and thank you again D for being so helpful," she responded as they disconnected.

He figured he would take his time showing her around and helping her find a place. *Maybe she won't move at all,* Big D thought hopefully. He always had his girls to keep him sexed, but he wanted a woman to keep him loved. Maybe he was getting a second chance with Jackie. Big D smiled and began whistling as he walked out the door headed for the store.

●●●

Jackie was thinking about D. *I wonder what his real name is, for goodness sake,* she thought, chuckling aloud. He was a nice guy from what she observed. *Not bad looking either,* she thought wickedly. It was a while for her. Jackie and Chris were sexless together for the last six months. She found out about his past, and about him and Kayla. She would never tell Kayla, of course.

Jackie didn't harbor any ill will toward her friend. What Chris did to Kayla wasn't her fault. Jackie wasn't even as upset with Chris about that as she was that he hid it from her. Of course there was also his infidelity. He slept with at least two women she knew of, during his visits to Georgia. *Good damn riddance,* Jackie thought, concerning Chris.

She hoped that Kayla kept her word, and talked to Dante. Jackie knew the man was totally in love with Kayla, and he would definitely help her pack to go to his house. She laughed aloud from her musing. Jackie needed to attend to a few more errands. She gathered her purse, but stopped to call Kayla.

"Hey girl," she greeted her.

Kayla laughed, and returned her greeting.

"You're up and out early," she told Jackie.

"Couple of loose ends before I leave tomorrow."

"Oh, OK girl. What's up," Kayla asked.

"Nothing, I just wanted to tell you not to wait until the weekend to talk to Dante. Talk to him today, or tomorrow, okay?"

Kayla wondered what the urgency was.

"Why?"

"I just feel it in my gut," Jackie sighed. "You need to be gone by the weekend, Kayla."

She couldn't explain it any better. She just felt it.

Kayla was slightly alarmed. Jackie was a very levelheaded woman, but she could tell her friend was really concerned.

"Alright, I'll talk to him tomorrow. Right after I say goodbye to you. Is that OK?"

"Yes," Jackie exhaled. "Now I won't be out of my mind with worry about you," she replied.

They chatted a little while longer, and hung up.

●●●

Dezi turned on the monitor, just as Kayla placed the phone back in the cradle.

"I wonder who she's talking to this early," he remarked.

Dezi turned his attention to the monitors in Collins house, finding him also on the phone.

"Yeah, Thomas," Collins was saying. "We're having lunch today."

"Please try and find out where her mind is for me," Thomas asked him.

It's on getting the fuck away from you, dickhead, Dezi thought frostily. These two were beginning to really piss him off.

Dezi already set up his plans for Collins. He wouldn't be a problem anymore in a couple of days. *Now, I just need to decide what I'm going to do for good old preacher man,* he thought again, his blood boiling.

"Tell you what," Collins began again. "Call me, and let me know if you can get back. If you can good, I'll make sure Kayla's home," he went on. "If not, then I'll get her to hang out with me again. At least you'll know where she is."

"Sounds like a great idea, Maurice," Thomas told Collins.

"Ok, then I'll expect to hear from you tomorrow," Collins finished.

"Yes, definitely," Thomas replied, and they ended their call.

Dezi was staring at the monitor coldly.

"We shall see about that, Mr. FBI agent," he said flatly, picking up the phone.

"Hi there," Dezi greeted her, as she answered the phone.

Kayla smiled, and returned his greeting.

"Hi, Dante," she said pleasantly.

He was still watching her on the monitor.

"Do you have any plans for tomorrow?"

She chuckled lightly.

"Actually," she began, and Dezi steeled himself for her answer. "I was going to call you, and ask if we could have our talk."

He smiled at himself, thinking how silly he just was.

"Yes, of course," Dezi replied smoothly.

"I'm going to see Jackie first, tell her goodbye," Kayla told him. "I can come by later, say around eight?"

"That would be perfect," Dezi told her giving Kayla directions to his house again.

"Good, I'll see you tomorrow," she told her cheerily.

"Have a wonderful day Kayla," Dezi admonished.

"Thanks Dante, same to you," Kayla smiled.

Dezi watched her thinking, as she placed the phone back into the cradle. She went upstairs to the attic. He watched her pull out a trunk. Kayla opened it, and began searching for something. Her back was to Dezi, blocking his view of the trunk. Whatever Kayla was looking for, she obviously found. Evidently satisfied, she returned the other items to the trunk. The one she kept, she placed close to her body. When Kayla stood to return downstairs, Dezi still couldn't see what she took out. *What that was all about,* he wondered. Dezi decided that he needed to finally end this charade. *It's time for her to go,* he thought. Jackie would be gone. Mariah and Aidan were already in place. There was no real need for Kayla to still be here. Dezi picked up his cell, he needed to check on the kids in the Parish, and make sure all was well.

●●●

"Hello, Mr. Enzo" Miguel greeted him, when he called.

Dezi returned the man's greeting, and asked how everything was going.

"Well, there has been a bit of trouble, but it's handled now," he replied.

"Tell me," Dezi asked Miguel to elaborate.

"Mr. Aidan and his wife were out at the market, when a man approached her," Miguel began.

Dezi already had a pretty good idea of where this was going, but he prompted the man to continue.

"Mrs. Aidan, she tells the man she is married, but he continues to accost her," he took a breath before continuing. "Mr. Aidan, confronts the man, and asks him to leave. The man swears at him, and challenges him to a fight. Mrs. Aidan, tells her husband to please go, so they can take the baby home," Miguel paused briefly, and then continued. "He left with the wife, but I see the look in his eye, that he will find the man later, and finish what was started."

Dezi smiled into the receiver. Seemed his son was definitely beginning to come into his own.

"Then what happened," Dezi inquired further.

Miguel took another deep breath and began anew.

"Mr. Aidan left the house later that night and I followed him. He found the house of the man who insulted him and his wife. He entered the house through the window. Again, I follow, quietly and invisibly. He found the man sitting in his kitchen, drinking. Mr. Aidan attacks him and beats him viciously. The man is unconscious. I hear the sounds of someone coming and see that Mr. Aidan hears it too." Miguel took a breath and continued.

"He left the man and went back out of the window. I remain and watch as the man's brother comes in and finds him. He takes him to the hospital, but it's too late. He is dead." Miguel finished, allowing Dezi to question him further.

"So who else, besides you, knows Aidan killed the man," he asked contentedly at the end of Miguel's story.

Dezi was proud of his son. He was feeling better and better about Aidan taking over the legacy he built.

"Who was the man anyway," Dezi queried further.

"The man was brother of one of the local businessmen. Highly respected, but known for his flirtatious ways. The brother, unfortunately saw Mr. Aidan leave, and gave a description to the police," Miguel told Dezi, who sighed lightly.

He knew there would be no repercussions; Dezi basically owned the police force there.

"So what happened next," he asked, wanting Miguel to get to the end of his story.

"The police chief came to see Mr. Aidan, but I intercepted him and explain to him who Mr. Aidan is," he said calmly.

Dezi chuckled. He knew that effectively ended any formal inquisition that would have come about. Dezi was pleased. *I knew his blood would finally come full circle*, he thought of the young man's actions.

"Thank you for handling things Miguel, and keeping them under control," Dezi spoke. "I should be returning relatively soon," he told Miguel, before the two ended their conversation.

●●●

Rachelle was finally able to return to work. *He was crazy!* Rachelle thought internally. Thanking God constantly for letting her find out before she managed to get pregnant from him.

"Why are all the good looking ones psycho," she mumbled aloud.

Rachelle didn't forget about her run in with Thomas either. He totally flipped on her. Granted she tricked him into the kiss, but he reacted crazily. *I always knew there was something dangerous smoldering down inside him.* Rachelle thought as she opened the letter. She didn't notice until after she opened it that it was marked personal. It was from Florida.

Well it's opened now, she thought as she took the letter out. It was from the state probation department. *What the hell?* Rachelle wondered as she began to read it. The letter was informing Thomas that his probation period was now ended with the state of Florida. She continued reading and saw that he served time and was on probation for assault with a deadly weapon. *This sure as hell wasn't on his resume!* Rachelle thought completely shaken.

Rachelle hoped Kayla never did anything to make that monster come out. She thought Thomas capable of seriously violent behavior and now she held proof to back it up.

Rachelle carefully put the letter back into the envelope and slipped it into her purse. *I may need this later,* she thought, making a mental note. She was getting ready to walk out of her office when the phone rang.

"Good morning, Pastor Bradford's office," Rachelle answered politely.

Thomas greeted her and her blood ran cold.

"Oh, good morning Pastor," she replied.

"Can you give me an update on what's going on at the church this week," he questioned.

"Everything is fine and running smoothly. No worries," Rachelle told him.

"That's good Rachelle," Thomas told her pleasantly. "Is everything alright with you," he asked. "Doris tells me you were sick a few days."

Doris was Rachelle's replacement when she was out or on vacation.

"Just a bug, I'm feeling fine now," she told Thomas.

"That's good," he replied. "Well I'll check in with you again later in the week."

"Have a good day Rachelle," Thomas told her as he hung up.

She stared at the phone for a few moments after he hung up. For the first time in her years as church secretary, Rachelle started thinking about a new job. She also thought about Dante again. She missed him. *Surely he's not still mad is he,* she thought longingly. *He was probably hurt because he thought I was different,* she told herself. Rachelle sighed softly and picked up the phone.

•••

Dezi looked at the display. "Is this bitch crazy?"

I might still need her though, he thought. *She may actually be useful at a pivotal point.*

"Hello?"

Rachelle let out the breath she'd been holding.

"Hi Dante," she said quietly.

Dezi decided to feign indifference.

"What do you want Rachelle," he asked matter-of-fact.

She was a little hurt that Dante was being short, but he didn't sound angry at least.

"I wanted to apologize for the last time we were together," Rachelle started. "I also wanted to ask you to please give me another chance to be your friend," she continued. "We could start all over."

Dezi supposed he could suffer her company but he needed to make one thing clear first.

"No sex Rachelle," he said plainly.

Rachelle understood. She expected as much. She would need to work at rebuilding his trust, but at least he agreed to see her again.

"All right Dante," she replied. "We'll take it one step at time, OK?"

"That's fine, I suppose," Dezi told her.

"When can I see you?" Rachelle asked.

Dezi had plans tomorrow night, so he decided lunch would be all right.

"Lunch tomorrow?"

"That will be good," Rachelle answered.

They set the time and place.

"Do you forgive me Dante," Rachelle asked softly.

"Yes," Dezi sighed lightly.

"Thank you," Rachelle replied and told him she would see him tomorrow.

They disconnected as Dezi headed to his car.

Smoke & 18 Mirrors

Thomas we know this process has been strenuous," Bishop Montford told him, "But we're pleased to see that you endured, and even more pleased to tell you, you've been selected to head the Eastern Division for the entire Church For Christ Body."

Thomas was elated. This was what he spent almost a full year working on. He was established now and he could finally turn his attention to his marriage.

"We'll make the official announcement tonight and do the installation next Sunday at the convocation," Bishop Montford was saying. "Why don't you bring your lovely wife out to be with you and spend the week with us before the installation?"

"Yes, I will definitely do that," Thomas told them. "Thank you so much gentlemen for having faith in me," he added.

They all embraced him and talked for a few more hours. He was still smiling when he arrived at his hotel, calling Kayla immediately.

●●●

"Hi baby," he said gently once she answered.

"Hi Thomas," Kayla replied pleasantly enough.

"I have some wonderful news for you honey," he went on.

"Oh? What is it?"

Thomas told Kayla about his appointment and what it meant to their future. He told her about the convocation and the installation next Sunday.

"I've booked your flight baby," Thomas continued telling her.

What?! Kayla thought, panicking. What was she going to do now? She had to go. She hadn't talked to Dante yet so she couldn't leave. Kayla sighed lightly and tried to sound happy.

"That's wonderful honey," she replied. "When am I leaving?"

"In the morning," Thomas told her.

"OK, I need to let my clients know I'll be out of town for a few days," Kayla replied.

"Baby, I promise to show you the time of your life this week," Thomas told her.

"I'm sure you will," Kayla responded.

"It's not too late for us Kayla," he told her softly.

Kayla didn't share that feeling, but she didn't enlighten him either.

"I'll see you in the morning Thomas," she replied instead.

"OK baby, get a good night's sleep," he told her. "I love you Kayla," Thomas declared before he hung up.

Thomas knew there was a lot of work to do still. He shook the thought and called Elise. He needed to see her one last time. He wanted to tell her in person he couldn't see her anymore, Thomas felt he owed her that much.

"Hi," he greeted her.

Elise smiled. She loved hearing from Thomas.

"Are you busy?"

Elise chuckled.

"Never too busy for you."

"Good, can you come over and see me," Thomas asked.

"I'll be there in forty-five minutes," Elise replied as they disconnected.

Thomas headed for the shower readying himself for her visit..

●●●

Elise was still thinking about him. *I've got to tell Thomas how I feel,* Elise thought as she dressed. She needed to stop and get them some wine. Thomas liked to have at least a glass or two while they spent time. Elise sighed gently. *This isn't supposed to happen,* she thought again knowing it was already too late.

She was in love with Thomas Bradford and she wanted him all for herself. Elise arrived a few minutes later and Thomas invited her in. They talked for a moment then began kissing passionately. She was lying in his arms now content and satisfied from their lovemaking.

"Elise I need to tell you something," Thomas began softly.

She turned to look at him as he spoke.

"I can't see you anymore," he told her gently. "My business is concluded and my wife is joining me tomorrow."

Elise didn't want to hear this. She knew Thomas was married. She knew that someday he would say the words he just said, but she still wasn't ready. Her eyes immediately filled.

"Please don't cry Elise," he told her. "I never meant to hurt you," he went on. "I've always been honest with you haven't I?"

Elise smiled weakly.

"I know Thomas," she began. "But that doesn't make it hurt any less," she continued. "Surely you know I've fallen in love with you don't you," she went on. "I would give anything to be in your wife's place right now," she finished softly and turned away letting the tears fall.

Thomas felt terrible. He never intended to hurt Elise and she was a very sweet young woman. He continued to hold her saying nothing else. There were no words that could bring any reasonable comfort to either of them right now. Elise left about an hour later. They said goodbye and kissed each other passionately for the last time.

"Thomas," she said walking out. "If you ever need me, please pick up the phone okay," she finished and left, not waiting for his reply.

Thomas showered and went to bed. He wanted to be refreshed and ready when Kayla arrived in the morning.

●●●

"This is a lot harder than I thought it would be," Kayla told Jackie trying to hold back tears.

She was saying goodbye. Jackie had everything packed into the car and they were embracing for the last time.

"Take care of yourself Kayla," Jackie told her. "I mean it!"

Kayla assured her she would.

"I'm heading out myself," she told Jackie. "I'm flying to meet Thomas and be with him for the week."

Jackie was livid.

"Why the hell would you do that?"

Kayla explained his call last night and his appointment and installation, adding that she didn't really have a choice because she hadn't talked to Dante yet. Jackie didn't like it. She wanted Kayla to get away from that man as quickly as possible. Jackie knew Kayla was right though. She had to continue playing the good wife role. It was vital to her safety.

"OK," Jackie said reluctantly. "But you talk to Dante as soon as you get back. Do you hear me," she admonished Kayla.

"Trust me, I will," Kayla promised.

"Call and leave me a message when you get there, okay," Kayla told Jackie.

"I will," Jackie told Kayla.

She hated lying to Kayla. She would tell her truth after she knew Kayla talked to Dante. Jackie got in and started the car. They gave each other another quick hug and Jackie headed out to the interstate.

●●●

Kayla waved until she was out of sight, then returned to her own car and headed to the airport. She called Dante from her cell. Kayla got his machine so she left him a message explaining her trip and telling him she would call him when she returned. She arrived at the airport went through check in and boarded her flight. Kayla thought about Thomas all the way there. She didn't want to do this anymore. She wanted a divorce. They were so far apart. She was happy about his appointment, knowing it was something Thomas really wanted. Kayla just didn't think their marriage could be mended. She really resented how he neglected and abandoned her all these months. Then there was him hitting her and threatening her.

Kayla was afraid of Thomas now. She knew he would want sex too and she absolutely abhorred the idea of him touching her. Kayla thought about Dante. *There's something not quite right there too*, she thought. He reminded her so much of Dezi. It scared her. It also forced her to remember, which wasn't so bad. Dezi wasn't always been scary to her. It was only after she learned his other activities in full that she began to fear him. *But he never hurt you Kayla or threatened you*, she thought to herself again.

Kayla sighed gently as the plane landed and captain came on the loudspeaker. She shook herself and got off the plane. Kayla made her way through the terminal. Thomas was waiting for her. He smiled and waved when he saw her. Kayla forced herself to smile back after spotting Thomas.

"Hi baby!" he cried excitedly hugging and kissing her.

Kayla greeted him and hugged him back. *Get it together girl*, she told herself. *You've got an entire week with this man.*

"You hungry," Thomas asked still smiling and holding her hand.

"Yes."

"Good. We'll go have breakfast," he told her. "I'm so happy you're here baby," Thomas told her looking into her eyes.

Kayla smiled again.

"I'm glad to see you too Thomas," she replied simply.

Thomas saw the pain in her eyes. He saw the sadness too. He already knew he had a lot of work to do, so he wasn't deterred by her attitude. *I'm going to make you fall in love with me all over again baby*, he thought as he opened the door for Kayla to get into the car. They went to a small café he found during his stay. The food was absolutely wonderful and it was warm and cozy inside with all the people conversing and smiling. There were children giggling as their parents tried to coerce them into eating their food. Kayla smiled as she watched them, thinking of Livvy.

"I'm proud of you Thomas," she told him as they ate their breakfast.

Thomas smiled warmly. That meant a lot to him coming from her.

"You know baby," he began. "You can travel with me more now."

Kayla was careful not to show her true reaction. She held no intentions of going anywhere with him.

"Well that's certainly a welcome change," she replied turning her attention back to the wonderful vegetable omelet she ordered.

Thomas smiled again glad that Kayla was at least trying. They finished their breakfast and headed back to the hotel. He took her up to his room. He asked the maid to clean it while he was out. He was with Elise last night and he wanted it fresh and clean when Kayla arrived.

●●●

She loved the room. It was beautiful with the antique chairs and the oversized desk. The view was magnificent. You could see the entire downtown skyline from it.

"This is really nice," Kayla remarked as she watched the people walking from buildings and stores and shops that were below.

Thomas hugged Kayla again and kissed her. He held her after the kiss and stroked her hair. He kissed her again passionately and began to undress her.

"No," Kayla said pushing him away.

Thomas was hurt.

"Baby I know I've neglected you," he began, trying to touch her again. "I'm sorry for that. It's over now and we never have to be apart again."

Kayla was looking at him hard. Thomas could tell she was angry, but he also saw something else in her eyes.

"What are you thinking,' he asked a slight edge to his voice.

Kayla knew she couldn't tell Thomas she was going to leave. He would definitely hurt her.

"Nothing," she replied looking away.

"You're lying," he said plainly. "Listen to me Kayla," he began trying to reason with her. "I understand your anger. I understand it completely, but baby I'm not letting you go," he went on. "I've already told you that, so please stop thinking it. There will be no divorce," he finished and pulled Kayla to him.

He began kissing her again.

"Thomas please, stop it!" Kayla said pulling away from him.

Thomas was getting angry. She was trying to leave him and now she didn't want him to touch her. He was going to have to restore order to this situation and do it quickly. Thomas grabbed Kayla and threw her onto the bed. He straddled her and held her arms above her head as he talked to her.

"Listen to me!" Thomas said angrily through clenched teeth. "You are not leaving me! You are not divorcing me and you as sure as hell are not denying me sex!" he finished as he roughly undressed her.

Kayla was terrified. She didn't resist as Thomas took off her panties. He pushed her legs apart and entered her. He was hurting her.

Kayla wanted to cry but she didn't. Thomas began to thrust into Kayla as he spoke in her ear.

"I love you, why can't you understand that," he said still thrusting into her. "I don't know what you're thinking and I don't care," he told her as he continued his assault. "But I'm the only man who will ever be inside you so you may as well get used to it and enjoy it," Thomas finished, thrusting into Kayla even harder.

She did cry this time as he continued to punish her. Thomas finally came and collapsed on top of her. He got up, kissing Kayla as he did.

He looked her in the eye and spoke again.

"Do we understand each other," he asked evenly.

Kayla was too scared to talk. She simply shook her head that she did.

"Good," he said softly.

Kayla stood in the shower and tried to wash the hurt away. *How am I going to get away from him,* she thought. Kayla finally gathered herself and got dressed.

"You look beautiful baby," Thomas told Kayla as he hugged her. "I'm sorry it had to be that way honey, but you left me no choice," he said softly in her ear as he caressed her.

"I love you," Thomas spoke as he kissed Kayla softly.

They headed out the door to the meeting with the council.

Smoke & **19** Mirrors

Dezi was irritated. He missed seeing Kayla this morning. He went out to handle business that should have taken and hour but ended up taking most of the morning. He turned on the monitors and saw the house was empty. He flipped them off and headed upstairs. He was having lunch with Rachelle. Not that Dezi wanted to spend any time with her; he simply needed information and a favor from her. It was tonight that Dezi was most looking forward too. *I'll finally find out what she wants from me*, he thought and chuckled.

Jackie left him a message telling him she would be at D's and gave him the number. Dezi laughed again thinking how sweetly he set them up. Dezi needed to check on Collins when he went back downstairs. Thomas was supposed to call Collins and let him know his plans. Dezi was very much interested in those himself. *He better not mess up our meeting tonight*, Dezi thought to himself as he headed back downstairs.

He flipped on the monitors just as Collins was answering the phone.

●●●

"Hello?" Collins spoke into the receiver.

"Hey Maurice!" Thomas replied.

Collins laughed and told Thomas it was good to hear from him again.

"So, were you able to get back?"

Thomas laughed.

"No, but that's okay. Kayla is here with me." he said.

"How did you manage to pull that off," Collins laughed.

"My business was finally concluded, so I sent for her," Thomas explained. "She arrived this morning."

Dezi was livid. *Kayla didn't even tell me*, he fumed then checked his cell again. She left him a message. *A fucking week and a half?!* Dezi thought furious all over again. *What if she decides to give her marriage another try?* The thought hurt Dezi admitted. He loved Kayla and he thought she was falling in love with him. He knew she loved Thomas and they were married almost two years.

Would she really throw that away to be with me, Dezi wondered internally turning his attention back to their conversation.

"Great!!" Collins told him "I know Kayla was happy to see you."

Thomas laughed and said she was.

"We're getting ready to have lunch," he told him, "We worked up quite an appetite if you catch my drift," he finished laughing.

Collins joined him. Dezi loaded the other .10mm he bought. *So Kayla's still sleeping with him*, he thought then chastised himself. *Of course she is. What choice does she really have right now?*

"Well I'm glad you two are working things out," Collins told Thomas.

"Thanks Maurice," Thomas told Collins.

Dezi was ready to kill them both.

●●●

Kayla was trying to act normal. She managed to make it through the meetings and now they were sitting in the restaurant. Thomas was crazy. If she ever doubted it before she didn't now.

"Baby what are you having," Thomas asked looking at her.

He was acting as if everything was fine and nothing happened earlier.

"A salad will be fine," Kayla replied quietly.

She wasn't hungry.

"You need more than that," Thomas told her. "I'll order for you."

Kayla simply nodded. *OK Kayla, think,* she told herself. *You can pull this off. You can't act any other way than loving to him. You've got to get through this alive.*

"Honey," Thomas was calling her again.

Kayla was so deep in thought she didn't hear him.

"Yes?"

"Do you need a drink refill?"

She shook her head no and the server left.

"Why are you so distracted," Thomas asked looking at her closely.

Why do you think, Kayla wanted to say but didn't.

"I'm sorry," was all she could manage.

Thomas sighed deeply. "Listen, I know what happened earlier was intense."

That's a freaking understatement, Kayla thought.

"Baby, you weren't being rational and I had to make you realize that," he told her.

Kayla was looking at Thomas and wondering who he was. This was not the loving, kind, man she fell in love with. This man was crazy and she carried no doubt in her mind he would kill her.

"Are you going to do that to me again Thomas," Kayla asked quietly.

Thomas stopped drinking his tea. He knew what she was talking about. He looked at Kayla for a moment before he answered.

"Only if you force me too," Thomas replied darkly.

Kayla swallowed hard and tried to keep the tears from coming. She would have to force herself to give in. She didn't want Thomas to hurt her again like today.

"I won't," Kayla said softly and he smiled.

"That's my baby," Thomas told her gently.

Their orders arrived and they began to eat. He ordered her salad with chicken instead of plain.

"Don't pick it either," Thomas told Kayla laughing.

She smiled weakly and began to eat the salad.

●●●

Dezi and Rachelle walked into Champions Green together. She was impressed that he wanted to bring her here. *This is definitely top of the line*, she thought as the hostess led them to their seats. Dezi was still thinking about Kayla and her being gone. He was scared. What if Thomas talked her into staying with him? He couldn't bear the thought of leaving without her again. *She loves me. She has too!* Dezi thought trying to reassure himself. He thought of the times they were together. *I should have made love to her then*, he chastised again.

"Hellooo?" Rachelle was saying trying to get his attention.

Dezi felt himself become annoyed and took a deep breath. He was here with her after all. They ordered and began to chat.

"Does the church have a projection screen," he asked Rachelle.

She thought it was a very odd question, but told him yes.

"I went to a movie at a church once," Dezi told Rachelle explaining why he asked about the screen.

Of course Dezi possessed a movie of his own he was planning to show. He caught himself before he began laughing. Dezi told her about his new broker.

"Oh that's Kayla. Pastor's wife," Rachelle told him.

"Yes, I found that out when I met here," he smiled.

"Do you know if Pastor Bradford is violent," Dezi asked after they were eating for a while.

Rachelle stopped eating and looked at him.

"Why? Did Kayla say something?"

"No, it's just a feeling I get," Dezi replied.

"It's funny you should say that," Rachelle replied.

He looked at her quizzically. She reached into her purse and showed Dante the letter. Dezi read it and looked at her.

"I bet your church didn't know this when they hired him did they?"

"Of course not," Rachelle told him.

"I sure hope he hasn't done anything to Kayla. She acted sort of afraid the last time I spoke with her," Rachelle said.

"Well she's gone out of town with him for a few days. So I guess everything is alright with them," Dezi told her.

"It's about time I would say," Rachelle replied. "He's always leaving her alone. He's lucky she hasn't found someone else."

She has. I just have to get her away from him before he hurts her, Dezi thought. They finished their lunch and rose to leave.

"Thank you so much for lunch Dante," Rachelle told him as he walked her to her car. "And thank you for forgiving me and giving me another chance."

Dezi smiled. "You're welcome Rochelle."

•••

His cell rang as he started his car. It was the business he was handling.

"Everything is set," Cedric told him.

Dezi smiled.

"That's good," he replied. "I want it done tomorrow understand?"

"No problem," Cedric replied again.

"Call me," Dezi told him as they disconnected.

So this fucker thinks he's going to make her stay with him does he, he thought recalling what Rachelle showed him.

"Not gonna happen," Dezi said aloud coldly.

His cell rang again. It was Jackie.

"Hi there," He greeted her.

She returned the greeting.

"Did Kayla mange to reach you?"

She wasn't sure if Kayla would be able to follow through and Jackie still had that bad feeling.

"Yes, and I'm not happy about her being with him," Dezi told her.

"Neither am I," Jackie said plainly.

"What if they work it out and she wants to stay with him?"

"That can't happen Dante," Jackie said flatly.

"I don't know what I can do about it if she truly wants to be with him," Dezi replied fishing.

Jackie sighed.

"Look I wanted Kayla to tell you this, but her life is at stake and I can't let Thomas hurt her," she replied. "Kayla wants to leave Thomas. She wanted to ask you if she could stay at your house in Bermuda until you came back. That would give her enough time to figure out what she wanted to do."

Dezi smiled.

"Of course she can," Dezi said simply. "Kayla doesn't have to leave until she's ready to go."

Jackie smiled. She knew as much.

"Then we've got to find a way to get Kayla out of that house and away from him," Jackie said.

"Thomas is going to watch Kayla like a hawk," she told Dante. "I told you he's very possessive and jealous," she continued. "I just hope he hasn't hurt her already."

Dezi hoped so too for Thomas's sake.

"I'll try and reach her later today," he told Jackie.

"Me too," she said. "I'm sure Kayla has her cell, but Thomas may be right there when I call," Jackie finished sighing lightly.

They both knew this was going to be hard.

"Jackie, I'm going to find a way to get her out of that house," Dezi said plainly.

There was something in Dante's tone that frightened Jackie, but she knew he would keep his word and get Kayla out.

"Thank you Dante," she told him.

They talked a little while longer and Jackie told him she was getting settled and everything was good with her and D.

"He's a really nice guy." She told him.

"Good, I'm glad everything is working out," Dezi smiled.

"I'll call you tomorrow," Jackie told him.

Jackie was worried about Kayla and she wouldn't rest until she knew Kayla was safe.

"That's fine," Dezi told Jackie and they hung up.

Dezi headed back to the house. He needed to think.

•••

Thomas was sitting in his meeting his mind wandering. Kayla went back to the hotel. He thought back to earlier. *I know she's scared right now. But she'll see that I really do love her,* he rationalized. Thomas couldn't let her leave him. He loved her. Kayla was all he ever wanted. He knew he neglected her, but he was trying to secure their future. Now with that taken care of, he would be the best husband he could possibly be. *She's got to stop thinking crazy thoughts though,* Thomas thought to himself about Kayla wanting to leave. He didn't mean to hurt her this morning. He only wanted to make love to her. *She promised not to make you do that again*, Thomas reminded himself. He smiled slightly. Maybe Kayla was slowly forgiving him. He certainly hoped so.

•••

Elise saw the woman walk in. She received a general description from Thomas as they talked one evening. This was his wife. She didn't move immediately as to not call unwanted attention to herself. She was actually a very beautiful woman Elise grudgingly admitted. *I'm still better for him and younger too,* she boasted inwardly. Now that Elise held an idea of what she was up against, she would pull out all the stops to take Thomas from her.

•••

Thomas was exhausted. He headed back to the hotel. Kayla heard him come into the room. She continued to lay still with her eyes closed. *Please let him think I'm asleep,* she prayed silently. Thomas slid in beside Kayla and pulled her close. He inhaled her scent deeply. *I can never let you go,* Thomas thought as he began to stroke her hair. Kayla didn't stir. He rolled her onto her back and began kissing her. Kayla wanted to cry but she promised she would do what he wanted. She kissed him back. Thomas was pleased and smiled at her.

"I love you baby," he told her.

Kayla smiled in response. Thomas felt his heart lifting. He began to arouse her and she seemingly responded. He licked Kayla gently all over and told her he was sorry for hurting her this morning. She stroked his face softly. Thomas kissed her again and pulled Kayla on top of him. She did what Thomas wanted and he soon spent himself. Kayla bent and kissed him softly on the lips as she climbed off him. She headed to the bathroom as Thomas closed his eyes and drifted off.

Smoke & **20** Mirrors

Dezi woke refreshed and in a wonderful mood. He thought about the task he planned for today and smiled.

"It's going to be a good Thursday," he said cheerfully as he headed to the shower.

Dezi thought about Kayla as he showered. He wondered how she was. He wanted to talk to her but she turned her cell off and he was scared to leave a message for fear Thomas may get it. Dezi sighed deeply.

"Well today is the beginning of the end," he said aloud stepping out.

He made plans and he was going to methodically carry them out. Dezi knew now that Kayla wanted to be with him. He was a man on a mission. *Nothing is going to keep us apart this time baby*, Dezi thought as he picked up his cell and turned on the monitors.

● ● ●

"Yeah?" Cedric answered.

"Is everything ready?" Dezi asked instead of a greeting.

"Oh sorry Mr. E," Cedric returned once he recognized his voice. "Yeah, everything is ready."

"That's wonderful," Dezi smiled. "I'll see you both shortly."

"Okay," Cedric replied as they hung up.

Dezi reflected on the two men and smiled at how fortunate he was to find them. Big D recommended them from one of his girls. One of them was her cousin, the other just a friend. They were extremely professional and helpful since the first assignment. Dezi was pleased thinking back to their reaction when he asked about this current task.

"Either of you ever kill anyone," Dezi asked.

Neither man flinched.

"Yeah," K.C. answered.

Cedric shook his head in agreement. Dezi looked at them for a moment before proceeding.

"Do you have any objections to doing it again?"

Cedric smiled and looked at K.C.

"Man no!" they both emphatically replied.

Dezi smiled. He liked them. They reminded him of a time long ago. He didn't think of the Front 5 often. K.C. did remind him of Monster a lot though. He was quiet and reserved but you could tell the underlying danger that lurked within him.

"Who you need us to take out," he asked matter-of-fact. Dezi told them and again neither man flinched.

"When you want it done?" Dezi told them and they made plans. He didn't actually want them to do the killing. Dezi waited a long time and he planned to close Collins's eyes personally. His cell ringing brought him back to the present. The number didn't display on his screen.

"Hello," he answered carefully, accent in place.

"Hi," Kayla said softly almost whispering.

Dezi was so glad to hear her voice.

"Hi Kayla, are you all right," he said all in one breath.

"Yes, I'm okay," she responded. "I'm on a payphone," Kayla told him. "He checks my cell," she said simply. "I just wanted to see if you got my message."

Dezi smiled again.

"Yes Kayla I got it," he said softly. "I miss you."

Kayla smiled. "I miss you too."

"I need to talk to you when I get back," she told him.

"I'll be waiting," Dezi replied.

"I have to go. Thomas will be looking for me," Kayla told him.

"Alright, but please be careful," Dezi told her. "I don't want anything to happen to you."

"Thanks, I will be very careful," Kayla told Dante.

They disconnected and Dezi sighed again. He returned to the task at hand. Collins was still asleep. Dezi knew from monitoring him, he worked the night shift now. He usually didn't get up until well after noon. Dezi looked at his watch. It was time to go.

•••

Cedric and K.C. doubled checked all their equipment. They were getting paid handsomely from this job. They talked at length last night deciding they would get out of North Carolina after this was done.

"Man I'm sick of this town," K.C. said plainly. "I'm going out to the coast."

Cedric agreed.

"Definitely more money to be made," he told K.C.

Neither of them had an issue with killing. They did more than their share, running with the various crews they hung with.

"This is big time shit right here," Cedric remarked, knowing that the target was a federal agent this time.

"Makes me no never mind," K.C. replied.

For him death was death. Mr. Enzo wanted this guy dead and that's what he was paying them for.

"Well technically we ain't killing him anyway," Cedric returned after thinking about it.

He remembered that Mr. Enzo wanted to do that himself.

"Wonder what this fool did to piss Mr. E off?"

K.C. shrugged. "I don't know but whatever it was, he's going to be sorry as hell today."

They both burst into laughter and headed out the door. They arrived shortly afterward parking in the alley two blocks from the complex Collins lived in. His was a ground floor unit, which would make the job that much easier. K.C. used the remote he copied during their last visit to unlock the door and disarm the security system. They crept inside and sent the text message to Mr. Enzo.

Dezi looked at his cell as it buzzed and saw the message. He smiled, finished his coffee and paid his tab. He hailed a cab and headed for his destination.

●●●

K.C. and Cedric put on their ski masks complimenting the gloves they already donned and headed for the bedroom. Collins was sleeping peacefully they discovered once they crept into his room. K.C. located his weapon lying on the nightstand and gingerly removed it. Cedric trained his gun on Collins as K.C. hit him to wake him up.

"Get the fuck up man," K.C. yelled as he slapped the sleeping man.

Collins jumped and reached for his gun.

"Get your ass up," K.C. repeated as Collins realized his gun was gone.

"What do you want," he asked the masked men trying not to show any fear.

"We're doing all the talking here asshole," Cedric told him.

"Get your ass in the living room," Cedric ordered again.

K.C. backed up into the living room gun trained on Collins as Cedric followed him out, gun in his back. *What is this shit?* Collins thought. *Home invasion? They gonna rob me or what?* he continued to wonder as they forced him into a kitchen chair they brought into the room and handcuffed him to it.

"Fucked up to get cuffed with your own shit huh," K.C. said menacingly.

Collins was embarrassed yes, but he was more curious than anything. They gagged and taped his mouth. Secured his feet and began ransacking the house. *Hopefully they'll just rob me and leave,* he thought. Collins couldn't identify them so they didn't need to kill him.

Cedric felt his cell buzz and looked at it. He signaled K.C. and they both headed back to the living room.

Dezi had the cabbie to drop him at the strip mall down the street. He carefully and meticulously made his way the four blocks to Collins house. He'd entered through the back door of the garage. He was now ready to make his presence known.

K.C. opened the door to the house allowing him access. Collins back was to the door but he heard another person come in. *Maybe it's their driver or something,* he thought getting a very bad feeling. Dezi stood looking at Collins's back, the rage building in him. He calmed himself and headed for the kitchen, removing a glass from the cabinet and helping himself to the scotch Collins placed on the counter.

Collins was curious. The man said not a word since he came in. The other two were calmly sitting in the living room looking at him like a bug under glass. Dezi finished the drink, shattered the glass then looked at K.C. and Cedric signaling them to remove their masks. They did and looked at Collins. *Shit!* he thought. *Now they definitely had a reason to kill him.* Dezi walked slowly into the room and stood behind Collins in the chair. He walked around the chair and sat down in the one they place directly in front of Collins.

Collins looked at the man and wondered what this was all about. He wanted to ask but the gag prevented him from talking. Dezi studied him for a while and saw that Collins was indeed clueless to who he was. Dezi took a deep breath and sat back in the chair. K.C. and Cedric watched intently. *Mr. E is cool as hell with this shit,* K.C. was thinking as he took note. He liked Mr. Enzo. He had style and flair, something K.C. wanted to learn.

"I understand you've been looking for me," Dezi said evenly never taking his eyes from the man.

Collins frowned. *Who the hell is this guy? What is he talking about?* He never saw this man before in his life. Dezi laughed.

"You don't even know who I am, do you?" Dezi asked coldly.

Collins, clueless, shook his head no. Dezi chuckled softly.

"Kayla is still as beautiful now as she was twenty years ago," Dezi said calmly.

Collins heart sunk. *Please God no,* he thought as recognition flooded his face. Dezi laughed again.

"Oh, I see you recall now, hmm?"

K.C. and Cedric were enthralled. They never watched anyone like Mr. Enzo. *This guy is a fucking professional,* Cedric thought, hoping they would see more they could emulate later.

"You and your damn friend cost me her love a long time ago," he told Collins. "Now I'm back to get what's mine."

Collins was breathing hard. *What the hell can I do now,* he thought, *This crazy bastard is going to hurt Kayla and there's nothing I can do about it.*

Dezi began to talk again.

"It really wasn't very fair of Agent Black to do what he did you know," he told Collins coldly. "He lied to my baby, and made her afraid of me, because he wanted her for himself. That's why the fucker is dead now. Serves him right," Dezi spat bitterly.

Collins couldn't do anything but listen to Gianni. *Damn! He's still crazy as ever.*

Dezi smiled again.

"Did you know Kayla and I have been together?"

Collins expression was disbelief, which made Dezi laugh again. *This fucker is lying. Kayla wouldn't come within ten feet of him,* he thought but corrected himself because she wouldn't know who he really was.

"She's going to leave Thomas for me," Dezi said flatly.

This much Collins believed. He knew from Thomas himself they were having problems. Dezi continued as he took the .10mm from his pocket.

"Your friend Thomas is not all you think he is," he said coldly. "Did you know he hit her," Dezi said harshly. "You and Black made Kayla think I would hurt her, but I would never put my hands on her like that," he continued. "You coming here trying to play the hero was a big mistake on your part," Dezi told Collins. "You should have left well enough alone and let me be dead in your mind," he continued. "After all, you lied to your partner up until the day he died, so why not," Dezi finished seeing the words stung Collins, who now held tears in his eyes.

He's right and now I'm going to die, and for what? I couldn't even save Kayla from him, Collins thought sadly as the tears rolled down his cheek.

Dezi was genuinely amused. K.C. and Cedric were fascinated. *This man has talent like I've never seen,* K.C. thought again continuing to watch Mr. Enzo.

"Well, this has been a very pleasant stroll down memory lane, but I have other things to do today, and you have an appointment with death," Dezi said plainly.

Collins felt his body shiver. He didn't want to die and he certainly didn't want this to be the man that killed him. Collins resigned himself to the fact that it was indeed about to happen however.

"You can say hello to your buddy Agent Black when you see him in hell," Dezi spat coldly as he put the silencer on the gun and took the safety off.

Collins thought of his life. Thought of all the mistakes he made, the good times he experienced. He thought of Black, Kayla and their daughter. *I'm sorry man,* he thought sadly as Gianni put the gun to his head. *I failed,* was the final conscious thought Collins formed as Dezi shot him twice point blank in the head. The force of the bullets knocked Collins backwards and the chair fell over. Dezi kneeled and shot him twice in the heart for good measure.

"There you go fucker," he said coldly. "Bet you wish you hadn't found me now."

K.C. and Cedric smiled broadly. They'd never seen anything like that, except in movies or on TV. This guy was the real deal. Dezi told them to get their souvenirs and let's go. They all left together. Dezi went back the way he came and K.C. and Cedric went theirs. They would meet later and he would pay them the remainder of their money. *One down, one to go,* Dezi thought as he sat in the cab he hailed headed back to the coffee shop.

●●●

"Did you see how cold that muthafucker was," K.C. asked Cedric, referring to Mr. Enzo.

He shook his head in agreement.

"That's what I'm talking about!" he said laughing. "Yeah I'ma be like that," K.C. said wistfully. "I'm going to build myself an empire," he continued looking out the window as they drove.

Cedric knew K.C. was serious and he believed he would.

"I'ma be there too man," he told him.

K.C. laughed.

"Of course man," he replied. "We like batman and robin," he said laughing. "Can't have one without the other."

●●●

Dezi picked up his car at the coffee shop and returned home.

"That went well," he thought, chuckling.

He couldn't check to see if anyone found Collins yet. He instructed K.C. and Cedric to remove any equipment they installed. Dezi didn't leave anything to link it back to him. They ransacked the house so everyone would simply assume it was a home invasion robbery. *I told that fucker I was going to kill him. He should have believed me,* he thought coldly.

Dezi thought about Kayla and that brought a smile to his face. He was glad to hear from her this morning.

"Well preacher man, your help is gone. It's just me and you now," Dezi said aloud heading to his office to make some new arrangements.

Smoke & **21** Mirrors

Kayla was almost at her wits end. Thomas was absolutely impossible now that they were back. They returned and immediately left again headed for the coast to attend Maurice's funeral. She still couldn't believe he was dead. *Why did they have to kill him,* Kayla questioned sadly. The police surmised that he was the victim of a home invasion robbery. She sighed softly at the thought. She called Mariah and told her and of course she was upset. She wanted to come home immediately but Kayla persuaded her not too.

Now Thomas wouldn't let her out of his sight. Even when Kayla worked he insisted her clients come to the house. Thomas didn't have an issue with any of them, except Dante. He absolutely loathed him, and was trying to get Kayla to drop him as a client.

"Thomas you're being ridiculous!" she told him.

"I see how he looks at you," Thomas said. "I know when a man wants a woman," he continued angrily.

"Look, haven't I done everything you've asked of me Thomas," Kayla threw back "Any yet you still don't trust me? Why is that?"

She sighed heavily and told Thomas he needed to stop it. He was putting more strain on their marriage. He dropped the subject and hadn't brought it up again. *He's still watching me like a hawk though,* Kayla thought again. She couldn't even have a private phone conversation. Thomas went to market with her, shopping, errands, whatever. Kayla felt like a prisoner. She wasn't able to talk to Dante for the last two and a half weeks. She had to get out of here.

Kayla was tired of pretending Thomas was Dante when they had sex. He even made her go with him to his pastor's conferences the last two weeks. Kayla prayed that this week she wouldn't have to go. She needed to see Dante desperately. She wanted to leave this place. The phone rang.

"Hello?" she answered.

"Hey girl!" Jackie squealed into her ear.

Kayla laughed and saw Thomas out of the corner of her eye come into the room and sit down, making sure he was within earshot of the conversation. She sighed lightly.

"Are you okay?" Jackie asked concerned.

She knew Kayla was virtually his prisoner and couldn't get away.

"Yeah mostly," she replied.

Jackie knew that meant Thomas was somewhere close.

"Is he listening?"

"Yes, of course," Kayla replied laughing lightly.

Jackie was angry. She didn't want her friend going through this.

"Is he making you go with him again Friday?"

"I don't know, I hope not," Kayla replied.

"So how is Georgia," she asked trying to change the subject.

"It's cool girl," she replied casually. "Listen Kayla," Jackie went on. "You've got to find a way to get out of there. Thomas will hurt you eventually, you know that."

"Yes, I know and I'm going to get there," Kayla told Jackie.

Thomas assumed Kayla was talking about visiting Jackie. He thought it might not be a bad idea for them to take the trip there. He made a mental note to call Chris later and check on it. Kayla saw Thomas was still sitting and listening. She wouldn't be able to get any help from Jackie right now.

"Well I guess I should go," Kayla told her. "I need to make lunch for us."

Jackie sucked her teeth and Kayla tried hard to stifle the giggle.

"You should poison the dog," she said harshly.

Kayla giggled again and Jackie joined her.

"Call me the minute you get to Dante's, do you hear me?"

"Yes, and I'll talk to you again soon," Kayla told Jackie.

They said goodbye and disconnected.

●●●

"How is Jackie?" Thomas asked making it obvious he heard her conversation.

"She's fine," Kayla said smiling. "I'm going to make our lunch now, okay?"

He smiled. "Yes, that's fine."

132

Thomas watched Kayla go into the kitchen mind racing. *You really should stop hovering over her,* he began thinking. *She's been nothing but perfect since you got back. You're going to drive her away again with this nonsense,* Thomas sighed and decided he wouldn't make Kayla go to the conference this time.

●●●

Big D watched Jackie as she read her magazine. She was really steamed when she got off the phone. He knew all about Kayla's situation. Dezi was keeping him informed and he was keeping Dezi from killing Thomas. Big D really liked Jackie being here. They clicked from the moment she arrived. He took her everywhere and showed her everything.

He asked about her husband and she told him about the divorce. He helped her find an attorney to work everything out. She cooked for him and they enjoyed dinner together. She found her way into his heart real quick. Big D just couldn't figure out if Jackie felt the same way. She was cordial to him as always, but she didn't give away anything.

●●●

Jackie felt Big D watching her, but she refused to look up. He completely unnerved her. She was so attracted to him. She felt ashamed of herself for thinking the things she did when she saw him. *I want to know what he feels like,* Jackie thought again sighing softly. Big D was really a nice guy. Fun and outgoing he took her everywhere. They really enjoyed each other's company. Jackie just wasn't sure how Big D felt about her.

●●●

I wonder what she's thinking about, Big D thought watching Jackie read the same page for the last fifteen minutes. They were definitely compatible. Jackie was brash and sassy. She spoke her mind but knew how to listen too. *I would love to spend a little time nursing from those breasts,* Big D thought and chuckled lightly. Jackie looked up at the sound of him laughing and their eyes met. He looked at her intently until she smiled and looked away. Big D was getting totally turned on sitting here looking at Jackie. He got up and stretched.

"I'm going to take a little nap," he said looking at her.

Jackie looked up and smiled.

"Okay, sweet dreams."

Big D began walking past her and stopped. She looked up at him once more.

"You wanna come with me," he asked softly.

Jackie was speechless. She honestly admitted she really did. She didn't reply as Big D took her hand and helped her from the chair and led her to his bedroom.

●●●

"I thought we were taking a nap," Jackie said as Big D kissed her neck.

He chuckled.

"We are," Big D replied. "After."

She smiled as he looked into her eyes and began kissing her. Jackie was completely aroused after his kiss. *This man is no joke,* she thought as Big D began to find erogenous zones she didn't know she possessed. Finally, he kissed her again deeply as he entered her. Jackie thought she died and gone to heaven. *My god,* she thought moaning loudly, *he's wonderful.*

She was breathing hard as Big D brought her to orgasm again and again. He kissed her once more and began his own assent to release. Big D held her tightly and thrust into her deeply. Jackie cried out in ecstasy as she reached her peak yet again, this time Big D groaned deeply with her as he finished. They held each other afterward kissing and caressing each other.

"Damn," Jackie said looking at him. "Where have you been all my life," she finished, laughing softly.

Big D kissed her. "Right here, waiting for you."

They both laughed and continued to hold each other, drifting off finally into a fitful contented sleep.

●●●

Elise knew she shouldn't be here, but she had to see him. He managed to elude her the entire week his wife was with him at the convocation. *Well you won't escape me this time,* she thought as she unpacked her suitcase. She arrived a couple hours ago and ate lunch. She found his church and watched it for a while. Thomas didn't come in, but she saw the secretary. Elise didn't stay, as she didn't want anyone to notice her and ask questions. She managed to learn Thomas conducted a weekly meeting with his other pastors, and this time the members, on Friday.

Elise was planning on being in attendance. *I need your sweet love one more time Thomas.*

Elise wanted to get pregnant. She knew it was the oldest trick in the book, but she didn't care. She wanted this man and she would do whatever it took to get him. *Maybe I should call him,* she thought. *He doesn't have to know I'm here,* Elise figured as she picked up her cell and pushed the button she programmed with his number.

•••

Thomas heard his cell. *Who in the world,* he thought as he answered.

"Hello," he answered and Elise smiled at the sound of his voice.

"Hi Thomas," she said softly.

He looked around. Kayla was upstairs fortunately. He closed the door to his study.

"Hello Elise," Thomas said calmly.

Why is she calling me, he fretted nervously. He didn't need Kayla to walk in on this conversation.

"I just wanted to hear your voice and tell you I miss you," she said sweetly.

Thomas exhaled deeply. He missed Elise too. More than he thought he would. He was more attached to her than he originally imagined he would.

"I miss you too Elise," he replied honestly.

She was elated to hear that.

"But you really shouldn't call me anymore," Thomas told her.

Elise frowned slightly. That was not what she wanted to hear.

"Well why don't you tell me your schedule and I promise to call only when I know you're alone," she pleaded.

Thomas thought about it for a while. He didn't see the purpose.

"Why?" he began. "We won't see each other again."

Elise sighed gently.

"We could if you wanted to Thomas," she told him evenly.

Thomas was intrigued. He loved his sessions with Elise and while Kayla was willing she wasn't as passionate with him anymore.

"Let me think about it, OK?"

Elise was excited. She wouldn't push.

"OK Thomas," she replied. "You've got my cell, so just call me."

"Alright, I will," he told her and disconnected.

Thomas sat at his desk thinking about her. *She feels so damned good when I screw her,* he reminisced. He wasn't in love with her, but the sex was wonderful, and it made him feel fifteen years younger. *Maybe I will call her at that,* he thought smiling as he rose to go down to the church. Thomas checked on Kayla before he left. She was fast asleep. *Are you going to leave her here, alone?* Thomas sighed deeply as he roused Kayla from her sleep. He wasn't ready yet. Friday was still two days away.

●●●

They arrived at the church about an hour ago. Thomas felt like a real heel. She immediately went to Chris's old office and lay down. Kayla was still fast asleep as he checked on her. *Why did you make her come,* he asked himself feeling stupid at the answer. Thomas sighed deeply and made up his mind to stop treating Kayla this way. He was still just so worried about her leaving him. *I can't let this end up like Debbie and I did,* Thomas thought tiredly.

Debbie was his last serious girlfriend. They endured a tumultuous relationship arguing and fighting. She caught him cheating and threatened to leave. Thomas loved Debbie and she was his. He wasn't going to let her go. He supposed he was always possessive about his things and she was no exception. *I didn't mean for her to get hit,* he remorsefully thought another time. He was waving the gun around just to scare her. Debbie called his bluff and tried to walk out the door. Thomas was aiming for the wall but somehow hit her. The injury wasn't life threatening but it was enough to get him an assault charge. He was still on probation now. *That should be up by now,* Thomas made a mental note to check on it.

He looked at Kayla sleeping again and pushed the bad thoughts out of his mind. He sighed deeply and headed back to his office. Once he arrived he picked up the phone and called Chris. He wanted to touch base with him and find out when they would be ready for visitors. Thomas knew Kayla wanted to see Jackie and he of course wanted to see his old friend too. He didn't get an answer so he left a message.

Guess they're out getting acquainted with the city, Thomas thought as he began to go over the itinerary for the meeting Friday night. His cell rang.

"Hello," he answered absently still looking at the notes.

"Hi Lover," Elise purred into the phone.

She decided to call him again hoping to push him to a quick yes and the return of their relationship. Thomas smiled in spite of himself.

"Hi," he returned. "What are you doing?"

"Thinking of how nice it would be if you were inside me," she replied and Thomas found himself getting turned on at the thought.

"That might be difficult considering the distance," he replied chuckling lightly.

Elise decided to take a chance.

"Well, I'm only about five miles away from you right now," she returned softly.

Thomas was intrigued.

"You're here," he asked excitedly.

"Yes baby," Elise told him again hearing the excitement in his voice.

That's right. I'm here waiting for you, she thought waiting for his reply.

"Tell me where you are," Thomas said matter-of-fact.

Elise told him the hotel she was staying in and the room number.

"What time should I expect you," she purred.

"I can't tonight baby," Thomas replied. "But if you stay until tomorrow, I promise to make it worth your while."

Elise was disappointed that it couldn't be tonight but she would wait.

"OK," she said softly. "But you have to spend some time with me," she pouted.

Thomas smiled. That would definitely not be a problem. Kayla booked appointments all day tomorrow and she was at the children's hospital tomorrow night for a charity event they were having. He would know exactly where she was at all times.

"You got it," he replied happily. "I'll see you tomorrow around ten."

Elise laughed delightedly.

"AM or PM?" she asked still laughing.

"AM of course," Thomas joined Elise chuckling.

They said their goodbyes and hung up.

●●●

Thomas was delighted thinking of the wonderful sex he would have with her tomorrow.

"This might actually work out," he chuckled returning to check on Kayla.

She finally awakened from her nap. She was sulky because he roused her and made her come.

"I'm sorry baby," Thomas told Kayla softly. "I promise you don't have to do this anymore," he continued. "And Friday you don't have to come to the meeting with me."

Kayla looked at him but didn't react. Finally she took a deep breath and gave Thomas a small smile.

"Thank you," she said softly.

He smiled and kissed her passionately.

"I love you baby," Thomas told Kayla as he pulled away and they headed for the car.

Smoke & **22** Mirrors

Kayla was elated. She was careful not to let Thomas know how happy she was. *Finally I can see Dante and get away from here*, she excitedly thought. She couldn't see him tomorrow. Kayla was swamped and there was her charity event in the evening for the children's hospital. *I'll call him and set it up for Friday while Thomas is at his meeting*, Kayla began planning her escape. She wasn't taking anything with her other than a change of clothes and her photos.

She still had plenty of her own money. She always kept her own investments current and hidden. Thomas was without idea the wealth that she amassed during the years. She got a hefty head start with all the money she got from Dezi in addition to her own. Black knew about her investments but never where the capital came from. Kayla thought about Dante and got excited. She missed him. She hadn't been touched or held like that since that last time they were together.

Kayla wanted to be with Dante and make love with him. *We'll have time*, she thought. Thomas wouldn't know where she was. She made a mental note to make hotel reservations for herself. Kayla would use her maiden name. She didn't think he remembered what it was. Thomas usually left for his meeting around seven or so. She would give him about forty- five minutes in case he decided to turn around. Then she would go and meet Dante, get everything settled, then head to her hotel. *It's almost over*, Kayla told herself.

● ● ●

She made Thomas's favorite dinner tonight. They enjoyed it with a wonderful desert.

"Come on your missing the movie!" he called out cheerfully as Kayla was getting their coffee.

"I'm coming honey," she replied happily.

Thomas knew Kayla was happy. He wouldn't treat her like a prisoner ever again. Thomas loved her and he knew Kayla loved him back.

"Sit down; you're going to miss it," he said playfully pulling her into his lap.

Kayla laughed and slid down off his lap sitting beside him. She leaned on him and Thomas held her in his arms as they watched, each of them entertaining their own thoughts.

"How many clients are you seeing tomorrow," he asked her after the movie was over.

"I have three of my regulars and I have four prospective ones," Kayla told him.

"Is Mr. Enzo one of them?"

Kayla knew he was extremely jealous of Dante.

"No, not tomorrow," she replied. "I'll probably meet with him next week," she finished sipping her coffee.

Thomas breathed a sigh of relief. He didn't like the guy plain and simple. Thomas could tell he was interested in Kayla. She was so sweet and trusting, she didn't see it, but he certainly did.

"Well you're going to be a busy bee tomorrow," Thomas told her laughing.

Kayla joined him and said yes she would be.

"What are you doing tomorrow?"

"I've got meetings all day," Thomas replied frowning slightly.

"Aww, I'm sorry," Kayla told him and hugged him.

Thomas laughed. "It's okay, I'll survive."

You better hope she doesn't ever catch you, he thought of his plans with Elise tomorrow.

"What time is the charity event?"

"Starts at eight and isn't over until after midnight," Kayla told him.

Thomas made a mental note to be home by eleven.

"What are you wearing," he asked Kayla again stroking her hair absently.

"Oh, come upstairs and help me choose something," Kayla said excitedly pulling Thomas up off the couch.

Her excitement was contagious and he found himself laughing as he followed her.

●●●

So she's going out tomorrow night hmm, Dezi thought still watching the monitor. He hoped Kayla would call and they could finally get together. His cell rang. Dezi knew it wasn't her she was still talking to her husband.

"Hello," he answered never taking his eyes off the screen.

"Wassup man?" Big D boomed in his ear.

Dezi smiled and began to laugh.

"Hey man what's up?"

Big D told him all about him and Jackie.

"Glad to hear it worked out with you two," Dezi chuckled.

"So what's the plan on your end," Big D asked.

"He's been like a damned shadow, " Dezi told him. "She's going out tomorrow night so I expect to hear from her."

Dezi thought about something he wanted to talk to Big D about.

"Hey, listen man," he began. "Why don't you and Jackie come on over to the island with us?"

Big D was quiet as he listened.

"I mean I have a serious operation going on over there," Dezi went on. "You wouldn't have to handle the girls personally, we got underlings for that shit," he continued. "You would just be there as the overseer and collector if you know what I mean."

Big D thought about it.

"Hey, it sounds good to me man, I just have to sell Jackie on it," he replied. "I mean hell, ain't shit keeping me in the states," Big D went on. "Damned cops always trying to knock a brutha's hustle. It might be nice to just relax in the sun and enjoy my life."

"I don't think it will be that hard a sell once Jackie knows that Kayla is with me," Dezi told him. "we just have to tell her the truth of who I am."

"Alright man it's on," Big D told him.

"Did you find us a flyer," Dezi asked.

"Yeah, getting confirmation tomorrow," Big D answered.

"Good," Dezi replied. "Call me once we got that."

"You know I will," Big D told him and they said goodnight.

Dezi returned his attention to the monitor and found Kayla showering. He watched as the soap ran down her beautiful body.

"Call me tomorrow baby," Dezi said gently.

Kayla looked up at the camera like she could see Dezi looking at her and smiled. He looked into her eyes and saw she was genuinely happy.

"What are you up to baby," Dezi said chuckling to himself.

He knew she was plotting. Dezi watched until she dried herself and got dressed for bed. Thomas came into the room and Dezi thought he would have to endure watching him torture Kayla sexually again. Instead Thomas held her and they both drifted off to sleep. *Interesting*, Dezi thought and finished his drink. He flipped off the monitor and headed up to bed. Tomorrow was a new day and he hoped to get some good news.

●●●

K.C. and Cedric were chilling and getting high.

"I wonder what Mr. E got for us to do now," Cedric asked as he released the smoke from the hit he'd just taken.

"I don't know, but whatever it is, I'm down," K.C. said matter-of-fact.

They both were enjoying their new wealth, not to mention the knowledge and skill they were acquiring for what they planned to do with their lives.

"I wonder what Mr. E used to do for real," Cedric asked.

The man was entirely too smooth at the game to have ever been legitimate.

"I bet he used to kill people large scale," K.C. said.

"What makes you say that man," his friend asked.

"It's just that swagga he has about him," K.C. replied. "Have you noticed he don't even break a sweat about killing them," he went on. "It's like he steps outta himself and ain't even there."

Cedric thought about it and agreed. Mr. Enzo could be as cold as ice when he needed to be.

"That takes talent man," K.C. commented again.

"Yeah, and I want him to tell me how he does that shit," Cedric piped up.

So did K.C. He liked Mr. E. He bet there were a lot of things he could school them both on. They talked a little here and there but he didn't release much. K.C. understood. It was hard to trust people in this business. He hoped that after this job though Mr. E would feel enough at ease to tell them what they wanted to know.

Smoke & **23** Mirrors

T homas kissed Kayla goodbye as he headed off. He stopped by one of the convenience stores outside of town and picked up some condoms. *Must be safe,* he thought laughing. He couldn't wait to get inside Elise. Thomas found the hotel with ease and parked in the rear. He didn't want to chance anyone seeing his car and wondering what he was doing there. Thomas found Elise's room and knocked. He was glad it was an open entrance hotel. No front desk to go through and have the clerk able to identify you.

Elise opened the door and smiled broadly when she saw Thomas.

"Hi!" she squealed and pulled him into the room kissing him.

Thomas kissed Elise back and told her hi, once he got his bearings back.

"I'm so happy to see you," she told him.

"I'm happy to see you too," Thomas laughed.

I can't believe he's here with me, she thought happily.

"Did you have breakfast yet?"

"Yes, I did."

"Elise," Thomas began looking at her seriously.

What is he thinking, Elise thought uneasily, holding her breath.

"I don't want you to get too far gone with our arrangement," he said evenly.

"I don't understand," she told him confused.

"I'm not going to leave my wife, ever," Thomas told her plainly.

Elise was crushed. This was not what she wanted to hear.

"I've never asked you too, have I?"

Thomas saw she was hurt, but he had to make her understand.

"No, you haven't," he replied. "But I'm not stupid either."

Elise looked up at him but said nothing.

"I already know you're in love with me," Thomas told her plainly.

"Now, while I do care for you, I love my wife with all my heart."

Elise sighed dejectedly.

"I understand that Thomas," she went on. "I just want whatever time you'll give me," she continued. "Can we just do that?"

"Of course we can," Thomas smiled.

He kissed her and hugged her tightly. Elise couldn't stay mad. She loved the way he felt and the smell of him. She smiled and they began to caress and arouse each other.

"I want you to make love to me Thomas," Elise said as they were enjoying foreplay.

She continued to arouse him with her mouth. She mounted him and he slipped easily inside her wetness without the condom. *She feels incredible,* Thomas thought as he began thrusting into her. Elise was in heaven. He was making her feel sensations that went past wonderful.

"Oh Thomas," Elise moaned softly as she continued to ride him.

Their rhythm got faster and faster until she cried out in orgasm and felt him cum inside her. *Thank you Thomas,* Elise smiled internally. She would hopefully get what she wanted now. Thomas realized he made love to Elise without a condom. *Well you can't get her pregnant. So no harm no foul,* he thought as she climbed off and kissed him softly.

Thomas held her for a few moments until they began to kiss re-igniting their passion again. "Thomas you are absolutely fantastic," Elise told him as she lay on his chest.

He smiled. *This woman is wonderful for the male midlife crisis ego,* Thomas thought as he held Elise. He looked at the clock and saw it was after three. He needed to call Kayla and at least check in.

"I need to go in the bathroom and call my wife," he told her.

Elise was careful not to let her emotions show.

"Go ahead," she replied. "I'll go grab us some lunch," she told him as she dressed.

Thomas smiled and kissed her. Elise smiled back and headed out the door.

●●●

He stepped into the bathroom and closed the door.

"Hello?" Kayla answered.

"Hey baby," Thomas said smoothly.

"Hi Honey," she replied.

Thomas felt an instant wave of guilt and shame wash over him.

"How's your day going?".

"Everything is good, and I should be finished with the meetings around six," Kayla told him.

"That's cutting it close honey," he told her.

"I know, but I'll still get to the function on time," she giggled.

"OK baby, have a great time," Thomas told her.

Kayla sighed softly.

"Thomas?"

"Yes baby."

"Thank you," she finished softly.

"Have fun tonight and I'll see you when you get home," he told her as they said goodbye and hung up.

Thomas heard Elise come in as he hung up. He pushed the guilt out of his mind and returned to the bed to enjoy lunch and afterwards more sex.

●●●

Kayla returned to her client and apologized again for the interruption. The gentleman told her that was fine. She continued to explain his portfolio to him and gave him the name of the broker who would be handling his accounts since she was going to stop working now. After the client left Kayla called Dante.

"Hello?"

Kayla smiled. She was so glad to hear his voice and finally be able to talk freely to him.

"Hi Dante," she replied.

Dezi smiled at the sound of her voice.

"Hi there stranger," he teased.

Kayla told Dante all about her adventures and that this was the first free moment she found to call.

"I wanted to know if we could finally have our talk tomorrow," Kayla asked, explaining all that was going on today and tonight.

"Of course Kayla," Dezi replied smoothly, careful not to let her hear how excited he was at the prospect.

"When would you like to come by?"

"Well Thomas is leaving around seven so I could be there around eight I suppose," Kayla told him.

Dezi had plans. There were some loose ends he needed to tie up.

"That will be fine Kayla," he told her. "However, I won't be home. I have a meeting," he continued. "But you come on in and make yourself right at home. I'll return as soon as I'm finished."

Kayla wasn't sure she wanted to intrude on his home without him being there. Dezi chuckled softly as if he could hear her thoughts.

"I don't mind Kayla, really," he went on. "I think you'll find my home very interesting."

The statement intrigued her.

"Well if you're sure it's OK," Kayla replied hesitantly.

Dezi assured her again it was fine.

"Perhaps I can even convince you to stay the night once I return home," he said softly.

Kayla secretly admitted the thought crossed her mind.

"Well, we'll see how it goes," she said in reply.

Dezi smiled again and told her all right.

"My next client is coming in the door," Kayla told him.

"Alright, but I expect you tomorrow night," Dezi said going on to give her directions again as well as the location of the garage remote and keys.

"Thank you again Dante," Kayla said softly.

"For what," he replied. "Wait until I've actually done something for you first," Dezi finished chuckling again.

Kayla joined him. "Have a great day."

Dezi thought about her after he hung up.

"It's almost time," he said as he dialed a number on his cell.

●●●

Kayla smiled at the client as she left. She jumped into her own car headed for home. It was six thirty. She needed to get home shower and change heading out to the children's hospital. Kayla thought back to her conversation with Dante.

"There is something just not quite right there," she said aloud.

He reminded her so much of Dezi. *Too much to be a coincidence, but Dezi's dead Kayla,* she told herself. Still, she couldn't shake the thoughts she was having. *Ask him then,* Kayla gave serious consideration.

"Let's just see what happens tomorrow," Kayla said aloud as she entered her house.

She changed dresses. She didn't like the black one Thomas helped her pick out. It sported a high neckline, long sleeves and flowed into a hugely blossomed skirt at the waist. It also made her feel old, and tonight she didn't want to feel old. Kayla wore the red one. She knew Thomas hated it because it showed off her curves, but Kayla wanted to be noticed tonight.

Kayla grabbed her purse and headed out the door. *I've got to be home by twelve thirty,* she thought to herself. If she stayed out any longer Thomas would be suspicious. She would already have to deal with him about the dress. Kayla pushed those thoughts out of her mind as she arrived and the valet took her car. She noticed immediately the stares she was getting from some of the men in the crowd. Kayla smiled demurely and headed for her table.

●●●

Dezi, watching the monitors, looked at her in the dress and smiled.

"You look beautiful baby," he said approvingly.

Dezi picked up his cell after she left the house calling K.C. and Cedric.

"Hey Mr. E," Cedric greeted him.

"I have a job for you two."

"We're all ears," he replied and Dezi began to lay out the plans for tomorrow night.

"That actually works out perfectly," K.C. said chuckling.

He could easily handle what Mr. E was asking of him.

"I got the other end covered," Cedric told.

"That will work out just fine gentlemen." Dezi told them both.

They continued to talk and work out every detail. Dezi couldn't afford any slip-ups on this one. It was going to be the grand finale and it had to go right.

"You both will be completely set if you do this right," he told them.

"Mr. E?" K.C. inquired.

"Yes?".

"Look, I know you're into some shit that we couldn't even fathom, but I want to get some of that wisdom, if you know what I'm saying," he offered.

Dezi smiled. He was genuinely flattered.

"Tell you what K.C." he began. "You and Cedric pull this off and I'll give you both a serious crash course."

"That's definitely a deal," K.C. told him.

They went over the plan one more time and said their goodbyes.

●●●

Dezi dialed the next number.

"Hello?"

"Hi Rachelle," Dezi greeted her.

She smiled. It was so nice of Dante to call.

"I wanted to call and tell you that I'm going to have to leave," he said evenly.

Rachelle didn't want to hear that.

"Why Dante?"

"I just got an urgent call that I'm needed at home immediately," he told her again.

She sighed heavily. "Well I'm at least glad you called and told me," she replied.

"Well I also wanted to leave you a gift," Dezi said.

Rachelle was intrigued.

"You remember I told you I saw a movie once in church?"

"Yes, I recall you saying that."

"Well, I found the film, and thought I would share it with your church," Dezi replied smoothly.

"Oh, that would be wonderful Dante," Rachelle answered. "Actually Friday would be perfect. The entire church will be here for a meeting."

Dezi smiled wickedly.

"Perfect," he told Rachelle. "I'll send it by messenger in the morning," he told her. "You have to promise not to peek though."

Rachelle laughed.

"I promise I won't," she told him.

"I'll give it to the technician before service and have him cue it. I'll have the remote so I'll just start it from the floor," Rachelle explained.

Dezi was almost beside himself with glee.

"All right Rachelle," he told her. "Take good care of yourself and maybe I'll see you again when I get back this way," Dezi finished smoothly, knowing he would never come back to the states.

Rachelle sighed again.

"Take care of yourself Dante. I'll miss you."

"Everything is almost ready," Dezi said again as he disconnected and made himself another drink.

You picked the wrong woman to hurt preacher man, Dezi thought ominously as he sipped his cognac.

●●●

Kayla was having the time of her life. The children were absolutely marvelous. The other performers, a mime troupe, were giving a great show as well. The auction portion was getting ready to start. They were doing very well raising money for the hospital. Kayla was happy that at least she wouldn't leave them in debt. She genuinely loved the kids she helped here.

●●●

I wonder if Rev knows she's out in that dress, Detective Dwayne Marchant wondered as he took the woman in admiring each and every curve the form fitting red dress allowed him to see. He knew Kayla was the local Pastor's wife. She was also drop dead gorgeous.

"Nice, huh," his partner said as he saw the object of his stare.

Marchant smiled; embarrassed he was caught looking.

"Rev. must really trust her, to let her out of the house looking like that," his partner remarked again.

"She seems like a very nice woman," Marchant replied.

His partner shook his head.

"She is," he replied. "She's up here with these kids all the time. She really does a great job," he went on. "The auction was all her idea."

Marchant continued to look at Kayla. She was absolutely stunning. *Wonder if she knows about her husband's record?* The probation department for the State of Florida sent him paperwork confirming Thomas's probation was ended.

●●●

Kayla felt a stare and turned to find the source. She finally found the man standing against a wall, drink in hand. Kayla looked at him until he looked away. She smiled and turned around again enjoying the auction.

Great! Now she thinks you're a king sized pervert, Marchant chided himself. *She is just so damned pretty,* he thought again as he left. He was on duty in thirty minutes.

●●●

Kayla enjoyed herself at the charity function. She saw Thomas's car as she drove up. *Well here we go,* she thought as she entered the house. Thomas was waiting for her in their bedroom.

"Hi honey," he told Kayla as he greeted her with a kiss.

"Hi baby," Kayla returned as she removed her coat.

Thomas saw the dress and was immediately annoyed. He didn't react though.

"You look beautiful baby," he said softly looking her over.

Kayla smiled, glad she wouldn't have to argue with him about it.

"Thank you Thomas," she said sweetly. "That means a lot to me coming from you."

He smiled and kissed her again.

"You have a productive day," Kayla asked Thomas as she undressed.

"Yes, I did as a matter of fact," he answered.

She climbed in beside him telling him she was exhausted. Thomas stroked her hair and rubbed her shoulders for her.

"Close your eyes and relax baby," he told Kayla gently.

Thomas rubbed her until she fell asleep. He lay beside her and drifted off too.

●●●

Dezi watched with interest. *This is the second night he's gone to bed without being with her,* Dezi thought and finished his steak. He smiled.

"Elise is here," Dezi said simply.

He picked up the cell and dialed.

"Hello?"

"When did you get here," he asked flatly after she answered.

Elise panicked. *How the hell did he know I was here?*

"Doesn't matter," Dezi replied. "Be at the church Friday night," he barked.

This guy scared her. She never met him but she talked to him before and met his representative. He definitely was no nonsense all the way.

"What time," Elise asked quietly.

"Eight," Dezi replied. "Did you tip him off," he asked coldly.

"No," she replied.

Dezi was quiet for a moment.

"You better be telling the truth for your sake," he finished evenly and hung up.

●●●

Elise was breathing hard. This guy was crazy. She didn't want to go to the church. She saw Thomas and they spent time together. She didn't want to hurt him or his reputation. *What choice do you have?* It's what she was paid to do. She sighed heavily and climbed into bed knowing sleep wouldn't come easily tonight.

●●●

Dezi smiled at how well things were coming together. He finished his drink and headed up to bed. He wanted to be refreshed and ready for tomorrow. *The final act,* Dezi thought chuckling fitfully as he climbed the stairs.

Smoke & **24** Mirrors

Jackie was curious about what it was D wanted to talk to her about. Even though she learned his real name she still called him that. He was really evasive when she tried to find out earlier. Jackie was waiting for him to come back from the store and tell her. She thought back to her conversation with Kayla earlier today.

"When are you talking to Dante?"

"Well now that Thomas has finally stopped treating me like a prisoner, I made plans to see him tomorrow," Kayla told her

"Good," Jackie had replied. "Don't go back to that house Kayla for anything," she admonished her.

"I have no plans too," Kayla told he. "I'm leaving a letter and my rings for Thomas to let him know it is over."

"What about your divorce," Jackie asked.

"Dante said he would help me with that," Kayla replied.

"I'm just happy your finally leaving," Jackie told Kayla. "You call me the moment you make it to Dante's."

Jackie was still worried something might go wrong.

"I promise," Kayla responded, also informing her of the strange things Dante said and how she would be at his home alone.

"Take the time to snoop a little and answer the questions you have," Jackie advised.

"I just might," Kayla giggled.

The key turning the lock brought her attention back to the present. Big D walked in and smiled at Jackie.

"Hey girl," Big D greeted her as he kissed her gently.

"Hey baby," Jackie returned.

He smiled again, and sat across from her. Jackie waited until he made himself comfortable.

"So what's on your mind baby," she asked amiably, looking at him as she spoke.

Big D knew Jackie was curious. He wasn't sure how he should begin, but he took a deep breath and tried.

"Listen Jackie," Big D began "There are some things about me you should know."

He went on to tell her about his true occupation and his days with Dezi. Jackie listened intently.

"Baby I understand everyone has a past," Jackie told Big D as he stopped talking for a moment. "It's OK, that was then and whatever you do now, well, it's what you do."

Big D smiled again. "I have more to tell you though baby," he began again. "This is about us, about our future, about Kayla and Dante," Big D told her.

Jackie was totally confused. He told her the entire story of Kayla and Dezi from back in the day until now. Big D told Jackie the truth about his connection to Dante, and who Dante Enzo really was, and why he was back. Jackie was completely blown away.

"Oh my god," she said softly.

Big D hoped he didn't overwhelm her.

"That is incredible," Jackie spoke again still trying to absorb the magnitude of what she just learned.

"So Kayla was right," she said half aloud.

"What did you say," Big D questioned.

Jackie repeated what she said adding that Kayla suspected it since she met Dante.

"Does she know," Jackie asked.

"Not yet, but I'm pretty sure she will after tomorrow night," Big D told her.

"Dezi must really love Kayla," she said gently.

"Without a doubt," Big D assured her.

"What will he do to Thomas?" Jackie asked.

"That depends on Thomas," Big D told her. "Dezi only kills people if he has too, but he has no qualms about killing them either."

Jackie shook her head that she understood. She was quiet for a while and Big D was worried.

"Baby, are you OK with all this," he asked her quietly.

Jackie looked at him shaking the thoughts and webs from her head. She smiled at Big D.

"Yeah, we're great," she told him beginning to chuckle. "Guess I should get me some island gear huh?"

Big D got up and came over to Jackie pulling her to her feet.

"Yeah baby, we're going to enjoy life in the sun," he told her kissing her neck gently.

Big D was turning Jackie on and she really wanted some of him.

"Dezi will get Kayla out of there won't he," she asked him seriously.

"Baby, you can take that check to the bank," Big D told Jackie. "Once Dezi makes up his mind, it's all done except the singing."

"Okay, that makes me feel better," Jackie told Big D.

 He began to kiss her again and she soon found herself aroused again. Big D took her hand as they went into the bedroom together.

●●●

Dezi was up and out early. There was a lot to do today. He made his first stop and approached the receptionist's desk.

"Good morning," she greeted Dezi giving him the once over.

"Good morning," he returned smoothly. "I have an appointment this morning with Greyson."

She nodded. "And your name sir?"

"Dante Enzo," Dezi said again smiling.

She returned his smile and buzzed Mr. Greyson alerting him that his appointment was here. The man came out and personally greeted Dezi.

They shook and returned to his office.

"Is everything finished," Dezi asked once they were seated.

"Yes Mr. Enzo, it's all done," Greyson replied. "I must say it is highly unusual for it to be done this way," he told him looking at him steadily.

Dezi smiled.

"Well, as I told you when I hired you," he began. "This is a very unique situation and needs to be handled with the utmost tact and confidentiality," he went on. "Considering the parties involved I'm sure you understand my position," Dezi finished looking back at the man.

Greyson nodded he did indeed understand.

"They must be signed and filed before they are legal you realize," he asked Dezi.

Dezi nodded that he understood.

"How long after filing will everything be finished?"

"Hmm, due to the extenuating circumstances, I could ask for an emergency ruling, and have everything said and done in a matter of hours," Greyson told Mr. Enzo.

"Excellent," Dezi replied smiling again.

Dezi removed the bulky envelope from his inner suit pocket and handed it to the Greyson.

"Here is the first payment," he told him. "As soon as it's done you'll receive the other portion."

Greyson greedily reached for the envelope. Dezi chuckled inwardly preparing to leave the man's office.

"I'll be in touch as soon as the necessary signatures are in place," Dezi told him.

"I'll be anxiously awaiting your call Mr. Enzo," Greyson replied smiling.

They shook again and Dezi left the office. He told the receptionist goodbye as he passed her desk. Once Dezi was alone in the elevator he took out the papers and read them. He smiled at the content and put them back into his pocket. Dezi began to whistle lightly as he exited the building heading for his next task.

●●●

Thomas was getting ready to leave. He called Elise and let her know he would be stopping by. *She seemed a little down this morning,* he thought. Thomas attributed it to what he said to her yesterday about not leaving his wife. He sighed lightly. Thomas headed downstairs to find out what the heavenly smell was he picked up. He found his wife in the kitchen making breakfast.

"Are we having guests," he asked chuckling.

Kayla turned and smiled.

"No silly," she replied. "I made us breakfast, that's all."

Thomas hugged Kayla and kissed her deeply.

"Do you know how much I love you," he asked as he held her looking into her eyes.

Kayla smiled again and it warmed his heart.

"Yes Thomas, I know," she replied. "Now sit down," she playfully ordered.

Thomas did as he was told. Kayla brought him his breakfast, all of his favorites; hash browns, eggs, bacon, grits, and homemade biscuits. Thomas ate heartily as Kayla ate with him.

"Is that all you're having," he asked looking at her sparse serving.

"Yes," Kayla replied. "And I'll be quite full thank you," she added pretending to be offended.

Thomas laughed. She was in such a good mood this morning. He knew it was because he stopped squeezing the life out of her.

"Do you have plans for today," Thomas asked casually.

"I'm going to enjoy a girl day," Kayla told him.

"And what exactly does that entail," he laughed.

"Well, I think I'm going to the all day spa," she told him.

Thomas nodded with his mouth full.

"Sounds nice," he told Kayla once he swallowed his food.

"You deserve it baby," he added softly looking at her.

She took his plate and asked if he were full.

"God yes!" Thomas replied. "Now I need someone to carry me to my car," he joked.

Kayla laughed as she walked him to his car. Thomas stood there for a moment looking at Kayla feeling like a complete dog for what he was about to go and do. He leaned in and kissed her again.

"Have a good day at the spa baby," Thomas told her softly. "Will you be home before I go to my meeting?"

"Certainly," Kayla smiled.

"Good," he replied. "I'll need some sugar before I go face the crowd," he laughed.

He got into the car and started it up. Kayla waved as he left the driveway. Thomas saw her return to the house from his rear view.

●●●

He got on the interstate and headed to the motel where Elise waited. Arriving, Thomas knocked gently on the door. She opened it and smiled. *How can I do his to him,* she thought as he entered her room. She stayed up half the night wrestling with whether she should tell him the truth. Elise knew it would end her professional career if she did, but she also got the feeling it might end her life as well. She finally decided she had to play it out to the end. *I only hope I can salvage something with him after he finds out the truth,* Elise hoped knowing it was a long shot.

"What's wrong Elise," Thomas asked her gently seeing how distracted she was.

"Nothing Thomas," she replied trying to smile again.

"Come on, I can see something's wrong," he told her. "What is it?"

Elise sighed deeply.

"Well it's just I know this is our last day together, and I'm not sure when I'll see you again," she replied, only partly telling the truth.

Thomas smiled. "Don't worry about that right now."

"I do have another trip coming up in about three weeks Elise," he said looking at her.

She brightened a little and he felt better.

"Really," Elise asked smiling still.

"Yes, and of course you know I want you to be there," Thomas told her.

Elise wanted him so much. She felt miserable knowing his world was about to crumble. *Well you can make these hours with him count,* she told herself and began to make love to him with renewed fervor. Thomas felt the change in her behavior and figured she was feeling better about what he told her. Thomas relaxed and allowed Elise to have her way with him. She brought him to climax with her mouth. Thomas was in heaven. As soon as he relaxed a few moments Elise was arousing him again. Finally Thomas gave her what she wanted. Elise screamed her pleasure as he brought her to orgasm, sighing deeply as they held each other breathing hard.

"Thomas," she said finally.

He was dozing lightly.

"Hmm," he answered his eyes still closed.

"Promise me that whatever happens between us, you'll always remember the good times we had, OK," Elise said softly.

Thomas opened his eyes and looked at her. *Where did that come from*, he wondered. *Was she trying to tell him something?* Thomas saw from the look on her face it was important to her that he make this promise.

"I promise Elise," he said, gently stroking her face.

She smiled. Thomas kissed her again as his hands began to explore her body setting Elise on fire again. They made love one last time before Thomas showered to leave. Elise lay in bed after he left thinking of her task tonight, and began to cry.

●●●

Kayla arrived at the spa about an hour ago. She was enjoying a warm seaweed body wrap right now, her mind on what she still needed to do. *He doesn't suspect a thing*, she thought, recalling this morning. Kayla wanted to make sure nothing went wrong or alerted Thomas that she was planning to leave. She was afraid of him now. He scared her so badly while they were at the convocation. He hurt her again and again.

Kayla thought back to how he basically raped her in the hotel the first day she arrived. *How could he hurt me like that*, she questioned internally another time. Thomas changed. He became so possessive and jealous. He wasn't that way at first. *Maybe I did something to make him like that*, Kayla thought. She thought about Jackie and their conversation last night. Kayla chuckled thinking of Jackie telling her to snoop in Dante's house.

She admitted she was curious. *He is like Dezi reincarnate. This cannot be a coincidence*, Kayla thought again. She sighed deeply. *I went to his funeral. I saw him in that coffin*, she thought, rationalizing. *Maybe he's a relative*, she tried to reason once more. Kayla knew that was a long shot. She needed to know. She made up her mind she would indeed do some looking while she was there alone. *So what if he is Dezi?* She didn't know what to think. She loved Dezi dearly at one point. She allowed herself to become afraid of him, but she honestly was forced to admit she still cared even then. *Why would he be back? Why is he pretending to be someone else?* Kayla asked, already knowing the answer to both questions. She pushed it from her mind deciding she would deal with it later if need be. Kayla thought about Thomas again and how furious he would be once he found her gone. *I've got to make sure I can get on a plane before he finds me,* Kayla thought, shivering.

She remembered the threat he made. He always said he would never hurt her, but she wasn't so sure. She was going to wait until Saturday and leave because she knew Thomas would be all over the airport and train station tonight. He would look for her everywhere and he would call the police and report her missing. They would detain her and then she would never get away. No, she couldn't allow that to happen. *Just stick with your plan Kayla. If Dante is indeed Dezi you know he's going to get you out of here,* Kayla told herself and began to relax again. If she didn't know anything else, Kayla knew Dezi would move heaven and earth to make sure she was safe. She closed her eyes and began to nap.

Smoke & **25**Mirrors

Jackie was nervous as hell. She was all thumbs today. She was worried sick about Kayla and desperately hoping she got away this time. *Please God help her,* Jackie prayed. She knew Thomas would do something bad to Kayla if he caught her. *He's crazy and he's on a short fuse,* she thought. She watched him become more and more possessive of Kayla over the course of their marriage. He started making her dress like an old woman and wouldn't let her go out much anymore. He told Kayla it wasn't proper behavior for a pastor's wife to be out all the time.

Jackie loathed how Thomas controlled Kayla. Chris tried that crap with her and she hurriedly told him to step off. Kayla was such a sweet person and she genuinely loved Thomas. *Well you blew that didn't you buddy,* Jackie thought bringing a smile to her face. She knew Kayla was very much infatuated with Dante. *Once she finds out who he really is, she's gonna flip,* Jackie thought again. Her cell rang and she was dismayed to see it was Chris.

●●●

"Hello?" she answered.

"Hey Jackie," Chris said calmly.

She knew why he was calling. The messenger service alerted her that they delivered the divorce papers.

"What can I do for you Chris?"

He sighed deeply. He really didn't want to deal with this. He thought Jackie was bluffing when she told him she was going to divorce him.

"What's up with these papers," Chris asked and she heard the edge in his voice.

"Chris, we've been through all this before," Jackie replied tiredly.

"I didn't think you were serious," Chris replied flatly.

"Maybe you should have," Jackie threw back.

What did Chris want from her? He had his other women. He had his church now. Why couldn't he just sign the papers and leave her alone?

"I'm not going to sign these papers Jackie," he told her evenly.

She sighed lightly.

"Why not Chris?"

"Because I still love you," he told her.

Jackie chuckled at that statement.

"Oh really?" she asked becoming angry. "Did you love me while you were screwing those women," she asked angrily.

Chris sighed. He knew Jackie was still hurt and angry. He hoped this time apart would help but he saw that it didn't.

"I'm not giving you this divorce Jackie," he told her again. "Not until you agree to meet with me and talk."

Jackie sighed heavily. She didn't want to do that.

"I'm on my way to Chapel Hill anyway," Chris told her. "I've been trying to reach Thomas to let him know."

Jackie was immediately alarmed. She didn't want Chris talking to Thomas. Neither he nor Kayla knew they were apart and she was sure this would make Thomas stay at home tonight or at the very least make Kayla come with him to church. Jackie couldn't let that happen. Kayla needed to get out of that house.

"OK Chris," she replied. "But not in Chapel Hill."

Chris guessed Jackie didn't tell anyone about the separation which to him was a good sign.

"Where then," he asked.

"South Carolina," Jackie told him. "It's mid-point for us both."

"Okay, that's fine, what time?

She knew it would take her about six hours to drive.

"Hang on a second," Jackie told Chris.

 She quickly checked the internet and found a flight she could get.

"I'll be there around four," she told him.

They agreed on a place.

"I'll see you around five," and Chris told Jackie.

She hung up to find Big D standing there.

"What was that all about," he asked looking at her hard.

Jackie explained the call and why she agreed to meet Chris.

Big D relaxed. "I get it."

"You want me to come with you?" he asked.

"Yes," she smiled.

"But let me talk to him alone, OK," Jackie asked carefully.

"I have no issue with that," Big D told. "But I'll be right there in sight the whole time."

"If he makes a move, that's his ass," Big D added plainly and Jackie believed him.

They embraced and she began to kiss his chest. She wanted him and he responded. They undressed and enjoyed each other right there in the living room. Jackie was lying in his arms afterwards thinking. *I would never give up this man for that bastard Chris, past or no past,* she sighed softly and Big D hugged her tighter. Jackie looked at the clock and closed her eyes. They had a few hours till their flight.

●●●

Rachelle was stressed and it was too early in the morning for all this drama. She was fielding calls all morning from the various pastors and ministers who would be in attendance tonight. She heard the bell ring for the delivery door and sighed.

"What now," Rachelle mumbled as she headed to the door.

She opened it and found the messenger there.

"Ms. Rachelle Fields?"

"Yes."

"Sign here ma'am," he responded.

She signed and thanked him as he closed the door.

"What is this," Rachelle wondered as she opened it.

She found the note inside, smiling as she began to read.

'Dearest Rachelle', it began. 'Here is the DVD I promised. Remember no peeking, and I hope everyone enjoys it. Take care and I miss you. Love, Dante,' Rachelle sighed deeply missing him even more.

She was particularly pleased that he signed it love. *If only we had more time*, she thought. Rachelle took the DVD upstairs and loaded it into the player. She looked for a title so she could have it on the screen. It was simply labeled 'The Truth Revealed'. Rachelle shrugged and thought that must be it. She entered it into display before the DVD began and cued it for 8:00 when everyone would be seated and called to order. She left the sound room, locking the door behind her.

Rachelle returned to her office seeing Thomas come in as she did.

"Good morning Pastor," she said amiably.

Thomas looked up from his mail and returned her greeting smiling.

"Do I have any messages?"

Rachelle laughed and replied, "Only about a million."

He laughed.

"Bring them to me would you?"

She was so busy running around she forgot all about Chris's call. *Well he said he would call back, so whatever,* Rachelle thought again as she went to complete yet another task for tonight. She checked on Thomas again an hour later.

"Pastor," Rachelle asked gently.

His back was to her and she couldn't tell if he was on the phone or not. Thomas turned and she saw he was indeed on the phone. He held up a finger signaling her to wait a moment as he wrapped up the call.

"Yes Rachelle?".

"The film I told you about arrived, and I've cued it to play already," she told him.

"That's fine. How long is it," Thomas inquired.

"Only about thirty minutes I think." Rachelle replied. "I'm going out to lunch now, do you want me to bring you anything?"

"No," he smiled. "You enjoy yourself though."

"I'll be back in about an hour and a half," she told him as she left. "The auto answer is on, so you shouldn't be disturbed," she finished as she saw Thomas pick up the phone to return yet another call.

●●●

Dezi, K.C., and Cedric, were meeting for the final time to go over tonight's festivities.

"Did you get what I asked for," Dezi probed looking at Cedric.

He was searching all day for what Mr. E wanted and only managed to score it an hour ago.

"Yeah, I just found it," Cedric replied.

Dezi smiled. He knew it would be hard to get but he was proud of the young man for securing it.

"How are things on your end," he asked K.C.

"Right as rain," the young man smiled.

"If she doesn't do what she's supposed to, you handle her," Dezi told him plainly.

K.C. knew what that meant and he was down for whatever.

"Not a problem Mr. E," he replied calmly.

Dezi liked K.C. a lot. He reminded him of himself back in the day when he and Dirty were just getting started.

"I'm giving you both one last chance to back out if you want too," Dezi told them evenly sipping his tea.

Both K.C. and Cedric emphatically declined the opportunity.

"The plan is almost the same as before." Dezi started again. "Is everything wired and in place?" he asked K.C. again.

He was the electronics whiz of the two. Cedric was muscle.

"Yeah, it will all be operating when Rev. gets there," K.C. replied. "He won't be able to turn it off."

"You want him tied up," Cedric asked.

That's where he came in. It would be only Thomas and Cedric for a while until K.C. arrived from the church.

"Yes that will be fine to start," he replied.

They continued to talk as they ate lunch. K.C. turned to Dezi and looked at him.

"Mr. E?"

Dezi knew the young man had something on his mind.

"What is it K.C.?

"Me and Cedric are out of here once this is done," he told him. "I don't know where you've been in the world, but we were thinking about going to the coast," he went on. "I was just wondering what you thought about that?"

Dezi sat back in his chair and thought about that time in his life. It was very good to him and Dirty when they were there and he was pretty sure there was still money to be made.

"It sounds like a good idea," he replied.

Dezi went on to tell them a few other things they needed to know about the lifestyle they were choosing to lead. They listened intently taking in every word. K.C. thanked him for the knowledge.

"Well we gotta get up and get moving," Cedric said rising. "We got to get everything and everyone in place so it rolls right."

Dezi nodded his approval.

"Remember gentlemen," he said quietly looking at both of them hard. "Precision and timing are everything."

They nodded their agreement and left the restaurant. Dezi paid the bill and headed to his car. He dialed Big D.

•••

"Wassup man?" Dezi greeted him after he answered.

Big D told him nothing and that they were on their way to the airport.

"Why," he asked concerned.

"The soon to be ex," Big D told Dezi.

He explained how Jackie was deflecting him from calling Thomas and blowing their plans for the evening.

"Good looking out," Dezi replied. "You gonna take him down?"

"Not unless he loses his fucking mind," he replied coldly.

Dezi laughed hoping for his sake; Chris acted like he had some sense.

"That's straight," he replied. "Shout at me when you two make it back to Virginia."

Big D told Dezi he would.

"Have you made a decision yet," he asked referring to their previous conversation.

"We'll be right there on that plan with you and Kayla," Big D laughed.

Dezi laughed too, and then got serious.

"Does she know who I am," he asked, referring to Jackie.

"Yeah, she does," Big D replied.

"Put her on the phone," Dezi said calmly.

Big D handed his cell to Jackie.

"Hi," she said amiably.

Dezi returned her greeting.

"So are you alright with all of this?"

"Dezi, I'm alright with any man who loves Kayla enough to go through all you've gone through to be with her," Jackie replied calmly.

"Just please get her away from Thomas, and don't let him hurt her," she finished softly.

Dezi knew she was scared and upset.

"Count on it Jackie," Dezi told her with that same tone of finality that chilled Jackie before.

She handed the phone back to Big D.

"Alright man, we're at the airport, so I'll hit you up in a few hours," Big D told Dezi as they disconnected.

Jackie thought about how happy Kayla would be once she found out who Dante really was. *Please let everything work out,* Jackie thought as she and Big D boarded their flight headed for South Carolina.

●●●

Chris wanted to make sure he was on time. He made reservations at the hotel closest to the airport. They were meeting at a restaurant not far from there. *If I can just get her back to the hotel,* he thought. Chris knew if they had sex he could hold up the divorce even longer. That's exactly what he wanted. He needed more time. More time to convince Jackie he would change and that he still loved her. Chris sighed deeply thinking of the task ahead as he exited his car and entered the terminal.

167

● ● ●

Thomas called Elise. "Hey," he said cheerfully.

She returned his greeting.

"How's Florida?"

She told him she was flying out after he left headed for the sunshine state.

"It's very nice, hot actually," Elise lied, looking out the window of her hotel room in Chapel Hill.

"Well I just wanted to call and tell you again how much I enjoyed our morning together," Thomas said sweetly.

Elise felt two inches lower than dirt.

"I really enjoyed it too Thomas," she told him softly.

"Thomas," Elise called out, as he was about to disconnect.

"Yes?"

"I love you," she replied almost inaudibly.

Thomas sighed heavily. He knew she felt this way. He wondered if he should just leave well enough alone now and not call Elise anymore.

"I know you can't say it back to me," she told him. "But I just wanted you to know."

"Okay, I understand," Thomas told her. "I'll call you again in a few days."

He hung up still deep in thought.

"What have you started?" he said aloud as he entered the barbershop to get his hair cut.

"Hey Pastor!" Mario, his barber, greeted him.

"Hey Mario, how's it going," Thomas replied smiling and taking a seat.

Thomas was looking forward to tonight. He would make the announcement of the new Assistant Pastor as well as his own announcement of being elevated. He thought of Kayla and decided to check on her.

"Hello honey," she answered cheerfully.

Thomas smiled broadly and Mario teased him.

"You must be talking to Mrs. Bradford," he laughed.

Kayla heard him and starting laughing herself.

"Hey baby," Thomas replied still smiling. "How was the spa?"

She sighed deeply and told him it is wonderful.

"Oh, you're still there," he asked looking at his watch.

It was after three.

"Yes, I'm leaving in about an hour," Kayla replied. "Don't worry I'll be home before you leave tonight."

Thomas laughed and told her okay.

"I love you baby," he said softly and Mario made kissing noises.

Kayla laughed. "Tell Mario to behave."

She disconnected and Thomas told Mario what she said, not realizing she didn't return his declaration of love for the second time today. After his haircut Thomas decided he needed to stop and pick up a new pair of shoes.

He headed to the mall to find the ones he kept in mind. *Guess I'll wear my gray suit tonight,* he formatted as picked up a new tie set. Thomas found the shoes at the last shoe store he visited. *Figures,* he chuckled as he paid for them. He stopped at the jewelers. He wanted to get her something nice. Thomas picked out a lovely gold bangle, having it gift-wrapped. *I owe her this and so much more,* he thought as he took his purchases and headed for his car.

Thomas arrived home shortly afterward and put the gift on the bed. *I can't wait to see her face,* he thought laughing. He looked at the clock. It was five forty-five. *Kayla should be here any moment,* Thomas continued as he stepped into the shower.

Smoke & **26** Mirrors

Dezi arrived home and headed straight for his bar. He endured a long day and he needed a drink. He checked the clock and saw it was after five. *I better get started so I can get outta here,* he internally processed walking upstairs with his drink in hand. Dezi went into his bedroom and pulled out the box he brought with him. He opened it and examined the contents. He took them out and arranged them carefully on his dresser.

Dezi knew Kayla would look around while she was here and he wanted her to see these things. He flipped through the album himself looking at all the photos of them together. Dezi looked at the pictures of the four of them. He thought about taking those out. He didn't want to upset Kayla. In the end he left them, since there were only a few. *Tonight we'll finally be together again baby,* Dezi thought wistfully.

He picked up his cell and called the guys again. He wanted to check one more time. This was too important for anything to go wrong. Her life depended on it and that meant the world to him. Cedric answered and told Dezi everything was indeed still a go.

"I got everything in order Mr. E," he replied. "Believe me this is gonna go down just like you want it too."

"Good, I'll see you later," Dezi thanked Cedric.

He didn't hear from Big D. He hoped there wasn't any trouble. Dezi knew Big D would kill Chris and not think twice about it. He actually chuckled at that thought. Dezi was still itchy to kill Chris himself for what he did to Kayla years ago. Dezi took his cell into the bathroom with him as he prepared for tonight. He pulled out the razor and his contacts holder. *Tonight, Dezi Gianni returns from the dead,* he thought as he began to shave off the beard.

•••

He checked his reflection now that the beard and contacts were gone. *Well, she is definitely going to know who you are now,* he posed. Dezi knew no one else would, but Kayla knew him and she would recognize him in an instant, surgery or no. He continued placing items throughout the house, for her to find, leaving notes giving various directions.

Dezi surmised one of two things would happen. He would find Kayla either waiting for him when he returned home, or, she would leave him a note and be gone. Personally, he was hoping for option number one. Dezi chuckled again and went to gather his toys for the evening. He found the mountain bike in the garage he purchased earlier upon his arrival. He wasn't taking his car. He explained to Kayla that he was riding with a friend, so she wouldn't think his car being here was odd. Dezi began to get excited.

The time was drawing near and all his labor would finally come to fruition. He checked the clock again. It was after six. Dezi went inside and relaxed again. He wanted to check the monitors, but he made it a habit never to see Kayla before he handled business and tonight he was going to definitely be handling some business. Dezi turned on the TV instead and began to watch an old gangster movie he found. *Here's to the good old days,* he thought smiling as he watched.

●●●

Jackie saw Chris get out of the cab and head into the restaurant. Big D was sitting at the end of the counter with a bird's eye view of her table. *If he touches her he's dead,* he thought coldly as he stirred his coffee. Chris spotted Jackie when he walked and headed to her table.

"I'm so sorry I'm late baby," he told her.

Jackie gave him a look but said nothing. She almost left considering Chris was roughly an hour late.

"Well I'm here Chris, so what do you want?"

Chris was pretty much expecting this attitude.

"Baby, please don't be like this," he pleaded gently, giving Jackie his best smile.

She wanted to slap it off his face. Instead she simply sighed and waited on him to speak again.

"Listen I have a room at the hotel about two blocks from here," Chris began as he ignored the look spreading across Jackie's face. "Let's go there so we can talk in private. You know how animated we both can get."

She looked at him for a while and didn't speak. *I know what he really wants to get me there for. Still it might work to our advantage,* Jackie thought.

"I have to run to the restroom Chris," she told him. "I'll give you an answer when I come back," Jackie said, halfway civil.

Chris figured she wanted to mull it over and was buying time.

"Sure baby," he told her smiling.

•••

Jackie got up and headed for the ladies room. Big D saw her and gave her a minute then slipped unnoticed off the stool and headed there too. She pulled him into the ladies room.

"Girl, you trying to get me killed," Big D chuckled.

"No one's in here silly," Jackie giggled.

She told him what Chris wanted and what she thought.

"Sounds like you might be right," he told her.

In a room they could control Chris and keep him on ice until Dezi got Kayla and they knew she was safe.

"OK, here's what we're gonna do," Big D told Jackie as he bent close to her ear.

She exited the ladies room first, gently knocked on the door to let Big D know it was clear, and he eased out. Jackie returned to the table where Chris was enjoying his coffee.

"OK, we can go," she told him then gave him a look. "But don't try anything Chris," she warned.

He smiled warmly and told her that was fine. *Girl, when you see what I've done to that room, oh you'll give me what I want,* Chris thought gleefully. He paid his check and she gathered her purse.

"It's not that far, we can actually walk," Chris told Jackie.

She followed him out the door and they began to walk. Big D already left and was hanging out on the corner as they passed by. Jackie was careful not to look at him. Chris gave him a hateful look and pulled Jackie closer. Big D smiled at Chris and turned his head. He slowly counted to twenty, turned and followed them.

•••

Chris was right. The hotel was only a couple blocks away. Big D watched them to see which room they entered. They agreed he would wait a few moments and then knock on the door. Jackie was to let Chris answer. Big D would take it from there. Chris opened the door and Jackie walked in. *Wow, this would really be nice if I still gave a damn*, she thought seeing all the care he put into making it romantically appealing. He bought her a dozen long stem red roses that were beautifully arranged in a vase.

There was wine on ice. The bed was covered in a single layer of pink rose petals. The drapes were still drawn and he put candles around the room to give it a softly romantic glow.

"This is nice Chris," Jackie said trying to sound convincing.

He smiled, happy that she liked it.

"It's all for you honey," Chris said softly coming up behind Jackie and putting his arms around her.

"Stop," she said simply and stepped away.

He was hurt but undeterred.

"Would you like some wine," Chris asked cordially.

"Sure," Jackie told him and he went to get it for her.

Big D checked his watch. Eight minutes passed. *That's long enough buddy*, he thought as he headed for the door knocking forcefully.

"Who the hell could that be," Chris asked testily heading for the door.

He tried to look out of the peephole but couldn't see anyone. He cracked the door and Big D pushed Chris back forcefully. He was in and top of him before Chris could react. Big D put the knife he lifted from the restaurant to his throat, effectively ending any thoughts of a fight he may have had.

"Get up," Big D ordered him coldly.

Chris looked at Jackie who was calmly sipping her glass of wine. *What the hell is this*, he wondered.

"You got that tape baby," Big D asked Jackie.

She got up and pulled the duct tape out of her purse. They bought it earlier upon arrival, just in case. Chris was incredulous.

"Tape him up," Big D told Jackie.

She taped his hands and feet binding him to the chair he was sitting in.

"Why are you doing this," Chris asked Jackie as she bound him.

She didn't answer until she finished.

"Because you were once again about to mess everything up," Jackie replied evenly.

He looked at her quizzically.

"Chris I am divorcing you," she said plainly. "Whether you sign or not is irrelevant," she continued. "I'll still get it," Jackie finished for a moment as she walked over to Big D.

They kissed and Jackie handed Big D the other glass of wine. *Who the hell is this guy,* Chris wondered looking hard at him.

"What are you talking about mess everything up," he asked looking at Jackie again.

"Kayla is finally going to get away from Thomas," she said plainly.

Chris was confused. Jackie laughed seeing his face.

"Oh, you didn't know?" she said and they both laughed.

"Thomas is a bastard," she said plainly. "He's been abusing Kayla on a daily basis. He's hit her. He's kept her prisoner for the last month, but tonight she is going to get out and be free," Jackie told him. "You calling Thomas and telling him about our divorce would have only made him keep her that much closer," she went on. "I couldn't allow that Christopher," Jackie stared at him hard.

"Between the two of you there has been a lot of pain to me and Kayla," she started again. "I know what you did to her too," she told Chris coldly.

His mouth dropped.

"Yeah, I've known about it for a while now," Jackie continued. "You were a dog then, and you're a dog now."

Big D came and put his arm around Jackie.

"It's okay baby," he told her gently.

Big D came over to Chris and stood directly in front of him.

"You're going to sit right here until I make a call and find out that Kayla is safe, and out of that house," Big D told him matter-of-fact. "Then, Jackie and I are going to leave you loose enough to free yourself," he went on. "Now, you can do something stupid, like try to follow us, or call the folks, or you can do the smart thing, and go home with your life still intact," Big D finished coldly.

Chris looked at the man and knew he meant what he said.

"Do you really hate me that much Jackie," he asked quietly.

She turned to Chris, acid in her eyes.

"Yes," she told him

Big D smiled and shrugged. He gagged Chris and went to join Jackie on the bed. Chris couldn't believe she was doing this to him. *Thomas has lost his damned mind,* he thought. *How could he do all that stuff to Kayla,* he thought again. Chris remembered Thomas did time on a charge against him and was on probation. He just never thought Thomas would ever harm Kayla. Chris heard giggling and looked up to see Jackie and Big D playing with each other. He turned his eyes to the TV. He didn't want to see that. Jackie found herself getting aroused as Big D played around with her. He saw it and called her on it.

Chris heard them begin to kiss. He heard Jackie moaning softly. Then Chris heard the familiar sounds as they made love. Chris closed his eyes to block the image in his mind as the tears rolled down his cheeks.

Smoke & 27 Mirrors

Thomas emerged from his shower finding Kayla sitting on the bed admiring her new gift.

"Thomas it's beautiful," she breathed smiling at him.

He smiled back as he went to hug her.

"You're more than welcome baby," Thomas told Kayla as he kissed her. "Mm, you smell good."

She giggled.

"It's the seaweed wrap," Kayla replied.

"Makes me hungry," Thomas replied starting to get aroused.

"Baby you'll be late," Kayla gently rebuffed him.

He looked at the clock and saw she was right. It was already 6:20. *Damn!* Thomas thought. He really wanted to make love to her, but it would have to wait until he got home tonight.

"So what are you going to do with yourself tonight," he asked as he continued to dress.

"I have two movies set for watching," Kayla giggled. "I'm going to make myself some popcorn and climb into bed," she finished still admiring her bangle.

Thomas was amused. Kayla was so much like a child sometimes. He loved it. She was totally innocent to some things and he liked that quality about her. He finally finished dressing as she came back upstairs with her bowl.

"You look good, Pastor Bradford," Kayla said sensuously.

Thomas hated that he didn't have time to be with her. He really wanted to be.

"Thanks baby," he told her in between kisses.

"You better go now," Kayla told him softly.

Thomas saw the lust in her eyes and decided he better go too.

"Promise you'll be up when I get home," Thomas asked as she walked him downstairs.

"Only if you promise the same," Kayla told him mischievously.

He laughed and told her she had a deal.

"Bye baby, have a great evening watching your movies," Thomas told Kayla giving her one final hug and kiss.

She watched him get into his car and waved as he backed out. She closed the door and ran up the stairs. *OK, Kayla get yourself together,* she thought grabbing her bag and throwing in her change of clothes and night things. Kayla grabbed a few toiletries, the albums and mementos she vowed to take. She looked at the bracelet he just gave her. *Guilt offering no doubt,* Kayla thought as she put it back on the dresser. She took out the letter she wrote last night and carefully hid. Kayla removed the wedding rings and began to walk downstairs. She looked outside and saw Thomas hadn't returned.

"Thank you," she said quietly aloud.

Kayla looked at the house they shared together these last three years. Her gaze fell on their wedding portrait. Her eyes filled thinking how happy she was that day. She sighed sadly thinking how totally wrong it all went. Kayla shook herself before she got melancholy and changed her mind. *You can't stay Kayla. He won't change,* she told herself sighing again. Kayla placed the letter on the table, with the rings on top of it. She went to her car and got in; deciding she would swing by the hotel first and check out her room, maybe turn on the air so it would be comfortable when she returned. Kayla took one last look at the house and drove away. She couldn't stop the overwhelming sadness she felt or the tears that fell. She took a deep breath and continued driving until she reached the hotel.

●●●

Kayla stopped at the front desk to retrieve her key.

"K. DeWitt," she told the clerk when he inquired about the name the reservation was in.

The clerk smiled and handed Kayla a key. She paid in cash as to not leave a trail for Thomas to follow. Kayla found her room easily and saw there was another stairwell that would lead her directly to the parking lot. *I'll leave that way,* she thought, not wanting to call any more attention to herself than necessary. She was nervous even though she knew he didn't realize she was even gone yet. She turned down the bed and put the air on low. She filled her ice bucket and put the top back on it, grabbed her room key and headed back out. She was on her way to Dante's.

Kayla found the house easily, shocked at how close Dante actually was to her all these months. She found the remote and keys where he told her they would be. She opened the garage and parked inside. She wasn't surprised by his car being there, he told her about his meeting and him riding with someone else. Kayla opened the door and walked in. The house was absolutely marvelous. She loved the Italian marble tile and the custom window treatments. She found a note on the counter. 'Kayla, please make yourself at home. If you wish to lie down, my room is the first one on the left.' She smiled at Dante's obvious attempt to get her in bed. She wasn't sure it wouldn't happen; she just needed to talk to him first. Kayla saw the pineapple on the table. It was fresh and sitting in ice waiting for her. She saw another note telling her the same. She was confused again. *How did he know I love fresh pineapple?* Kayla thought again. *Dezi knew,* her mind answered for her. She took it and went into the den.

She loved the layout. There was huge projection TV and two overstuffed recliners with a matching love seat. *It was exactly like –,* Kayla stopped, realizing the entire house so far, was almost identical to either hers or Dezi's house back in the day. She pushed it from her mind. She didn't want to deal with the possibility right now. Kayla ate her pineapple and watched TV. She looked at the clock it was 8:15. She guessed Dante would be home soon.

After she finished her fruit, Kayla decided she wanted to go upstairs. She stood at the bottom of the spiral case, which was also identical to the one from Dezi's home before. *Are you ready for what you may find when you ascend these stairs,* Kayla questioned, taking a deep breath, placing her foot on the first step.

●●●

Thomas was calling everyone to order. They started a little late. Elise watched him intently. She found a seat in the back out of the light. She didn't want to be here, but it was what she was paid to do. K.C. was sitting a row behind Elise. He saw her come in. He was here to make sure she did her part, and to make sure the electronics worked correctly for tonight.

K.C. smiled. Once the DVD began to play no one except him would be able to stop it. He looked at Pastor Bradford standing there looking all sanctimonious and upright. *Fucking hypocrite,* K.C. thought to himself. Mr. E was kind enough to enlighten him to what was on the DVD. *Everybody will see the real you tonight Mr. Man,* he thought again waiting on the lights to dim.

●●●

Rachelle was impressed with the turnout. *Guess everyone is curious who our new Assistant Pastor will be,* She thought. *Thomas is looking pretty good tonight himself,* she thought looking him over. Rachelle wondered where Kayla was. He usually made her come with him lately. *Guess she found a way to get out of it this week,* she thought chuckling lightly.

"Tonight everyone, we've been blessed with a wonderful spiritual film, which will help us recognize our purpose and mission in this walk with God," Thomas was telling the audience as the giant screens began to descend from the ceiling.

There were three identical screens so that everyone in the sanctuary held a bird's eye view of them. Elise began to feel sick. *Please let something, anything, go wrong right now,* she prayed not wanting this to happen. K.C. sat up on the edge of his seat. He was waiting for the lights to dim and his aunt to hit the play button. *Come on let's do this,* he thought excitedly. K.C. remembered what Mr. E told him and calmed himself.

"Anxiety will mess up a perfect plan and get you killed quickly," he told them both about this business.

K.C. took a deep breath and continued to listen to Thomas drone on. He checked his watch. It was 7:59.

"So, everyone sit back and enjoy this short feature," Thomas went on. "I'm sure we will all find it enlightening," he continued. "It's entitled, The Truth Revealed," he finished and asked that the house lights be dimmed.

K.C. almost laughed out loud when he said the name of the film. *Boy you have no idea Rev,* he thought cheerfully. The lights finally dimmed and Rachelle pressed the play button. First a black screen came up with the name of the film and that it was a G-man production.

The next frame splashed on the screen and there in living color and stereo sound, Pastor Bradford was having sex with Elise in his hotel room. *Here we go,* K.C. chuckled inside as the audience began to erupt with gasps, screams, heckles and even a few curses. Mothers were covering their children's ears and eyes. Most of the men stared enraptured or obviously envious of the action they saw their pastor getting.

Rachelle was speechless. She was trying to stop the movie, but her remote wasn't working. She looked up to the sound both trying to tell them to cut the movie. Larry couldn't understand. He was continually pressing the stop button but the DVD just kept going.

Elise was in tears as one of the members sitting near her recognized her and called her out. Thomas's mouth was hanging open. His eyes were glazed over. He was absolutely livid. *The bitch set me up!*

"What do you have to say for yourself Thomas?!" one of the visiting Bishops was yelling at him.

He turned to the man, the look on his face making him back off and leave him alone. Thomas turned and strode purposefully from the pulpit to his office. K.C. saw him and figured he was headed for home. Thomas went into his office and retrieved the handgun he kept in his desk. *I'm ruined. My career is in shambles. My reputation is gone,* he thought as his glance fell on the photo of Kayla he kept on his desk.

"Oh my god," Thomas said alarmed.

What if they sent her a copy, he thought, terrified of the prospect. Thomas bolted out of the office and ran into three of the deacons.

"Pastor, we want to talk to you right now!" the one said.

Thomas gave the man a look and showed him the gun. They all scattered quickly and let him pass. He headed for his car and gunned it heading for his house.

K.C. rescued Elise from the mob by now and was waiting with her in his car. He saw Thomas leave and called Cedric.

"Yeah?"

"He's on his way," K.C. told him.

"Got it," he replied and they disconnected.

K.C. glanced at Elise as he drove to the Bradford home. She was still crying softly.

"What you crying for," he asked harshly. "Ain't this what you get paid to do?"

Elise didn't answer him. He could never understand how deeply she felt for Thomas. She just sighed and continued to look out of the window.

"Weak ass bitch," K.C. said half aloud.

●●●

Cedric heard the car screeching to a halt in the driveway. He stayed in his hiding spot. He had a clear view of the area he knew Thomas would be in.

They put everything in the den so they would know where he was and have clear advantage and leverage. Thomas came tearing into the house.

"Kayla!!" he screamed. "Honey, where are you?!"

Cedric saw the gun in Thomas's hand and knew he would have to be careful. Thomas was frantic. He heard noise coming from the den. He headed in and stopped in his tracks. The DVD was playing and he and Elise were repeating again and again.

"Oh god, please no," Thomas said stunned.

He saw the rings first, then the letter.

"Baby no," he said again still subdued.

She's gone Thomas, he thought as he laid the gun on the table and picked up the rings. Thomas held them in his hands. *Kayla never takes these off,* he thought. *She saw this damned movie and she left.* He remembered Kayla telling him she could never forgive him cheating on her.

"I've got to find her," he said aloud.

Cedric continued to watch. Thomas gingerly put her rings down and picked up the letter. He sat in the chair, his back still to Cedric, and read it. Kayla was indeed gone and she wasn't coming back. She told Thomas how much he hurt her, and she couldn't forgive him for it. She wanted her own life back, and to please leave her alone.

"I can't do that baby," he said, his voice full of pain.

Cedric decided it was time, creeping up behind Thomas and hitting him hard over the head with the butt of the gun. The big man went down like a crumpled bag. Cedric struggled but got him transferred to the kitchen chair and securing him to it, called Mr. E.

"Yes," Dezi answered pleasantly.

Cedric chuckled at how calm he was yet again.

"He's ready for you," he told Mr. E.

"Excellent," Dezi told him. "Call me once K.C. and Elise, arrive."

"You got it," Cedric told Mr. E and hung up.

Cedric took out the rest of the equipment as he waited for K.C. He put the things in order on the table as Mr. E instructed. He looked at the drug and the syringe and shivered. *I don't know what he's gonna do to you man, but better you than my ass,* Cedric thought, looking at the unconscious man. He heard K.C pull up. They entered the house shortly afterwards.

•••

Elise ran to Thomas and checked him.

"He's alright," Cedric said testily. "He's just unconscious," he added, sucking his teeth.

She rolled her eyes at both of them. They laughed.

"Bitch whatever," Cedric said.

They both took a drink from the bottle K.C. brought with him. Mr. E told them to only have one though. You never wanted to be lit when you handled business. It made you sloppy and less precise.

"You made the call," K.C. asked still giving Elise an evil look.

Cedric hit the dial pad again.

"Yes," Dezi answered still pleasant.

"The gangs all here," Cedric replied and they both chuckled.

"I'm on my way," Dezi said coolly.

Cedric looked at K.C.

"Well it's on now," he replied and they both exchanged knowing smiles.

Elise felt a cold chill run down her spine.

Smoke & 28 Mirrors

Big D and Jackie were still sleeping. Chris methodically worked his way out of the tape. He looked at them to make sure they didn't see him. *I've got to get the hell out of here,* Chris thought. He needed to call Thomas and warn him of Kayla's plans. He figured they may be having problems, but Chris knew Thomas loved her without a doubt. He deserved a chance to try and work it out.

He felt the last of the tape give and his hands were free. Chris carefully removed the tape from his ankles and feet. He needed to get to the door and out of it without them waking. They didn't put the chain or the bolt on, so all he would need to do would be to turn the knob. He still held his cell and his wallet in his pocket. They hadn't bothered to take anything from him.

Jackie stirred and Chris sat back up in the chair. She didn't wake and soon was still and breathing evenly again. The man never stirred at all. Chris slowly rolled the chair closer to the door. He was close enough now to reach out and touch the knob. He slowly put his hand out.

"Feeling lucky are we," Big D said evenly looking at him, the knife in his hands.

Chris turned to face the voice.

"Why don't you just relax? This will all be over soon enough," he said again without emotion.

Jackie was awake by this time.

"I bet you were gonna call Thomas and warn him weren't you," she asked looking at Chris hard.

He didn't say anything.

"Baby, go and get us something to eat," Big D told her.

"Are you sure," Jackie asked looking at Chris.

Big D smiled.

"Yeah," he replied. "Cause unless hubby here wants you to be a widow, he'll behave himself," Big D finished as he sat up against the headboard.

"OK," she replied getting dressed, and grabbing some money from her purse.

"What do you want honey," Jackie asked Big D.

He gave her his order.

"What do you want Chris," she asked him amiably enough.

He answered and Jackie said she would be right back. Once they were alone Chris started to talk.

"Who are you anyway?" he asked curiously.

"I'm Jackie's new man," Big D smiled.

"Why are you helping her ruin a marriage?"

Big D laughed again.

"Man, please," he replied. "Your boy did that all by himself," he went on. "I've known Kayla since the coast."

Chris was stunned. This wasn't one of the men who came to his apartment, he knew that much.

"She's good people, and she didn't deserve none of the bullshit your boy was dishing," Big D finished angrily.

Chris decided to leave well enough alone.

"You know you can walk away from this shit," Big D told him. "We aren't looking to do anything to you. Just sign the papers man and live your life."

Chris admitted right now it didn't look very good for him.

"I didn't bring them with me," he said honestly.

Big D sighed.

"It's OK. Jackie has her set," he replied as she came back with their food.

They ate silently.

"Jackie," Chris said quietly.

She looked at him with raised eyebrows instead of an answer.

"Give me the divorce papers," Chris told her.

Jackie looked at Big D. He didn't say anything. She got up and took the papers from her purse and gave them to Chris. He asked for a pen, which she also supplied. Chris took the papers and laid them on the table flipping to the ones that needed his signature. He signed them all and handed Jackie the papers and the pen back.

"There," Chris said simply and returned to his soft drink.

She was stunned. *What the hell happened in here while I was gone?*

"Thank you Chris," she said kindly.

"You wanna watch the game," Big D asked Chris.

He nodded yes, too full of emotion to speak. Big D flipped the set and they all began to watch. *Please let me get out of here alive,* Chris prayed as he watched the blur in front of him.

●●●

Kayla sat down on Dante's bed. The room made her dizzy. It was almost identical to hers from long ago. The chaise lounge, the colors, everything was almost exact. Kayla saw the album on the dresser. She picked it up and began to flip through the pages. She saw photos of them together. Kayla saw photos of Taea and she began to smile. There were pictures of the four of them together. Her mind began to go back and she began to remember. Kayla felt the tears stinging her eyes.

"It is him," she said softly aloud.

She didn't know how to feel. Kayla thought Dezi was dead. She made her heart accept that. Now he was back and wanted her to open it again. She thought of what he told her time and time again. *I'll never let anyone hurt you baby,* he said with that look of determination. Everything began to make sense. He came back for her. *Thank goodness he did,* Kayla thought wondering what she would have done if she never met him again. Thomas was making her life hell. Jackie was gone. Mariah and Aidan were gone. *Oh my God Aidan!* He didn't know who Dezi was. How would he react when he found out? Kayla laughed softly thinking how Dezi worked everything out. She was almost positive he was the one to pay for their school and their home. Kayla looked at the other things he left for her.

"He's really here," Kayla said again belief starting to sink in.

Where is he now, she wondered, a frightening reality settling in. *Thomas.* Kayla knew Dezi would kill Thomas if he thought he hurt her. She thought about it and relaxed a little. Dezi didn't know any of the cruel things Thomas did to her. He only knew that Thomas was over protective. So maybe he was actually out handling business. Kayla looked at the clock. It was after ten. She was starting to get tired. She went to the car and retrieved her bag and headed to the shower.

●●●

185

Dezi arrived and entered the house. K.C. and Cedric greeted him. They were taken aback at his appearance. He shaved the beard off and they saw his eyes were gray not green.

"Wake him up," he said calmly glancing at Thomas then turning his attention to Elise.

She saw Dezi look at her and the blood ran cold in her veins. Cedric took the smelling salts and held it under Thomas's nose. He woke with a start finding himself bound to the chair. Both K.C. and Cedric wore masks. Dezi didn't. Thomas saw them all standing around. He spotted Elise sitting on the couch and glared at her. Dezi saw him and laughed.

"Well now, that's no way to greet your lover, now is it," he chastised Thomas.

Elise looked away. She couldn't bear the hatred and raw anger she saw in Thomas's face. She knew he felt betrayed and she was guilty.

"Who are you," Thomas asked evenly looking at the man in front of him.

Dezi chuckled.

"Your worst fucking nightmare," he said plainly.

K.C. and Cedric laughed.

"What is this about," Thomas asked again, undeterred by the man's attitude.

"What's this," Dezi asked ignoring him, picking up the rings and letter.

"Looks like the missus saw the movie, huh," he asked laughing again.

Thomas was livid.

"Look, whatever the hell you want just take it and let me out of here!"

Dezi feigned indignation.

"Well!" he replied. "Such language, and from a man of the cloth no less," he got right up in Thomas's face and spoke.

"This is over when I say it is and not a moment before," Dezi told him coldly.

Thomas looked at the man and saw there was no emotion in him. His eyes were cold and flat and his tone was ice cold continually. Even when he laughed there was no warmth.

"Please," Thomas said quietly.

Dezi knew what was on his mind.

"Bet you would like to get out of here and go look for Kayla wouldn't you?"

Thomas looked at him hard.

"How do you know my wife," he asked through clenched teeth.

Dezi returned the stare.

"Because Kayla was mine before you, or that bastard Black, took her from me," he replied evenly.

K.C. and Cedric exchanged glances again. No wonder Mr. E was so meticulous about the plans. This was the second old score he wanted to settle.

"What the hell are you talking about," Thomas spat, angry all over again that this man was even talking about his wife like this.

"You know who I am," Dezi told him. "You may not know much about me, but I know Kayla has mentioned me."

"The eyes remind you of anyone you know," he asked coldly.

Thomas felt a shiver run down his spine. Dezi saw him remember.

"That's right Preacher man," he said, sitting down and crossing his legs. "I'm Dezi Gianni."

"That's not possible," Thomas returned flatly.

But look at those damned gray eyes. He's got to be who he says he is, Thomas thought. Dezi laughed again.

"Well it is preacher," he returned simply. "Would you like to know where your wife is right now," he asked, looking at him intently.

Thomas didn't want to think about it. Dezi connected the cell to the amplifier K.C. made for it and dialed Kayla's number.

"Hello?"

"Hi," Dezi said softly never taking his eyes off Thomas.

"Where are you," Kayla asked.

"Still in my meeting," he replied. "Are you alright?"

"Yes, I'm fine," she replied.

Thomas thought his heart would explode from the pain he was feeling right at this moment knowing Kayla was at this man's home.

"What part of the house are you in," Dezi asked still watching Thomas intently.

K.C and Cedric were once again enthralled at the expertise this man possessed. Elise was hurting for Thomas, but secretly hoping he would turn to her now.

"I'm in the bedroom," Kayla said simply.

Thomas gasped.

"What was that," she asked, hearing the sound.

"Nothing," Dezi replied giving Thomas a warning look. "Did you find what I left for you?"

Kayla sighed softly.

"Yes," She replied.

"I'll be home soon," Dezi told her.

"OK, I have a lot of questions," Kayla told him again.

"Are you staying with me tonight," he asked, still watching Thomas's pain.

She was quiet for a moment. *Please say no Kayla,* Thomas was pleading in his heart.

"Yes," Kayla said softly.

"You know I love you, don't you," Dezi asked, further driving the stake into Thomas's heart, hopes and dreams.

"Yes Dezi, I know," she replied.

The tears Thomas tried to hold spilled down his cheeks. Satisfied that he successfully proved his point Dezi told Kayla he would see her soon.

"The remote for the TV is in the drawer of the nightstand," Dezi told her, and Kayla giggled.

"How did you know I was looking for it?"

"Because I know you," he told her smiling.

Kayla laughed and hung up. Elise noticed for the first time, what an attractive man Dezi was, especially when he smiled. *Too bad he's certifiable and dangerous,* she thought, turning her attention back to Thomas.

Dezi looked at him. He was obviously miserable.

"Believe me now," he asked still watching him.

"Why," Thomas asked his voice filled with pain.

"Because she should have never been without me," Dezi went on. "Obviously you didn't know how to treat her. Look at the shit you did to her," he told Thomas coldly. "Hitting her? What the hell were you thinking," he said still calm. "You practically pushed her back into my arms. Or should I say into Dante's arms," Dezi finished, chuckling, as Thomas looked at him again.

"So, now what," Thomas asked.

Dezi looked at him for a moment.

"Well first you're going to sign these divorce papers and give Kayla her freedom," he said evenly, motioning Cedric, who brought the papers to Thomas.

He didn't want to sign them. To sign them would mean he lost and Thomas didn't want to admit defeat. He wanted, no needed, another chance to make it right with Kayla.

"What if I refuse to sign them?"

Dezi sighed.

"Well that's up to you. Me personally, I hope you don't. Then I can just kill you and make her a widow. Much easier and quicker," he continued calmly. "Really, it's up to you."

Thomas thought about it and decided if he could stay alive, he could always find Kayla and get her back. She didn't love this guy, she was just scared and he took advantage of her. He sighed deeply.

"Alright I'll sign," Thomas said dejectedly.

Dezi signaled Cedric who removed the cuffs, while K.C. kept his .10mm trained on him. Thomas took the papers and the pen given, signing them. Cedric cuffed him again and handed the papers to Dezi who looked them over and put them back into the envelope.

"That's very good Thomas," he said coldly.

Dezi looked over at Elise.

"Why don't you tell the good Reverend who you are really?" he told her calmly. "He deserves that much don't you think," Dezi finished eyeing her evenly.

She didn't want to do this. Elise was hoping that someway somehow she could salvage her relationship with Thomas. She looked at Thomas to find him still glaring at her. She dropped her gaze to the floor.

"I'm a professional decoy," Elise said quietly.

"Tell him what that means Elise," Dezi said plainly.

She took another deep breath before answering.

"I try to seduce men for their wives or girlfriends to see if they'll be faithful," Elise said again.

She hated every minute of this. Dezi smiled at her discomfort.

"What's wrong Elise?" Dezi baited her. "You've never been like this on any of your other jobs."

She began to cry softly.

"Tell the man why you're crying," Dezi told her.

She shook her head no.

"Tell the man why you're crying Elise," Dezi said again, colder than before.

His tone scared her. Elise looked at Dezi and the look scared her even more.

"He already knows," she replied, but said it again anyway. "I'm in love with him."

Thomas was still looking at Elise hard. *She has cost you everything,* he thought as he looked at her. He hated her. *She was the worst thing he ever did in his life,* Thomas thought miserably, not wanting to take responsibility still, for his own actions.

"Well, what do you think about that Preacher man," Dezi asked Thomas looking at him as he watched Elise.

"She's not Kayla," Thomas said flatly, which made Elise cry even more.

"Well, on that we agree," Dezi told him.

Dezi picked up the medicine bottle and filled the syringe. He walked over to Thomas and rolled up the sleeve of his shirt. Dezi injected him and stepped back.

"What was that," Thomas asked afraid, thinking it was some type of poison.

Dezi looked at him again but didn't answer. He sat down and closed his eyes for a moment. K.C. and Cedric were almost beside themselves with glee. *This is great!* Cedric was thinking.

"I've given you a drug that will paralyze you," Dezi said matter-of-fact. "You won't be able to move but you'll be able to see, hear, and feel everything that happens to you and around you."

Dezi stood up and strode over to Elise. He snatched her to her feet and brought her toward Thomas.

"This is what you gave up Kayla for," he told him calmly as he pushed Elise to her knees.

Thomas gave her a distasteful look and turned his attention back to Dezi.

"Undress him," Dezi told her looking at Thomas.

Elise pulled his pants and shorts down saying she couldn't finish because of the restraints. Dezi told Cedric to remove them. He knew the drug was in effect now. They removed the restraints and Thomas couldn't move. Elise finished taking his clothes off. Thomas was completely naked now.

"So fuck him," Dezi told her coldly.

Elise sighed and began to arouse Thomas. She got him hard in a matter of minutes and mounted him. Elise looked into his eyes and saw nothing. She was heartbroken. She rode Thomas until she felt him finish. Elise softly caressed his face and looked into his eyes again trying to show him the love she felt for him. Thomas stared back blankly. Dezi snatched Elise off and threw her to the floor.

"Now, I could just go ahead and kill you, couldn't I," he asked quietly.

Thomas was scared.

"But that would be too easy," he finished. "I have something far better in mind," Dezi told him smiling slyly.

Thomas relaxed a little as his mind went back on the day's events. He was effectively ruined in ministry, ruined financially since that was his livelihood, his marriage was ruined, what else could this man possibly do to him, he continued thinking. Dezi looked at Thomas, again effectively reading his thoughts.

"Oh trust me, it can get worse," he told him. "And for you, it will. See the nice thing about this drug, its untraceable in your blood stream," he went on. "It will wear off in about half an hour and no one will ever believe your story," Dezi finished smiling coldly again.

What is this guy plotting?.

"They'll find you in your wife's house, with your dead mistress," he finished plainly.

Elise looked at Dezi, comprehension dawning. She tried to get up and run. K.C. pushed her back into the room and to her knees.

"They'll find your semen inside her, and decide you killed her in the heat of passion," Dezi continued. "You'll be locked up for the rest of your natural life."

Thomas tried to speak, it was difficult, but he managed.

"I can't," he struggled to get out.

Dezi laughed.

"Of course you can," he said as he put the gun in Thomas's hand and held it with his own, gloved hand.

Dezi aimed it at Elise.

"No!" she screamed "Please don't do this!"

Dezi pulled the trigger, and the first bullet hit her in the stomach. Elise gasped for air. He pulled the trigger again, and hit her in the chest. She fell back spread eagle on the floor. A single tear rolled down Thomas's cheek. Dezi told K.C. to check Elise. She wasn't breathing, and he couldn't hear a heartbeat when he put his ear to her chest.

"She's dead," K.C. said plainly, as he picked up their equipment.

"Well preacher man, I would love to stay a while, but there is a very beautiful woman waiting at home for me," Dezi told him.

"Remember, I can get to you if it crosses your mind to try and bring Kayla into this," he said acidly. "You can feel free to tell them about me though," Dezi laughed.

Thomas knew why he said that. *Who's going to believe me when I say a dead man came into my house, drugged me, and killed my mistress*, he thought sadly as he watched them get ready to leave.

Cedric dialed 911 before they walked out and hung up. He knew that would bring them out and they would find what they were intended to find.

Dezi walked back to his bike. The two men left together all three meeting at the arranged spot. Dezi handed them the briefcase he put there and thanked them.

"Good luck fellas," he told them.

They told him thanks and they appreciated everything he'd taught them. They took the bike for disposal and Dezi walked the half-mile back to his house. They already removed all the surveillance equipment from the house so there was nothing to link back. Dezi quietly went to the fridge and got the strawberries. He smiled and headed upstairs to his room.

Smoke & **29** Mirrors

Kayla heard Dezi come in. She made it a point to stay awake. She wanted to see him, to touch him, to make him tell her what in the world was going on. She heard the door open and looked up. Dezi looked into her eyes as he entered the room. He smiled lovingly and walked over to her. He put the tray on the nightstand and turned to her. Kayla put her hands on Dezi's face and looked at him.

"It's really you," she said softly looking into his eyes.

He smiled again, and she traced the dimples with her fingers. Her eyes filled, and the tears were threatening to overflow.

"Yes baby," Dezi returned gently. "It's me, I'm here for you," he told Kayla, as he kissed her softly.

The dam broke and she began to cry. Dezi took her into his arms and held her, letting her release. Kayla pulled herself together and looked at him again.

"I don't understand," she said quietly, her eyes searching his.

Dezi sighed softly, and kissed her again.

"I promise to answer all your questions," he told her. "I want to get a shower, OK?"

Kayla nodded yes and Dezi kissed her once more. He got up and began to undress as he headed into the shower.

"Call Jackie and let her know you're here and you're safe," he told her as he went inside the bathroom and closed the door.

Kayla was still so confused. *He's alive. My God all these years he's been alive,* she thought still slightly askew. She sighed deeply and picked up her cell. Kayla looked at the clock as the phone connected. It was almost midnight. She knew Jackie would forgive her.

●●●

Jackie heard her phone go off. She looked at Big D and they exchanged looks. She saw that it was Kayla.

"Hello," Jackie answered anxiously.

"Hey girl," Kayla replied.

"Are you alright," Jackie asked again still concerned.

"Yes I'm fine. I'm here with –," Kayla stopped not knowing what to call him now.

"Dezi," Jackie finished for her.

Kayla was stunned. She knew too?

"How," was all she could manage to ask.

"He told me," Jackie responded.

Jackie also told her about herself and Big D, and that she was actually in Virginia all the time she was gone. Kayla sighed. It seemed everyone was throwing her off balance.

"I'm so confused right now Jackie," she told her honestly.

"I know you are, but listen," Jackie began. "This man loves you like nothing I've ever known in my life," she went on. "I know at one time you loved him too, and obviously from the instant chemistry when you thought he was Dante, you still do."

Kayla sighed again knowing Jackie was right. She was just scared.

"Everything is so perfect Jackie, I'm just scared it's not real," she told her.

Jackie smiled. She knew what Kayla was feeling.

"Honey, you know it's okay to feel that way," she began. "Just don't allow it to take you over. Enjoy what this man has done for you, and how he makes you feel," she told her. "In a few days you'll be gone from there and you'll never have to look back."

Kayla told her she was right.

"I can't wait to get to the sun, and sand, and water," Kayla told her wistfully. "I can't wait to see the kids and Livvy," she giggled.

Jackie laughed and told her she understood.

"I have a surprise for you," she said slyly.

Kayla was intrigued.

"What," she asked excitedly.

"I'll be seeing you soon," Jackie told her.

Kayla squealed with delight.

"Really? You're coming to visit?"

"Something like that," Jackie chuckled.

Kayla caught what she wasn't saying.

"Really Jackie," she breathed, not wanting to be wrong.

"Yes, really," Jackie replied.

"You and D," Kayla asked again.

Jackie told her yes. Kayla was beside herself. She hadn't been this happy in a long time.

•••

She heard the bathroom door open and looked up. Dezi was emerging clad only in a towel. Kayla took in him lustfully. *My god he is just as fine as the first time I met him,* she thought. He walked over to the bed and sat by her as she talked. Dezi began kissing her neck softly, and she found it harder and harder to concentrate on her conversation.

"Are you listening to me," Jackie asked Kayla after she didn't answer for a moment.

"Huh? Yeah I'm listening," Kayla replied as Dezi began kissing her lips.

Jackie heard the sounds and chuckled.

"I think I should let you go now," she began still laughing. "Looks like you're about to be very busy."

Dezi took the phone and spoke.

"Bye Jackie, tell D I'll call him tomorrow," he said and disconnected.

Dezi threw the phone on the nightstand and returned to her. He was kissing her and touching her. Kayla was completely engulfed in the things Dezi was doing to her. Her hands were caressing his body. He felt so good to her again after all these years.

"I've missed you so much baby," he said softly, as he gently licked her nipples.

Kayla was totally aroused. Dezi began to move lower, pleasuring her in a most sensual way. She was breathing hard trying to control herself. He was driving her wild.

"Dezi please," Kayla said breathlessly.

He smiled and continued pleasing her. She pulled him up to her. Dezi began kissing her again as she guided him inside her. He couldn't describe the depth of emotion he was feeling as he made love to Kayla again after twenty years. They were both deeply enthralled in their passion moaning and clinging to each other. He held her tightly thrusting into her deeply as she screamed her pleasure. Their pace became frantic as Kayla climaxed first with him swiftly behind her. Dezi held her as her body trembled in ecstasy.

It was just as he remembered it being. He kissed her again and again. When they finally collected themselves, Dezi looked into her eyes. He saw once again the love that used to be there for him.

"Do you know how much I've missed you," he asked her softly.

Kayla smiled and caressed his face.

"I'm sorry," she said gently her eyes filling again.

"For what baby," Dezi asked concerned.

He hoped she wasn't having second thoughts and was going to leave him again.

"For not trying to understand all those years ago," Kayla started. "For letting everyone else influence the way I thought and felt about you."

He kissed her softly and told her all was forgiven.

"I love you. Do you hear what I'm saying," Dezi asked her looking into her eyes.

Kayla smiled and the tear fell. He wiped it and kissed her again.

"Tell me how all this happened," She prodded.

Dezi took a deep breath and looked at Kayla.

"Later," he said simply as he began to arouse her again.

●●●

Jackie told D everything was fine and they could leave now. Big D looked at Chris hard for a moment.

"Well this is all over now, man," he told him "Let it die."

Chris sighed deeply.

"I don't have a problem with that," he said flatly. "I've accepted my loss and it's my own fault," Chris said looking intently at Jackie. "I just want to live my life and hope that Jackie is happy."

197

Big D was satisfied with that.

"We're leaving first, you can leave twenty minutes after us."

Chris nodded in agreement. Big D went to the restroom leaving Jackie and Chris alone.

"So Kayla is gone," he asked sadly.

"Yes, and she's happy Chris," Jackie told him plainly.

"Thomas isn't going to give her up that easy you know," Chris replied.

Jackie sighed deeply. She knew that too.

"Well, he doesn't have a choice really," she told Chris.

He shook his head.

"Jackie," he began. "I know I've done some foul things to you," he went on. "I just want to say I'm sorry and I never meant to hurt you," he continued. "I'm glad you're happy with this man now and I hope you always will be," Chris finished looking at her lovingly.

Jackie didn't really hate him.

"Thanks Chris," she told him. "I hope you find happiness too," she went on. "But I know you won't until you come to terms with yourself first."

Chris understood what she meant. He just couldn't seem to be satisfied with one woman. He needed help and he knew it.

"I'll try Jackie," he replied smiling weakly.

Big D entered the room and addressed Jackie. "You ready to go baby?"

She stood and stretched.

"Let me go pee first," Jackie replied laughing and walking into the restroom.

Chris looked at Big D once she closed the door.

"Please take good care of her," he said amiably.

Big D looked at him.

"I definitely will do that," he told Chris. "She's a wonderful woman."

Chris nodded in agreement once again.

"You might want to check on your boy Thomas," Big D told him evenly. "He might just need a friend right about now"

Chris thought about it and knew he was probably right. Thomas would be devastated to learn Kayla left. Jackie returned and picked up her purse.

"OK," she replied. "Let's go."

Big D walked to the door and opened it for her. She started to walk out, before stopping and turning back to Chris.

"Be well Christopher," Jackie said softly and walked out, Big D walked behind her leaving him alone in the room.

Chris closed his eyes and breathed deeply. He replayed the day in his mind the fear and pain of loss overcoming him. He thought about Thomas and picked up his cell. He was in no hurry. Chris possessed nothing left to run back too. It just walked out the door with another man.

Smoke & **30** Mirrors

etective Dwayne Marchant was questioning Thomas. "What happened here Mr. Bradford?"

Thomas remained silent since the police arrived and found the woman dead. They called for detectives and he drew the assignment. He looked around the house. Everything seemed to be in order except for the dead body on the floor. He recognized the woman from the DVD they played at church. He was there himself, hoping to see Kayla again. He had it bad for her, and he knew it. Marchant shook the thoughts and got back to the business at hand.

"You're going to have to start cooperating with us," Marchant told Thomas. "You're in some serious trouble right now."

Thomas sighed deeply but he didn't say a word. Marchant looked around. He spotted the rings and letter on the table. He walked over and saw they were wedding rings.

"Where is your wife Mr. Bradford," Marchant asked, concerned. "Did you kill her too," he asked harshly.

Thomas looked at him, tears and pain in his eyes evident. "I would never hurt Kayla," he said plainly.

Marchant pulled out his cell. He called and asked dispatch to run her name through every hotel in the city.

"You won't find her," Thomas said plainly.

"Why is that sir," Marchant asked.

Thomas was quiet again. *What is this man thinking? He is in a shit load of trouble and he's playing mute,* Marchant thought disgustedly.

"Do you at least want to tell us the woman's name," he asked Thomas again.

They found no ID and would have to wait on fingerprints and dental records unless he helped them.

"Elise," Thomas said simply.

"Elise what?" Marchant asked.

"I don't know," Thomas told him honestly.

He never bothered to ask. *Guess it didn't matter while you were screwing her huh,* Marchant thought again. He thought about Kayla and how beautiful she was the other night and wondered why in the world Thomas would cheat on her. She was absolutely stunning. *Guess some guys are never satisfied,* Marchant thought as he walked through the house looking for clues. His cell rang. He answered. They found no record of her in any hotel. He thought for a moment. He doubted Kayla would use her real name if she were leaving Thomas. He needed more information. He returned to the room where Thomas sat. The coroner arrived finally and they were bagging the corpse.

"What's your wife's full name?"

Thomas looked at him and Marchant thought he wasn't going to answer.

"Mikayla L. DeWitt Black Bradford," he said quietly.

Marchant called back and gave her complete name, telling them to try again.

"Listen Mr. Bradford," he tried again with Thomas. "You're looking at murder one here," he went on. "You could get life; or even the death penalty for this," Marchant continued. "Please, make me understand what happened here tonight."

Thomas sighed.

"You wouldn't believe me if I told you," he said sadly.

He still didn't believe it and he was here, Thomas thought tiredly. Before Marchant could speak his cell went off again.

"Yeah?"

They found a K. DeWitt registered at one of the local hotels. He got the information and told the officer thanks.

"Do you want me to call your wife," Marchant asked Thomas.

"She won't care," he replied tiredly.

Marchant knew she left Thomas, probably because of the DVD. Still, he figured she wouldn't just abandon him.

"What's her number?"

Thomas gave it to him and Marchant dialed. Her voicemail came on instantly. *She must have it turned off,* he left a simple message of who he was and that it was important she call him back along with his phone number. Marchant returned his attention to Thomas.

"Do you have an attorney?"

"Yes," Thomas sighed.

"You need to call him and tell him to meet you at the station," Marchant replied.

Thomas complied and they handcuffed him after he hung up. They placed him in a car and took him down for processing. Marchant remained behind. He would question Thomas later at the station. Right now he wanted to examine the house. It just felt wrong to him.

Something is not quite right here, Marchant thought, but just couldn't put his finger on what.

●●●

Kayla was sleeping peacefully as Dezi watched her. *My god she is still so beautiful,* he sighed. Finally they were together again. Dezi kissed her gently on her cheek. Kayla stirred and awakened.

"I'm sorry baby," he told her softly. "I didn't mean to wake you."

She smiled as she looked at Dezi.

"You're really here," Kayla said again still not sure she wasn't dreaming this whole night.

Dezi smiled. "I'm here baby."

"Tell me what happened Dezi," she said softly still looking into his eyes.

Dezi kissed her gently and began to explain the last twenty years to her.

"But I saw you," she said still confused. "I touched you."

"Body double," Dezi told Kayla.

He told her about the government keeping him under lock and key.

"Why didn't you tell me," Kayla asked.

Dezi kissed her again. "Baby you were afraid of me then, remember?"

Kayla sighed and knew he was right. She wouldn't have listened.

"I thought you would hurt me," she said plainly.

"Why? Because of the baby," Dezi asked.

She looked at him again.

"Yes," Kayla replied softly.

Dezi smiled again.

"Don't you know I could forgive you for anything," he told Kayla caressing her face.

"I do now," she replied gently. "What about Aidan?"

"I've been thinking about how to handle that," Dezi sighed deeply.

"Do you think he'll accept me," he asked, concern showing on his face.

Kayla thought about it for a moment before she spoke.

"Well he's already extremely attached to you," she told him. "You two have spent time, you've given him advice," she continued. "You've basically been his father figure for all these months, so I don't see that it would matter. If anything it should bring you two closer."

Dezi smiled. She made him feel better, which of course she always did.

"Dezi," Kayla looked at him fearfully.

Dezi was concerned. *Why is she looking at me like that?*

"Yes baby," he answered.

"You didn't kill Thomas, did you?"

Kayla, baby you will never change, he thought, chuckling inside. She was always worried about everyone except herself.

"No baby, I didn't kill him," he replied. "Honestly."

Kayla was relieved. She knew how Dezi could be, and she knew he would have very good reason to hurt Thomas.

"OK," she said softly. "When are we leaving," she asked changing the subject to more pleasant matters.

Dezi laughed.

"I'm going to talk to Big D tomorrow and find out about the flight arrangements."

"Jackie told me the good news," Kayla said happily. "Thank you," she told Dezi softly touching him again.

He smiled.

"For you, the world on a silver platter baby," Dezi replied feeding Kayla one of the berries off the tray.

They began to kiss and touch each other, making passionate love to one another once more. Kayla was breathing evenly, once more sleeping peacefully. Dezi slipped from bed and headed downstairs.

●●●

He looked at the clock. It was four a.m. He dialed Big D, who answered fully alert. Dezi liked that about him, he was always on.

"What's up with the flyer," Dezi asked after they exchanged greetings.

"Everything is set man," Big D told him. "We can leave out tomorrow if you want."

"I need to take care of this legal business for Kayla, and help her get her passport and finances handled, so we will leave the day after tomorrow," he responded.

"That's cool man," Big D replied. "I'll call him and set it up," he went on. "You two driving down?"

"Yes, so we'll see you both in a couple of days," Dezi told him.

They disconnected and Dezi went back upstairs. Kayla stirred slightly as he climbed back into bed. Dezi put his arms around Kayla pulling her close and she quickly settled again. *I'm never sleeping without you again baby,* Dezi thought as he closed his eyes inhaling her scent and drifted off to sleep.

●●●

Thomas was conferring with his attorney.

"Thomas you've got to tell me what happened in that house tonight," Maurice was telling him.

Maurice Alston was his attorney for years. Mariah dated his son David briefly and they became good friends.

"Maurice, no one is going to believe what I say," Thomas sighed gently.

"Please Thomas. At least tell me as your attorney, so I know how to plead this thing," Maurice told him again.

Thomas sighed deeply and told him exactly what happened. Maurice was looking at him in stunned disbelief.

"See," Thomas told him. "I told you."

Maurice admitted the story was farfetched, but that's what made it believable in his mind. He knew Thomas couldn't sell it to a jury though.

"Look Thomas, because I know you, I believe you," Maurice went on. "But you know I can't sell that to a jury, so we're going to have to come up with something better."

Thomas sighed and asked him what he had in mind.

"We're going to plead manslaughter," Maurice told him. "OK, the girl came over and you talked, she seduced you and you had sex. Then you argued and you shot her in the heat of passion," he told him.

Thomas didn't like it, but he didn't like the idea of the death penalty or the rest of his life in jail either.

"Do you think the prosecutor will go for it?"

"You're an upstanding citizen who hasn't been in trouble, so I don't see an issue," Maurice explained.

"What about that charge from Florida," Thomas asked casually.

"That was years ago," Maurice replied. "You're a minister now for God's sake."

"This girl's job was to seduce men, so proving she took advantage of your emotional state will not be hard," he went on. "You came home to find your wife, whom you love dearly, gone. Then this woman comes over at your lowest point and drags you back into the mess that started it all in the first place," Maurice finished once again.

Thomas thought it was beginning to sound pretty good. *Maybe I won't be in prison forever and I can still find my wife and explain.*

"How long am I looking at doing?"

"Hmph, when I'm finished I'll say time served and probation," he told him.

Thomas hoped he was right. He knew Maurice was no joke in the courtroom. He got many men off and they walked. For the first time tonight Thomas held some hope he might have a life left to salvage.

Detective Marchant walked in ready to question Thomas. Maurice remained present.

"Mr. Bradford," he began. "Was your wife at home when you arrived," he fired first.

Thomas sighed. "No."

"She'd left already?"

Thomas sighed again, taking a deep breath to stay the tears threatening to come again.

"She was already gone," he said plainly.

"Why did she leave?"

Thomas looked at Maurice.

"That's irrelevant," he told the detective. "She wasn't at home when he arrived, and thus wasn't there when Elise Hudson arrived," Maurice continued. "Why she left is not the point."

Marchant was annoyed. He knew he wouldn't get anything worth using out of Thomas with his windbag there.

"I'm going to need to talk to your wife," he told Thomas looking at him evenly. "Where can I find her?"

"I don't know," Thomas replied honestly.

"Is there anything else Detective," Maurice asked.

He was anxious to wrap this up so he could get with the prosecutor and start the plea bargaining process.

"For now, no," Marchant told him no.

Maurice arranged bail for Thomas. They wanted to hold him without it, but he argued Thomas was not a flight risk being a cornerstone of the church community. They finally acquiesced and set a high bail. Maurice easily arranged it once Thomas supplied him with his account information.

They were leaving the precinct now.

●●●

"Thomas," Maurice stopped him. "Don't do anything stupid like go looking for Kayla," he told him evenly. "Go home."

"I can't," Thomas told him. "It's a crime scene, remember?"

"They've collected everything they need," Maurice told him. "You can go home."

"Okay," Thomas sighed.

"Please Thomas," Maurice told him again. "I'm trying to save your life," he finished as they got into the car.

Smoke & **31** Mirrors

Maurice dropped Thomas at his home and headed off to his own. It was almost eight a.m. now. He spent all night at the police station. Thomas hurried into the house and checked the machine hoping Kayla called. There were several messages. Most were from church members voicing their belief in his guilt or innocence. One was from Chris telling Thomas he knew about Kayla, and to call him. None of them were from her.

Thomas was deeply pained that she didn't even think to call him. *Did I hurt you that much Kayla,* Thomas wondered sadly. He refused to go into the den. He thought of Elise. He was angry with her for what she did, but he would have never killed her. At least that's what he told himself. *Dezi is alive and he's got my wife,* Thomas thought angrily. He was helpless. He had no idea where to begin to look for Dezi or for Kayla.

●●●

Dezi was at attorney Greyson's office bright and early. He gave the papers to him and Greyson checked for a signature.

"Very good Mr. Enzo," he said looking at him curiously. *He shaved the beard,* Greyson thought. Dezi however, did put the contacts back in.

"How soon," Dezi asked shortly.

"I can file them now, and request the emergency hearing with the judge, based on the circumstance," Greyson told Dante.

Dezi nodded.

"Good, that's exactly what we want to happen."

He gave Greyson yet another money filled envelope.

"I expect to hear from you later today."

They shook hands and Dezi left his office.

He was getting in his car when his cell went off. It was Kayla.

"Hey baby," he said pleasantly.

She was crying.

"What's wrong baby," Dezi asked alarmed.

"I'm supposed to go to the police station," Kayla said, still sniffling.

"Why baby," he asked, getting angry.

"Thomas was arrested for killing some woman, and they want to ask me about it," she told him. "I don't even know what they're talking about Dezi."

He could tell she was really scared.

"Baby, take a deep breath. I'm on my way home OK," Dezi told her.

"OK," Kayla said and disconnected.

He needed to get home and calm her down. He had an idea what the police wanted. She truly was innocent. He just needed her to relax. *They're trying to figure out where she was when everything went down,* Dezi thought. He made it home in fifteen minutes. He found Kayla in the den still visibly upset.

●●●

"Hey baby," he said softly sitting down beside her.

"Why would Thomas kill someone," Kayla asked genuinely confused.

Dezi sighed deeply.

"Baby, there are some things you need to know," he told her.

Her heart sank. Kayla didn't think she wanted to hear any of what was about to come out of Dezi's mouth.

"I found out this morning," he lied smoothly and gave her the newspaper.

It was front-page news. Kayla saw the headline and her mouth dropped. 'Local pastor kills mistress' the headline read.

"Oh my god," she said softly shaking her head in disbelief.

Kayla read the article as Dezi got up and retrieved himself some juice. She was finished when he returned.

"So why do they want to talk to me," she asked. "I wasn't even sure he was having an affair, although I guess I am now, huh?

Dezi looked at her for a moment before speaking.

"They want to know what you know," he told her. "Which frankly is nothing, so you have nothing to be afraid of baby," he told her. "Just tell them the truth."

Kayla sighed heavily.

"I really don't want to do this," she replied looking at him.

Dezi smiled and kissed her gently.

"I'll take you, and I'll be there to pick you up, OK," he told Kayla looking into her eyes.

"Okay," she smiled.

"Come on and get dressed, let's get this over with," he told her.

"Dezi," she stopped him. "I have an order against Thomas," she told him. "You don't think he'll be there do you?"

Dezi could see the fear in her eyes.

"No baby, he won't be there, trust me," he told Kayla hugging her tightly.

He couldn't wait to give her the final decree this afternoon once Greyson called him back. Kayla smiled as he released her. They headed upstairs together.

"I only have one change of clothes," Kayla told him once they arrived at the bedroom. "I wasn't expecting to still be here."

Dezi laughed and pulled her into the other room. He opened the closet and Kayla was shocked to see it filled with clothes and shoes.

"I took the liberty of doing a little shopping while I was here," Dezi told her laughing.

Kayla smiled and kissed him.

"You are so good to me," she said softly.

Dezi looked into her eyes.

"And I always will be," he replied helping her to select something to wear.

Kayla finally settled on an electric blue wrap dress. He loved the way it hugged her.

"Mm nice," Dezi said smiling as he looked at her in it.

Kayla loved how Dezi made her feel. Thomas spent the last three years making her feel like her figure was a bad thing and she should cover it up or be ashamed of it. Dezi on the other hand, loved it, and was always buying her things to show it off.

"I hope I don't hafta kick no police butt today about you in that dress," he said looking her over.

Kayla laughed. "You're my only man."

"Damned right," he said playfully as they headed to the car.

He dropped Kayla off at the station, kissing her as she got out.

"Call me and I'll be right here," he told her.

Dezi wasn't going far. He spied a coffee shop at the corner.

●●●

Kayla took a deep breath and entered the station. She walked up to the desk and asked for Detective Marchant. The officer told her to have a seat. A few moments later the Detective emerged. He spotted the attractive woman sitting in the otherwise dismal waiting room. She was in stark contrast to the gray and gloom of the metal chairs and scattered debris lying on the floor here and there. *Again, I ask why would you cheat, with something that gorgeous laying in your bed,* Marchant thought as he made his way to her.

"Mrs. Bradford?"

Kayla was a bit startled. She was reading a magazine she found in the waiting area, trying to soothe her frazzled nerves, and not paying attention.

"Yes," she replied rising.

"Thank you so much for coming down," he told her smiling as he took in the dress and her in it.

Wow, he thought appreciatively.

"I'm Detective Marchant," he introduced himself.

Kayla took his outstretched hand and shook it.

"Please follow me," he told her and she dutifully obliged.

Kayla took the detective in as they walked to the room. He was an attractive man. Tall, well defined body. She surmised he was of Creole descent because of the accent, the fair complexion, and emerald green eyes. They entered a small interrogation room. There was a simple metal table and a couple of matching metal chairs. Marchant took the opportunity to really look at Kayla again in the dress she was wearing. *She is absolutely amazing,* he thought longingly.

Marchant guided Kayla to one of the chairs and asked her to sit down. He sat at the end of the table, she on the side.

"Mrs. Bradford, I need to ask you some questions about your whereabouts last night," Marchant told her, watching her reaction.

He could tell Kayla was extremely uncomfortable.

"Where were you between nine and midnight?"

She breathed deeply.

"I was at my hotel," Kayla lied.

That's true, Marchant said internally. They ran a key check and found she entered the room at 8:00 and not left. The encoded key recording every time the pass key was used to enter it.

"All night," he asked for good measure.

"Yes," Kayla replied again not looking at the man as to not give away the lie she was trying to tell.

He was satisfied with that.

"Did you know about your husband's affair," Marchant asked. Kayla flushed.

"No," she said plainly.

Marchant could tell Kayla was hurt.

"When did you find out?"

He saw the tears in her eyes. He really wanted to reach out and hold her right now. Marchant took a deep breath instead.

"This morning," she said plainly. "I read it in the paper."

Marchant felt badly for her. She seemed like a genuinely nice woman.

"So, that's not why you left your husband?"

Kayla sighed softly.

"No, it's not," she replied.

"May I ask why you left," Marchant questioned.

She sighed again.

"Thomas and I had a lot of problems," Kayla said simply.

"Was he violent," Marchant asked interested in her answer.

"Yes," she said quietly.

He knew about the restraining order. Marchant wanted to see if she would admit it. So far she was very forthright with him.

"Do you think your husband could have killed this woman deliberately?"

Kayla closed her eyes and sighed again.

"Two years ago I would have said absolutely not," she began. "But now, I honestly don't know," she told him as the tears rolled down her cheeks.

Marchant handed Kayla a tissue hating that he made her cry.

"Have you seen the DVD in question," he asked after she collected herself.

"No," she replied.

They found a copy at her home. *She must have left without watching it,* Marchant thought.

"I know you don't want too, but I need you to look at it and tell me if you recognize the woman in it," he told her.

Kayla didn't want to see it, but she agreed. Marchant ask the officer to bring in the TV. He started the DVD. She saw the black screen then the feature started. Kayla was shocked and hurt thinking of all the lies Thomas told her about being faithful. She began to cry earnestly. Marchant shut off the DVD, seeing how it affected her. Kayla sobbed uncontrollably as he took her into his arms and tried to comfort her. Marchant felt like a clod for doing this to her, but he happily admitted holding Kayla was one of the most wonderful experiences of his life. After she calmed down and collected herself, Marchant released her.

"Do you recognize the woman?"

Kayla shook her head still unable to speak, that she didn't.

"Thank you for coming down Mrs. Bradford." Marchant told her as he escorted her out. "I'm sorry for any unnecessary pains we've cause you today," he apologized again.

"Thank you," Kayla said softly.

I wish I met her before the good Pastor, Marchant thought as he watched her go outside the station. *You better know I would never cheat on her,* he thought again returning to his office.

Dezi picked Kayla up in front of the station. He got out and opened her door as Marchant was watching from the window. Dezi kissed her softly as he helped her in.

"Well, looks like Mrs. Bradford has already replaced the good Pastor," Marchant said aloud.

He was a little disappointed. He was thinking of approaching her himself after a reasonable period of time.

"Wasn't meant to be I guess," he said aloud again as he returned to his work and waited on the prosecutor to call and tell him what they bargained down to.

Smoke & **32** Mirrors

I have a surprise for you," Dezi told her smiling.

Kayla brightened. She was still thinking about the images on the screen in the station.

"What is it," she asked, looking at Dezi closely.

He chuckled softly.

"Quit it!" Kayla squealed and hit him playfully.

Dezi was teasing her and he knew she hated it.

"OK, if you're going to be violent, I'm not giving it to you," he said playfully.

"You are going to make me hurt you Dezi Antony Gianni," Kayla replied.

He was impressed she still remembered his whole name. Dezi laughed and handed her the papers.

"What's this," Kayla asked looking at Dezi quizzically.

"Well open them and see, duh!"

Kayla rolled her eyes and he laughed. She smiled again and carefully opened the envelope. She unfolded the papers and read them. Kayla looked at him, tears in her eyes.

"How did you do this?".

Dezi looked at Kayla.

"Do you really want to know that," he asked.

She thought about it and decided she didn't.

"Is it really over," Kayla asked not wanting to get excited yet.

Dezi looked at Kayla seeing the worry in her face and smiled.

"Yes baby, it's really over," he told her.

Kayla sighed deeply and Dezi knew she was relieved.

"We need to stop by the bank and arrange your transfers," he told her.

She shook her head yes and they pulled in. Kayla walked in with the handsome man on her arm. She got looks ranging from pity to outrage. She ignored them all as she sat at the customer service desk.

"Good morning Mrs. Bradford," Charles greeted her.

He took Kayla in noting he never viewed her in anything quite as form fitting. Charles also wondered who the man was she was with. She did business here since she moved to Chapel Hill.

"Hi Charles," Kayla smiled back. "It's DeWitt now," she told him showing the divorce papers granting her maiden name be returned.

He was surprised, but he remained professional. *Man, wait till I tell the deacons she's divorced him,* Charles thought as he listened to her. Kayla told him what she needed done. Dezi supplied Charles with all the account numbers and information he needed. They were done in less than an hour. Their next stop was to pick up Kayla's passport, and update her mail forwarding. They took care of that in less than an hour also.

"Well baby," Dezi began. "We're ready to go," he told Kayla. "That is if you still want to leave with me," he finished looking at her evenly.

She turned to him and looked into his eyes.

"What kind of stupid question is that," Kayla said as she put her arms around Dezi and kissed him.

He smiled and held her close.

"I've waited twenty years for that yes," Dezi told Kayla softly.

"So let's go then," she told him laughing.

Dezi kissed her again passionately. His cell rang.

"Yeah?"

It was the movers telling him everything was ready to be shipped. He had them working triple time on the house while they ran their errands.

"Good. We'll be expecting them when we arrive," Dezi told them and hung up.

Once they were in the car heading to Virginia, Kayla pulled out the satin case.

"What's that baby," Dezi asked softly.

"Can you pull over for a minute," she asked, which he did.

She opened the pouch and poured the contents into her lap.

"Do you remember this," Kayla asked as she handed Dezi the picture.

He looked at it and smiled. It was a picture of them together the first night at the club.

"Of course," Dezi told her. "It was one of the happiest nights of my life," he finished looking at Kayla evenly.

She showed him the ring.

"Do you remember what you told me when you gave me this?"

Dezi kissed her passionately.

"I told you that I loved you with perfection, like this flawless diamond, and that love, like this diamond, would endure until the end of time," he said softly.

The tears rolled down her cheeks.

"You've kept that promise Dezi, and now, I want to promise you that same thing," Kayla said softly.

Dezi took the ring and placed it on her finger then kissed her passionately again and again.

"Let's go home," he said softly and Kayla smiled her agreement as he put the car back into gear and got back onto the highway.

●●●

Thomas heard his cell ring. He answered it absently, his mind still on Kayla and her leaving.

"Hello?"

"Hey Thomas," Chris greeted him.

Thomas sighed lightly. He was glad to hear from Chris. *Probably the only friendly voice I'll hear all day*, he thought.

"How you doing Chris?".

"I've seen better days," Chris told him.

"I guess you have too though, huh?" he asked gently.

Thomas sighed again.

"How much do you know," he asked him tiredly.

Chris told Thomas he knew about Kayla leaving and he received a call from one of the deacons about the murder charge.

"They want you to come back and Pastor huh?"

Chris detected no hostility or anger in his friend's voice.

"Yes," he replied gently. "But I'm in no position to do that myself."

Thomas was confused.

"Why?"

"Jackie and I are divorcing," Chris explained. "I signed the papers last night, so I assume she will file them today.

"Wow," Thomas said softly. "I had no idea."

"Yeah, no one did," Chris told him. "I was hoping we would work it out."

"Of course she let me know in no uncertain terms that wasn't going to happen," Chris added.

"I'm definitely sorry to hear that man," Thomas told him. "I don't even know where Kayla is."

Chris heard the pain and hurt in his friend's voice.

"Chris, I messed up bad," Thomas told him quietly, close to tears.

Chris felt for him.

"I'm on my way there to you," he told him.

Thomas was grateful for that. He needed a friend right now.

"I have to tell you what happened, even though I doubt you believe me," he told him.

"You would be surprised what I might believe right about now," Chris replied.

"I'll see you in a few hours," he told Thomas as he prepared to hang up.

"Cool, I'm looking forward to seeing you," Thomas told Chris and they disconnected.

●●●

As soon as he hung up, the bell rang. *Now what,* he thought, sighing heavily as he went to answer it.

"Yes, can I help you," he asked the deputy when he opened the door.

"Thomas Bradford?"

"Yes," he replied.

"Please sign here sir," he told him handing him a clip board.

He signed, not sure what it was, and the deputy handed him the papers. Thomas returned to the sunroom and opened the sealed envelope. He began to read, his disbelief growing with each line.

"No! This is not happening," Thomas yelled in the empty house.

This was a final divorce decree. He knew he signed the papers last night. *That bastard Dezi made me sign them,* he thought angrily.

"How did she get this done so quickly," Thomas asked again.

He went to the phone and called Maurice.

"Hello?"

"Maurice I need you to tell me something," Thomas replied after he greeted him.

"I'm all ears," The attorney replied.

Thomas told him about the decree he just received and that he signed the papers last night.

"How did Kayla get this done so quickly and is it legal?"

"She probably pleaded extenuating circumstances and fear for her safety," Maurice told him.

"Is there an order against you," he asked Thomas.

"Yeah, I guess there is," Thomas told him.

Maurice sighed.

"Well then that's how, but," he began and Thomas was hopeful. "We can go and try to fight it," he went on. "Have you been intimate with Kayla in the last seven days?"

"Yes, of course," Thomas told him.

He didn't bother enlightening the attorney however, that most of the occasions were by force.

"Hmm," Maurice replied.

"What," Thomas asked.

"Let me do a little research," Maurice told him. "I'm pretty sure I can get an injunction and force Kayla to at least come back and deal with you." He went on. "Maybe even force her into counseling before a divorce will be granted."

Thomas was elated.

"Please find out, and do whatever you need too," he told Maurice.

"I'll call you later and let you know what I find," Maurice assured Thomas.

"Please let this work," Thomas said aloud after he hung up.

He needed another chance. He wouldn't fail this time. He would make her see how much he loved and wanted to be with her. For the first time since this storm hit, Thomas could actually see a pinpoint of light.

Smoke & **33** Mirrors

Hey man what's up," Big D greeted Dezi.

"Hey Kayla," Big D greeted her smiling.

She smiled and told him hello. Dezi introduced them. She always heard about him, but she never met him before. *He's a good looking man. No wonder Jackie is all hot and bothered,* Kayla thought smiling internally.

"Where's Jackie?"

She was anxious to see her friend and spend some time with her.

"She ran to the store. She wanted to get something or other she said you liked," he replied chuckling.

Kayla laughed. "OK."

Big D and Dezi left her in the living room watching TV.

●●●

"So how did you leave it," Big D asked when they were alone in the bedroom.

"I didn't kill him," Dezi said plainly.

Big D nodded.

"I left him holding the bag on a murder rap."

Big D chuckled. *Definitely old school Devastator,* he thought.

"I still have a feeling I'm going to end up having to kill him though," Dezi said flatly.

"Why," Big D asked.

"He just doesn't seem to get it," he replied before changing the subject and asking Big D about their adventure.

Big D told Dezi about Chris and the whole hotel thing.

"So you're telling me, you and Jackie were getting busy, with him sitting right there," Dezi asked, laughing hard with tears now rolling down his cheeks.

Big D was laughing just as hard.

"Yep, he was right there," he replied breathlessly.

"Man that was cold as hell!" Dezi roared.

●●●

Kayla heard the lock turn and looked up.

"Hey Miss," she greeted Jackie.

Jackie squealed and dropped her bag running to hug her friend.

"Girl, let me look at you," she told Kayla pushing her back and taking her in. "I'm so happy you're alright," she told her eyes misting.

"Me too," Kayla told Jackie.

"Where is Dezi?

"He and D are in the room talking and laughing from what I can hear," Kayla replied chuckling herself.

Jackie gathered herself and grabbed the bag headed for the kitchen. Kayla followed and sat at the table as she put up her purchases.

"Girl, D is a sexy man," she said slyly, giving her friend a look.

"Oh shut up!" Jackie laughed.

Big D and Dezi heard them talking and decided to join them.

"Hey baby," Big D said hugging and kissing Jackie.

Dezi walked around the corner as she was disengaging from Big D.

"Hi Jackie," he greeted her.

Jackie looked around Big D and saw him. She dropped the jar in her hand and it shattered.

"Oh my God," she said shocked looking at the man who could be Aidan's twin.

Dezi smiled. He forgot she didn't know what he actually looked like.

"Jackie, are you alright," Kayla asked.

They all forgot she didn't know his relationship to Aidan.

"You look just like my nephew, gray eyes and all," Jackie replied somewhat subdued.

Dezi sighed softly and walked over to her.

"I should," he replied. "He's my son," he finished evenly looking at her intently.

Jackie gasped.

"I don't understand," she finally said.

Dezi sat down and told her the story of how he met Olivia and their times together, of course making them seem a bit more humanistic than they actually were. He also added a long overdue apology to Kayla for cheating on her. She immediately smiled and told him all was forgiven. Jackie understood now. Olivia often talked about Aidan's father and how wonderful he was.

"Does he know," Jackie asked referring to Aidan.

Dezi shook his head.

"I'm going to tell him when we get home."

Jackie shook her head yes.

"Wow," she said finally. "We are one big happy family huh?"

"Well, let's get dinner started," Jackie said again as she and Kayla ran Big D and Dezi out of the kitchen.

●●●

They were enjoying the game when Dezi's cell went off.

"Yeah?"

"This is Greyson," the man replied.

What the hell is he calling me for, Dezi thought crossly.

"What can I do for you," he asked plainly.

Greyson cleared his throat. This was a call he didn't want to make. He got the feeling this was a man he didn't want angry with him.

"Mrs. Bradford, I mean DeWitt, has to appear in court tomorrow," he began. "Bradford's attorney has filed an injunction, and is contesting the divorce."

Dezi frowned deeply and his eyes changed. Big D, watching him intently since he answered the phone, knew whatever was being said wasn't good news.

"Can he do that," he asked evenly, aware that Kayla was within earshot.

"Yes unfortunately, because they were sexually intimate within the last seven days," Greyson went on. "He's also claiming mental duress when he signed the papers."

Dezi took a long, deep, breath. *I knew this muthafucker was gonna make me kill him,* he thought coldly.

"So what happens if she doesn't show up?"

"Well the judge could hold her in contempt, and actually issue a warrant for her. He could also throw out her divorce, which would mean she is still legally married to Bradford," Greyson told him.

Dezi knew Kayla would be devastated to have to go back and see Thomas again.

"OK, what time," he asked already making plans in his head.

"The hearing is at ten o'clock," Greyson told him.

"OK," Dezi said sighing deeply and hung up.

Greyson looked at the phone, *I wouldn't want to be Thomas Bradford right now,* he thought and shivered.

Dezi looked at Big D motioning him out of the room. Once they were alone Big D asked what was going on.

"The son-of-a-bitch has filed a motion to get the divorce thrown out," Dezi said flatly.

Big D knew that wasn't good news.

"So can Kayla fight it?"

Dezi knew she could and she would probably win, he just didn't want to waste the time it would take. He knew the judge would probably be sympathetic to Thomas and make them go to counseling or some other nonsense.

"I'm not wasting that kind of time," he replied calmly.

Big D knew what Dezi was thinking.

"So what's the plan," he asked, down for whatever.

"We're going back to North Carolina, and I'm going to tie up this loose end," he replied coldly.

"Are you taking Kayla back," Big D asked.

"Yes, and I know she's going to hate it, but I need the time she'll buy being in court to set everything up," Dezi replied.

"That's cool. Jackie can come, and of course she'll be her support," Big D replied.

They agreed and began to plan just what was going to happen this time. *I won't leave him breathing,* Dezi thought ominously as he gathered himself to go deal with Kayla.

●●●

Thomas was elated. Maurice called earlier and informed him that they won a hearing tomorrow morning and Kayla was required to be there.

"I get another chance," he said excitedly aloud.

He would make her understand. Thomas would show her how much he loved her. *To hell with Dezi! Kayla was his wife and she was going to always be his wife,* he thought angrily. Maurice also told him they were able to plea the charge down to involuntary manslaughter. He was confident he would get Thomas off without having to serve any more jail time. Everything was going great.

Thomas forced himself into the den and cleaned it thoroughly. He took up the carpet with the bloodstains, stripped and waxed the floors. He put fresh flowers all over the house and was going shopping later for the ingredients for their dinner tomorrow night. Maurice told Thomas there was a good chance of winning his motion. He heard the bell, interrupting his thoughts and went to answer.

"Hey man!" Chris greeted him cheerfully.

Thomas smiled and they embraced as he entered the house.

"How're you doing man," Chris asked after they sat with their coffee.

"I'm doing a lot better now," he told him smiling.

Chris asked what was going on and Thomas filled him in on the charges and about Kayla.

"So you think this judge is gonna throw out the divorce?"

"Maurice seems to think we have a good chance," Thomas told Chris.

"What if she decides not to come," Chris asked.

Thomas thought about it for a moment, but dismissed it.

"You know Kayla is not going to do anything close to breaking the law," he told him, and Chris agreed.

"Well, I hope it works out for you Thomas," Chris told him, "You do realize you have a serious amount of work to do don't you," he finished looking at his friend evenly.

Thomas sighed deeply.

"God yes, Chris," he replied tiredly. "I've messed up so royally," Thomas told his friend.

Thomas was glad Chris didn't ask him about Friday night. Now that he knew he would more than likely do little to no time, he didn't feel the need to share it.

"Chris," Thomas began.

He was remembering his and Kayla's history.

"Do you know anything about some guy named Dezi she was dating back in the day?"

Chris looked at Thomas hard. *Where the hell did he hear about that guy?*

"Yeah," he replied simply.

"Tell me about him," Thomas returned.

Chris took a deep breath and told him all he knew.

"Thomas, that guy was seriously bad news."

"Why would you ask about him?" Chris asked. "He's been dead for almost twenty years."

"I was just curious," Thomas said. "Kayla mentioned him in passing."

So everyone thinks this guy is dead. Well he may as well be, because I'm getting my wife back, he thought as he sipped his coffee.

"Thomas, do you mind if I go lie down for a while," Chris asked.

"No, not at all," Thomas told him and showed him the room he would stay in.

"Will you go to court with me tomorrow?"

Chris smiled.

"Oh course man, you know that goes without saying," he replied.

Thomas left him to his nap and headed downstairs. *I hope this works out the way he wants it too,* Chris thought remembering his own history with Kayla, and how once her mind was made up, there was no unmaking it.

●●●

Kayla was livid. "What?!" she screamed.

Jackie was also pissed.

"Why the hell does she have to go through this crap?!"

Dezi was trying to calm Kayla down, and Big D was doing his best with Jackie.

"I want to find him and rip his damned heart out," Jackie said.

Kayla was quiet now. Dezi could see she was seriously upset.

"Baby, please calm down," Dezi told Kayla softly as he took her in his arms.

"What's going to happen tomorrow Dezi," she asked fearfully.

Dezi knew Kayla was very fragile right now. There was far too much going on. He had to handle this quickly. *I'm going to kill this fucker tomorrow night and put an end to all this bullshit once and for all,* Dezi thought as he held her. Kayla was crying softly.

"Will they make me stay with him?"

"Don't worry baby, I'm going to take care of it," Dezi told Kayla.

She looked at him, staring deeply into his eyes.

"You won't let Thomas hurt me anymore will you?"

Dezi kissed her deeply. "Not ever."

Kayla smiled at him.

"I just want to go home and be with our kids and Livvy," she told him tiredly.

"We will soon baby, I promise," Dezi told Kayla kissing her again.

She was in so much pain. *Why is Thomas doing this to me,* Kayla thought miserably.

"Dezi?"

He stopped stroking her hair and looked down at her.

"I want to go lie down," she said quietly.

"Alone," he asked gently.

Kayla looked at Dezi fearfully again.

"No, never without you again," she told him.

"You never will baby," Dezi smiled.

They rose and headed for the bedroom. Big D and Jackie were already in theirs, having left a few moments earlier. Everyone was trying to make it through the night and get tomorrow over with. Dezi lay awake after she drifted off to sleep. He was thinking about Thomas now, and how he was going to kill him. *You shoulda listened to me preacher man,* Dezi thought as he closed his eyes smiling at the pain he was going to bring to Thomas before he killed him.

Smoke & **34** Mirrors

They left early morning and drove back. Dezi dropped Jackie and Kayla off at the hotel telling them he and Big D had business to take care of.

"Baby, don't worry, I swear no matter what happens in that courtroom today, this is over," Dezi told Kayla looking her in the eye.

She knew he meant what he said and she didn't ask any questions. At this point she honestly didn't care how he did it, as long as he did it.

"I really don't want to do this Jackie," Kayla told her as they showered and changed for court.

"Girl I know, but hey, let's just keep our heads up," she replied.

"I dread even seeing Thomas again, Jackie," Kayla said tiredly.

Jackie made Kayla dress in one of the outfits she got from Dezi. It was a form fitting purple dress that flared at the knee. Kayla looked stunning in it.

"I don't want that dog to think you're down or upset concerning his trifling self," Jackie told her.

Kayla giggled. "I wholeheartedly agree."

"Well," Kayla said taking a deep breath. "Let's go get this over with."

They left headed for a cab to take them to the courthouse.

Thomas and Maurice were conferring when Kayla and Jackie walked in. Greyson was at the other table waiting for her. Chris saw Jackie. *Damn she looks good,* he thought as he took her in. She spotted him and gave him an 'I should have known' look. Chris wished he could talk to Jackie and tell her he was faultless in this.

Thomas looked up and saw her. Kayla looked absolutely beautiful in the dress. *I should never have tried to change her,* Thomas thought looking at how peaceful she looked. Kayla greeted Greyson and they sat down together.

"Maurice, are you sure I have a chance," Thomas asked suddenly nervous.

Maurice chuckled. "Calm down, let me handle this."

●●●

"Mrs. Bradford," Greyson began. "Let me do all the talking and we should be out of here in an hour."

"I will gladly let you handle everything," Kayla smiled.

The judge entered the room and they all stood.

"The case of Bradford vs Bradford is called to order," The bailiff announced.

The judge told them they could all be seated.

"Mr. Alston," he began. "Your client is here to have the divorce that was granted, overturned, is that correct," he asked addressing Maurice.

He stood. "Yes your honor, that is correct," he replied.

The judge sat back in his chair.

"On what grounds counselor?"

"My client was under extreme mental duress when he signed the documents in question, not to mention he, and Mrs. Bradford, were sexually intimate three days before this was filed," Maurice told the judge.

Kayla blushed. She couldn't believe their sex life was going to be discussed like this.

"Your honor," Greyson piped up.

The judge regarded him.

"Mr. Bradford signed the papers. He is also guilty of adultery, and my client is afraid for her safety, given the charges pending against him," he replied.

The judge looked at Greyson thoughtfully.

"Mrs. Bradford," the judge addressed her.

Kayla looked up at the man.

"Yes your honor?"

"Are you afraid of your husband," he asked looking at her intently.

"Yes. Completely," Kayla told him.

"Tell me why," the judge addressed her again.

Kayla took a deep breath and told him about Thomas hitting her, and how he sexually abused her, and kept her prisoner in her own home, as well as lying about his affair.

"I'm scared that he may kill me too," she finished quietly.

The judge listened intently, and then turned to Thomas.

"Mr. Bradford," he addressed him.

Thomas swallowed hard and answered the judge.

"Tell me why I should overturn this divorce, when your wife has obviously decided she wants no part of a marriage with you anymore," he said calmly.

Thomas sighed gently.

"Because she never gave me a chance, us a chance," he told the judge. "I've made some mistakes, and I did a lot of things I'm not proud of, but I love my wife with my whole heart," Thomas went on. "I would never hurt Kayla, not ever, and I would never have signed those papers if I were in my right mental state."

His honor was looking at Thomas intently.

"You may sit if you're finished," he told him.

Thomas returned to his chair. The judge sat back in his chair and closed his eyes for a moment.

"I'm going to go to my chambers for fifteen minutes," he told them. "When I return, I will give you my decision," he finished and left the courtroom.

Greyson told Kayla he needed to make a couple of calls, and he would be right back. She nodded. Jackie came and sat beside Kayla once he was gone.

"What is Chris doing here," Kayla asked noticing his presence.

Jackie rolled her eyes.

"All dogs stick together don't they," she hissed.

Kayla almost laughed but she was so nervous.

Thomas was watching her intently. *Please let him give her back to me. I'll be so different this time,* he thought as he continued watching Kayla.

"I'm afraid of him Jackie," Kayla told her trembling.

Jackie let out a long sigh.

"I know, but it's going to be OK. You'll see," Jackie told her.

Greyson returned just as the judge came out of his chamber. They all stood once again until he told them to sit.

"I've thought about what's been said today and I've come to a decision," he started. "Mrs. Bradford, I believe that some things were done to you that shouldn't have been, and I believe you're afraid," he paused for a moment.

Thomas was getting a bad feeling.

"However, I don't believe Mr. Bradford would cause you any intentional harm. Perhaps a lot of the incidents you described were simply a difference of viewpoint. As for his current situation, I cannot base my decision on that, since he has not been convicted of any actual crime," he went on.

Kayla was feeling ill.

"I'm going to order that the divorce be overturned, and require that you and your husband enter counseling for ninety days. During that time period, you will be required to maintain residence with him," he told her.

Kayla's head was swimming. She couldn't believe what this man was saying. She felt it coming from the depths of her soul and she couldn't stop it.

"No!" she screamed, "Don't do this! Don't make me go back with him," she continued even though the Judge was asking for order.

"I can't!" she screamed again and again. "He'll hurt me again! He'll kill me this time! Please don't do this to me," she screamed crying hysterically.

The judge felt horrible doing this to her, he didn't want to overturn the divorce. He believed Kayla and what she said about Thomas, but he owed Maurice a favor. A big one; and he called that favor in this morning when he found out he was the presiding judge on the case. Kayla was still hysterical. She finally crumpled to the floor almost passed out. Greyson was shouting for them to call an ambulance. Thomas was over to Kayla in an instant.

"Leave her alone," Jackie screamed at him. "Haven't you done more than enough?!"

Thomas didn't care about her yelling, the judge just gave him his wife back and he was going to take charge.

"She's my wife Jackie," he told her evenly. "Now, I want you to back off and let me handle this," Thomas said unpleasantly.

Jackie almost attacked him but Chris grabbed her and told her to come and sit with him. She was livid. *I hope Dezi blows his fucking brains out,* Jackie thought miserably. Kayla was babbling incoherently and crying.

"Shh, baby it's alright," Thomas told her softly as he held her and stroked her hair.

•••

The paramedics arrived and got Kayla ready for transport. Jackie and Chris followed the ambulance. Her mind was on Kayla, and calling Dezi and Big D, the first chance she got. They arrived and Dr. Lindsey met them there. He was Kayla's personal physician. Jackie called him on the ride over. He took over Kayla's care once she arrived and ordered everyone, including Thomas, out of the room. Jackie was looking at Thomas with all the hatred she could muster. Thomas felt her eyes on him, but he didn't care. He was still elated that he received another chance. Thomas knew Kayla was upset, but she would rest here a few days and he would be here to nurture her and their marriage.

Dr. Lindsey emerged a few moments later. He found them all in the waiting room.

"Kayla is exhausted, and not far from a complete breakdown," he told them looking directly at Thomas. "I'm keeping her here for a couple of days, heavily sedated," he continued. "I want her to rest. No visitor's period. Not even you Thomas," he told him.

Thomas started to protest but Dr. Lindsey stopped him.

"What's more important Thomas? Your ego or her health," he asked looking at him hard.

Jackie smiled inside. She loved Dr. Lindsey. He was no nonsense. Thomas backed down.

"Can I at least see her for a few minutes," he asked.

Dr. Lindsey sighed softly.

"Alright, five minutes," he told Thomas. "She won't know you're in the room."

"Thank you," Thomas replied and left.

•••

He entered her room quietly and saw her sleeping. He walked over to her and stroked her face. *I love you so much Kayla,* Thomas thought looking at her. He kissed her gently on the mouth. Kayla didn't stir. Dr. Lindsey entered and told him his time was up. Thomas kissed Kayla again gently and told her goodbye. Dr. Lindsey checked her and left instructions at the nurses' station as he continued rounds.

"I'm not leaving," Jackie told Chris.

"But you can't see her Jackie," he tried to reason with her.

"I don't care," she replied. "I'm not leaving," she told him again adding she would call a cab when she got ready to go.

"Where are you staying," Thomas asked walking up on their conversation.

Jackie looked at him distastefully. "Why?"

"Because I need to have my wife's things brought home," Thomas replied looking at her hard.

"I'll have them sent when Kayla wakes up and says to send them," Jackie shot back daring him to ask again.

Thomas sighed and walked away.

"Bastard," she said flatly.

Chris shook his head and followed Thomas knowing he wouldn't get through to Jackie now. When she was sure they were gone, she called Dezi.

●●●

"Hey Jackie," he answered. "How did it go?"

Jackie told Dezi everything that happened and where Kayla was now. For a moment she wasn't sure he heard her. It was deadly silent on the phone.

"I'm on my way," Dezi said calmly.

His tone scared the hell out of her. They arrived twenty minutes later. Big D hugged Jackie.

"You good," he questioned.

"I'm fine," Jackie told him. "His buddy Chris was at the hearing too."

Dezi turned when she mentioned his name. Jackie saw a look in his eye that told her everything she would need to know about how he planned to handle this situation.

"Which room," Dezi asked.

Jackie told him as she and D headed to the nurses' station to keep them distracted. Dezi slipped inside her room unnoticed. Kayla was still heavily sedated. He kissed her forehead.

"My sweet baby," Dezi said gently in her ear.

She stirred slightly but didn't wake.

"This is all going to be over tonight baby," he whispered again in her ear.

Dezi gently kissed her and left. Jackie saw him return to the waiting room and signaled Big D. They all talked together.

"I need you to stay here Jackie," Dezi told her evenly.

She looked at him then at Big D. They both shared the same look and she was afraid to even ask.

"OK," Jackie said quietly.

"You need some money or anything," Big D asked.

"I'm fine," Jackie told him.

"Be careful, both of you," she said softly, looking at them both.

They nodded and left. *This town is about to be rocked to its core,* Jackie thought as she picked up a magazine and began to read.

Smoke & **35** Mirrors

Dezi pulled out his cell and dialed. Cedric looked at the display.

"Hey Mr. E," he greeted the caller.

Dezi greeted him then got down to business.

"Seems we left some unfinished business the other night," he told Cedric. "Would you gentlemen be interested in finishing it?"

"Yeah man, we're down for whatever you need," Cedric told him.

"Good to hear," Dezi smiled and told them where to meet him.

•••

They pulled up to the house he owned when he was here and entered the garage. It was empty since the movers already shipped everything. The two other men arrived, joining him and Big D. They all sat on the staircase and talked.

"This is Big D," Dezi told K.C. and Cedric.

They greeted him and listened attentively as Dezi outlined how everything would play out this time.

"It's going to be worse than before," he warned the two men.

K.C. spoke this time.

"If the outcome is that fake ass preacher being dead, then I don't care how bad it is," he said plainly.

Big D laughed.

"Well damn," he said still chuckling. "Seems this brother just can't buy no friends in this town," he finished still smiling.

Dezi thought about Chris.

"I'ma kill that fucker that was in court with him today too," he spat venomously.

Big D looked at Dezi hard.

"I want that pleasure personally if you don't mind man," he told him evenly.

"Why," Dezi asked looking at Big D.

"We tried to leave his ass with his life last time, and he turned around and ran up here helping Thomas pull this bullshit," Big D went on. "He's hurt Jackie and lied to her. I figure I owe his ass."

Dezi smiled.

"He's all yours man," he told Big D.

"You gonna do it at his house," Cedric asked.

Dezi mulled that over for a moment. He couldn't think of a better place. Thomas would after all feel safe there.

"Yeah," he replied. "We still have the element of surprise. Him nor his boy Chris knows we're here."

"OK, we've got four hours to pull all this shit together," Dezi told them as they all got up to leave.

"We'll have everything and be ready, count on it," Cedric told them both.

"Say Big D," Cedric inquired.

He looked at the young man.

"What's your game," he asked, genuinely interested.

Dezi told him about the young men and their ambitions earlier before they arrived. Big D smiled.

"Pimpin', youngblood," he replied smoothly.

K.C. smiled at Cedric. Here was someone else who could give them advice and expertise.

"We need to talk man," K.C. told Big D.

"Yeah maybe we will after everything goes down tonight," he laughed.

They nodded and each dispersed to their own destinations making note of what time they would reunite to commence the activities of the evening.

●●●

Thomas was on top of the world. The judge effectively gave him his life back. He was concerned too. Kayla was emotionally unstable right now. He was glad she was hospitalized and would get well. *I'm so sorry you've had to endure any of this drama baby*, Thomas thought as he looked out over their deck. The lake was tranquil and he noticed the ducks huddled contentedly together. He thought of how much Kayla loved watching the sunset, while sitting out here listening to the frogs in the reeds, singing to each other.

The wind was blowing softly, almost whispering its pleasure at the spectrum of nature it surrounded. Thomas sighed gently thinking of what he did in court today. He couldn't just let Kayla leave him. He loved her too much. He knew he did a lot wrong, but he needed this chance to make it right for her again. Thomas thought back to her reaction in the courtroom. Kayla was actually terrified of him. *What a monster I must be in her mind,* he thought sighing heavily.

●●●

Chris walked out onto the deck where he was standing.

"How you holding up man?"

"I'm okay," Thomas sighed gently.

"Well you must at least be glad that she's still married to you," Chris said absently as he looked out at the tranquil view illuminated by the warm orange glow of the sun beginning to set.

"But she hates me and is scared to death of me," Thomas replied sadly.

Chris shook his head. There wasn't much he could say about that.

"Well Thomas, you knew it wouldn't be easy," he reminded him. "Just try and make her see, and remember, the man she fell in love with."

Thomas thought about that and knew Chris was right. He became a stranger to Kayla over this past year, always gone out of town from one month to the next. He left her alone far too often. *No wonder she turned to Dante or Dezi or whatever the hell his name was,* Thomas thought bitterly. He couldn't be angry with her for that either. He engaged in a full-fledged affair during their marriage. Then he further disgraced Kayla, and himself, by the woman being killed in their home.

"I need to buy another house," Thomas said plainly.

Chris understood. There was no way Kayla would want to stay in this one.

"Let's go grab something to eat," Chris suggested.

Thomas didn't really have an appetite but he did want to get out.

"Sure," he replied. "Let's go."

Chris stopped him one final time.

"Thomas it's going to work out," he told him looking at his friend evenly.

Thomas smiled slightly and told Chris he believed. They went back inside headed out the front door to the car.

●●●

Dr. Lindsey came back to check on Kayla. He went into her room and found her still very much asleep. *What the hell has been going on with this woman,* he thought remembering her state when they brought her in. He never cared much for her current husband.

"Sanctimonious prick," Dr. Lindsey said under his breath.

He checked Kayla's vitals. She was doing better. She started to stir and awakened. It took her a minute to focus and recognize Dr. Lindsey.

"What happened," Kayla asked quietly looking at the doctor.

He smiled gently.

"You're in the hospital," he told her. "You collapsed and they brought you here."

Kayla thought about the court hearing and the things the judge said to her.

"How do you feel," Dr. Lindsey asked bringing her out of her thoughts.

"Tired, but otherwise fine," Kayla told him.

"Yes, that's what I figured," he told her. "I'm keeping you heavily sedated and keeping you here for a few days."

Kayla didn't argue she just wanted to sleep.

"Is Thomas here," she asked fearfully.

Dr. Lindsey saw her fear.

"No, I sent him home," he returned evenly.

"Thank you," Kayla sighed heavily.

"Your friend is here. Do you want to see her?"

She knew he was talking about Jackie.

"Yes, please," Kayla replied.

Dr. Lindsey nodded and smiled as he left to get Jackie.

●●●

He found the woman sitting in the waiting room watching the TV.

"Jackie," he called.

She turned at the sound of her name.

"Kayla is awake, and she wants to see you," he told her.

Jackie jumped up and headed for the room. Dr. Lindsey stopped her before she got there.

"You can only stay a few moments, and try not to upset her," he told Jackie. "She's still very fragile."

Jackie smiled.

"Doctor Lindsey I would never do anything to hurt Kayla, or her recovery," she assured.

He smiled and walked away.

●●●

Jackie entered the room and found Kayla waiting.

"Hey girl," Jackie said softly smiling at her friend.

"Hey," Kayla smiled back.

"How are you feeling?"

"Tired but okay otherwise," Kayla told her.

"Did you tell Dezi?"

"Yes, he and D were here to see you," Jackie told Kayla.

"I guess I was still out," Kayla replied. "He's going to do something really bad to Thomas."

Jackie didn't reply. She knew it as well. Kayla sighed deeply.

"I used to ask Dezi to spare people who hurt me, and not kill them," Kayla went on quietly. "But I can't bring myself to ask him that this time," she finished and was quiet for a few moments. "Does that make me a bad person Jackie," Kayla asked softly, looking at her friend.

Jackie smiled before replying.

"No," she told her calmly. "It makes you human."

Dr. Lindsey returned and gave Kayla another shot.

"This is going to make you sleep the rest of the night," he told her. "If I'm satisfied you're better in the morning, I'll let you go home OK?"

"Okay," Kayla smiled.

He allowed Jackie to remain with her until she fell asleep.

"Can I stay in here with her please?"

Dr. Lindsey saw the worry on her face, and decided she could if she promised not to wake her.

"I promise," Jackie told him smiling.

He smiled back and left her there. Jackie felt better being here with Kayla. She was scared of what was going on outside the hospital, and equally sure she didn't want to know what it was.

●●●

Thomas and Chris were returning from their day out. They stopped by the hospital, but the nurse wouldn't allow them to see Kayla. Dr. Lindsey left specific orders, and they weren't budging.

"Well at least tell me how she is," Thomas told the nurse.

She sighed deeply and told him his wife was resting comfortably. Her vital signs were excellent and she was doing well. He curtly thanked her and they left.

They didn't see Jackie and Chris assumed she went back to her hotel room. Now they were going to watch a couple of games trying to relax for the rest of the evening. The phone was ringing when they entered. Thomas rushed to it and answered.

"Thomas, this is Maurice," the man boomed as soon as he answered.

"Hey Maurice," he replied. "Man thanks again for today. I seriously owe you one."

Maurice laughed.

"Well you're gonna owe me two, after I tell you this," he replied.

Thomas was intrigued.

"What is it?"

Maurice proceeded to tell Thomas that they were going to forego a trial, and simply sentence him on the lesser charges. It seemed that Elise Hudson had a few charges and criminal history of her own. Even her own parents weren't surprised at her death, knowing her history and line of work.

"The prosecution knew they would have a hard time finding any jury that would convict you, with your reputation in the community," Maurice finished waiting for Thomas's response.

"So it's really over Maurice," Thomas asked hoping it was.

"Yes, for all intents and purposes," Maurice told him.

"Thank you so much," Thomas replied happily.

It was all coming together for him. He was given his wife back and now he had his life back too. They could start again, and be happy this time, with no dark shadows reaching out to engulf them.

"We'll get together tomorrow morning, bright and early, go downtown and take care of your sentencing," Maurice told Thomas.

"That will be fine, Thomas replied thanking Maurice again before he hung up.

Thomas was grinning ear to ear when he returned to the den where Chris was watching TV.

"What gives," Chris asked him seeing his expression.

Thomas told him everything Maurice just told him.

"Man that deserves a drink," Chris told him grabbing the bottle of wine that was delivered earlier with the well-wishes basket.

They opened it and began to drink celebrating the victorious day they enjoyed. Halfway into the bottle they both began to feel light headed.

"Man this is some serious wine," Chris told Thomas his words slurred.

He couldn't understand it. Wine usually only gave him a slight buzz, but this stuff was knocking him off his feet. Thomas was feeling the effects of the drink too. He was trying to focus and finding it extremely difficult.

"Who sent this stuff," he said trying to see the card that was attached to the basket.

He couldn't make it out and asked Chris if he could see it. Chris didn't answer. He was out. Thomas called him a couple more times feeling further and further away himself. He finally passed out too. Neither of them heard or saw the two men enter the house.

Smoke & 36 Mirrors

K.C. and Cedric looked at the unconscious men and chuckled lightly. The wine was laced with a powerful quick acting sedative.

"They are so stupid," Cedric said plainly as they began their task.

It took them a little while because of the men's size but they finally accomplished their tasks. They blindfolded each of them and taped their mouths.

"You want something to drink," Cedric asked K.C.

They were both semi winded from the work of dealing with the two men.

"Yeah that might be good right about now," K.C. replied heading to the kitchen.

They each found soda in the fridge and popped them open.

"Man that Big D is cool as shit," Cedric said, drinking deeply from his can.

K.C. belched loudly and agreed.

"It's amazing the shit they both know," he told Cedric.

They were leaving tonight for sure. He already told his Aunt Rachelle goodbye. She was sad and even cried a little, but told K.C. she understood he had to go be a man.

"I'ma get his ass for my auntie before I leave here though, believe that shit," he told Cedric hatefully.

Cedric understood. He liked Rachelle himself. She was always cool with him staying over all the time and stuff.

"So are we calling them now," Cedric asked.

"Let's get our trophies first," K.C. told him as they began to ransack the house.

●●●

Later after they took what they wanted and put it in the car, they made the call. Dezi answered on the second ring.

"Everything is in place Mr. E.," Cedric told him.

"We're on our way," Dezi smiled and disconnected.

"I can't wait to see what shit these two pull out of the bag tonight," K.C. chuckled looking again at the bound men and shaking his head.

"Whatever it is it's gonna to be good," Cedric said with certainty.

They both sat down and relaxed waiting for Dezi and Big D to arrive.

"You bring the smelling salts," K.C. asked knowing Mr. E was going to have them wake the men up when they arrived.

"Oh shit!" Cedric replied. "It's in the car."

K.C. rolled his eyes. "Go get it!"

"You know how Mr. E is," he told him, as the young man got up to go get the item.

No sooner than Cedric returned Dezi and Big D came in the back door. They never saw them drive up, nor heard them, before they got inside the house. *These muthafuckers is good!* K.C. thought, a whole new respect coming for them both.

●●●

Detective Marchant was incensed. *I can't believe they are going to give this asshole a slap on the wrist,* he thought. He quickly developed a real dislike for Thomas Bradford. The man was an arrogant, self-centered, pompous, blowhard, with a real superiority complex. He especially disliked him after he talked to his wife. *Why would you hit a woman at all, much less someone obviously as nice as she is,* Marchant thought again as he finished up the paperwork on the case.

"Say Marchant, you still here," Detective Landing asked as he entered the station.

"Yeah, just finishing up the Bradford deal," he replied sourly.

Landing chuckled. He knew how much Marchant wanted to send this guy up for killing the girl.

"Well you're definitely not gonna like what I heard earlier either then," Landing told him waiting for his reply.

Marchant was curious.

"What did you hear," he asked guardedly.

"Get this," Landing began. "This arrogant son-of–a-bitch gets his attorney to file a motion, and gets the judge to agree to overturn his divorce, and force his wife back into the house with him."

Marchant's mouth dropped.

"Are you kidding me," he asked still filled with unbelief.

Landing nodded trying to swallow the coffee in his mouth.

"Yeah," he said then shook his head.

"Poor woman couldn't take it," he told him sighing slightly.

Marchant was alarmed.

"What happened," Marchant asked Landing.

The detective sighed deeply before answering.

"She suffered a breakdown," he told him "They took her to the hospital. She's still there under sedation from what I understand."

Marchant was blown away.

"That guy is a true piece of work," Marchant said angrily.

Landing shook his head in agreement.

"Well, I gotta get outta here Marchant," he told him rising to leave.

"Thanks for the update man," Marchant told him as they bid each other goodnight.

I hope she's alright, Marchant thought internally about Kayla. He reluctantly admitted he found himself already more than slightly attracted to her.

Marchant gathered his things from the paper cluttered desk, and rose to leave. He looked around the station at the worn furniture, the outdated computers, and scarce manpower. *No wonder the damn criminals keep winning,* he thought tiredly as he headed out the door to the hospital where Kayla Bradford was.

•••

Marchant arrived at the hospital quickly, parking in an emergency lane space. His car was marked, so no one would question him about his choice of spaces. *The law does have its privileges,* he chuckled, entering the emergency entrance. He saw the hospital was as usual, busy. He saw several people waiting to be seen. Some were obviously ill or hurt, while others seemed to just be looking for a cozy place to sleep. Marchant sighed gently thinking of all the homeless and uninsured the hospital was forced to take in. *The system really sucks,* he thought disgustedly as he went to find out what room Kayla was in.

The reception volunteer advised Marchant of Kayla's room number and he headed upstairs to find it.

"May I help you," the nurse asked Marchant as he approached the station.

"Um yes," he replied. "I'm Detective Dwayne Marchant," he told her showing his badge "I'm checking on Kayla Bradford."

The nurse gave him a look, but she didn't question him.

"Mrs. Bradford is resting comfortably," the nurse replied amiably.

Marchant wanted to see her. He wanted to know for himself Kayla was all right.

"Is it possible for me to see her," he questioned again all business.

"She is unconscious," The nurse informed him.

"Dr. Lindsey has left strict orders that Mrs. Bradford have no visitors, besides which she is heavily sedated," the nurse finished looking at him evenly.

Marchant didn't miss a beat.

"Well I need to see for myself, and document, that Kayla Bradford is indeed in that room sedated," he told her looking back at her.

"Go ahead," the nurse sighed. "Please don't remain for more than five minutes Detective," she admonished.

Marchant shook his head and left headed for her room.

●●●

Jackie was coming out the restroom when she heard the door. She quickly turned out the light and stepped back in leaving the door open so she could see. Marchant entered Kayla's room quietly and walked over to her bed. She was indeed asleep. He looked at the woman and sighed deeply.

"Why would anyone want to hurt you," he said softly, reaching out and stroking her hair.

Jackie was intrigued. *Who is this guy,* she wondered.

Marchant was getting angrier the longer he stood here. He wanted to see Thomas Bradford locked up and rot in prison for the rest of his life.

"Be well Kayla, and I hope your husband gets what's coming to him," Marchant said softly, as he leaned over and kissed her forehead.

Kayla stirred slightly but didn't wake. Marchant sighed again and turned to leave. Jackie stepped back out of his line of sight. She emerged from the restroom and returned to her chair. *What the hell was that all about?*.

"Looks like Thomas has made all sorts of new friends," she said sarcastically aloud and went back to reading her magazine.

Smoke & **37** Mirrors

ezi and Big D looked at the two men and smiled their approval.

"Wake them up," Dezi said evenly taking a seat.

Cedric waived the smelling salts under the men's noses one at a time waking each of them. Their heads turned back and forth, pulling against the restraints. Dezi chuckled, as did Big D.

"Take the blindfolds off," Dezi told K.C. who readily complied.

Once the blindfolds were removed the men blinked continuously trying to focus. Finally they were able see their captors.

"Good evening gentlemen," Dezi said pleasantly.

Thomas looked at him with a mixture of hatred and contempt. Chris was scared, plain and simple.

"I see from your reaction preacher man, you remember me," Dezi said impersonally his eyes taking on their usual cold flatness.

Big D was watching Chris intently. Chris wanted out of there. *I should have never come and I definitely should have never gone to court with him,* he was thinking as Big D got up and walked over to him. He stood and looked at Chris for a long time not saying anything. Big D turned just as silently and walked away, sitting back down in his chair and relaxing. Chris was petrified. Thomas's gaze never faltered. He was looking at Dezi with all the hatred he could muster. Dezi was amused with Thomas's gaze.

"Take the tape off," he told Cedric.

He walked over to Thomas and snatched the tape off, pulling out several hairs from his mustache as well. Cedric laughed when he saw them on the tape.

"Oops, sorry Rev," he chuckled.

Dezi smiled and looked back at Thomas.

"It would seem you have something on your mind that you would like to get off," Dezi told him calmly.

"I'm still married to Kayla you bastard!" Thomas spat venomously. "She's my wife and she's going to stay my wife!"

Dezi laughed heartily.

"Do I look like I give a fuck what a court, or a piece of paper, says about who Kayla belongs too," he asked calmly after he stopped laughing.

"In case you haven't noticed preacher man, you're in no position to give orders or ultimatums," Dezi finished.

Thomas wasn't deterred. He wasn't going to let this guy come in and take Kayla away again.

"Why don't you let me down from here and face me like a man, you asshole," Thomas challenged.

Dezi exchanged looks with Big D. He smiled and shrugged. Dezi looked at K.C.

"Let him loose," Dezi said flatly.

Cedric and K.C. were shocked but intrigued. They wanted to see this. Dezi stood as they loosened the last binding.

"So, here we are," he told Thomas calmly regarding the man.

Thomas looked hard at Dezi thinking of the bodily harm he intended to inflict on the man.

He stepped closer and spoke, "I'm going to kill you"

Dezi didn't flinch. Cedric and K.C. were watching closely fascinated with the man's demeanor. Big D was still sitting comfortably watching Thomas. Chris was shaking his head hoping his friend wouldn't do this. He remembered the beating Dezi inflicted the last time they met. Thomas lunged at Dezi, who caught him in the midsection and dropped him hard. K.C. smiled at Cedric as they continued to watch. Dezi stepped back and allowed the man to get up.

"Try again," he said calmly looking evenly at Thomas.

Thomas rethought his strategy this time and tried boxing. Dezi calmly ducked or deflected each of the blows that Thomas threw. After the last swing Thomas took, Dezi caught him with a hard right and a left uppercut. Thomas staggered backwards but didn't go down. He charged again and Dezi caught him once more with a hard right. His mouth was bleeding. Thomas spit the blood onto the floor and came at Dezi again. Big D was amused, knowing his friend was only toying with the man.

Chris wanted to yell at Thomas and tell him to stop. Thomas was furious. He couldn't get a good punch in anywhere it seemed. He couldn't let this guy beat him. Thomas lunged at Dezi again aiming to take his legs from under him. Dezi read his move and kicked him hard in the gut. Thomas crumpled and Dezi kicked him again.

"Give it up preacher man," he said calmly as Thomas tried to catch his breath.

Dezi gave K.C. and Cedric the signal to bind him again. K.C. took the opportunity for a little payback himself. He kicked Thomas viciously in the face, breaking his nose. Dezi chuckled lightly. They secured him and Dezi spoke to Thomas once again.

"Oh, that was K.C.," Dezi told him, explaining the kick. "He's a little pissed that you hit his aunt and threatened her."

Thomas looked at Dezi blankly, having no idea what he was talking about.

"Rachelle," Dezi told him.

Recognition flooded Thomas's face.

"I see you remember who I'm talking about," Dezi told him. "Is there anything in the fridge to drink," Dezi addressed Cedric.

"Sodas," he replied.

Dezi chuckled.

"Yes, I forgot, Kayla detests beer," he said and Thomas gave him a look.

"Bring me one would you," he told Cedric who left to get it. "All that excitement worked up a thirst," Dezi said calmly as both Big D and K.C. laughed heartily.

Cedric returned with his drink and Dezi opened it taking a long drink from it.

"Whew, that's better," he replied. "Well, hello Christopher," Dezi said finally turning his attention to the man.

"Take it off," he told K.C. as he went to remove the tape from Chris's mouth.

"Long time no see," he said again.

Chris was careful not to say anything.

Dezi chuckled.

"I see you've learned a lot from our last meeting," he replied. "Too bad you didn't learn from the other night hmm," he replied and returned to his drink.

Thomas looked at Chris. He wished he asked more about Dezi and their history. Maybe he would have known how to better handle this now. Big D rose and walked over to Chris.

"Didn't we give you a fair shake the other night," he asked evenly never taking his eyes from him.

Chris shook his head vigorously.

"It's not what it seems," he replied trying to sound steadier than he felt.

Big D crossed his arms on his chest.

"Really," he queried. "From what I've seen, you're here. You were in court, and you were at the hospital with your best friend here."

Chris swallowed hard.

"I didn't know anything about the court thing until I got here," he told Big D. "Please, I swear I didn't."

Big D regarded him a moment then continued talking.

"Why should I believe that," he countered. "This is your boy, your friend, you two been road dogs for a long time haven't you?"

Chris was trying to think. This looked bad, and even though he actually was innocent, he was caught up.

"Yeah we're friends and stuff, but I swear, I had nothing to do with this," he finished his voice cracking.

Big D half believed him, but that was beside the point. He was in the wrong place with the wrong guy.

"Well I won't pass judgment," he replied "I'll leave that for your maker to do," he finished as he hit him hard in the midsection.

Chris coughed and tried to catch his breath. Big D proceeded to work him over hitting him again and again until he was almost unconscious.

"Please," Chris begged still trying to catch his breath.

Big D didn't react. He flipped out the switchblade and locked it. The blade glistened in the light, sharp and unyielding. K.C. and Cedric were entranced as they watched him. Dezi was watching Thomas intently and saw the fear that was now in his eyes. He turned his attention back to Big D and Chris.

"Please don't kill me," Chris was pleading, tears running down his face.

"You had that chance already, remember," Big D replied coldly.

He cut him with the blade and Chris screamed. Dezi smiled. K.C. and Cedric's mouth dropped. Blood poured from the wound. Big D cut Chris again and again. None of the cuts were life threatening on their own, but combined he was losing too much blood. Chris felt himself begin to lose consciousness.

"No buddy, not yet," Big D told Chris softly as he stood close to his ear.

"I hear salt works well," Dezi suggested still smiling.

Big D turned and grinned at him.

"Yeah, but alcohol stings more," he replied and they both burst into laughter.

"Find the alcohol," he told Cedric, who scampered to the bathroom.

He returned moments later with the bottle in hand.

"Oh God, please don't do this," Chris whispered softly.

He was bleeding heavily and weakened from it. Big D opened the bottle and held it above the man's head. He poured it all over his body. The liquid found its way into each of the cuts and began to burn. Chris screamed and tried vainly to get out of his bindings. Big D smiled and stepped back.

"Very nice," Dezi told him.

Chris was screaming and crying, his nose was running, and he pissed himself from the pain.

He was hanging by his arms and his legs were tied and bound to the wall. He couldn't render any sort of aid to himself. Chris began to quiet down as the pain began to subside. He was gasping for air. Big D and Dezi knew he was going into shock.

"Look what you've done preacher man," Dezi said evenly looking Thomas in the eye. "You've gotten your best friend killed."

Thomas stared at Chris.

"Let him go," he said plainly.

"What was that," Dezi asked.

Thomas sighed heavily.

"Let him go, please," he repeated.

Big D looked at Thomas.

"Why would I do that," he asked simply.

Thomas looked at the man. *Do all these damned psychos just hang out together and hurt people?*

"Because he's telling the truth," he replied. "He didn't know about any of this. He even tried to talk me out of it."

Big D gave Dezi a look. Dezi shrugged and finished his drink.

"Well," Big D began. "If he is truly innocent, it will make his getting into heaven that much easier," he replied, as he stabbed Chris in the heart.

K.C. and Cedric gasped. Dezi smiled and looked back at Thomas.

His mouth was agape and his eyes watered.

"I told you he didn't do anything," he screamed.

Big D turned to Thomas and regarded him coldly.

"Maybe not to you, but I owed his ass," he said evenly as he turned and cut Chris's throat for good measure.

What the hell is he talking about? Thomas thought before realization kicked in. *This was the man Jackie divorced him for.*

K.C. and Cedric gave each other high fives. Dezi still watched Thomas intently. The tears rolled down his cheeks. *Oh God Chris, I'm so sorry. This is all my fault,* he thought miserably as he watched his friend take his last breath. Big D cleaned his knife and closed it. He returned to his seat and sat down. Thomas thought about Kayla. He knew he would never see her again. He was going to die here tonight. Dezi rose and walked over to Thomas.

"Do you like the way I bound you," he asked smiling slightly and looking deeply into Thomas's eyes.

"It's fitting don't you think? Considering the complex you have," he told him.

He bound Thomas with both his arms out to his side and his feet together, exactly as Christ was crucified on the cross.

"Why don't you just kill me and get it over with," Thomas replied unimpressed.

Dezi chuckled.

"And deprive myself of the fun of watching you suffer," he questioned walking over to the bag lying on the table.

What sick games does this nut have in mind, Thomas fearfully wondered watching the man retrieve items from the bag. Dezi took out the hammer and nails he requested. They were long four-inch spikes. He turned to Thomas. When Thomas realized what Dezi was about to do, he panicked.

"Why are you doing this," he asked looking afraid again.

Dezi sighed gently.

"Well, you should actually feel honored shouldn't you," he asked. "I mean, this is what happened to your God correct," he asked again as he took the first spike and drove it through Thomas's right hand.

He gritted his teeth and managed to not cry out. Dezi was impressed. He chuckled lightly as he did the same thing to his left hand. Again, Thomas managed to not cry out. *I will not give him the satisfaction,* he thought bitterly. Dezi admitted he was very impressed. Still he took the other spikes and drove them through both feet. Tears trickled from Thomas's eyes but he didn't cry out.

"You're a very strong willed man preacher," Dezi said softly.

He stabbed Thomas in his side and cut him deeply. Thomas cried out from both the pain and the surprise of the blow. He began to bleed profusely.

"There," Dezi said stepping back. "What do you think," he asked all the other men in the room.

They all voiced their approval that he did an excellent re-creation. Thomas was feeling lightheaded.

"After I leave here I'm going to the hospital and get Kayla," Dezi said evenly looking at him.

Thomas mustered all his strength and spat in his face. Dezi cut him deeply across the chest causing even more blood to spring forth. Thomas screamed again.

"That wasn't very nice preacher man," Dezi said calmly after he cleaned his face. "Kayla and I made love last night," he told him softly in his ear.

"She was wonderful," Dezi told him again causing more pain in Thomas's heart.

"Just kill me," he pleaded.

Dezi chuckled softly.

"No, not yet," he replied.

"Did you like the dress she wore to court today," Dezi asked anew. "I picked that out and bought it for her," he told Thomas. "I like to show off that flawless figure Kayla has, because unlike you, I'm not insecure," he chuckled. "Did you know that every time she was with you she was thinking of me," he taunted.

Thomas was miserable. His heart felt like it was about to explode.

"I'm going to take Kayla away from here and away from all the pain you've inflicted on her," Dezi told him matter-of-fact.

Thomas was sobbing openly now. He didn't care what any of these men thought of him. He was weeping for Kayla and for his loss. Dezi walked back to his bag and got out the last spike. This one was ten inches long, three inches thick and solid steel. He walked back to Thomas and looked at him again.

"I promised you death if you hurt her ever again," Dezi said coldly never taking his eyes off Thomas.

"You fucked up for the last time preacher man. Take a good look at my face and know that I'm the man who will be with Kayla for the rest of her life," he finished and drove the final spike through Thomas's heart.

His face was frozen in shock and pain as he died. Thomas's eyes stayed fixed on Dezi even after he took his last breath. In one final act of desecration, Dezi emasculated the dead man. K.C. and Cedric were still entranced. They never, in their wildest dreams, imagined they would see anything like the sight they just witnessed.

Cedric once again dialed 911 and hung up. They doused the house with the gasoline they brought and Big D flicked the match inside. They stood and watched for a moment as the house began to go up in flames. K.C. and Cedric said their goodbyes and jumped in their car, tires screeching heading for the coast. Dezi looked at Big D.

"Let's go," he said simply.

They left headed back to the hotel to shower, change and rest.

Smoke & **38** Mirrors

etective Marchant heard the call go out on his scanner. He was close to the house and decided to go to the scene. *What the hell has happened at this house now,* he wondered as he arrived on scene finding the house almost fully engulfed and firefighters trying to put out the blaze.

"What happened," Marchant asked the uniformed officer out front.

"Looks like someone started a fire," he replied.

"Anyone home," Marchant asked again.

"We can't get in yet, fire is too hot, so we don't know for sure," the officer told him.

"This is the same guy we had that murder at a few days ago right," the officer asked Marchant.

He absently nodded yes looking at stately house as it burned. Marchant got the distinct feeling they would indeed find a body when the fire was put out. He couldn't explain it, it was a just a feeling in his gut. He remained until firefighters brought the blaze under control, which didn't take them as long as he originally assumed it would. Marchant looked at the remains of the once magnificent structure and shook his head. *Well at least she won't have to come back to this house now,* he thought of Kayla.

"We got two bodies inside," the Fire Chief told him plainly.

Marchant told him okay and followed him. The fire seemed to have miraculously missed the major portion of this room and he could plainly see the two men bound to the wall. Marchant knew he had a murder scene on his hands. He immediately called his team as he made his way gingerly over to the two bodies. They were virtually undamaged by the fire. He recognized the one man, hung crucifixion style as Thomas Bradford. The other man hanging by his arms he didn't recognize.

Detective Landing made it to the sight first. He joined Marchant in the room and looked at the bodies.

"Jeez!" he said aloud looking at the carnage. "Who the fuck did this guy piss off?"

Marchant was curious himself. *Who would be angry enough to do this kind of harm to the man,* he wondered. He thought back to the station and the man that picked up Kayla Bradford. Marchant made a note that he needed to talk to her and get more information on her boyfriend.

"Well I recognize Bradford, but I don't know who this other guy is," Marchant said nodding toward the other man.

Landing looked at him.

"His name is Chris Lynch" he replied, telling Marchant he recognized him from the church.

"Damn," Marchant replied. "Maybe he was just in the wrong place at the wrong time."

The coroner and CSI's arrived and he and Landing left them to do their work.

"Well at least his wife doesn't have to live with him again," Landing replied flatly.

Marchant was thinking the same thing.

"You don't think she had anything to do with this do you," Landing asked.

"No," Marchant told him. "I checked the hospital and she is still completely unconscious."

"No doubt whoever did this had a score to settle, but hell that could have been anyone in his church or outside that we didn't know about," Marchant told him.

Landing nodded in agreement. Thomas definitely wasn't Mr. Popularity in the last few days. They each returned to their cars agreeing to meet at the station later. Merchant told Landing he would begin the paperwork. *Well, he got what he deserved no doubt,* Marchant thought. *Now Kayla could get on with her own life and never look back.* He started the car and headed to his apartment. He needed to sleep for a few hours. Marchant decided he would be the one to tell Kayla about Thomas in the morning. It was also an opportunity for him to see her one last time.

●●●

Big D called Jackie and let her know they were okay when they arrived back at the hotel last night. She didn't ask any questions other than when they were leaving.

"We'll leave tomorrow," he told her. He and Dezi knew the police would come and inform Kayla of Thomas's death and question her. Once they were satisfied she knew nothing he would come and get them and they would leave. Jackie was understanding and told them she would remain with Kayla and call them once everything was settled.

She heard Kayla stirring and it brought her back to the present. She looked at her watch. It was after nine.

"How long have I been asleep," Kayla asked stretching.

She looked better, peaceful even.

"All night miss thang," Jackie quipped. "It's the next day already," she teased.

Kayla chuckled.

"I sure feel better," she said lightly.

Jackie called the nurse and told them Kayla was awake and wanted to shower. She asked Big D bring them both clothes last night. The nurse entered and helped her from the bed.

"Can you stand on your own," she asked.

"Yes, I'll be fine," Kayla smiled.

The nurse nodded and left them alone. Kayla showered and dressed first, then Jackie followed.

"What time is Dr. Lindsey coming by," Kayla asked.

"He didn't give a specific time," Jackie told her.

"I hope it's early," Kayla said, "I really want to get out of here."

"Amen to that," Jackie replied.

●●●

Detective Marchant approached the nurse's station again. "Hello I'm Detective Dwayne Marchant," he told the new nurse now on duty. "I need to see Kayla Bradford please."

Dr. Lindsey was just about to go see Kayla and heard the man inquire after her.

"I'm Kayla's doctor," he told Marchant as he introduced himself. "What exactly is this about?"

Marchant gave him a brief rundown of what he needed to tell Kayla. Dr. Lindsey was shocked.

"I knew he wasn't the nicest man, but I never expected anything like this," he said subdued.

Dr. Lindsey thought long and hard about letting him tell Kayla.

"She's very fragile right now. I don't want her pushed over the edge," he replied. "Hold on a moment," he said and retrieved a syringe, filling it before they went in. "Just in case," he told Marchant who was looking at him quizzically.

•••

Kayla and Jackie were still laughing and talking when the two men entered the room. Jackie recognized him as the man who came in last night and of course Dr. Lindsey.

"Hi Dr. Lindsey," Kayla said amiably.

He smiled. "Hello Kayla."

"Hi," she said looking at Marchant. "I remember you," she said trying to recall his name.

"Yes, I'm Detective Marchant," he smiled.

"I'm sorry I didn't remember," Kayla apologized.

"It's fine," Marchant told her.

"Did I forget something at the station the other day," she asked trying to figure out why the Detective was here.

Jackie was curious herself, seeing the man's behavior last night. She already knew he had a serious crush on Kayla. *That's not a healthy occupation*, Jackie thought and almost laughed.

"Well, Mrs. Bradford," he began. "I actually need to tell you something," Marchant finished looking at her evenly.

Kayla began to be afraid. *I hope nothing's happened to Dezi or D*, she thought. Marchant saw the worry and anxiety in her eyes. He didn't want to upset her and cause her to relapse, but he needed to tell her.

"What," Kayla asked "What's wrong," she asked again becoming slightly excited.

"Kayla, I need you to calm down," Dr. Lindsey told Kayla. "Breathe deeply or I'm going to sedate you again."

She nodded yes and started to slow her breathing.

"Mrs. Bradford, I'm sorry to have to tell you, your husband is dead," he said gently.

Kayla gasped, as did Jackie. *Dead? Oh my God,* she thought as she held her hand to her mouth. Dr. Lindsey was watching her intently ready to use the syringe if necessary.

"How," Kayla said quietly never taking her eyes off Marchant.

His heart was hurting for her. He wanted nothing more than to take her into his arms again and hold her.

"He was umm, murdered it seems" Marchant told her.

Kayla clamped the other hand over her mouth, tears spilling from her eyes. *Even after all the hurt he put her through she's still upset at his death,* Marchant thought, watching the woman suffer.

"I hate to ask you, but do you know Christopher Lynch," he asked and Kayla immediately looked at Jackie.

"I know him," Jackie spoke up, not thinking she wanted to hear what came next.

"How do you know him," Marchant questioned.

"He's my soon to be ex-husband," she replied.

He sighed heavily.

"Mrs. Lynch, your husband was killed also," Marchant told her gently.

Now it was Jackie's turn to be shocked. Marchant saw the tears come to her eyes and spill out.

"Oh God," she said softly and dropped her head.

They saw her shoulders shuddering and knew Jackie was crying silently. Kayla went to her and they hugged each other crying and trying to find comfort. Dr. Lindsey suggested they leave them alone.

"Mrs. Bradford, Mrs. Lynch," Marchant began. "I'm truly sorry," he said softly as they left them alone.

Once they were sure the men were gone, they pulled away from each other and dried their tears.

●●●

"I guess it really is over now," Jackie said softly.

Kayla agreed.

"I guess we have to at least plan their services," Jackie said again.

"I'll arrange it all for Thomas, but I'm not going to be there," Kayla told her.

Jackie understood and she couldn't blame her friend. She went through hell and back with Thomas. What little Kayla was doing was actually a huge deal considering the circumstances. Dr. Lindsey came back into the room.

"Are you both alright," he asked them looking concerned.

"Yes, we're fine," they both assured.

"Can I go home today," Kayla asked.

Dr. Lindsey looked at her evenly for a while before nodding yes.

"I'll sign your paperwork," he told her. "Please take care of yourself Kayla," he told her gently.

"I will Dr. Lindsey, I promise," she smiled.

Jackie called Big D.

"The police have come and gone," she told him.

"We're on our way," Big D replied, disconnecting.

"They're coming to get us," she told Kayla.

She smiled and nodded. Kayla pulled out her own cell and began making calls tying up Thomas's service and burial. She made calls to the insurance company concerning the house. Jackie did the same for Chris. Kayla was just finishing when Dezi and Big D walked into her room. Dezi took Kayla in his arms and kissed her. She hugged him tightly.

"Thank you," she said softly looking deeply into his eyes.

He kissed her again.

"I told you I would never let anyone else hurt you ever again," Dezi replied softly caressing her face.

Big D was still kissing Jackie. She pushed him away gently, giggling.

"You're gonna get something started in here," she chuckled.

"Hey, I'm down for whatever," Big D laughed.

"Do you know how much I appreciate you," she asked him softly as she stroked his face.

"It's you and me baby and that's the way it's gonna be," he replied kissing her again. "Let's get the hell outta here," Big D said loud enough for everyone to hear "We got a plane to catch."

They all laughed and started walking out together.

●●●

Marchant had hung around a while. He saw Kayla and the boyfriend. He also saw Jackie and her friend. He had a pretty good idea of who killed both the men and why. Marchant looked at Kayla and saw how happy she was in the arms of this man she was with. His cell vibrated and he answered.

"We couldn't find any useful prints to work with, so we're effectively back to ground zero," the officer told him.

"Thanks," Marchant told him absently and hung up still watching the couples as they made their way to the elevator.

He took one last look at Kayla as the door closed. He turned around and walked back down the stairs. This case in his mind effectively closed.

Smoke & **39** Mirrors

The entire town was in a state of shock. The church was filled to overflowing for the services. They were being held together, the funerals of Pastors Thomas Bradford and Christopher Lynch. Marchant came out of curiosity. He wanted to see if either of the wives would show. Marchant looked out at the sea of people who came to pay their last respects when he saw her.

She and Lynch's widow were together. Kayla looked absolutely beautiful. She was clad in a tailor cut navy dress, with her hair up, and sapphire accessories completing her look. The shoes were 3-inch stilettos and they accentuated her already beautiful legs. They were both escorted to the front pew and seated. The duel mahogany coffins were directly in front of them. Thomas's was covered with an expansive yellow, red, and white rose spray. Chris's was covered with white mums, blue and yellow carnations.

Marchant was intrigued watching the women. Neither of them showed much emotion, simply sitting stoically, as if at a performance or lecture they would rather not be in attendance of. He also wondered where the men were he saw escorting them out of the hospital two days ago. He didn't expend a lot of energy worrying about it. He enjoyed the opportunity to once again see her and allow his imagination to run freely.

•••

Kayla was sitting and looking at the coffins. Mariah and Aidan didn't know about the deaths. They decided to tell them once they all arrived home. Coming to the service was Dezi's idea. Kayla was glad it was over, and she was finally free. She didn't want to come here and pretend. She really wasn't sorry Thomas was dead. She already went to the cemetery to say her goodbyes to Black. Kayla wanted to leave and live her life now, with the man who loved her more than life itself. She wanted to see the kids, and play with her granddaughter. She didn't want to be here in this church, with these people, pretending to mourn for a man she didn't love anymore.

Kayla sighed deeply as a single tear rolled down her cheek. The more she thought about the past year, the more she cried. Jackie put her arm around Kayla and tried to comfort her. Kayla was finally spent and stopped crying. Jackie continued to hold her and she put her arms around Jackie. They looked up as the minister took the podium. They contacted Pastor Al

Maxwell who was a lifelong friend of both Chris and Thomas from Florida to come and do the eulogies. They gave him their full attention as he began.

●●●

Al couldn't believe he was standing here doing this. Both his friends were dead, murdered brutally by unknown assailants. *Who would want to kill them*, he thought all morning. What the hell went on with Thomas and Chris here in Chapel Hill? He heard all sorts of rumors in the three days he was here. They were asking him if he would be interested in coming on as Pastor. He looked at the two women sitting on the front row. He recognized each of them from photos. He could tell they were trying hard, especially Kayla, Thomas's wife. He watched her break down. Now she was holding onto to her friend, trying to stay composed. He looked at Jackie, Chris's wife. She was staring unbelieving at the coffins, trying hard to stay strong for herself and her friend. His heart went out to them. *Lord, please give them the strength to go on*, he prayed silently.

The audience listened as Al spoke, alternating between joy and sorrow. He told them about the men's characters and how they lived their lives. Kayla and Jackie simply endured. They had stories of their own they could tell. Finally Al was finished and the funeral attendants came and opened the coffins for everyone to have a final viewing. Kayla sat with her eyes tightly shut still crying softly. She didn't want to see Thomas again. She just wanted this to be over. Kayla endured the viewing, the trauma of seeing Thomas again being almost too much for her to bear even now. She vaguely remembered being escorted to the waiting limousines. Once inside she and Jackie began to talk.

"Are you alright," Jackie asked concerned.

Kayla looked back at her for a moment before answering.

"I was angry even seeing he was dead, Jackie," she told her quietly "I thought about all hurt, and pain, and I felt guilty for hating him still," she finished shrinking into the seat.

Jackie shook her head. *My God the hell she must have endured this last year with Thomas,* she thought looking at the hurt in Kayla's face even now.

They finally arrived at the gravesite.

"Come on girl, we're at the homestretch," Jackie told her trying to lighten her mood "Don't quit on me now!"

Kayla laughed lightly.

"OK, let's get this done," she replied.

Kayla wanted to get out of here and Dezi promised they could leave once she did this. They were all standing at the gravesites. They were being buried alongside each other with the spaces on either side of them reserved for their wives. No one was the wiser that neither wife was ever intending to be buried there. Kayla and Jackie sat attentively as Al said the final words of internment, and they began to lower the coffins into the ground. Kayla watched until Thomas's was completely interred before leaving.

Marchant still watched her intently. Jackie saw him and waved. He waved back, embarrassed once again, to have been caught looking.

"That's your secret crush," she told Kayla softly, nodding toward the man.

Kayla turned and looked at him. She thought about what Jackie told her, about the man coming into her room while she slept. Kayla waved and gave him a warm smile. Marchant waved back and returned the smile. *If only,* he thought as he watched her get into the car and be driven away.

● ● ●

They were all on the plane heading home. Dezi was holding Kayla as she slept. She fell asleep almost immediately upon takeoff. He chuckled inside looking at her. Dezi sighed; glad to finally be on their way. He was happier than he could recall in twenty years. He looked at Jackie and Big D, both of whom were also napping. Dezi smiled again, content that the plan came together. They would all be together, happy, rich, and enjoying life in Pembroke Parrish. He owned almost seventy percent of the island and his businesses thrived.

Dezi thought of Aidan. He knew it wouldn't be easy telling him who he really was. He just hoped that his son accepted him, and they could have a relationship. Dezi looked at Kayla again. She stirred for a moment, adjusting herself in his arms, and then went back contently to sleep. She was a wreck after returning from the funeral. He made her go. He knew she needed to keep up appearances to ward off suspicion.

"Nothing but happiness for you from now, until forever, my baby," he said softly.

They were still almost two hours from arrival. Dezi leaned his head back and closed his eyes drifting off into a fitful sleep.

● ● ●

Mariah and Aidan arrived at the house and got out of their car.

"Wow," Aidan remarked looking at the huge mansion standing in front of them. "Dante has got to have reserve money bags," he exclaimed laughing.

"I can't wait to get inside," Mariah laughed

"What time are they getting here," she asked excitedly.

Dante called and told them they were on their way.

"I can't wait to see mommy," Mariah said again.

Livvy squealed and they both laughed.

"Looks like someone else is ready to see grandma too, huh," Mariah said as Livvy smiled brightly.

They rang the bell and the door opened.

"Hello, how are you," the housekeeper greeted them with a thick accent.

She was a heavy set black woman, with big beautiful eyes and an infectious smile.

"Come in! Come in!" she told them, immediately taking Livvy who giggled.

Aidan and Mariah were astounded when they entered the house. Chandeliers hung in the three expansive great rooms they could see from their vantage point. There were beautiful sculptures and artwork everywhere. The oriental rugs were authentic and absolutely breathtaking.

"Come with me," the housekeeper told them.

They finally caught up long enough to ask her what her name was.

"Oh I'm sorry, my name is Celeste," she told them.

They smiled and greeted her again using her name this time.

"I'm Aidan, this is my wife Mariah, and the little one is Livvy," Aidan told her.

"Yes, I know who you are," she smiled.

Mr. Enzo called and told her they were coming. Mariah smelled the food cooking.

"Mm, it smells wonderful in here," she remarked as they headed to the kitchen.

Celeste laughed.

"It's for your lunch," she told them, busily giving Livvy papaya as she talked to them.

The baby loved it and kept reaching for more.

"What time is it," she asked Aidan anxious all over again.

He laughed.

"Relax baby, they will be here soon," he added.

"Look around if you want," Celeste told them. "Mr. Enzo won't mind."

"Thank you," they returned, leaving her with Livvy, and going exploring.

●●●

They both gasped when they saw the rear deck. It was sitting directly on the ocean. The view was even more spectacular than theirs. Mariah looked down and squealed.

"Look," she told Aidan.

He looked down and saw what she saw. The entire floor of the deck was clear. You could see the fish swimming under your feet.

"Oh mommy is going to absolutely love this," Mariah said excitedly.

They left the deck and began exploring other rooms. Aidan went into Dante's office. It was nicely decorated with antique furniture and a huge mahogany desk. He kept all sorts of books on philosophy, law, and the like. Dante also kept a box of Cubans on his desk. Aidan chuckled thinking it was so much like him.

Mariah was intrigued when she entered what must be Dante's bedroom. There was a picture of her mother from years earlier on his dresser. *How odd,* she thought, interrupted by the sound of the car pulling up outside.

"They're here!" Mariah squealed running back downstairs, Aidan close on her heels.

●●●

Kayla, Jackie and Big D were in shock.

"This damn house is amazing," Big D remarked.

"It's just a little something," Dezi laughed.

"Do you like it baby?" he asked Kayla softly.

She shrugged.

"It's alright," Kayla replied smiling mischievously at him.

Dezi laughed again and kissed her.

"Come on," he said taking her hand.

Celeste met them at the door and welcomed them.

"I'm going into my office for a moment," Dezi told them as he left them.

Celeste took their things and ushered them into one of the expansive great rooms. Jackie was still looking at the house in disbelief.

"OK, Dezi has to print his own money right," she said laughing.

They all laughed with her.

●●●

"Mommy!" Mariah squealed finally making it to them.

Kayla turned at the sound of her voice and rose. They embraced each other tightly, smiling and crying at the same time.

"Let me look at you," Kayla said still crying.

Aidan finally made it in with Livvy.

"Aunt Jackie? D?" he said excitedly. "Wow this is great," he exclaimed hugging everyone.

"Hey Mom," Aidan told Kayla hugging her too.

"Why didn't you guys tell us you were coming," they both asked in unison.

Everyone laughed and said they wanted to surprise them.

"Where's Dante," Aidan asked.

His back was to the office and Mariah was engrossed in conversation with Jackie. Neither of them saw him walk in the room.

"I'm right here, Aidan," Dezi said softly.

Aidan turned to the sound of his voice and looked directly into his own gray eyes. He was stunned speechless. Mariah looked up and saw him too. Her mouth dropped. Kayla rose and walked over to Dezi, who put his arm around her.

"Aidan," she said softly, never taking her eyes off him.

He looked at her questioningly.

"This is your father. This is the man I loved twenty years ago and the man who came back and saved my life," Kayla went on. "This is Dezi Gianni."

Aidan was blown away. There were so many emotions going on within him right now.

"They said you were dead," he told Dezi looking back at the man who could have been his twin.

Dezi smiled and Aidan saw the dimples.

"It's a very long story Aidan," he said gently. "I never knew you existed until Big D sent the photos," he told him "But once I did, I wanted very much to get to know you, your wife, and my granddaughter."

Aidan was still trying to digest the fact that his father was alive.

"You did this," he asked referring to them being here, their home, school and financial stability.

"Yes," Dezi replied softly. "I wanted us all here, together."

Aidan looked around the room at all the people in it. Everyone here was family. He looked back at Dezi.

"You have got to be the most unique man I've ever met," Aidan told Dezi looking at him evenly.

"I wanted to get to know you. Especially after mama died. I wanted to know why I am the way I am sometimes," he finished, emotional now as the tears started to come.

Mariah came and hugged Aidan.

"I'm glad you're not dead," he told Dezi looking at him once again.

Dezi smiled feeling the weight of the world lift from his shoulders.

"I'm looking forward to us all learning each other, and living a wonderful life here, together," he told Aidan.

"I would like that a lot," he said softly.

Dezi stepped to his son and they embraced holding each other, finally allowing all their emotion to overtake them. Everyone left them alone and headed out to the deck.

●●●

"Mommy you look so happy," Mariah, told her as they talked alone.

Big D and Jackie were in the kitchen with Celeste and Livvy.

"I am baby," she told her daughter smiling and looking out at the ocean. "Happier than I've been in a very long time," she said softly.

"What about Thomas," Mariah asked concerned. "Are you getting a divorce?"

Kayla sighed deeply. She knew Mariah didn't know anything that transpired the past few months.

"I think we'll all talk about that together," Dezi interrupted, as he and Aidan emerged.

Kayla smiled at him, grateful he arrived at that moment.

They all gathered again in the great room and began to talk. Kayla told Mariah and Aidan all that she endured with Thomas during the past year, all about his affair, the woman being murdered in their house, the court proceedings, her near breakdown, and finally his own death.

Jackie told them of her similar ordeal with Chris. They both listened enraptured, as the women spoke. Mariah was crying softly when Kayla finished.

"Mommy, Aunt Jackie, why didn't you tell us," she asked.

Kayla smiled.

"I didn't want to burden you, or worry you," she replied.

Aidan was angry.

"How could they do those terrible things to you both," he said coldly, knowing that his father and Big D were more than likely responsible for their deaths.

"It's the past now Aidan," Jackie smiled.

"We're all here together, and we're going to live a wonderful life," she said and they all agreed.

Dezi watched Aidan, looking at a mirror image of himself. He saw the coldness come into his eyes and heard it in his voice. Big D looked at Dezi and they exchanged knowing glances. This was indeed his son. *I'll teach him the business later when he's ready,* Dezi thought as he sipped his drink, knowing Aidan was already two kills in.

"Well, I for one want to go swimming, before lunch," Dezi boomed rising from his chair.

Jackie and Big D were staying with them for the week as they prepared their home.

"We didn't bring swimwear," Aidan laughed.

"Oh no you don't," Dezi laughed.

He called to Celeste and she materialized with the bags he stopped and picked up on the way here. He handed them to everyone.

"Ladies and gentlemen," Dezi announced. "Swimwear."

They all burst into laughter and headed to their rooms to change.

●●●

"Your father is amazing," Mariah laughed as she took out the tiny suit he bought for Livvy.

Aidan smiled.

"Yes, he's remarkable," he replied. "He must really love your mother," he said wistfully.

Mariah thought about it and agreed.

"I know he does," she replied as she slipped on her own suit.

"Very nice," Aidan remarked eyeing her lustily. "Livvy may just get that sibling yet," he said as he kissed her.

Mariah giggled. "Stop perv, and come on."

●●●

Kayla looked at the suit Dezi bought for her.

"Where's the rest of it," she giggled.

He looked at her slyly.

"That's a regulation size swim suit," Dezi replied.

"Mm hmm," Kayla replied as she left to put it on.

She returned moments later.

"Damn girl," Dezi said looking her over. "You might not make it to the ocean looking all good like that," he finished, licking his lips.

She laughed and kissed him.

"Come on or we won't make it outside," Kayla giggled.

Dezi laughed and followed her out. Everyone was having a great time. He and Kayla were playing with Livvy who was thoroughly enjoying the water.

They all came in to the patio for lunch. Dezi fed Livvy, who delighted in feeding him back. Aidan smiled seeing how much his father was enjoying himself. The day turned into evening and Mariah and Aidan were preparing to leave.

"Mommy, I'll be back tomorrow, and we'll go shopping!" she told her excitedly about all the shops she found.

"Jackie and I will definitely be ready," Kayla laughed.

They embraced again.

"I'm so glad you're here, and you're safe, mommy," Mariah said softly her eyes full of love.

"Yes, Mariah, so am I," Kayla smiled and told her.

They waved goodbye and returned inside. Jackie and Big D bid them goodnight heading to their room and Kayla and Dezi retired to their own room.

●●●

Kayla showered and put on a lacy pink nightie. She went outside on the balcony while Dezi showered. She breathed deeply and basked in the freedom she now felt. Dezi saw her standing there, the wind blowing her hair softly. He loved this woman so much, and he waited twenty years, to see her standing in this room. He went outside and put his arms around her. Kayla smiled and laid her head back onto his chest.

"This is so beautiful," she said softly looking out across the water at the moon that looked as if it were sitting in it.

Dezi turned Kayla to him and looked into her eyes.

"Not as beautiful as you," he said softly, kissing her passionately.

He undressed her, and made love to her on the balcony, as they lay on the chaise lounge.

"I love you so much," Dezi told Kayla afterwards holding her in his arms.

"I love you too," she replied and smiled at him.

EPILOGUE

Dezi and Kayla got the chance to talk, and she shared with him, some of the more heinous things that Thomas did to her during the course of their marriage.

"After Thomas hit me, I knew he was dangerous. I decided while he was out of town, to go and have my will drawn up," Kayla told Dezi quietly. "He was a walking time bomb. I honestly thought he would kill me," she told Dezi, crying softly.

"I'm so happy now, being here with you again," Kayla told him. "I hope you have truly forgiven me for all the hurt, and pain, I must have caused you all these years."

Dezi smiled and hugged Kayla tightly.

"Baby, I love you," he told her. "I forgive you completely. That's the past. We have so much to look forward too now," he kissed her softly, before beginning again.

"We have Livvy, and soon we'll have our newest edition," he told her chuckling.

Mariah was expecting her and Aidan's second child in six months.

"I'm just glad to finally have you home baby," Dezi finished, kissing Kayla passionately.

Kayla smiled.

"Thank you again for rescuing me, Dezi," she spoke lovingly.

Dezi kissed her again. "You're more than welcome."

"I'm leaving for a little while baby," Dezi said rising from the chair. "I'm meeting with Aidan, but I won't be late," he finished as he kissed Kayla goodbye.

She smiled and told him okay.

●●●

"So do you regret any of it?" Aidan asked his father candidly.

They were discussing his business and Dezi's desire that Aidan change his last name to continue the legacy.

Dezi considered the question for a moment before answering.

"The simple answer would be no," he replied looking his son in the eye. "I only killed people when it was necessary to the survival of my empire," he went on. "I never mistreated those who worked with me or for me. I made sure they lived the good life just as I did," Dezi continued, his gaze never wavering. "And I made sure that the woman I loved always knew it," he finished and took a sip of his drink.

Aidan admitted he enjoyed the lifestyle that Dezi's money afforded them. He didn't want to go back to struggling like he did when he was in Virginia Beach. He wanted himself, and his family, to always have plenty. He already killed two people, and felt completely justified in doing it. Aidan wanted a love like the one his father and Kayla shared. Kayla trusted Dezi completely, and Dezi made sure she never wanted for anything. Aidan sighed deeply and answered his father's earlier question.

"I don't see a problem with my switching my names," he told him amiably. "As for the business, well, I'm not sure I'm ready to step into the huge shadow you still cast," he replied honestly.

Dezi smiled.

"You don't have to take over today Aidan," he told him calmly. "I'm going to teach you everything you need to know, and of course, by the time you do take over, you'll be implementing your own spin," Dezi took another breath. "And if we're lucky, our newest arrival will be a boy, and the legacy will continue for another two generations," he finished still smiling wistfully to himself.

"Well, since you put it that way," Aidan began, filling his glass again. "Let's toast to the Gianni empire," he chuckled as Dezi joined him and lifted his glass.

●●●

Two weeks later, Aidan Gianni Preston became Aidan Preston Gianni, and the lessons began. Five months later, Dezi Aidan Preston Gianni II was born and the legacy was assured to continue.

Also, check out these other offerings from the Author KR Bankston available www.krbankstononline.com and other online retailers: Amazon.com (https://www.amazon.com/author/krbankston), BN.com, and more.

THE GIANNI LEGACY:
A Deadly Encounter
Sins of the Father
Smoke & Mirrors
Life After Death
Aftermath
Sinister Alliance

THIN ICE – THE SERIAL:
Thin Ice
Thin Ice 2- Hide & Seek
Thin Ice 3 – Armageddon
Thin Ice 4- Resurrections
Thin Ice 5 – Checkmate
Thin Ice 6 – Hangman & Socrates
Thin Ice 7 – Echoes of Reckoning
Thin Ice 8 – Separazione Finale
Thin Ice 9 – Epiphany
Thin Ice 10 – Ambition
Thin Ice 11 – Homecoming
Thin Ice 12 – Siren Song

NOIR FROST SERIES:
Shattered
Evolutions
Darker Shades of Light
Crosshairs
Reawakening

THIN ICE GENERATIONS:
Blood Legacies
Dark Confessions
Malevolence
The Wedding
Eldest Son

OTHER BOOKS:
X-Mafia: The Rise of Pirate & Creeper
Unholy Empire (pt1 & 2)
Christian
Atomic
Shattered Peace
Interception
Three The Hard Way
Now You're A Star
The Agency
The Master Orchestrator
King of the Game
One of the Boys
No Take Backs
Gold Plated Dreams

About the Author:

K.R Bankston is an established Romantic Suspense author with some 40 published works to her credit, including the highly successful Thin Ice and Gianni Legacy series. KR is the CEO of Kirabaco Media Group, LLC which houses her works. In addition to being an author KR is a Publishing Consultant, and Public Speaker. KR also writes Contemporary Romance under the pen name Kay Raneé within the Cayenne Drama label.

KR's "BookOpera" series Thin Ice was voted Serial Novel of the Year and Urban Fiction of the year. Her other series The Gianni Legacy has been touted as The Godfather of modern day. Her novel, Christian was voted #75 of Top 100 Books of the year. Her novel X-Mafia was voted Urban Fiction of the Year. KR invites you to step outside the box of assumption and pop open a title and allow the stories to enrapture you.

You can find the Author on the following networks:
https://twitter.com/KRBankston
https://www.facebook.com/KRBankstonAuthor
https://www.patreon.com/KRBankston
https://youtube.com/@KRBTheAuthor
https://www.amazon.com/author/krbankston
https://www.instagram.com/bookoperalegacy

www.ingramcontent.com/pod-product-compliance
Lightning Source LLC
Chambersburg PA
CBHW032054050726
47590CB00001B/264